# LOXWOOD

The complete series

By Grace Wilkinson

First edition

Copyright © 2016 Grace Wilkinson

All rights reserved.

LOXWOOD..................................page 3

A PERFECT STRIDE......................page 111

BETWEEN THE FLAGS..................page 220

ROAD TO SUCCESS......................page 342

LAP OF HONOUR........................page 451

# LOXWOOD

## BOOK 1

# Chapter 1

There are three thousand horses in this town. Not only do I see these Thoroughbreds, going out on the gallops every morning, but I get to ride them. While most people are still asleep, there is another world starting the day.

I raise my whip to hit the light signal, then wait and watch as the cars in front of me slow to a stop. Frank is already walking into the road, his hand in the air as an instruction for us all to cross. The early morning sun is directly in my eyes as Loxwood takes his first step onto the tarmac, and I nod at the cars either side of me to thank them, even if I can't make out the drivers as I squint. I can only see racehorses in the distance.

But as I ride the horse of my dreams, it isn't races that are on my mind. I imagine us galloping on a cross country course, with a mutual trust strong enough to carry us over the wide tables and through the water complexes. I see the beautiful chestnut Thoroughbred flying over every fence with ease, and then sailing around the show jumping to claim the Badminton title. But that's just a fantasy…

I love the sound of shod hooves walking across tarmac, the consistent rhythm as satisfying as popping bubble wrap. Loxwood steps between the white railings, his chestnut mane bobbing with every step he takes, and once we reach the track, with the other horses safely behind us, I push him into a canter. Not a full out gallop, just a warm-up. The full on gallop comes later. In the distance, there are other horses going up Warren Hill, their outlines like shadows as they power across the turf, with a colourless sky behind them.

Frank is ready for us when we finish the warm-up, hands in his coat pockets, and blond hair making him look like an oversized child.

'You three,' he says, nodding at me and the two horses behind Loxwood. 'Go up first. Easy, don't push them.'

'Yes, boss,' I say. The two other exercise riders mutter something similar, though their limited English makes me doubt whether or not they ever understand what they are told.

'Take the lead, James.' Frank adds.

I nod, before Frank walks off to watch from the side of the track, where other trainers are gathered. Frank Zermot, both one of the most successful and most respected racehorse trainers in Newmarket. Growing up in a town famous for horse racing, you learn a lot about the industry. And Frank is one of the special few involved. One of those trainers who actually cares about his horses, and works to get the best out of them, not just to make owners happy. At nearly fifty years of age, he still gets up at five o'clock every day, and is generally at the gallops only moments later.

A click of the tongue is all it takes for Loxwood to strike into a canter, my hands resting lightly against his neck. We all have our favourite horses, the ones we ride more willingly than others. For most of the riders, a lot of whom had only ever ridden a handful of times before getting a job here (somewhere anyone under the weight of ten stone can rock up and be guaranteed ten pounds an hour), it is whichever horse tries to kill you the fewest times. And while, granted, I don't fear for my life on Loxwood as much as I do when riding others, that's not what makes him special. He has a certain quality you can't pinpoint. There's something about him that just stands out. I don't think that a single horse I ride by on a daily basis cost less than five figures, yet so many of them resemble mules. Often, a horse will show up at Frank's, a son of so-and-so, and a full brother to whichever winner of whatever title, bought for the bargain price of two hundred and fifty thousand, and the animal that gets off the truck looks like it's just come out of a knacker's yard. Last time this occurred, and I happened to make a comment about it, Frank turned to me and said, 'You'd think they'd actually bother to look at what they're buying, wouldn't you?'

We start out in a steady rhythm, Loxwood's stride increasing with the incline of the hill. The first time I rode a horse out on the gallops, I had to fight the instinct to lower my seat and collect the pace, but I don't think about it anymore. It's like two separate lives - my job exercising race horses, and my passion for *real* riding and schooling. The elements of dressage and jumping I spend weeks and months trying to perfect are non existent here. All that exists is speed.

'Do you want to go get a pizza? I'm bloody freezing,' Lizzie says from behind me.

I turn around from Loxwood's stable, where he is being

cooled off and cared for by a groom. 'Yeah, I'm starving.'

'I'll ask Graham if he wants to come. GRAHAM!' Lizzie begins wandering off down the stable block, retying her dark hair as she does so. 'DO YOU WANT TO GO GET LUNCH WITH ME AND GEORGIA?' Her voice dies down as she disappears from sight.

One circuit around the walk-and-trot track is enough to warm me up, but since getting back to the yard my limbs have already started to turn numb. Not to mention my toes, which I haven't felt since stepping foot outside at six o'clock this morning. The worst part is that it's only the beginning of January, and we all know that the cold spell has yet to come.

Pulling my knee socks up higher beneath my chaps in a hopeless bid to warm myself up, I turn back to Loxwood. The sun is shining directly into his stable, reflecting off his bright chestnut coat. He has a wide head, slightly dished, with the smallest white star on his forehead. He also has four small, white socks, which you tend not to notice unless you're staring at them.

Loxwood's groom, Luís, is busy strapping sweat sheets onto him, whistling as he does so.

'Handsome boy,' I say quietly over the stable door.

'Thank you,' Luís replies smugly with a grin.

'You know who I meant,' I say with a glare.

Luís laughs. 'But is he fassst?'

I draw in a breath to answer, only to let it back out again. What am I supposed to say to that? He knows as well as I do that Loxwood is nowhere near the times of the fastest horses on the yard, and probably never will be. I think he's wonderful, but that doesn't change the fact that he won't be winning races any time soon. He only placed once as a three year old last year, yet Frank still managed to convince the owner to give him another shot.

Nobody can deny that Loxwood is a class horse, but that means nothing in this world. I'm not even that fond of racing myself, but being a racehorse is better than the alternative. I learnt early on that I can't save them all, and while I don't like to turn a blind eye, it's all I can do if I want to get up every morning and go to work without feeling guilt ridden. Some of the owners and trainers do everything they can to ensure the horses that are too slow go on to have second careers and good homes. But that doesn't make up for the number that don't. And so long as Loxwood is racing, he is safe. Beyond that, nothing can be predicted or protected. Even if I do have some crazy fantasy about turning him into an event horse.

'We should get paid double for being out in this weather,' Lizzie says as we walk into the warmth of Pizza Express.
'You wouldn't be cold if you'd ridden that black filly,' says Graham. 'It tried to get me off three times - reared right when we were crossing the road!'
A waitress appears and starts directing us towards a table, while Lizzie goes into a rant about how the colt she rode tried to kill her. My feet lead me behind them, but my mind is elsewhere. Frank must have spoken about Loxwood's speed (or lack of, I should day) if the grooms are discussing it. This isn't news, I've always known he isn't a sprinter. He doesn't power across the turf in a single burst of speed. He has a long stride, which goes upwards and builds impulsion as he goes. When Loxwood first came to the yard, a few weeks after I started working there, I was convinced he was an event horse. I still am, but back then I had wanted him not to be fast enough, and for the owner to give up on him. It seemed simple - nobody would want Loxwood, and then he would be mine. But I have seen more horses disappear

since then, and over analysed the reality of owning a horse. Being told, aged sixteen, that you're being paid over minimum wage to ride is surreal, but I know it's not enough to live off. Not when you're working an average of two hours a day before school it isn't, anyway.

'Earth to Georgia!' says Lizzie. She and Graham are both seated, and I'm still standing by the table.

'What?'

'Thinking about that horse?' Graham says with a laugh.

'Just thinking,' I say defensively as I unzip my coat before sitting down.

Lizzie turns to Graham. 'She's thinking about *real* riding. More pirouettes this afternoon?'

I shake my head, forcing a smile. Neither Lizzie or Graham mean anything by their comments, they just don't get how there can be any other side to horses than racing.

I am spared having to say anything else as Lizzie's phone starts ringing. Followed is the cursing that comes as she starts unzipping her many coat pockets in search of the device.

'Uggh,' she says when it is finally found, before tapping the screen and clearing her throat to answer. 'Yes, Mum?' she says brightly. 'Just finished. Getting lunch.' There is a moment's pause between each of her responses, presumably when her mother is speaking. 'With Georgia and Graham. Pizza Express. What do you mean we can't eat pizza at eleven o'clock!? It *is* lunchtime when you've been up since five! Uh huh, okay.. See you soon. Yep. Bye.' She hangs up the phone with another *Uggh*, slamming it down loudly onto the table. 'Just for that I'm ordering dessert, too.'

'I'm starving,' I say, picking up the menu in front of me, and hopefully diverting the conversation away from my riding pursuits.

'You eating this week?' Lizzie says to Graham. At five foot seven, Graham is already at a disadvantage for being a jockey. Coupled with his supposed naturally solid build, he practically lives on air to make weight. When he first told me and Lizzie this, we couldn't believe it. Anyone who saw Graham now would think that he is one of those people who keep a child's frame their entire lives, and can eat whatever they want. But since the three of us became friends, a couple weeks after I started riding out, when we all gravitated towards each other for no reason other than the fact that we were the only English-speaking jockeys at the time, the extremes Graham puts himself through have become clear. Unlike Lizzie and me, he wants to make a career out of being a jockey, and therefore has to live most of his life on a diet. I feel bad for him as it is, never mind the fact that he is always eating out with the two of us, who, between us, eat enough to feed an army. Especially Lizzie, who is so short that it would take a lot for her to exceed the ten stone exercise rider limit, and has no desire to be a competitive jockey. 'Forty pounds a morning to gallop about on a hill,' she is always saying, 'and you finish work by eleven o'clock. Why would I ever want to do anything else?' I never argue when she says this, but Graham is forever pointing out that she still lives at home, and therefore has no bills to pay.

'I'll eat one of those light ones,' Graham says. 'I'm going running later.'

'If you rode *pirouettes* you wouldn't have to worry about what you eat,' I say with a smirk.

'Where's the fun in that?' says Lizzie.

'Don't speak too soon,' says Graham, 'what's that big competition you're always going on about?' He looks at me now.

'It's called something like volleyball?'

'Badminton?' I venture.

'Yeah, that's the one,' he says, turning back to Lizzie. 'Those jumps are huge! Have you seen them?'

'Another reason to stick with racing!' she cries. 'You're less likely to get yourself killed!'

'I'm too tall to be a jockey,' I say dismissively.

'You'd make the weight if you ditched the pizza,' Graham says with a childish grin, and I slap his arm with my menu.

'Ignore him,' Lizzie says. 'But, seriously. No, really, I'm being serious,' she adds, seeing the amused looks on our faces. 'What is it about event..whatever it's called, that racing doesn't have?'

At that moment, the same waitress who showed us to our table appears with a pad and pen, quickly scribbles down our orders, and then walks away. Lizzie's eyes are on me again the second she leaves, still expecting an answer.

'In racing..' I pause as I struggle to find the words to explain. 'You have no say over what happens to the horse. You don't even know the horses you're riding most of the time! You just get on and go. But in eventing - or dressage or show jumping - you train with the horse, every day. It's not about just one of you winning, it's both of you.'

The waitress comes back again with a jug of water, which she places wordlessly in the middle of the table. I pour myself a glass, and gulp it down quickly. 'Racing isn't in the Olympics, anyway,' I add, seeing Lizzie's bemused expression.

'Uh huh,' she says unsurely. 'Oh, I just remembered!' She pushes her chair back from the table suddenly, and bends to lift her rucksack from the floor, swinging it onto her lap and shuffling through its contents. 'These are for you,' she says, taking something out and placing it in front of me.

'What the heck is that?' I say. It's a bag of mini cream eggs.

'There are Easter eggs everywhere,' she says. 'What!?' she cries, looking at my annoyed expression. 'You said you liked cream eggs!'

'Christmas was last week! What's wrong with you!?'

'Excuse me for being nice,' Lizzie mutters. 'I won't do it again.'

'It's January!' I continue. 'What is wrong with the world!?

'I saw someone putting Valentine's decorations up today,' says Graham.

Lizzie drops her rucksack back down onto the floor. 'At least Valentine's day is before Easter.'

'Since when are you supposed to decorate for Valentine's day?' I say. 'What kind of person has the time to do that? What kind of decorations count as Valentine's day decorations, anyway?'

'Heart wreaths,' says Graham, pouring himself some water. 'I saw two different people swapping Christmas wreaths for them.'

'That's why I work with horses,' I mumble. 'I don't want to deal with those sorts of people.'

'Just wait until Frank starts putting decorations up at the yard,' Lizzie jokes.

'Never,' I say. 'Thank you for the eggs, anyway.'

'You're welcome.'

The greyness of the morning has lifted by the time I'm walking up to the Murphys' front door. It's barely a couple degrees above freezing, but the sky is blue. There is still ice along the shady areas of the pavements where the sun has not been able to reach, and I walked the whole way with my eyes focussed on my feet.

Clara answers on the second knock. 'It's freezing,' she says.

'I know,' I say, huddling past her into the warmth of the corridor.

'You can keep your boots on,' Clara adds, knowing how long it takes to remove, and then put back on, chaps.

I follow her down the hallway, through to the kitchen at the back of the house. I know the way, having done it too many times to count. I pull a chair out at the table, and take a seat. Clara's kitchen is warm and familiar. The vast space, with clutter flowing over all the mismatched unit surfaces. The plaster walls, where paint is pealing away at the corners. The constant smell of tea and toast. And, more importantly, the small clues that suggest an interest in horses. A bridle hangs from the back of a chair, gleaming the way it only does when it has just been oiled. Amongst the previously mentioned clutter lies an old rosette, the ribbons creased. A dressage test is piled with various bank statements on the table in front of me, and on the fridge, held up by letter-shaped magnets, are photographs of Clara riding.

I turn in my seat at the sound of footsteps, and Clara's mum, Hope, appears through the kitchen doorway. There's a tape measure around her neck, suggesting she's been sewing. It's what she spends most of her time doing, in a small room in the attic. She made me a patchwork horse for my birthday once when I was little, and I still have it on my bed.

'Hello, Georgia, dear,' she says warmly.

I've known Clara for ten years, since we bonded at school over our mutual "pony mad girl" statuses. Even back then, Clara already had a horse of her own, even if it was a small Shetland. It was two years ago that she got her current horse, Spirit, and started eventing more seriously. And since then she has kept her horse in a livery yard run by a three-star event rider, Rose Holloway, only four miles away. I would go and watch her ride whenever I could, until I mustered up the courage to ask Rose for lessons. I had ridden before, both with Clara and on shaggy ponies in local riding schools, but it wasn't the same as riding at a place like this. Although she still competed a little, Rose was more focussed on her children now, and gave out private lessons on her two schoolmasters to earn their keep. I thought I knew the basics of riding, but I soon discovered that knowing how to stay on and knowing how to work a horse were two completely different things entirely. I started working at the track a year after I started training with Rose, and between the two I progressed quickly.

Clara is the best friend I've ever had, but I still worry that there will come a day when we'll drift apart. I want to make horses my life, whereas she has plans for university and travelling. Until that day comes, though, I'm grateful for her friendship.

'Ready to go, girls?' Hope says, removing the tape measure from round her neck, and picking up a set of car keys from the kitchen table.

I stand up. I'm ready, I'm always ready to go to my favourite place I know.

# Chapter 2

There are two sides to Newmarket. The turn off the motorway, where suddenly you are thrust into a world of wide hedges and white railings. Race horses walk along the pavements, and cross the road, and there are the small glimpses of stable yards that lie beyond the walled barriers. Even in the High Street, where plenty of people look as though they have never even so much as touched a horse, there is a racing presence. Whether it be the sight of an exercise rider grabbing a post training coffee, or a glance down at one of the horse shoe tiles that are scattered across the pavements, each one a tribute to a great legend, or because you are unable to walk through the town without stopping outside the racing museum to admire the bronze statue of Hyperion. Not to mention when it is the time of year during which the sales are held, and Ferraris and Porches and four-by-four vehicles, all with blacked-out windows, dominate the traffic, as enthusiasts prepare to outbid each other of hundreds and thousands of pounds, most of them investments that will never be returned.

This side of Newmarket is special, but there is another even more so.

Minutes away from the town centre, when you start driving along the smaller roads, there is another world. The white railings are gone, replaced instead with post and rail fencing, and long, sweeping driveways that lead to the kind of barns and paddocks I thought only existed in Kentucky before witnessing the sight with my own eyes. The studs are closed off by huge iron wrought gates, hanging from stone bollards, and most with twenty-four-hour security. Hardly surprising, when some of the stables are home to stallions so valuable they can't even be insured.

There are small villages to drive through, each consisting of a pub called something like *The red lion* or *The new inn* or *The white horse*... and the streets are lined with thatched cottages, and there is usually a red phone booth in some corner. And all this some three miles from the town centre. I love Newmarket with all my heart, but it is to this side that I give it.

Clara and I swing open the car doors at exactly the same time. Out of habit, as we have done ever since we were little, we both sit in the back, leaving the passenger seat beside Hope empty. Immediately upon setting foot outside I am greeted by the familiar scents of the yard. There is something so comfortable about this place - while the racing world always feel rushed, everything here is peaceful.

From the car park we turn the corner into the stable block, as Hope can be heard driving away in her old jeep. Dark, wooden structures, with low, tin roofs, and painted white doors. Whilst we aren't that far from the road, the trees that conceal the buildings make it feel as though it were a mile away. There are sixteen stables in total, in addition to various outbuildings, some of which are used to store straw and hay. The paddocks extend away from the lane, and beside Rose's house, a two-story, hundred year old, white building, is an outdoor arena, with lights on telegraph poles surrounding it.

As Clara wanders over to Spirit - Song of Spirit, a twelve year old, fifteen three Thoroughbred Connemara cross - I begin to look over the horses that are in, when there comes the sound of feet running towards me.

'GEORGIIIIIA!'

A child's body slams into me, wrapping its arms around my waist.

'Hey, Kenzie,' I say, returning her embrace by placing my arm lightly around her shoulders.

'Will you come watch me ride?' Mackenzie asks excitedly, looking up from where she is still holding on to me, all dark eyes and freckles. 'Or will you ride *with* me!?'

'I'll have to check with your mum,' I say, as she finally releases my waist.

'You can take Paddington out,' a kind voice says. Mackenzie and I both turn to see Rose coming towards us. As usual, she is dressed in jodhpurs and a fleece, with knee socks poking out from beneath her chaps, and brown hair in a short ponytail. 'If you really want to spend an hour with this terror,' she adds, taking hold of Mackenzie's coat hood.

'Hey!' cries Mackenzie. 'I'm not a terror!'

'You are to your mother,' Rose says with a smile. 'If only you were as nice to me as you are to Georgia.'

I think it was the third time I came here, back before I was brave enough to ask Rose for a lesson, that I met Mackenzie. I was wandering around the yard while Clara tacked up, looking at the horses, when a small figure appeared beside me as if out of nowhere.

'Who are you?' Mackenzie said. Although I had never met her, I knew who she was from the resemblance to Rose, paired with the fact that two daughters had been referenced. Mackenzie was six years old at the time, making her sister, Jemima, four.

'Umm, Georgia. I'm a friend of Clara's,' I said, pointing to Spirit's stable. Mackenzie was staring at me intently, and I began to worry for a moment. The main reason was that I had never thought I was particularly good with children, possibly because I am an only child myself, and as a consequence tended not to like them. I usually tried to avoid eye contact, so that they would lose interest before I had time to say or do the wrong thing.

'Will you come see Cinder?' Mackenzie said. I didn't even have time to answer before she had taken hold of my hand and started dragging me to the farthest stable.

I didn't even see Clara ride that day. The whole time I spent with Mackenzie, meeting Cinder, a lovely chocolate coloured Connemara, and then discovering other things about the yard. I don't know what it was about Mackenzie that I liked. More to the point, I don't know why she liked *me*. That alone was enough for me to like her. Ever since that day, I have been unable to come here without finding myself spending most of the time with Mackenzie as a shadow, and I still don't know why she ever took a liking to me. But even Jemima, who is certainly much shier, seems to be asking me to pick her up whenever she is around, so maybe I am just good with some children. Saying that, Mackenzie and Jemima are the only kids I know who have ever looked at me with any interest, so it could just be fluke.

It also often occurs to me that Mackenzie's infatuation is the reason that Rose has always been so nice to me. After my first lesson with her, when I tried to hand over my three crumpled ten pound notes, she had refused. Hard as I tried, I couldn't get her to take the money. She insisted that I was helping her out, exercising one of the horses, and that I was welcome to any time. I still kept trying to pay every week. After all, Rose would stand in the school for over an hour teaching me, but I never got through. I wonder what it was in my fifteen year old face she saw that gave away the fact that the money I was wanting to pay with was the result of various car cleaning payments and Christmas presents. That didn't matter to me, though. Riding was all I wanted, and, in my eyes, there was nothing better I could spend the money on.

By the time it became clear that I would never get Rose to accept a single penny from me, I settled for making sure I was helping out around the yard whenever I was here.

'You aren't as nice to me as Georgia is,' Mackenzie says.

Rose smiles at me. 'I'm sure that's it.'

Mackenzie and I tack up our rides while Clara prepares for her lesson with Rose. Paddington is a chestnut Irish Sport Horse, seemingly plain at first glance, but a pleasure to ride, and possibly one of the kindest event horses you'll ever come across. The contact in the reins is always as light as a feather, a sharp comparison to the mouthy Thoroughbreds I'm now well used to. He has already competed up to two-star level with Rose, which is probably where he will remain.

It's easy to access bridle paths from the small lane. We walk along the road for a while, and if a car comes near it slows right down until we signal for it to overtake. Both Paddington and Cinder are completely traffic proof, unlike some of Frank's youngsters - while most of them are used to vehicles, there are also plenty that have a tendency to cross roads on two legs.

'Did you ride Loxwood this morning?' Mackenzie asks as we turn off down a path that borders one of the main estates in the area.

'Yep,' Mackenzie is one person I can gush about a horse to without being taunted for it.

'You should buy him,' Mackenzie says. 'Then you could keep him with us, and we could ride together all the time.'

I smile. 'I don't think it's that simple.'

'Grownups always say that. Everything's simple if you let it be.'

'I wish,' I say, and before Mackenzie can push the matter further I ask if she wants to trot. Of course, her answer is yes, and we push our horses forward up the grass path.

An hour later, when we ride back into the stable yard, both horses happily on a long rein, Clara and Spirit stand at the sand school gate. Rose is beside them, and though I can't hear what she is saying I can tell from the way her arms move that she is talking. It's what she does at the end of every lesson - spend a few minutes going over everything. Though usually by that time you're so tired that whatever Rose does say only half registers.

'You have to try one of my fairy cakes!' Mackenzie says excitedly to me when I come out of Paddington's stable, having untacked and rugged him. I heard Spirit's steps on the concrete as Clara led him back to the stable, but haven't had time to speak to her yet.

'Okay.'

'Do you want to come inside, or shall I bring them?' Mackenzie asks, in a way suggesting that the matter is far more important than it actually is.

'Bring them here?' I say. 'I don't know how much time I've

got.'

Mackenzie runs off towards the stone house, her arms flailing either side of her.

'Nice ride?' Rose asks, emerging from the tack room.

'Yeah, thanks. They were both really good.'

Rose smiles. 'Are you still coming show jumping with us next Saturday?'

'Definitely. If you still don't mind?'

'Of course. You're a massive help. And we don't need to leave until lunchtime, so you can still go to the track in the morning.' She pauses to look around. 'Where's Kenzie?'

'She went to get some, umm, fairy cakes?' I say.

'Oh, yes, *the fairy cakes.*' Rose says with a laugh. 'She made them this morning. Wouldn't even let Ben have one,' she adds, referring to her partner. '*They're for me and Georgia,*' says Rose in an imitation of Mackenzie's voice. We still have the smiles on our faces from laughing when Mackenzie runs up with a plastic Tupperware container.

'Are those for me?' says Rose. 'Thaaaank you, you shouldn't have!'

'Don't!' Mackenzie scolds as her mum goes to take one. 'Georgia gets to choose first.'

The perfectly iced cupcakes are held out to me, each covered in pink buttercream, hundreds and thousands, sugar flowers, and additional pipping. One stands out for the letter *G* that has been written in purple icing.

'Is that one mine, by any chance?' I say, directing my finger towards it. Mackenzie grins widely, nodding as she does so. 'Thank you.'

When Hope arrives to pick us up, I'm on my second cupcake, as is Mackenzie, and Clara is making her way through her first.

It's not yet four o'clock, but the sky is already dark, and it will be pitch-black within the hour.

Leaving Rose's yard always leaves me with the same feeling I get when I hand Loxwood over to one of the grooms. I'm unaware of the feeling at the time, but as soon as I am gone I feel like I've left home. And it's time to go to where that's supposed to be.

'I'm back!' I yell, closing the door of the terraced town house behind me. It's small, with the narrow hallway I'm in now leading into the open plan living room, an adjacent kitchen at the other end. The floor is tiled - not original tiles, worn with age, but new and plasticky looking ones. The furnishings are all new, bought from some cheap interior design shop nearby, and there are too many useless items scattered around.

I can hear the sound of the TV as soon as I step inside, the familiar voice of a commentator on a gameshow. Pulling my boots off by the door, I listen out for any warning signs. No clutter of pans that would suggest guests coming round, or restless voices that should want some important discussion.

While I want nothing more than to soak in a hot bath, in spite of Mackenzie's two cupcakes I am still starving. I seem to always be either completely stuffed, or hungry enough to have a whole bag of crisps to myself. Inevitably, the second feeling always ends up resulting in the first.

'Hey,' I say as I walk into the kitchen, where my mum is sitting at the table with her laptop. Her hair, somewhere between blond and brown - the way mine was before I let Clara's sister (who wants to be a hairstylist) use me as a practice dummy, since when it has been closer to a colourless, pale brown - is held back by a clip. There are a couple bags beside her, each printed with the logo of her favourite knickknack shop. Or, as I think of it, emporium of the utterly useless.

'Good day?' she says, with her eyes still on her computer screen.

'Fine.' I walk up to the table, where the plastic bags are, and start looking through her purchases. 'What did you get all this stuff for?' I snap.

'Just things I fancied.'

'We're broke,' I say. 'We can't afford to waste money like that.'

'It's not a waste,' my mum says. 'And we're not broke.'

*I'm not, maybe.* Money is what causes us all to clash. For as long as I have known her, my mum hasn't had a job that has lasted longer than a few weeks. She will apply to any position that takes her fancy, mostly sales assistant positions in local shops, only to quit for no reason. She has her own reason, of course, usually along the lines of, 'It wasn't what I was expecting' or 'They didn't appreciate my skills' and 'It was a waste of my time, really', all of which come to the same conclusion that she considers herself above that kind of work. My dad is no better, working minimal hours and then spending any time he isn't in front of the TV. If he has any ambition then I haven't seen it, and he despises the wealthy. The owners of most of the horses I ride at the track probably have enough money to buy the entire town twice over, and my dad will always make a snotty comment on the matter. Unless I manage to hold my tongue, I'll point out that people work hard to obtain that kind of lifestyle, but the concept is lost on him. At least both my parents have something in common. Plus the fact that neither of them seem to take the pile of bills on our kitchen counter seriously. They aren't cruel, though, and whilst I don't think they would ever try and take any money from me, I don't share the numbers on my paycheques with them.

'It's still a waste of money,' I say, pulling a porcelain lizard figurine out of the bag.

'There's nothing wrong with wanting to make the place look nice,' my mum says. 'Just because *you* wouldn't care if we lived in a shed.'

I pull the lizard's matching purple friend free from the rest of the monstrosities, and decide that I would chose a shed any day.

'I don't know how you can talk about wasting money,' my dad says as he walks up to us from the sofa, empty glass in hand, 'when those racing people spend millions on ponies.'

'It's not a waste, it's called earning a living.' I say coldly before taking a glass out of the cupboard and filling it with tap water.

'If they can afford to buy horses at that price, then they already have money to begin with,' he says.

I down the entire glass in three gulps. 'Passion, then,' I say, putting the glass in the sink, and wiping my mouth on my sleeve.

'Then what's the difference?' he asks, gesturing at my mum's purchases.

I struggle to keep a straight face. 'Horses, and horse racing, are a passion, porcelain reptiles are not.'

'You can't always be so hypocritical,' says my mum. She is still fixated on her computer screen, probably playing bingo, which I'm sure she'll try to argue is a passion, too.

'Whatever,' I snap, picking an apple from the fruit bowl on the table. 'I'm going to have a bath.'

Even upstairs isn't far enough away from my parents. Lying in the bath, I can still hear the sound of the TV through the floor. The annoying presenter's voice, cheers and gasps from the live audience, the sound effects that come with the questions.

I wander out ten minutes later, washed of the day's dirt, wearing a pair of tracksuit bottoms and my favourite hoodie. Luckily, my bedroom is the one room that my mum hasn't touched. It's small, and I can cross it in three strides, but at least it's mine. The carpet is old and beige, and in places I can still hear the floorboards beneath it creak. The walls are equally colourless, with an odd eventing photo pulled out of a magazine taped up on it. My chest of drawers is cluttered, unfolded clothes piled upon it, and my schoolbag and books occupy a corner of the floor. There's a single bed in the middle of the room, unmade.

My entire body aches, my lower back in particular from when the filly I rode before Loxwood spooked at a lorry speeding by, sending a shock down my entire spine. I know that as soon as I lie down I won't want to move, but I do so anyway, pulling the duvet up to my waist, and propping two pillows against the wooden headboard. I thought to put my phone in my pocket before throwing my clothes on the floor, and I take it out now. My screensaver is a photo of Warren Hill, as seen from the saddle. Loxwood's chestnut ears frame the shot, his coat dim in the early morning light. There aren't many horses on which I would dare pull my phone out of my pocket, but he is an exception.

Looking at the simple picture makes my eyes well up, and as the sound comes of my dad laughing at something on the TV, I suddenly feel cold and alone. I'm safe, and well fed, with a sturdy roof over my head, and parents who do look after me. Yet, lying here, staring at some stupid picture, I want to cry. I'm in a house, but I'm not home.

# Chapter 3

'You all right?' Clara asks as I hobble towards her.

'Tired,' I say, lifting my arm to slide my schoolbag further up my shoulder.

'What time did you start this morning?'

'Rode the first one at six. Was up at five.'

'I don't know how you do it,' she says.

The bell rings, the sign that it's time to go to our first lesson, and we hurry through the corridor to find the right classroom.

'Getting up to ride is easy,' I mutter as we push our way through crowds of people, 'it's coming to this place that's hard.'

I manage to stay awake through my first morning class, mostly by doodling on the corner of my notebook. Occasionally, I would remind myself to concentrate, only to give up a few seconds later. If the legal school age hadn't changed, I would already be done, and working with horses full time. But they *had* to go and give us an extra two years of education. That's when I stopped paying attention in class (or started paying even less, I should say). I can never shake the feeling that every hour I spend at a desk is another I could put to use improving my riding. I'm behind as it is, being almost seventeen and having never competed. Most riders my age, at least the ones who aspire to ride professionally, already have a decade of experience and a few team appearances under their belts. The kind of people who are always told they have natural talent, or a gift. It's bad enough for those like me, who have to work three times as hard to achieve what seems to come easily to others, and no support from family. I don't even have a horse. But if I didn't have to go to school, then at least I would be able to work extra hours, and afford said horse. There have been many times in the past couple years that I have seriously considered it, buying a horse of my own. I spend very little of my salary, and therefore have more money than most my age in the bank. But I've never brought myself to seriously scour classified adverts, and start searching within my budget. Even if I did that, I'm not naive enough to believe that the purchase cost of a horse is the only thing to worry about. I've done the maths before - in maths class, coincidentally. I thought Mr Moore (I think that's his name) would appreciate it above random doodles. And what I earn at the track would just about cover feed, bedding, and DIY livery costs, but it's still tight.

There's another reason, I suppose, why I haven't found a way to acquire my own horse up to now. I try and tell myself it is solely the above, but I know it isn't. *Loxwood.* He came to Frank's a week after the idea of buying a horse seriously crossed my mind. I wasn't first to ride him, I (understandably) wouldn't have been considered good enough, but that just meant I got to watch him. One of the most experienced exercise riders was on Loxwood, and I was a few horses behind on the walk and trot track, my eyes on him the whole time. His build was larger than most of the spindly Thoroughbreds around him, his neck more muscular. He didn't stand out to me because he looked like he was going to win races, he stood out because he looked like an event horse. And I had some crazy idea that I would be the one to turn him into just that. I remember how excited I was the first time Frank told me to ride him. He needed a *woman's touch*, Frank's words, because although he was sane, he was also sensitive. When the stronger jockeys would rise the trot and land on his back with a thud, Loxwood would pin his ears and scoot to the side. It wouldn't have mattered if he at least spooked forward, but sideways didn't win races. And Frank's bright enough to know that I did know more about schooling than most of the other riders.

It's not as though I sat on Loxwood and he was suddenly perfect. Although, from the moment I was given a leg up into the saddle, everything certainly felt *right*. But when he spooked or misbehaved, I knew how to react, and he responded. Some horses take no notice of you, but Loxwood did. If I asked him something, he would try to do it. It wasn't some instant spark, shooting up in an explosion, but a slow building flame that never went out. No other horse came - *comes* - close to him. It never occurred to me to find another, because it already felt like I had my own. Loxwood certainly owned part of me. But he isn't mine, and that's the worst part. Loving something so much, and being completely and utterly powerless. Even Frank doesn't decide what happens to him. The only person who has a say is someone who lives countries away, and probably has countless horses. I know his name, *Schofield*. Mr R Schofield. Only he makes decisions. It's crazy... Does he know that Loxwood needs a bucket of water in his stable, because he'd rather get dehydrated than drink out of an automatic? Does *he* know that his horse hates to be patted, and will pin his ears if done so, but would happily have his ears scratched all day long? Almost worse than the thought of him being re-homed is that of Loxwood being sent to another racing yard, one even larger, where each horse isn't seen as an individual. Racing gets a lot of stick, but nobody can seriously look at Frank and his stables, and say that he doesn't love his horses. So long as Loxwood is with him, he is at least safe. The thought of him in one of the other trainer's yards makes me physically ill.

'Miss James? Are you listening?'

I look up from my lined notebook, where *Loxwood* has been scrawled across the entire page multiple times in green ink. Which lesson I am in has slipped my mind, but as the teacher in front of me appears to have been reading from a novel, I'm guessing it's English.

'Yes,' I reply. I should probably say, 'Yes, Mrs -', but I can't remember her name - I usually just think of her as the woman who wears hair clips better suited to Mackenzie's age group. I think it sounds like *chandelier*...

'We're reading,' she says, rather tartly, her thin, lipstick covered lips pressing into a tight smile.

'I can see that,' I say. The class snickers at my response, and Mrs Chandeliersomething glares.

'Have you got your copy?'

'Umm, yes,' I stammer, ducking to find it in my schoolbag. After too many seconds, I pull the little-cared-for paperback out from where it was wedged between two files.

'Would you care to carry on reading for us, Miss James?'

No, I would not care to, but somehow I don't think it's a question. I flick through the book to where I last turned over one of the page corners, and stare at the words absently. I look up at the woman with glittery flowers in her hair, feeling a sick hollow in my stomach. She knows as well as I do that I haven't a clue where I'm supposed to start reading.

'Page 85,' a voice on my right mutters.

Mrs whatshername looks irritated as I find the correct page and start reading. The words roll off my tongue, monotone, and I just wish that I hadn't left my hair up this morning, so that it could fall like a curtain between me and the rest of the room.

After the final lesson, Clara and I go to our favourite cafe to refuel. She orders a hot chocolate, with mini marshmallows, and a blueberry muffin, while I go for a cappuccino and a slice of red velvet cake. We do our homework at the same time, except that whilst Clara is actually doing hers, I'm just answering enough questions randomly to make it look as though I have. It's almost four o'clock when a worried Hope calls, wondering why her daughter isn't home yet. We pack up our things and begin walking home, side by side up to the point where we head in different directions. I wait until Clara is around the corner before carrying straight on, past the turning for my street.

It takes me five minutes to cross the main road. Newmarket is possibly the only place in the world where it is easier to get through traffic on a Thoroughbred than on foot. Vehicles stop immediately to let horses across, and you never have to wait. Dodging between cars on foot is infuriating in comparison, and I almost gave up and turned home. But when there finally was enough space between vehicles, I sprinted to the other side.

Cars whoosh past as I walk along the pavement, my gaze down, and my arms crossed against my waist for warmth. This morning was so cold that the bottle of water I took with me to the stables had frozen by the time I came back from my first ride. My limbs were so numb when I went home to change that I ended up going to school wearing three pairs of socks and two woollen jumpers.

I pass the warm-up track where we trot the horses, and the crossing to Warren Hill, until there are no longer white railings either side of me, but brick walls and security gates. Even against the sound of engines, I can hear the bustle of yard duties enclosed behind. Wheelbarrows rattling across courtyards, stables doors clinking shut. I keep walking until I reach Frank's, and come to a stop. Behind the red bricks, horses are being rugged up and hayed, ready to start again tomorrow. I would spend every afternoon there if I could, but it's not like Rose's where I can just pop in to say hi. Exercise riders show up in the morning to ride, end of. I get on well with Frank, but I hardly think he would appreciate me hanging around twenty-four-seven.

Standing just steps away from where I know Loxwood is brings me comfort. I come here often, if ever I have a bad day, or just need a break. It's one of those things that makes me feel two opposite emotions - which never seems possible until it happens. On the one hand, I feel close to what I love. But the wall that separates me from the horses is also a reminder that we live in two different worlds. Sometimes I'm not sure how I'll ever cross over for good.

# Chapter 4

It is pouring down when we pull into the venue, so much so that we don't even unload the horses right away. The smallest classes are up first, meaning Cinder is the first to go. It's only an unaffiliated show, but Mackenzie is kitted out in beige jodhpurs and a dark jacket, hair pulled back into a tight bun. She's been competing Cinder for a few months now - Rose refused to let her start any earlier - and together they have proved to be a steady combination. Cinder's going on eighteen, having done countless rounds with various children before coming to her current home two years ago. It was only the first competition, when Mackenzie struggled to contain her emotions and ended up resembling a deer in headlights in the ring, that didn't go too smoothly. Since then, I don't think Cinder has ever come out of the ring without a rosette swinging from her bridle.

I watch beside Rose at the edge of the indoor arena as Kenzie rides Cinder around the fifty centimetre course with ease, and is rewarded with a clear round. She walks the little Connemara mare in circles outside as we wait for the last few combinations to go, with a look of stubborn competitiveness. It stopped raining minutes before Mackenzie and Cinder went into the ring, but the two of them are soaked from their warm-up outdoors.

When the last rider has been, Mackenzie is called in third place. Rose and I clap as Cinder plods back into the ring with the other placed combinations, all of the children looking just as determined as Kenzie.

By the time we get back to the lorry, Hope and Clara have pulled in beside us, Spirit loaded in the trailer. I help Mackenzie cool off Cinder, while Rose helps get Spirit ready for his class. Clara is riding off by the time the bay pony is rugged up, at which point I get Mackenzie to change into some dry clothes before we go watch the class.

Clara is cantering Spirit round the warm-up, Rose standing between the two practice fences, and Hope nervously by the entrance. Mackenzie takes hold of my wrist and pulls us to a clear space by the railings, where she swings one foot straight up to climb up onto the lowest one. Knowing how accident prone she is, I quickly stand behind her, thus able to stick an arm out should she fall.

'Come over the cross,' Rose calls.

Clara barely looks up from Spirit's neck when she turns towards the obstacle, and her body remains just as limp when he chips in a short stride and stumbles over it. At that point, Rose gestures for her to come to the middle of the ring, and the two of them exchange a conversation I can't hear.

'Do you think she's telling her off?' Mackenzie asks.

'Shush,' I say quietly, nudging her waist.

It cannot be said that Clara is a bad rider, but she isn't brave. She rides well at home, and so long as she is within her comfort zone she is actually quite good, but everything goes wrong at competitions. It doesn't matter how small the show is, but the pressure gets to her, and she no longer reacts the way she should. Being as kind as he is, Spirit often saves her, but it isn't pretty. The difference between the two of us is that Clara doesn't want to ride professionally. She loves and cares for horses, but they aren't her whole life. It astonishes her the lengths I go just to ride, getting up at five in the morning to work at the track and cycling four miles to get to Rose's, but then she's never had to fight to have horses in her life. Her parents aren't professional riders, nor are they millionaires, but being able to have horses has always been straightforward. Hope had a simple country upbringing, involving Pony Club meets and Sunday hunts, and Clara has had a similar experience. She rides because she enjoys it, but it's not a passion. Not like me, or even Mackenzie who rides almost every day after school. The silly thing is that Clara could be amazing if she wanted to be. Her seat is natural, and she doesn't have to spend weeks perfecting elements of her position like I do, but she isn't interested. We'll watch eventing competitions together, and while I dream of sailing over the same fences, Clara looks petrified with fear.

'I don't know how they do it,' she said once while we were watching Badminton reruns. 'I'd faint or be sick or both.'

'I want to do that someday,' I said.

'But you're brave. I wouldn't get on any of those crazy racehorses you ride.'

I hadn't replied to that, because I didn't know what to say. Courage is a muscle, not an epiphany. I didn't wake up one day with a nerve of steel. It's something you build up, like points, one ride at a time. And you hope you never have one ride bad enough to empty everything you've worked towards.

After a few words from Rose, Clara acceptably jumps a few fences, at which point she makes her way to the ring. Hope walks beside her, offering comfort, and carrying a bottle of water, and Rose goes ahead.

'Let's go watch from inside,' Mackenzie says, holding my hand again. We start walking past where Spirit is standing, when Rose hurries up to us.

'You two all right?' she says, peering back behind her to glance at the current rider on course. She looks drained, the exhaustion that comes from having to fear for somebody else.

'We're going to watch from inside,' Kenzie says again.

'Here,' Rose stammers, searching her coat pockets. 'Get yourselves something warm,' she says, handing over a crumpled ten pound note.

'Yipee!' Mackenzie cries, tugging at my hand.

The sound of cheers makes Rose turn to where a round has just ended, and Spirit is trotting into the ring. 'Thank you, Georgia,' she says, sighing before heading over to Hope.

'Let's go,' I say to Mackenzie, 'before Clara starts.'

Our running gets us to the viewing area along the long side of the arena just as Spirit is cantering to the first jump. Clara looks none the more confident, but as soon as the starting bell sounds it usually gives Spirit enough buzz to sail over the course on his own, which is just what he does. It looked like they were going to go clear, too, but Clara tapped his shoulder with the whip at the final fence, resulting in the top pole of the upright falling. But at least they got round.

Mackenzie stood beside me at the window to watch the round, and she's now queuing at the concessions stand opposite us. 'I'm getting a hot chocolate and a cornflake crispy,' she says. 'Would you like the same?'

'Sounds good,' I say, going to stand beside her.

With our snacks, we settle at one of the plastic tables up by the window, and continue watching the rounds. Mackenzie is one of those kids who make you feel like you have no memory, as she seems to remember even more riders' names than I do.

'That's the girl who fell off two weeks ago when her horse spooked at an umbrella. Remember?'

'Uh huh.'

'Look, look,' Mackenzie says, chocolate covering the sides of her mouth, 'that's Helena Cullen!'

That is one rider whose name I don't need reminding. Helena Cullen is one of the best junior riders out there, being the same age as me and having already won two European medals, and coincidentally based not very far away. She has a team of three horses, each one better than the next, in training with Amanda Walton, a former event rider with a list of credentials as long as my arm. In addition to winning many four-star titles herself, Amanda has trained even more winners since retiring twenty years ago. I looked at the rates on her website once, and found that keeping a horse there costs the same as what I earn in three months. And while Helena is an accomplished rider, certainly better than me, I can't help but envy her. I wonder if I'd be the same, if my parents had been able to afford the same kind of tuition.

'She's amazing,' Mackenzie says, her eyes glued to the glass window. Helena is piloting a beautiful grey horse around the one-ten.

'She's all right,' I mumble.

The horse, who I know, from stalking articles, is named

Arturo, jumps the last fence to cheers. Helena is smiling, patting the grey's muscular neck, and music plays to announce the clear.

Mackenzie is clapping in awe. 'That was really good,' she says seriously.

Helena rides out of the ring on a loose rein, where she is met by her support team. A woman, who I now realise must be Amanda Walton - and also realise, with some panic, I was standing next to only moments ago - pats Arturo on the neck stiffly, and another, who I assume is Helena's mother, gives her daughter's leg a squeeze, and feeds the horse a polo.

It's stupid, but the sight makes me want to cry. I feel the usual guilt I always do when I start comparing my life to somebody else's. But seeing someone else live your dream, and having the image dangled right in front of you, is agony.

'Come on,' I say to Kenzie, clearing my throat. 'Let's go help your mum get ready.'

Rose steers Paddington to a steady clear, and we load for home immediately after. These small, unaffiliated shows are only training outings for the horses in anticipation of the start of the event season in spring.

I help with the evening stable chores until Hope and Clara are ready to leave, at which point I gladly accept their offer to drive me home. The four mile ride is less attractive in the evening, and I gratefully secure my bike onto the back of the four-by-four.

In addition to Rose's one full time member of staff, Leah, there are other DIY owners pitching up to finish off their horses. In all my time here, I don't think I've ever exchanged more than two words with any of them. Most are mother daughter shares, who do their own thing. It's something I can't ever get my head around - both sharing a horse with your mum, and actually having a mum to share a horse with. The concept is so alien to me that I've never even tried to interact with them. Nor they with me, I might add. Hanging around a livery yard without actually owning a horse is the kind of behaviour that earns you wary stares.

Of the eight DIY liveries, there are only two who don't belong in the category above. There's an elderly woman who owns an equally old dressage horse, and takes weekly lessons with Rose. While I've rarely spoken to her, she's earned a place in my good books in view of how well she treats her horse. I don't know much about him, other than the fact that he is referred to as Fly, and looks like a gentle giant. The woman, whose name is either Nora or Dora (I never have figured out), is one of the few to arrive at a sensible time in the morning to feed, unlike others who leave their horses waiting until ten, and clearly loves him.

The other is more of a mystery. Her name is Paige, I know that much, and she can't be much younger than me. Her horse is a scrawny bay, possibly a Thoroughbred, who follows her around the yard like a dog. Paige is more difficult to figure out than Nora/Dora. She is slim and frail-looking, and the first adjective that comes to my mind when I see her is flighty. Her hair is naturally dark red, and usually pulled back in some sort of ponytail-bun hybrid, with loose strands flying about. I probably would have tried to make conversation with her at some point during the few months she has been here if she weren't always looking away. It's almost like she doesn't want to risk having anyone start a discussion with her. Rose rarely speaks of her, but when she does she does so with affection. I would never push the matter, but if ever I ask about Paige she seems to be evasive. I've caught Rose giving her a lesson occasionally, trying to catch glances from the stable block. The horse is lacking condition and muscle, although less so than when he arrived, but Paige rides nicely. She seems to have no problem with keeping her hands together, and her shoulders relaxed. Natural talent, I thought the first time I saw her. The two words thrown around so loosely to everyone but me.

I catch a glance of Paige before climbing into the back of the car. She's carrying a bucket of water to her horse's stable, her skin especially pale in the cold weather. The coat she is wearing is at least one size too big, and there's a rip down the back of it.

The bay horse nickers when she goes near him, and even from where I'm standing I can see a smile spread across her face. She never smiles when she's walking around, she looks upset and anxious. With her horse she looks happy, and more confident.

I doubt that she can see me from this angle, and I almost feel bad for staring. But it hits me, in a flashing moment, that maybe her horse is all she has to be happy about.

# Chapter 5

'Come in, Miss James. Close the door behind you.'

I walk into the office unsurely, pulling the door to as instructed. My bag and coat are hanging off one arm, and I drop them on the floor beside the chair. Mrs Sanchez is sitting in her own seat behind the desk, looking at her computer screen, with a stack of papers in front of her. Ten minutes ago, I had no idea who Mrs Sanchez was. When the loud speaker announcement came that I and a few other names were to report to her office when possible, I then had to search my schoolbooks for some idea as to who that was. It was Clara who finally put me out of my misery, confused as to how I could not know the guidance counsellor's name. I can list countless riders' and horses' names, but my mind blocks out teachers'.

Why the guidance counsellor should want to see me went over my head, but going now meant missing the beginning of Maths, so I'm not particularly bothered.

'Sit down, Miss James.'

The room is bare, with only a desk and two chairs. I take a seat opposite Mrs Sanchez, tugging my sleeves down lower, and resting my clasped hands on my legs. For forty-seven seconds I remain like this, until finally she looks up from the computer, removing glasses from her nose.

'Right, Georgia,' she says. I want to ask what's prompted her sudden move to first name basis, but decide against it, instead noting the forced enthusiasm with which she enunciates each word. 'Is everything all right with you?'

'Define all right.'

Mrs Sanchez frowns. 'I'm sure you know your grades haven't been up to scratch lately,'

As this doesn't actually seem to be a question, I stare at her, rather than offer a response.

'Do you remember the questionnaire you filled out at the beginning of term?' Mrs Sanchez continues, 'About future plans, things like that!?'

'I don't know, I've filled out a lot of questionnaires. Any specific time in the future?'

She grins. 'See, now, you're a smart girl. If only you applied yourself to your studies with the same dedication.'

I haven't got a reply to this, so I continue to glare.

'Georgia,' Mrs Sanchez says despairingly. 'It says here,' she looks down at the stack of papers in front of her, and for the first time I notice that one of them is the questionnaire in question. 'That you want to be an event rider.' She pauses, and I nod in case it is for confirmation. 'I know you don't think so, none of you do, but we - educators - have your best interests at heart. I know you clearly have some plan, but that doesn't mean you don't need an education to fall back on.'

'All due respect,' I say, 'but Algebra isn't what's going to help me win medals.'

'Okay, Miss James,' Mrs Sanchez says, leaning back further in her chair. 'Tell me what does.'

'Sorry?'

'I don't know what I'm talking about, I know that's what you're thinking. So, tell me, what you have accomplished that gives you enough confidence to know that the Olympics are in your future.'

My limbs go numb, and a slight panic rises to my chest. 'I already work with horses,' I say carefully. 'Every morning. Today, I was up at five, and I rode twice before coming to class.'

'Yes.' Mrs Sanchez smiles. 'Go on. Do you compete on a regular basis? There was a girl here, a few years ago, I remember she represented Great Britain at the European Championships, something or other. She was often missing days of school to go to train with some team. Do you?'

'Umm,' I stammer, biting my lip to stop tears prickling at my eyes. 'I train with an international rider.'

'But do you have good results? How often do you finish first?'

'I'm not competing at the moment-' I'm interrupted by a knock at the door.

'Mrs Sanchez,' a boy says, sticking his head around the door. 'I was told to come to your office.'

'One minute,' she says to him with a smile before turning her attention back to me. 'Don't place all your eggs in one basket, Georgia. I suggest you start working a little harder. Don't leave it much later.'

I don't even look Mrs Sanchez in the eye when I leave the room, and I keep my glance down until I am out the building. There's no way I'm going to Maths class now.

I walk to the high street, where I order coffee and a millionaire shortbread to go, and start walking up to the racing stables. I only stop when I pass the first newsagents, and wonder whether they have the newest *Horse and Hound*. Inside, I find one copy left, and buy it quickly before setting off again.

There's an empty bench by the racetrack, and I decide to sit there instead of continuing farther up the pavement. With my schoolbag beside me, I drink my coffee while flipping through the magazine. There are plenty of articles on hunting and showing that don't interest me, but as I flick through there's one that immediately catches my eyes. It's a feature on Helena Cullen. *Seventeen year old Helena (Leni) Cullen, up and coming star, talks us through her plans for the year.* The main picture is a close up of her, standing between two horses, one of which is Arturo. She is smiling, pink lips pressed together, wavy blond hair pulled back, and green eyes matching the jumper she's wearing. The article goes through the main competitions she's aiming toward this season, as well as her long term goals. *The main dream is Badminton, Leni says with a smile. If things keep going as well, then this seventeen year old is well on her way.* Reading the words makes my stomach twist, and earlier's tears threaten to return. I bet Helena Cullen wasn't made a fool of when she told her guidance counsellor she wants to go to the Olympics. I bet she doesn't have to go to school. She gets to spend all day every day riding, with her parents' full support. For her, Badminton isn't just a dream, it's a goal. An achievable one.

I don't know how long I stay on the bench, reading the article over and over again, thinking of the injustice of everything .

'Heads up,' Graham says with a nod, 'the owner's here.'
I turn in the saddle, searching the side of the track for Frank.

Sure enough, beside him, standing in front of a parked BMW, is a man in a tweed jacket. Even from a distance, I can make out a stern expression.

'That's Schofield?' I say. I've no reason to be afraid, but I suddenly wish I was anywhere else.

'Yep. You were off the last time he came. Miserable sod. I don't think he knows what he's looking at.'

Instinctively, I drop a hand to Loxwood's neck. Not a pat, he doesn't like that. I just let it rest there. 'How many does he own?'

'As well as him?' Graham says. 'He's got one other one with Frank. The big grey filly. He's got a dozen others elsewhere.'

It's early morning, and still cold despite the sunshine. Being Saturday, I don't have to worry about being on time for school. I was looking forward to it when I woke up, a relaxing ride on Loxwood. Except it seems it's not going to go that way.

After exchanging words with Schofield, Frank comes over to us. The horses have already been warmed up on the small track, and we're waiting to take them up the hill. There are other owners parked beside Schofield, all enjoying an early outing to watch their horses run.

'Take him up front, James,' he says.

'Yes, boss.'

'Owner's in a bad mood,' Frank says tightly. 'Let him out, give him his head. The guy wants to see speed, give it to him.'

'Yes, boss.'

Loxwood's stride lengthens, and he lowers his head as he moves. His rhythm is beautiful, and his balance perfect, but it's not enough.

'Come on, boy,' I say, clicking my tongue.

His ears flicker backwards, and I push him on again. He responds by building impulsion, his body shortening like a spring.

The lump of coal rises in my chest, shortening my breath. He would be the perfect event horse, able to sustain a cross country course, and always be collected for the sharp turns. But that's not what matters now. What matters is that he run fast, so that his owner is happy, and leaves him with Frank, where he is safe.

'Come on,' I say again, moving my hands up his neck.

The cold air stings my eyes, and all I hear is the steady rhythm of Loxwood breathing. The closer we get to the top of the hill, the more he slows down, until the ground has levelled out and he has come back to a walk. As Graham and the other riders slow behind me, I feel sick. Loxwood is nice to ride from an event rider's point of view, but he doesn't go like the winners do. The youngsters who go out and win their first races have that sudden turn of speed you never see coming. You think you're going as fast as you can, but then suddenly there's this whole other gear you didn't know existed. Loxwood doesn't have that.

Frank has joined Schofied again, standing with him at the owners' watch point, midway up the hill. They're staring at our group as we walk down, but I know at least Schofield's eyes are only on me. His expression is unreadable, because it has that quality that suggests he always looks displeased.

I keep my glance down as we walk past them, not wanting to meet Schofield's judgemental stare. I wish I could turn Loxwood away from the other horses and gallop off into the distance, never to be heard of again.

We're at the road crossing when Frank catches up with us again. He runs his hand through his pale, greying hair every few steps, and I feel my heart rate increase. It's one of the giveaway signs with Frank, a way of knowing he's stressed.

'What did he think?' I ask. It's not my place to be concerned about one of the horses. I'm an exercise rider, paid to ride and nothing else and nothing more. But Frank knows I have a soft spot for this horse, to put it mildly. He does, too.

'Arrrg,' he sighs, shaking his head. 'The guy doesn't have a clue. But he's not impressed with his times. Especially not when that filly is going so well.'

'What's he going to do?' I say, struggling to keep my voice even.

'I don't know,' Frank says. 'He's going to let me know. Said he's considering sending him to Marlborough.'

'What? Why? If he won't run for you, then he won't run for anyone.'

Frank's shaking his head, but he grins at the compliment. 'This is the part I hate, James. I don't get much more of a say than you do. It's the way things go.'

I can't think of anything else to say, and Frank walks into the road to stop oncoming traffic.

# Chapter 6

Nothing more of Loxwood is mentioned during the week that follows, and I'm still none the wiser when I go with Clara to Rose's the next weekend. Every time I've ridden Loxwood since has been shadowed with a fear that it might be the last, and the worry has been making me sick. So much so that my mum even noticed something was up. And that's saying something.

Stepping onto Rose's yard makes my mind feel clearer than it has all week. The higgledy-piggledy stable block, with its tin roof, and happy horses looking out over each door. There's the occasional scurry of the barn cats, Map and Web, or the family dog. But mostly there's a feeling of comfort.

Clara is going on a hack with one of the other full liveries, and Rose offers to give me a lesson on the flat. I gratefully accept, and spend the next hour focussing on precise dressage movements, riding semi-retired schoolmaster Sterling. It's like a time out from real life, an escape. For a short moment, it's as though the aids for a half-pass are the most important thing in the world, and although I'm exhausted it leaves me feeling rested.

This week, Mackenzie swapped cupcakes for brownies, and she carries out six of them and two glasses of milk, setting the tray in the kitchenette by the tack room.

'How's Loxwood?' she asks when we're both on our second.

Just hearing his name makes me want to cry. 'Not so good,' I say quietly. 'He isn't very fast at the moment.'

'But that's a good thing!' Mackenzie says. 'That means you can have him!'

'It doesn't, Kenz. He might be given to another trainer, or sold.'

'He might not,' she says with all the confidence of a child who thinks that there's no such thing as an unhappy ending.

'It's best for him that he stay where he is,' I say, looking down at what's left of the milk in my glass.

I'm prepared for Mackenzie to tell me again that I don't know what I'm talking about, and that there's no reason I can't have a horse, or something else along those lines. But instead she gets up from her chair, putting the half eaten brownie down on the table, and walks round to put her arms around my neck, resting her head against my cheek. The tears I've been fighting to hold in the past couple weeks well up in my eyes, and I silently let them fall, with only Kenzie to witness them.

I don't particularly feel up to it, but Rose is going on another show jumping outing the next day, and Mackenzie made me promise that I would go along. I'm not working at the track today, but I awake early none the less. I go downstairs to the kitchen at six o'clock, make myself a cup of green tea, put a pop tart in the toaster, and then carry both back up to bed. There's no chance of me falling back to sleep, but it's nice to just lie there, without any obligations. This lasts forty-five minutes, by which point I can't take staying still any longer. That's when it occurs to me that I should find a way to thank Mackenzie for her regular baked goods, and so I decide to bake something. By eight o'clock there's a tray of flapjacks cooling on the oven, and my pyjama sleeves are soaked from washing up.

My parents still aren't up when I leave the house an hour later, the flapjacks in a Tupperware box in my rucksack. It rained during the night, and while the weather is clear now, I'm constantly dodging puddles on the road.

It takes over twenty minutes to cycle the four miles, but some days, like today, it feels like nothing. When I get to the yard, the last few stables are being mucked out by Leah, whilst some of the DIY horses are still waiting to be fed. Rose has offered to do so before, hating seeing them starve, but the owners refuse. One woman left the yard last year when she lashed out at Rose for giving her horse a slice of hay when she still hadn't shown up at eleven. That was just before Paige came, claiming the free stable. In the few weeks it was empty, I thought if ever I did get Loxwood there would at least be space for him, but not now.

As soon as she sees me, Rose insists that I go inside with her for a cup of tea. Mackenzie and Jemima are still in their pyjamas, and Ben, who doesn't work with horses, is flipping pancakes.

'Sunday is pancake day,' Mackenzie says excitedly.

We spend the next hour topping them with syrup and Nutella until we feel sick, before heading out again. I help Rose get the competing horses ready, and when Kenzie appears, now fully dressed, I help her groom Cinder. Clara is going too, but she won't leave until later.

It's sunny when we pull into the venue - the same venue as a couple weeks before. In addition to being only a fifteen minute drive away, it hosts both affiliated and unaffiliated shows on a weekly basis.

At some point during Rose's first warm-up, after Mackenzie and Cinder have already ridden a clear round, I'm leaning against the railing, when I notice one of the other riders in the class. It's Helena Cullen, on a different horse this time. He's a dark bay, without any markings, and I recognise him as Flintstone Cooper.

I lean up from the railing, cross my arms over my chest, and look around. It takes me a moment to spot her, but I see Amanda Walton near the entrance. She's not standing by the fences, like most of the coaches, but blending into the crowd.

'Leni,' she calls out, shortly after I've spotted her. Flintstone Cooper is trotted over to Amanda Walton, where Helena slows him to a halt.

Mackenzie is standing beside me, completely engrossed by one of the grey horses going round, and unaware of the conversation along from us. They're speaking quietly, but I can make out a few words.

'What's up with you?' Amanda is saying, 'you're riding like a sack of potatoes! You look half asleep!'

If what I just saw looked like a sack of potatoes, then that must be a compliment.

'Nothing. I'm fine,' Helena mutters. I notice, for the first time, that there are dark circles beneath her eyes.

'Get it together,' Amanda says bitterly, turning round to regain her spot by the entrance.

Helena seems to let out a sigh, shortening her reins to push her horse back into a collected trot. I scan the faces of the other spectators, but I can't make out her mother. Everyone always says that Amanda Walton is tough, but you put up with it because she is the best. End of.

I would have stayed and watched the rest of Helena's warm-up, but Rose is called to the ring just as Flintstone Cooper pops into a canter, and so Mackenzie and I make our way to the arena.

The TV is loud when I wheel my bike into the hallway, struggling to get it past the pairs of shoes that line the wall. Hope dropped me off again, Clara's clear round having left them both in a jolly mood. Back at Rose's, I had pulled the box of flapjacks out of my bag, and we all ate until we couldn't manage another bite.

'Georgia?' my mum calls.

I let go of the bike to close the front door, and the handle bars falls against me. 'No,' I yell back, between cursing to myself, 'a burglar.'

'Georgia,' she says again, despairingly this time.

'Who else is it going to be!?' I call, leaning my bike against the wall. I throw my rucksack onto the floor and wrestle out of my coat.

'Are you coming?'

'No, I thought I would move into the hallway permanently. What do you think I'm doing!?'

'Georgia!' she says my name angrily now. 'Come in here, please.'

Kicking my boots off as I walk, I make my way to the kitchen, where my mum is in her usual spot at the table, some papers beside her laptop. I don't look back at my dad, who'll be reclined on the sofa.

'What's up?' I say casually, wearing my most clueless look.

'You know, Georgia,' my mum says, sighing the first words, as though this conversation is going to require great effort on her part. 'We let you get away with a lot, your father and I. You're free to go out as you please, something you do take advantage of. We never restrict you from seeing friends, and we always let you have money when you go out.' (This refers to the what has become known as "the food jar", which lives on top of the microwave. It's where spare change and notes go, and I'm free to take from it as I wish to buy myself provisions, which gets everyone out of cooking. I must say that it's one of my favourite of mum's parenting techniques.) '…and all we ask on your part, Georgia, is a little respect, and some effort…'

I know we're almost there. She's sighing again. Talking to me is exhausting, apparently.

'A letter came from your principal.' *Bingo.* 'You're failing everything!' she cries, picking the letter up and then throwing it back down again. In the background, one of the contestants on the gameshow my dad's watching loses, and he yells at the TV.

'No I'm not,' I say, 'I'm top of the class in P.E.'

'P.E. does not count!' my mum screams.

'I do pretty well at Geography, too-'

'Stop being pedantic, Georgia. You know full well this is a joke.'

I cross my arms across my chest. 'Fine. Whatever. Can I go now?'

'No, you cannot go!' my mum says, standing up from the table.

Clearly the contestants on my dad's gameshow are useless, because there are more disappointed cries, followed by him insulting the TV once more. I use this as an excuse to look away, and my mum sighs loudly.

'John!' she calls. 'Can you come in here? This concerns both of us!'

I stay rooted to the same spot, while there's the sound of a glass being placed on the coffee table, and the sofa springs giving way as weight is lifted from it.

'What's the problem?' my dad says, walking lazily to stand beside me.

'Georgia's schoolwork.' My mum says tensely. 'We got a letter from her principal, remember?'

'What did the principal say, exactly?' I interrupt, in an attempt to approach the matter from a different angle.

She sighs dramatically. 'That you've stopped paying attention, and are not handing in your homework. They said you gave in a *blank page*, Georgia! What on earth is that about!?'

'What's the problem?' my dad says.

'There is no problem,' I snap.

My mum picks the letter up again and shakes it in the air. 'Clearly there is!' she says. 'Mrs Paterson thinks you should get some tutoring?'

'Who?' I say.

'*Who* what?' my mum says in an irritated tone.

'Who the heck is Mrs Paterson?'

'She's your principal, Georgia,' my mother cries. 'How can you not know your principal's name?'

'I have better things to do with my life than memorise the names of the college faculty.' I say.

'*Better things..* - I'm not going into that now.' she says. 'Anyway, Mrs Paterson, *your principal*, is suggesting that you go to after school tutoring classes.'

'Ha,' I laugh. 'Good luck with that.'

'Georgia,' my mum says, her gaze drifting to my dad. She's probably hoping he'll back her up, but he's standing with his neck craned in an effort to see the TV.

'I don't need tutoring, and I spend enough hours at school as it is.' I say.

'You're failing all of your classes-' she screams.

'Not *all*-'

'..and you think you don't need tutoring!?'

'I could pass if I wanted to,' I say.

'What is that supposed to mean!?' my mum says.

I look down at my socks and shake my head, wondering how far I should go. 'It means that if I wanted to sit down and do my homework I could. I don't need anyone explaining it to me, I understand fine on my own. It means that I can't even bring myself to do that, because it's not what I want to do with my life!'

My mum crosses her arms and lets out a breath. 'And what exactly *do* you want to do with your life that doesn't involve qualifications?'

'Dammit, Mum, I want to *ride*.' I say, my hands in fists. 'You know that's what I want to do. It's all I want to do. Why else do you think I get up at four o'clock every day? Why do I cycle four miles - eight in all - after school, most of which is in the dark in winter!? Do you know what it's like to have to watch other people live the life you dream of having yourself!?'

'Do you think your dad and I thought our lives would pan out like this!?' My mum yells. 'Do you think we dreamed of living like this when we were your age!? Of course not. And you're going to end up the same way if you don't go to school and get qualifications.'

'No, I'm not.' I say, my voice beginning to shake with anger. 'You live the lives you lead because you've never aspired to anything else. Not going to school doesn't mean I'm lazy, it means the opposite. Sitting at a desk and doing what you're told is easy. Having to give something your all, with no guarantee of success, is a different matter altogether. I don't want to just get by, I want to *achieve* things.'

'Wait until you're older,' my mum says. 'Life doesn't work like that. Wait until you have bills and a mortgage. Don't you have any idea how hard we work just to get by!?'

'You don't!' I yell. 'This is my point! There's a difference between working a few hours a day, and dedicating your entire life to a goal.'

My dad choses this moment to divert his attention away from the TV. 'I think that's enough.'

'Don't change the subject,' my mum says to me, coldly. 'We're not talking about us. We're talking about you. Failing subjects isn't going to help you with anything. You need to commit.'

'Homework isn't going to help my riding,' I scoff.

'Not doing it isn't going to help anyone,' she says.

'Don't you get that school is completely irrelevant to what I want to do for the rest of my life!? I have to watch other people succeed, and bringing myself to do homework when *I* can't live that kind of life is torture.'

'Who are these *other people* you keep referring to!?' my mum says. 'Anyway, Georgia, I don't want to keep discussing the matter. If you don't want to go to tutoring then you can jolly well get your grades up and that's that.' She sits back down in front of her computer as she says the final words, a way of showing that the conversation is over.

I look towards my dad, but he's already gone back to the sofa. Instead I'm left standing, while my parents stare at their respective screens.

'Whatever,' I mutter, turning to leave. I walk a few steps

before turning back to my mum. 'I'll stop talking about it if you can just answer me one thing,' I say. 'What if I had a horse, and paid for it myself and you never had to hear about it. Would you actually care?'

For a moment I think she hasn't heard, because her eyes remained fixated on her laptop. 'I don't care, Georgia,' she says. 'I really don't care.'

# Chapter 7

'Seriously, can we stop now!? I feel like I'm about to die. And my feet hurt.'

I come to halt, a few paces ahead Lizzie, and Graham, who is even farther out front, stops to turn back.

'We've only done two miles,' he says, looking at his heart rate monitor.

'Lizzie's right,' I wheeze, leaning forward to rest my hands on my knees. It's only four degrees, yet we're all in t-shirts. 'This is torture.'

'Thank you!' Lizzie says.

'I mean,' I continue, my breathing still rapid. 'I seriously don't know how you do this every day. Literally, the only reason I've made it this far is because I'm thinking about what flavour cake I'm going to eat in a minute. And you don't even get to do that.'

'I have to,' Graham says, looking at his watch again. 'I'm

pretty sure he's regretting ever asking us to join him on his daily run. I agreed because the idea of clearing my head sounded appealing, and Lizzie only so she wouldn't be left out.

'You can carry on,' she says, wiping the back of her hand across her forehead. 'I need a hot chocolate. You can meet us there when you're done.'

Graham shrugs, looks at his heart rate monitor again, and resumes his jog across the pavements of Newmarket.

'Come on,' Lizzie says to me when he is out of sight. 'I'm starving.'

Our favourite table is available, and we collapse onto the soft chairs, with a tray of hot drinks and slices of cake in front of us. We're in a corner, not conspicuous to other customers, but in the perfect place to do some people watching. My mouth is full of cake (bought with money from the food jar) when somebody's order catches my attention.

'Regular cappuccino and a slice of red velvet.'

I look up because it's my usual order, to the point that most of the people that work here know without asking me. But I glance towards the counter without thinking, absentmindedly, and it's only when I've turned back to my drink that something startles me, and my eyes go up again. You know when you recognise someone but don't know them? Something nags at your mind because they look familiar, yet you know you've never met. The girl looks about my age, and I flick through the nameless faces I pass in school corridors every day in a bid to place her. But the more I look, the more I know that's not where I know her from..

'What you looking at?' says Lizzie, noticing my distraction.

I snap my eyes away, turning my concentration back to my friend, and that's when it hits me. 'Nothing,' I say quickly. 'Just thinking.'

Lizzie stares at me a moment longer before taking another mouthful of her carrot cake. Once I'm sure she's no longer suspicious, I flick my gaze back to the counter, where the girl is waiting to pay. Where Helena Cullen is pulling a wallet out of her handbag.

I've only ever seen her either in photographs or on horseback, which is why it took me a while to recognise her. Her thick, dark blond hair reaches below her shoulder blades, in unbrushed curls. She is wearing dark jeans, her legs muscular from riding. I see now that the coat she has on is a horse one, a familiar logo on the navy blue sleeve. Her shoes aren't riding boots, but they look like them.

'Four pounds ninety,' the girl behind the counter says.

Helena unzips her wallet and begins lining coins up in front of her. She seems to get to four pounds easily enough, and then she starts counting pennies. Unbelievable. Amanda Walton's coaching rates are fifty pounds an hour, and here Helena is, counting pennies. Rich and a cheapskate, the worst combination.

There are close to twenty different coins on the counter by the time the amount is achieved, by which point the barista at the till looks well and truly annoyed.

'Thank you,' Helena says, not meeting her eye. She's probably completely unaware of what a nuisance she's been, clueless as she walks to a table.

I look away again, quickly, nervous that she'll see something in my face that suggests I know who she is. Or, worse, that she'll recognise me from competitions. Not that I imagine Helena Cullen paying attention to some nobody spectator.

Graham comes through the doors just as Helena is taking her coat off to sit down.

'Have fun!?' Lizzie calls, loud enough to make Helena glance in our direction, which makes me looks down shyly.

'Laugh now,' Graham says. 'Just wait until I'm the most in demand jockey in Newmarket.'

We sit in silence while Graham orders himself a drink - coffee, black, no sugar - and I do my best not to look at Helena. I glanced long enough to see her pull a thick paperback from her bag, and as far as I know she's barely looked up since.

'What's wrong with you?' Lizzie's voice says, cutting into my thoughts.

'Huh?'

Lizzie and Graham laugh. 'Your head in the clouds today?' Graham says.

I force a smile. 'Something like that.'

Another moment of silence passes before Lizzie frowns and says, 'Seriously, stop, you're weirding me out. Since when are you so quiet?'

I try to think up a witty response, but for once my mind is blank. At the track, and around Lizzie and Graham, I'm usually the loud, confident one. The one not afraid of offending somebody, or speaking their mind. I'm confident in my ability to ride whatever horse is thrown at me, and that self assurance translates in my attitude. But when I'm at Rose's it's not the same. It's not a world I'm part of, however much I want to be, and I feel like I don't belong. It's like have two different lives, and I'm not used to them crossing like this. Not that Helena Cullen is even part of my life, but her presence reminds me of it.

'That run exhausted me,' I say with a grin, and Lizzie laughs.

'See what you've done to her, Graham?' she says, and I let out a breath at the awkward moment passing.

Graham launches into a debate on how little we ran, and

how if Lizzie ran every day it would get better... Their discussion gives me a chance to zone out again, and I look back at Helena. She's still reading, pausing occasionally for a sip of coffee or a forkful of cake. I tilt my head in a bid to see the cover, though I doubt I'll have read whatever it is. It's not that I don't like reading - when I was little I read every pony book I could get my hands on - but it's something I do more and more rarely. The thing is that I don't like rubbish books. The kind my mum is always reading, with stickers on them like *Number one bestseller* or *Top book club choice*. They're the only sort we have lying around the house, and one page is all it takes for me to put them down. I only like good books, the really great sagas that are considered classics. I don't have time to read much anymore, I'm usually exhausted whenever I have an hour spare in the evening, and by then my brain is too fried for the concentration required to read the kind of book I enjoy. As a consequence, I tend to only read one book every few months, if I have the time to dedicate myself fully to it. I still remember spending three solid days in my room, before I started working at the track, devouring *Wuthering Heights* page by page. That's the kind of reading I do. I don't think I'll ever be able to do one chapter here and one chapter there just for the sake of it.

Leaning forwards in her chair, Helena closes the book, keeping her thumb between two pages as a bookmark, and reaches for her coffee cup. My eyes snap down, and I get a perfect view of the cover. I was expecting one of those light books my mum reads, with some generic title, or a pathetic cover photo of a bracelet, or a door, or whatever else is usually on them. But I'm surprised to not only see the title of a well known classic, but one I've read and enjoyed. *Far From the Madding Crowd* by Thomas Hardy.

The sound of Lizzie and Graham laughing turns my attention back to them. I don't know why, but seeing Helena read a decent book has annoyed me. Maybe because it's easier to hate her if I imagine her as being stupid. I mean, seriously, I must have read no more than twenty novels in the past five years, what are the odds of her holding one of them now?

I'm listening to Lizzie recount a recent argument with her mother over laundry when Helena walks past us. I look down at my watch discreetly, trying to remember what time it was when Helena arrived, and decide that she can't have been here for more than fifteen minutes. I don't know where she lives, but I know for a fact that Amanda Walton's yard is forty minutes away, and she can't be far from there. Of course, she could have been in the area, but it strikes me as strange that she should drive all that way, just to stay in a coffeehouse for fifteen minutes. Why am I even thinking about any of this!? It doesn't affect me, and it's not exactly interesting. For all I know she lives in this very town, and drives the forty minutes to Amanda's every day.

'..and, so, I was like, "Since when do you have a problem doing my washing? It's not like you have anything else to do…"'

I take a sip of my cappuccino, which is now nothing but cold froth. Graham is drumming his fingers against his coffee cup, looking gaunt and hungry. Maybe the hungry part is my imagination, but it's hard to look at him without thinking that he must be.

'What are you going to do when you leave home?' I say, in a bid to contribute something to the conversation. I know Lizzie well enough that I'm never offended or horrified by the way she speaks of her parents. Even if I have been doing my own washing since I was twelve. I just see it as amusement.

'Why would I ever move out?' she says. 'I don't pay rent,' She counts on her fingers. 'I don't clean, I don't cook. It's not like I ever want kids, anyway, so I only need to move out if I meet some millionaire who has a team of staff to do all that stuff for me once we're married.'

'You're terrible,' Graham, who rides four or five horses a day to pay the rent on his mouse infested flat, says.

'Jealous,' Lizzie says with a smile.

'Miss James?'

I stop in the hallway, turning to where a woman is standing. Her hair has been blow-dried to hang around her face like a bowl, and she wears a vile red suit, with lipstick to match. Is this the principal? I can't tell, they all look the same.

'Yes,' I say.

'I informed your parents of your struggles lately,' she says, confirming her identity, and smiling as though she's done me a favour.

'I know, we got your letter,' I say, with a smile as fake as her own.

'You know,' Mrs Paterson says, 'we only do this to help you.' God, teachers' favourite line. And the way they say *we*, like it's some secret sorority.

'I'm sure you do,' I say, dragging out each word.

'It's for your own good,' she says, still with that stupid smile.

'I'm sure it is,' I say in the same tone as my last response.

'Miss James,' Mrs Paterson says, annoyed this time. Something about the way she speaks and comes across makes me think of a political candidate. In fact, I would hardly be surprised to see her face next time a debate is on TV. 'You might think that you know what you want now, but if you change your mind in a year or so, and don't have any grades to fall back on, then you'll be sorry.'

'All due respect, Mrs,' I say, which I only ever say when I mean without any respect at all. 'But I know exactly what I want to do with my life, and whether or not I pass Chemistry has nothing to do with it.'

'I can't help but notice, Miss James,' she continues, as though I never spoke. 'That you aren't part of any after school activities. You know, there are many clubs you could join.'

I force a smile, biting my lips to stop myself from saying something I'll regret. 'I don't have time for extra curricular activities.'

'I don't know how that can be, it's not like you spend the time doing homework.'

Mrs Paterson's comeback catches me off guard. Teachers and staff don't usually get sarcasm or irony, let alone employ it. 'I have a job.' I say.

'It would do you some good to have interests.'

'I have interests,' I say coldly, as the bell rings in the background. 'Now, if you excuse me,' I say with a fake smile, 'I don't want to be late for Physics.'

# Chapter 8

Seeing the wide track in front of me feels like somebody has picked up the box of worries inside my head and emptied the contents over a cliff. It's my last ride of the day, on Nantucket Winter, a gorgeous grey, and possibly my second favourite horse to ride after Loxwood. Frank says he hasn't heard a word from Schofield, but even he did I'm not sure he would think to tell me. Exercise riders' feelings aren't exactly high up on his list of priorities. But I rode Loxwood this morning, and it was lovely, and I'm now on another horse I love, and simply enjoying it. Lizzie and Graham are riding in the same group - Graham up front, and Lizzie behind. We're going to grab lunch afterwards, and then I'm spending the afternoon with Clara at Rose's. And, for once, I'm not feeling pessimistic. I'm enjoying myself, galloping up a hill, and looking forward to stuffing my face with a mozzarella and tomato sandwich.

Nantucket goes well, though I'm not sure he'll be a racing

star, either. He's like Loxwood - beautifully made, with a great attitude, but not built purely for speed. Not like the filly Graham is riding, who is always way ahead. But she's almost completely crazy, and most jockeys don't like riding her. Maybe that's why Loxwood and Nantucket won't make good racehorses. It seems the fast ones all have a screw loose.

We walk down to the crossing, Frank ahead, ready to start heading back to the yard. There are cars rushing past, and we pull up as Frank steps out to stop them. Nantucket stops happily, as does Lizzie's horse behind, but Graham's chucks her head, prancing sideways, and threatens to go up.

'Easy,' he says, unfazed by what is common behaviour.

Lorries slow to a stop, and Frank waves his hand for us to cross. But even when he allows her to move forward, Graham's filly rears straight up. Not a little rear, a few feet off the ground for the sake of it, but a full on rear, body vertical.

Lizzie screams, Frank calls out "whoa" in a bid to calm the horse, and I just stare. Grahams throws his weight forward, successfully staying on until the filly brings her front legs back to the tarmac. But he isn't prepared when she goes up again, with even more power this time. Frank yells again, and I watch in horror as Graham is thrown backwards, taking the Thoroughbred with him. I hear Lizzie cry again as the two of them come crashing down onto the tarmac, Graham's frail body beneath that of the horse.

Frank doesn't falter, reaching the filly's head before she is even up, catching hold of the reins. She's more shocked than anything, not looking to be suffering from any grave injury. But Graham is still on the ground.

'Graham,' I yell. I daren't get off, that only ever makes things worse, but I walk Nantucket up as close as I can, knowing he's sensible enough not to strike out with a leg or anything like that. There was a groom nearby, who is now rushing over to take the horse, while Frank kneels by Graham. I make out another spectator rushing to the ambulance that is always parked nearby in case of incidents like this.

'I'm okay,' Graham says quietly, his body still and his eyes closed.

Drivers are now getting out of their vehicles, leaving doors open, and hazards flashing. We're sprawled out on the road as though it's our own private patio.

Franks is kneeling beside Graham, not worrying about the waiting motorists. 'Don't move,' he says. 'Take your time.' He looks down at Graham's pallor, and then up at me and Lizzie. 'You lot are friends, aren't you?' he says. 'When did he last eat or drink?' I can't believe Frank would be paying close enough attention to an exercise rider to see something like that, and it clearly shows on my face because he looks at me and says, 'Do you think I don't notice these things? He shrinks by the day. Did he eat anything this morning?'

'He doesn't eat,' Lizzie says hysterically, her ride prancing at his rider's panic. 'He never does.'

'He has to starve himself,' I say. 'To make weight,' I add, as though it isn't obvious.

More people are coming over now, including paramedics from the nearby ambulance. Frank is still kneeling beside Graham, the kind of concern on his face that is usually reserved for the horses.

'I'm fine,' Graham says shakily, trying to push himself up.

'Is he all right?' I say, to Frank.

'Would be if he had any strength,' he says. 'I reckon that's why he's passing out.'

A stretcher is being rolled towards us now, and the horses start shuffling even more than before.

'You lot need to take the horses back,' Frank says. 'He'll be fine, I'll stay with him, just get the horses back to the yard.'

I don't protest, and even though I sense she would like to, neither does Lizzie. It's the same in all equestrian disciplines, no matter how gravely injured the rider is, the horse must come first.

Lizzie is practically sobbing the whole ride up the sand covered pavement, earning us judgemental stares from cyclists and runners.

'He's going to be fine,' I say, my voice steady, and for a fleeting moment I'm reminded of the way teachers address me.

'It just happened so quickly,' Lizzie says, her voice catching in her throat. 'How do you stay so calm?'

I am wondering the same thing. This isn't the first time this sort of accident has occurred - with close to three thousand horses going out every morning it's kind of a regular occurrence. And it never flusters me. Not even when it's my own friend. Maybe I'm just heartless.

The ambulance is still parked in its regular spot when Lizzie and I reach the scene of the accident. Graham's horse had already been led back to the yard when we got there, and we handed our own to waiting grooms at top speed before rushing off, collecting our things on the way.

'I should have carried on with that stupid run,' Lizzie yelled, wheezing as we sprinted back down the pavement.

The road was clear, the constant flow of traffic resumed. At first we thought we were too late, and that the ambulance had already left, but then we saw it, and Frank's broad figure beside.

'Is he all right?' Lizzie calls to him as we approach. 'Where is he?'

Frank nods towards the ambulance. 'He's in there, he's fine.' He doesn't have time to say more before Lizzie hurries to the ambulance doors, behind which, on closer approach, I see Graham sitting up on a stretcher, sipping a carton of orange juice from a straw.

'What did they say?' I ask Frank, standing beside him, a safe distance away from the ambulance. I might be good in a crisis, but anything hospital related freaks me out.

'He was lucky. Had a body protector on, so that broke his fall, he was just winded for a bit. Probably more to do with the fact that he was close to unconscious as it was.'

'All he wants is to be a jockey,' I stammer. 'He left school when he was sixteen, I don't think he'd even know how to do anything else.'

Frank shrugged. 'I know. And jockeys starve themselves, we all know that.. It's still dangerous.'

After stalling for a bit longer, I stick my head round the door to say a quick word to Graham, before the paramedics insist on driving him to the nearest hospital just to be sure. By the time the ordeal is over, neither Lizzie nor I feel like going out for lunch anymore, so we each head home. I thought all I wanted was to stay put, and spend the afternoon lounging around, watching movies and eating ice cream, bur after an hour in the same house as my parents I realise that I'm not traumatised enough to choose their company over a few hours at Rose's.

A roan pony is plodding around the ring when we pull up. Hope and Clara were horrified when I told them about the morning's events, and seemed far more disturbed than I was on the drive over.

'Sit up, Jem,' Rose calls. 'Good girl, keep your heels down.'

Jemima trots Pheasant in circles, the elderly pony that once belonged to Mackenzie looking as laid-back as ever. Her brown hair is in a plait, which bounces against her back with every stride. Rose raises a hand to us in acknowledgement, and I wave back, a smile spreading across my face. I can't imagine what it would have been like to grow up like Mackenzie and Jemima, with a barn full of horses on your doorstep, and a mum there to teach you. For me, the idea is stored in the same box as what it would have been like to grow up in some Hollywood mansion, or a beach hut in the Bahamas. Pure fantasy.

'Would you like to jump Sterling?' Rose asks me when she comes back to the stables, Jemima following on Pheasant.

'If you're sure,' I say, to which Rose nods. Sterling is her former three-star horse, who at eighteen is now retired from competition, and earns his keep as a lesson schoolmaster. The first time I ever jumped him, I was so nervous of doing something to mess him up, but as time has passed I've realised he's so easy to ride that it's almost impossible.

After warming up over trotting poles and a crossbar, Rose sets up a grid. Clara and I then spend the next half hour taking turns to go down it, being corrected as we do so. And for once, not only can I be happy that Sterling was perfect, but Spirit and Clara are just as successful. Grids are best for her, as so long as she gets in on a half descent stride, Spirit can do the rest.

I've just finished cooling Sterling off when Mackenzie appears, rushing from the house with a tray of cupcakes. It's freezing outside, and along with Rose and Clara we huddle into the clubhouse, where we're drawn to the radiator like magnets.

'You girls did well today,' Rose says as we eat.

'Sterling always does well,' I say. And before Rose can try to compliment my riding instead, which really isn't what I was searching for when I said that, I add, 'I can't believe he never got to four-star.'

'Oh,' Rose says with a smile, 'I can.'

'But, he's amazing!' I say. 'And I've seen the pictures of him competing.'

'He is amazing, don't get me wrong. But plenty of horses can get to three-star, and it takes a whole other sort of horse to make that next step up. It's not that he was lacking anything on paper, it's just that extra...' Rose's voice drifts as she rubs her thumb to her index finger. 'You know?'

'Yeah,' I say. The same nameless quality I associate with Loxwood. 'Did you never find one like that?'

'God, yes,' Rose says immediately. '*Searching for Orion*. That was his name. I picked him up for peanuts from some local dealer. Now *he* had that quality.'

'What happened to him?' I say, doing little to hide my shock. In all the time I've known Rose, I've never heard her discuss this horse before.

Rose smiles sadly. 'The thing I've always dreaded. Someone made me an offer I couldn't refuse.'

'What?' I cry, having fully prepared myself to hear some tragic death scene.

'When I was little,' she continues, 'I remember hearing about stories like that, how a rider could sell their top horse for the right price, and be both completely horrified and adamant that it would never happen to me. But when it does, sometimes you have no choice.'

Mackenzie and Clara are silent, but I manage to say, 'And did he go four-star?'

Rose looks me in the eye, creases appearing under her hazel coloured eyes. 'What do you think?'

When I get home, Orion and Rose are still on my mind. I head straight to the kitchen for something to eat, where my mum is sitting at the table, more purchases beside her. I put an Oreo in my mouth before fishing out whatever she bought.

*You have got to be kidding me*, I think as I pull the first item out the bag.

'Isn't it a nice idea!?' my mum says, smiling ignorantly. 'I don't know why I haven't thought to do it sooner!'

I stare at the heart shaped wreath in horror, and swallow down the last of my Oreo. 'Mystery, indeed.' I mutter before scanning the monstrosity for a price tag. 'Twenty quid!' I yell. 'How can you waste twenty quid on something like that!?'

'Georgia,' she says. 'I've had enough of this. There's nothing wasteful about it, and it's my money to spend.'

'It's pathetic,' I say, slamming the wreath down on the table, and then turning back for the packet of Oreos. 'You know, some people have to give up the things they love more than anything in the world just to pay the bills, and there you are, wasting money on rubbish.'

'I will not be spoken to like that in my own house!' my mum yells, looking up from her computer.

'Whatever,' I say angrily, marching out the room with the packet of biscuits in my hand. 'It's not fair,' I shout as I stomp up the stairs, tears prickling my eyes. Absolutely nothing in life is fair.

# Chapter 9

'HAPPY BIRTHDAY!'

I frown at Clara, my right hand holding my rucksack strap in place over my shoulder. 'Don't,' I say.

'It's your *birthday*!' Clara says, loud enough for a group of guys I don't know walking past us to turn and look towards me.

'Seriously,' I say, 'I hate my birthday, and I hate people knowing that it's my birthday. The only bright side is that it's just one more year until independence.'

'And you can drive now,' she adds. 'Seventeen….' Clara muses as we begin walking down the hallway. 'When did we get so old?'

I glare at her. 'Don't,' I say again. 'You know how much I hate this day.'

Clara rolls her eyes, tucking her shoulder length hair back behind her ears, and jogs to keep up with me. 'You just say that,' she says, swinging her bag to her waist, unzipping it as we walk.

'Everyone likes their birthday-'

'I don't,' I interrupt.

'-And you know I'm not going to let it slide, anyway, so accept it.'

I've been power walking down the corridor, leaving Clara a few steps behind. I hear the zip of her bag again, followed by the sound of her jogging. 'Here,' she says, thrusting something wrapped in pink and silver paper into my hands.

'I hate you,' I grumble.

'You say that every year,' says Clara, 'and it's still not going to stop me from buying you a present.'

I don't just say it, though, I truthfully do hate receiving presents. If it's something I don't like, then I have to pretend to, and then feel guilty for whomever wasted their money, and if I do like it then I worry I won't ever be able to repay the gesture, and feel guilty again. So it's a no win situation. But I admit that I'm always touched by Clara remembering my birthday, especially considering how hard I try to never bring it up.

The first bell has yet to ring, so when we get to our classroom door, where we are the only two waiting, I discreetly unwrap the present. I shouldn't be surprised by what's inside, seeing how Clara knows me better than most people, but I'm still caught off guard - in a good way.

'You shouldn't have,' I say, a smile spreading across my face.

'Give it a rest,' Clara says.

We were in one of the local tack shops a few weeks ago to pick up a new set of reins for Spirit, whose own had been broken when he caught his leg in them, Clara's fall at a spread having resulted in him taking off for a lap around the school. Leaving Hope to wait at the counter, Clara and I had gone to admire the new stock, including a long-sleeved riding top I coveted. Now here it is in my hands.

I fold the top back into the paper, and slide the entire thing into my bag. 'Thank you,' I say.

Clara pretends to act shocked. 'I'm sorry, I didn't hear you...' She laughs. 'Was that really so hard?'

School is school, which is exactly what I say to my mother when I get home after having Clara treat me to a slice of birthday cake, and am confronted with the generic question. *How was school?* I wonder what parents (or anyone, for that matter) expect when they ask that. Answering honestly *(waste of time, torture, like being forced to watch an old woman thread a needle)* isn't ever considered acceptable, leaving the just as truthful *School is school* saying as the only option. There may be people who respond to this question differently, but I've never met them.

It was reluctantly agreed this morning that we would all go out for a birthday dinner. My mum is the one who suggested it, wanting to do "something special". I was immediately dismissive, having no desire to go out (and certainly not to a restaurant), only to be told off. 'Don't be so ungrateful,' she said. 'Honestly, Georgia, you really are spoilt sometimes.' *It's* my *birthday,* I wanted to scream. But I didn't. I tend not to back down in arguments, even when I know I haven't a chance, but this time I just couldn't be bothered. So after a post school snack, I go upstairs to have a bath, and get ready. When I come back downstairs, wearing the only dress I own and having let my hair loose from its bun, my parents are waiting.

I like eating out, and in fact do so almost everyday, I just don't particularly like restaurants. I love getting coffee and cake with Clara, or a lunchtime pizza with Lizzie and Graham, but evening meals are just dull. You're always tired, and hungry, and have spent so much time agonising over what to order and waiting, that by the time your plate comes you're fed up, and there's always something wrong with the food. This evening is no exception, when after a half-hour wait I'm presented with an unexceptional portion of vegetable lasagne. My mum seemed happy enough with the outing, though, rambling on about the actions of characters in some TV show the whole time.

When I get home, I unwrap my few presents. Everything from my parents are things I specifically asked for (having created an online wish list), so there is neither surprise nor disappointment. They're just small items, nothing extraordinary, but DVDs of eventing footage is fine by me. I take them up to my room, where after changing into my pyjamas and getting into bed, I slide the first disc into my computer. It was nine o'clock when we got back from the restaurant, and it's well after midnight by the time my eyes start flickering closed in front of the screen. I stare at the rolling credits for a while, until the words become blurred. Watching cross country footage is both a comfort and a burden. It's one of the few times when I feel like myself, side by side with what I want to do with my life, but I also worry at how far I have to go, and the fear that it may never happen.

But then there is a wonderful moment, when I've closed my laptop and put it on the floor, and I can no longer keep my eyes open. I see all those cross country fences, and a horse and rider galloping along, with the voice of a commentator in the background. Except that this time it's my name that's being said. And the horse on the other side of the camera lens is a certain chestnut Thoroughbred. There I am, on Loxwood, taking each fence that comes in its stride. I don't see the scene as though I'm riding, rather I'm watching as a spectator. *Georgia James on course,* the loudspeakers say, *riding the magnificent Loxwood. Now here is some good cross country riding if I've ever seen it. And on a self-made horse, as well. Here are two stars of the future.*

I keep playing the image in my mind, again and again, not wanting to lose the moment. Like rereading a passage in a book, or playing your favourite song on repeat, because you want to forget that there is anything else in the world. In that one moment, that image, or book, or song *is* the whole world. And then you fall asleep with it in mind, soaking up every aspect like oxygen, because until morning, you don't have to think or be anything else.

You know when you feel yourself wake up slowly, conscious of each time your eyelids flutter, only to suddenly be wide awake? I feel as though I've been dozing in and out of consciousness, but then a bolt of energy hits me, and suddenly I can't bear to stay still.

I wake up without assistance most mornings, minutes before my alarm is set to go off, but I still set in anyway. This morning, I have yet to hear it. Leaning up from my pillow, I see that it's only just gone four. I could lie back down and fall back into a slumber for half an hour or so, but already I know any attempt to do so would be useless. Instead I get up, and pull on the dirty riding clothes that are in a crumpled pile on the floor, overcome with the sudden need to go outside.

It's still dark, but not as cold as it has been these past few weeks. Don't get me wrong, it's still freezing (four degrees at the most) but at least I'm not dodging sheets of ice.

I walk to the track, where the horses of the trainers who start even earlier than Frank are already running. The first time I saw it, these Thoroughbreds galloping in the dark, for a fleeting moment I believed in magic. It was the only word I could think of to describe this secret nightlife that goes on every day, while the rest of the world is unaware.

At the edge of the white railings, I watch the outlines of horses until the earliest coffeehouse opening hour, by which point the dark sky has faded, giving way to daybreak. I knew I was cold, standing there, but I don't realise just how much until I walk into the heated building. I order a cappuccino and a millionaire shortbread (easier to eat on the go than cake), consuming both on my way back to the track. There are cars on the roads now, the sound of their engines cutting into my perfect silence. I walk past other exercise riders, some about to start the day like me, and others already leaving the track. We're all part of the same team, working in the same area, a common denominator between us. I'm always worrying about belonging, whether it be in the eventing world or my own house. And at times like this, when I'm not searching for anything, but am subtly reminded of it, I remember that I do. There is a community I belong to, where I'm accepted, but it just so happens that it's not where I want to stay.

I throw my coffee cup into a bin, before rounding the corner into Frank's yard. There's the familiar sound of wheelbarrows, and open stable doors reveal tacked up horses, waiting to be taken out. Grooms are already giving some riders a leg up, everyone retrieving their hats and matching silks.

Loxwood's door is closed, and I wander straight up to it and peer in. It takes me a second to realise what's wrong - there's Loxwood, standing and munching his hay. He looks happy enough, his ears pricked as he sees me. But he's not tacked up.

I turn around, panic dripping into my veins. Is he hurt? Has he gone lame? But Frank is here, coming towards me.

'Is he all right?' I say. 'Why aren't we taking him out?'

'Owner called last night,' Frank says, standing with his hands in his coat pockets. 'Wanted to know how he's been going, whether he should try sending him somewhere else.'

'What did you say?' I stammer, struggling to keep my voice from going high pitched.

Frank shrugged. 'I said I thought he'd only be wasting his time. The horse isn't a racehorse, we both know it. He's never going to win the big bucks.' He coughs to clear his throat. 'I told him he'd be better off cutting his losses.'

'What!?'

'We're getting rid of him,' Frank says.

'What!?' I cry again. 'You're giving him away? Where?' My words come out like babbling. 'You're not shipping him off to a dealer, are you?'

'Calm down, James,' Frank says, and a sly grin starts to spread across his face. 'I'm giving him to you.'

# Chapter 10

If it's possible for your thinking capacity to cease, then that's what happens. I'm dumbstruck, standing statue still, Frank opposite me.

'What?' I manage.

Frank laughs. 'What's wrong with you lot? Why are you always shocked when I notice things? Do you think I don't hear you all speak!? You're not exactly subtle!'

'I don't understand…'

'You want him, don't you?'

'Yes,' I almost scream it. 'Yes, I do.'

'Good,' Frank says. 'You know how things work in this world! Owner wants to get rid of a horse, we get rid of it. No questions asked. I sleep a lot better at night if I know a horse is actually in good hands. Now you can turn him into an event horse, or whatever. That's what you and the chatty girl are always saying, isn't it?'

'Maybe,' I say, turning to look at Loxwood, who now has his head over the stable door, watching the other horses go by. 'When do I need to take him?' I add quickly, the consequences of the current exchange now daunting me.

'You know how it is. As quickly as possible.'

There's the steady rhythm of shod hooves on concrete as more horses walk past. Loxwood whinnies as he realises his friends are going off without him, and with it he sets off an alarm in my head. 'I've got to go,' I say to Frank. 'I'm sorry,' I add, looking at what tacked up horses are left. 'But..'

'I understand,' Frank says, his eyes drifting to Loxwood. 'Go. Sort things out,'

'You ready, boss!?' someone calls out.

'Coming,' Frank yells. Then to me he says, 'I'll see you later,'

'Yep,' I say. I watch him march away, and it's only when faced with the back of his blond head that I call, 'Thank you,' as an afterthought.

As the horses disappear from sight, their receding steps accompanied by jockeys' banter, I turn back to Loxwood. He's still looking over the door, not anxiously so much as out off curiosity.

'Hey, boy,' I say quietly. 'It's okay.'

I walk up to the chestnut Thoroughbred and run a hand down his silky neck. Everything about him is familiar, but for the first time something is different. Something both terrifying and exhilarating. *He's mine.*

My legs are burning, and my jaw aches from breathing heavily in the cold. There are a few cars on the road, drivers overtaking me with angry looks on their faces, but I'm just focussed on going forward, cycling as quickly as I can.

After leaving Frank's, I hurried home in a daze, watching the horses go past me on the pavement as I did so. I had a flash of memory, where I could see myself and Loxwood riding down the same path. Like my daydream last night, I wasn't seeing the scene as I had witnessed it, but as an outsider. I knew where Loxwood would be in the row, his ears pricked. Lizzie and Graham would be there, of course, Lizzie probably in front of me, turned in the saddle to talk. And I'd be smiling, happy, riding my favourite horse. Then I blinked, and the image slipped from my grasp, until I was looking at the other horses again, no Loxwood in sight. And the wave crashed into me, reality. It wasn't going to be like that anymore. Suddenly, I was going to be able to make that other dream come true.

My parents weren't up yet when I got home. I went to the kitchen, where I put an apple in my coat pocket. The house was still, and for a moment I stood without doing anything. Then the enormity of everything I had to do came into my mind, and I hurried out of the house, pushing my bike, without a backward glance.

After the first two miles, I am well and truly stressed. I started going over a to-do list when I set off, and ticking off every item is beginning to look impossible. There aren't any spare stables at Rose's, where is Loxwood going to go? He can't go outside, can he? What if Rose says no? What if she's adamant there isn't room for another horse? And then there's the cost. I have my savings, earned from all those early morning rides. The only comfort is the knowledge that it should keep Loxwood going a while. But I'll still need to spend a fair amount on tack, and who knows when an unexpected vet bill is going to show up. And how will I get him to Rose's? If Rose even lets me keep him here. This thought pushes all the other worries (albeit temporarily) from my mind. Right now all that matters is that I have somewhere to put him.

I must look as though I've just run a marathon when I come round the corner into the stable yard. I dropped my bike in the car park, the handlebars slipping from by grasp and landing with a screech in the gravel. My breathing comes in short bursts, and judging by how hot I feel my face must be bright red.

I don't know what time it is, but Rose is still putting feeds through the doors. She turns at the sound of footsteps, and the surprise on her face shows that I am clearly the last person she expected to see this early on a weekday.

'Georgia,' Rose says, worry seeping into her voice as she takes in my frazzled appearance. 'Is everything all right? Are you okay?'

'I'm fine,' I stammer, 'I just.. Need to talk to you.'

'Just give me a second to finish this lot,' she says, nodding towards the pile of feed buckets beside her. 'I won't be a minute.'

On a normal day, I would be rushing to help her. But today my body doesn't seem capable of processing orders. So, I stand, until Rose has slipped the final bucket into Sterling's stable door, and is back beside me.

'Let's get a cup of tea,' she says, leading me to the clubhouse. The kettle is set to boil, and when two mugs of steaming tea are placed placed on the table, my words come spilling out. I tell Rose everything, about Loxwood, and how I've always dreamed of owning him, and Frank's words this morning.

'Do your parents know?' Rose asks.

'They don't care,' I say. My mum said so herself when I last brought the issue up.

'I don't know what we can do,' Rose says worriedly. 'Obviously, worst case scenario he can be turned out,' she says, more to herself than me.

I feel like my heart just stopped, only to be shocked back to life again. I thought Rose was about to say that there was no way she could take on another horse, or something like that. And I realise, seeing her manner, that she took it for granted that I would be able to keep him here, no matter what. Heavy guilt seeps through my veins when I think of my earlier worries. This is Rose, possibly the kindest person I've ever met. Of course she's going to do everything she can to help, she always does. If there isn't room, you make do. Simple as.

'I could always turn Cinder out,' Rose continues. 'She doesn't *need* a stable, really.'

'No,' I say. 'Don't, really. I don't want to start kicking horses out of their stables.'

Rose lifts her mug to swallow a mouthful of tea, looking deep in thought. I lift my own cup to do the same, when the table shakes, and I look up to see that it's due to Rose, who put her drink back down to stand up, unsettling the table as she did so.

'I've got an idea,' she says. 'Come on.'

I follow her out of the room, and past the row of munching horses, who are now being hayed by Leah. Rose is walking round the stable block, where a small outbuilding curves round to look over the back paddocks.

'It's a woodshed,' she says. 'We don't use it, but it's never been cleared out. It could work. What do you think?'

I peer over the wooden door, and squint as my eyes adjust to the light. It's dark and dusty, with various old, small, wooden beams and logs scattered around it, but I look past that to see solid walls, a high enough ceiling, and a view of the other horses. 'It could work,' I repeat.

'And look at this,' Rose says, sliding past me to open the door and go inside. She careful steps over various items, and heads to a side wall, where she starts hitting something. I have no idea what she's doing, and almost say so, but then something gives way, and light floods the four walls. 'There's a shutter,' Rose says proudly, standing on her tip toes to lean out of it. 'It looks over the stables, so he'll see all the other horses.'

'It's perfect,' I say.

Rose steps out to stand back beside me, shaking dust off her coat as she does so. 'I've got too much to do this morning, but I could start emptying it this afternoon. And I can ask Ben to help when he gets home.'

'I'll do it,' I say. 'You shouldn't have to. This whole thing's my fault.' I pause, before adding, 'Please.'

It takes a little time, but I finally get Rose to agree to let me start emptying the shed on my own, only with the promise of accepting her help in the afternoon. But I only did because I was certain I would be able to finish by then.

I've been moving logs for half an hour when Mackenzie appears in the doorway, dressed for school in her uniform.

'I can't believe it!' she yells. 'Mummy told me you're getting a horse! It's Loxwood, isn't it!? See, I *told* you everything would work out!'

Mackenzie chats to me, suggesting everything she can do to help, until her father calls her to leave. It's only then, when she disappears round the corner, that I remember that I'm supposed to be at school, too. I'll be in big trouble on Monday, and Mrs Sanchez or Mrs Paterson will tell me that I'm ruining any chance I have of having a future. But what they don't get is that right now, clearing out a stable for my horse, is the first time I feel like I'm actually working towards it.

At midday, by which point the hours of heavy lifting I've

done have passed surprisingly quickly, Rose drags me away from my work for some lunch. We eat baked beans on toast at her kitchen table, and I ask about how her horses were this morning. Sitting in this old farmhouse, with a yard of horses outside the front door, where my own will be very soon, it feels like I'm living somebody else's life.

As I had hoped, I have almost finished sweeping when Rose comes to help, having finished her riding for the day. There was so much dust, and every few minutes I had to stop and step outside for lack of oxygen.

While I'm clearing the last remnants of cobwebs, Rose wheels round some bales of straw, and once the stable is as clean as I'm going to get it, I build up a bed with big banks. I put in five bales (for which I will be paying Rose back, whether she likes it or not), and fill a large bucket with water. When she saw that there was in fact a light switch and socket, Rose found a spare lightbulb, so that the stable is now bright as the day darkens.

Mackenzie runs straight over when she gets home from school, determined to help in some shape or form. She ends up clearing a space for Loxwood in the tack room (all while still wearing her uniform) and making him his own name tag, Sellotaped above a bridle hook. A spare grooming box is also found, and filled with brushes just for him. As Mackenzie sets about searching for what items he could use, the reality of all I'm going to have to buy daunts on me - a saddle alone must cost half of my savings? But again, I push the issue to the back of my mind, stored in a box labeled *TO BE DEALT WITH LATER*.

It's almost four o'clock when I set off, just early enough that I can cycle back in daylight. Being Saturday tomorrow, at least I won't have to miss another day of school. I'll work at the track in the morning, and tell Frank I'll be back before midday to pick up

Loxwood. That's what Rose said, that she would drive us there in the morning, leaving him a good amount of time in daylight to settle in. It's hard to think that just this time yesterday, I was getting ready to go out for dinner with my parents, unbeknown to me what the next day would bring.

I text Lizzie and Graham when I'm a few minutes from town, asking them to meet me at our coffee shop. I added something along the lines of biggest news in the world, just to make sure Lizzie couldn't not be bothered to go - she would never be able to rest without knowing what it is. Though, knowing Lizzie, the promise of free cake and coffee is usually enough to lure her.

'What is this life changing news I just *have* to know about?' Lizzie says, waking into the cafe and throwing herself into one of the comfy chairs. I'm not surprised that she got here first.

'Graham's not here yet,' I say calmly. 'I can't tell you first, it would be rude.'

Lizzie frowns. 'Georgia Catherine James, you're driving me crazy.'

'Go order,' I say with a grin, my own cappuccino and cake already beside me. 'Graham will probably be here by the time you're done.'

I'm given another death stare, but the smell of coffee is enough to coax Lizzie to the counter. Graham arrives while she's queuing, looking much healthier than the last time I saw him, and soon the two of them are back at the table, with hot drinks and baked goods. I had planned to draw the story out, with agonising detail, to make them suffer. But as soon as I start I realise I'm just as anxious as them to get to the point, and the words come pouring out. Saying it out loud to my friends, who know how many times I've imagined this moment, makes it seem even more real. By the time I'm done, we're all grinning like idiots.

It's twilight when I start wandering up the street. Lizzie and Graham have each gone off in their respective directions, and I'm supposed to be heading towards mine. But I find myself walking past the turning for my street, continuing instead to the stables.

Before going to the coffee shop, I went home to drop my bike off. I didn't know whether my parents would suspect something was up, considering I don't cycle to school, but they didn't seem to. I was discreet, anyway, barely stepping past the front door to prop the bicycle against the corridor wall, and then yelling that I was meeting friends and would be back later.

Daylight is fading quickly, but I could do this trip blindfolded. The sounds, if nothing else, are enough of an indicator. And the overpowering feeling of familiarity I get when I reach the yard I'm heading towards. I still stand outside, on the opposite side of the wall, but I know they're all there. Frank, the grooms, Loxwood, Nantucket Winter… all the horses I've come to know over time. Even the ones I'm not fond of, like Cookiemoon, a bay filly who is a gift from the Devil himself. I love them all, I always have.

Standing here, thinking of everything that's going on behind that wall, there is a difference. Of the three thousand horses in Newmarket, one of them is mine.

# Chapter 11

I'm at Rose's by eleven. I barely slept last night, waking every hour to see if it was time to get up yet. When I finally gave up an hour before my alarm was set to go off, I climbed out of bed and pulled a cardboard box out from beneath it. Inside are the only mementoes I chose to keep from my childhood. I'm not sentimental, and there were only a few things I didn't send to Goodwill. One is a horse figurine, a beautiful chestnut standing with one leg raised, and his head turned so that it looks like the wind is blowing his mane. The other items are a couple pony books I read over and over again when I was little, wishing that like the heroines in them I could find some way of acquiring a horse of my own. This was the first time I've ever picked them up and had that be the case.

Walking into Frank's, knowing Loxwood was mine, was the best feeling. I went straight up to him, with the apple I had brought from home, and stood there stroking him until Lizzie and Graham showed up and started teasing me goodheartedly. It was Graham's first day back at the track, and to ease him back in the saddle he got to ride Nantucket, meaning most of the horses I rode this morning were crazy. But I didn't care. I really didn't care.

Rose already has the lorry out when I arrive. Leah is in the background, doing the last of the morning chores, and DIY liveries are still mucking out, with a few yet to show. Mackenzie is about, wearing purple jodhpurs and a waterproof coat a size too big for her.

'Why can't I come?' Mackenzie is whining to Rose. She can't see me from where they are, but I can just make them out.

'It's a racing yard, Kenzie. It's not somewhere anyone can just visit. We'll be in and out of there in seconds, we won't be hanging around.'

'Still,' Mackenzie says pleadingly. 'PLEEEEAAAASE can I come?'

'I said no, Mackenzie,' Rose says sternly.

I walk round to where they are standing, just as Mackenzie starts storming off to the house, not seeing me.

'Morning,' I say.

Rose looks at me and smiles, before turning her gaze back to Kenzie. 'That kid,' she says, shaking her head. 'Can't take no for an answer.'

Within ten minutes we are in the lorry, without Mackenzie, who has not been seen since walking off. Rose seems happy and laid-back, meanwhile the slight feeling of nausea I've had since yesterday is starting to become more and more apparent. While the idea of Loxwood being mine has settled in during the past twenty four hours, I know it's going to be a completely different matter once he's actually here.

As the horse box pulls out of the car park, I glance towards the sand school, where I can now see a horse. For a moment, I think he's loose, but I realise there is somebody on him, he's just tackless. No bridle, no saddle. It's only by looking at the rider more closely that I realise it's Paige. I'm taken aback for a moment, for no reason I can explain, but then I look more intently again. The horse is still thin, his coat shaggy, but he looks happy. Paige is trotting him in circles, arms at her sides. Despite how scruffy they both look, there's something wonderful about it. That mutual trust, certainly unconditional on her part. I could go on watching, but as the horse box pulls out a little further the horse is no longer in sight, and I'm reminded that now isn't a time to focus on that. I'm getting a horse of my own.

Arriving at Frank's in a horse box is strange. I've never not passed the gates either on foot or on horseback, never in a passenger seat. And never with Rose. It feels like the two lives I've been leading are about to collide, and it's just weird. Though I'm sure anyone else is clueless to this.

'This is lovely,' Rose says, looking at the stables through the windows. The red brick buildings, and painted doors, without so much as a blade of hay on the ground. Beautiful, but different to the comfort of Rose's. 'Where do you think I should park?'

'Over here,' I say, pointing at a spot beyond the windscreen. 'It's where the horse boxes normally go.'

I jump out the cab to direct Rose as she turns the lorry around, as jockeys and grooms start looking toward us. If I haven't exchanged words with all of them in the past, I've certainly spent enough time here that we all know each other by sight, and I can see their confusion at seeing me in a different context.

Frank appears in the courtyard just as Rose is climbing down from the driver's seat. Ever the gentleman, he goes straight up to her to say hello, and the two fall into easy conversation as I start getting things ready. I put the ramp down, tying back partitions, and find the travel boots Rose has provided for Loxwood. There's also a head collar and a fleece for the journey, with thicker rugs waiting for him back home. I don't know how I'm ever going to repay Rose for all she has done, even if she did easily accept money from me. We're in full on winter, and I didn't think to run out and buy a heavy duty cover straight away, which with Loxwood being clipped is essential. Borrowing travel boots and brushes temporarily is one thing, but Rose dug out not one but three covers for him, all hung on the rug rail she put up on his stable door. She's the one who understood that racing yards want horses that are no longer in training gone as soon as possible, and insisted on going the very next day, which cuts into her own riding time. And Rose does all this without expecting anything in return, she does it to help. It's thanks to her that my dreams are coming true, and I don't think I will ever be able to stop paying her back. And she doesn't even realise it, because she is so genuine that she would never expect a person to do anything different. She has got to be one of the most goodhearted people I've ever met.

Loxwood nickers when I go up to him, leaning all his weight against the stable door. Two days in for a horse like him must be awful, and it shows. Racehorses are fed up, bred to be fast and feisty, and when kept contained they go mad. I'm even more grateful to Rose than ever, because another day locked in a box would probably drive him to insanity.

'It's okay, Lox,' I say gently. 'We're getting you out of here.'

I put the head collar on, and set about adjusting the travel boots, a task I've done numerous times for both Rose and Clara. Loxwood kicks out each of his hind legs once when the boots are first put on, but he recovers quickly. I then swap his heavy duty rug for the fleece - anything more and he'll sweat during the journey.

In the courtyard, I can hear Rose and Frank laughing, each chatting happily. It's strange to see them both getting on, like old friends, but also logical. After all, they're both horse people, who have dedicated their entire lives to caring for the animals they love.

Frank breaks off the conversation when he sees me looking over the half door. 'All set?' he says.

I nod. This is the moment I've been waiting for, and now that it's here I'm terrified.

'Does he load well?' Rose asks.

'He won't if I say he does,' Frank says, and they both laugh.

I lead Loxwood out of the stable, feeling like a deer that has just walked into an array of oncoming headlights. The chestnut Thoroughbred, on the other hand, *my* chestnut Thoroughbred, walks out as though the whole world has stopped to look at him. His head carriage is high, but with his neck arched, not straight up in the air like a giraffe.

Rose and Frank each stand on one side of the ramp as I lead Loxwood up, who is more than happy to oblige. He buries his nose straight in the waiting haynet, and I tie him up while Rose closes the partitions behind me. I duck out once Loxwood is secured, and help Frank and Rose put up the ramp.

'Right,' says Frank when it's done, putting his right hand into his coat pocket. 'Here you go, he's all yours,' he says, handing me Loxwood's passport. My stomach flutters at the bold, printed letters. *LOXWOOD.* And he's mine. Frank turns to Rose. 'Pleasure to meet you, and bring those girls of yours round any time.'

Rose smiles. 'Will do. Thanks again - he'll be well taken care of.'

'Oh,' Frank says, 'I know he will.' He turns to me now. 'See you Monday morning, James?'

I nod. 'See you Monday, boss.'

Rose and I climb back into the cab silently, neither of us speaking as we drive out the yard, back up to the main road where the horse box slows to a stop as we wait for a gap in the oncoming traffic. I'm staring straight ahead, worrying about how Loxwood is going to settle in, when I feel a hand nudge my knee.

'Hey,' Rose says kindly, smiling widely. 'He's gorgeous.'

'You like him?' I say, unsure why I sound so surprised. I think he's beautiful, obviously, but I had no idea whether or not Rose would agree.

She grins even more. 'I think you've got a little star there.'

Mackenzie's stubbornness has obviously worn off, because she's waiting in the car park when we pull in. One of the horses neighs at the sight of the horse box, and inside I hear Loxwood reply, sounding like the highly strung racehorse he was supposed to be.

'We'll put him straight in the stable,' Rose says as she manoeuvres the lorry. 'And if he settles we can try turning him out for a bit later, do him some good. He won't have been turned out in years, we'll have to take it gently.'

'Okay,' I say.

'There's already hay and water in his stable,' Rose continues. From the way she's speaking, I get the feeling she's going through all these things to reassure *me*, as oppose to herself. 'He'll need his rug changing, but he might be too warm for a bit. We'll just keep an eye on him.'

It's been grey all morning, but now the sky has cleared, giving way to a canopy of blue. When I lead Loxwood down the ramp, the sun is shining off his chestnut neck, as though it only came out for him.

'He's so sweet!' Mackenzie squeals. 'Hello, Loxwood,' she says in a small voice. 'I love him!'

'Stay out the way, Kenzie,' Rose says. 'Let's just get him to the stable, and then you can say hello all you want.'

I can feel Loxwood is tense at the end of the lead rope, anticipation bubbling up inside him like a cauldron. This is a horse I have handled, and ridden, countless times, but my heart is in my mouth for the whole of the short time it takes to walk him to the stable. When I unlatch the lead rope clip inside, he spins around the stable once, looks out of his window for the other horses, and upon seeing them blows air from his nose, and turns his attention to the pile of hay.

'He's sensible,' Rose says, standing beside me at the stable door. 'He won't stay uptight for long.'

We leave him a couple more minutes before taking off the travel boots and head collar, and when it becomes clear that he is content eating hay, Rose tells me and Kenzie to follow her inside for some lunch. In the kitchen, Ben (who, from the few times I've eaten here, I have learnt is an amazing cook) is putting a mozzarella and tomato tart in the oven, while Jemima is drawing at the table. Their dog, an elderly West Highland Terrier called Alfred, who very rarely leaves the warm comfort of the house, is asleep in his basket. The refrigerator is covered in drawings similar to the one Jemima is in the middle of doing (it's of astronaut fish, apparently), and Mackenzie sits beside her to start one of her own. Rose gestures at me to sit down, taking a seat herself, as Ben asks how our expedition went. I rarely see much of Ben, who works as a literature professor in Cambridge, but he's one of those people you feel like you've known for years once he starts talking to you. He isn't into horses, but supports Rose's desire to be. The few times I'm with both of them together, like now, I wonder if Mackenzie and Jemima will ever realise to what extent they won the parent lottery.

By the time the delicious smelling tart is taken out of the oven, both Jemima's drawing of astronaut fish, and Mackenzie's of Loxwood, which she gave to me, are finished. I help Kenzie lay the table, and we all sit for our homemade lunch. The tart is delicious, and it's already the greatest lunch I've had in ages, and then Ben only takes an rhubarb crumble out of the oven. When the meal is over I am well and truly stuffed.

Loxwood is still munching on his hay happily when I go back outside. He's cool enough that I change his fleece for a thicker rug, and like the first it fits perfectly. I'm just sliding the bolt across the stable door when I see Clara (whom I texted with the news last night) walk into the courtyard, and she hurries over to meet the new addition, and we both jump around excitedly for a while. She starts rattling on about how we'll be able to go for hacks together, and it's such a simple thing, but as it's not something I've ever been able to discuss before it makes me ridiculously excited. I've watched Clara and others plan things like hacks for so long, that now I'm part of it too it just feels like the possibilities are endless.

Rose comes out of the tack room with a pair of brushing boots, suggesting that I take Loxwood for some grass, and that if I think he's relaxed enough I could turn him out for an hour. I carefully put the boots on his front legs, and swap his rug for a turnout one. It's hard to think he's the same horse as the one who came off the truck just hours ago. Already he looks like he's always lived here.

The paddock Rose had designated for Loxwood is flat, and fenced with post and rail. It's near enough his stable that I don't have too far to lead him, and within view of other horses. I reckon he gallops for a full five minutes when I let him off, and I nearly go catch him again, but then, without warning, he suddenly settles. Rose has been beside me the whole time, the only thing keeping me calm.

'Two years,' she says. 'He won't have been turned out since he's been in training. Two years without being free to move on his own. Can you really blame him?'

She's right. Loxwood has lived in a stable for years, only leaving it to be ridden. He hasn't been free to stretch his legs of his own free will during that whole time. Now it's my job to show him what it means to be a horse again.

I bring him back in an hour later, so as not to push it too much on the first day. Two years without being in a field also means two years without grass, and I can't risk him getting colic. I thought he might be apprehensive about coming back in, but as soon as I step into the field, he trots over happily.

Back in the stable, I groom Loxwood for close to an hour. It's silly, but I've never actually brushed him before. I show up, I ride, and hand him over to a groom - that's how it went. I never got to do any of this side of it, and it's not something I plan on neglecting. So I take my time, running a body brush over his coat, scrubbing his socks until they're sparkling white, and making sure his tail is tangle free.

When I've finished caring for Loxwood, I help Rose and Leah with the evening stable chores - skipping out, topping up water buckets, haying... When it's all done we prepare the feeds, with Rose coming up with one for Loxwood, to gently ease him away from what he's been fed at the racing yard up to now. I make a careful note of everything Rose puts in his bucket, and remind myself to write it down on the list of everything she has already provided, so that I can pay her back. She may refuse compensation for her time, but there's no way I'm going to not pay for feed and bedding.

Hope shows up for Clara just as the last feed bucket has gone through the door, and insists on meeting Loxwood before offering to drop me off at home. I haven't quite figured out how I'm going to cope with the fact that coming here twice a day to care for my horse will mean cycling a total of sixteen miles, but I'll deal with that as it comes.

The drive back to town makes me feel like I'm eight again. Clara and I in the back seats, giggling like children over what we're going to do with our horses during the week that comes. Tomorrow, Clara and Rose are going show jumping again, and me as a groom. But I don't mind. I don't mind at all, because now I know that it won't be long until I am the one riding too.

# Chapter 12

I'm dressed before even having breakfast. I pull my jodhpurs on as soon as I'm out of bed, pairing them with the top Clara gave me for my birthday, and wrestle my hair to the top of my head. Downstairs, I slice a cinnamon and raisin bagel, and put both halves in the toaster, before boiling the kettle. I find a flask at the back of the cupboard above the sink, and after rinsing it out three times deem it clean enough to fill with tea.

Before starting the journey to the yard, I go to one of the few shops open this early, and select a box of chocolates for Rose. It's not much, it's nothing compared to everything she's doing for me, but I can't think of anything else. I will, at some point, but for now it will have to do.

Rose has already started feeding when I arrive. She told me yesterday that she could feed Loxwood in the mornings, and that I didn't have to worry, but she was wasting her breath. DIY liveries are supposed to feed their own horses, end of. I'm not letting her pay me any more favours, she's done too much as it is.

My heart swells at the sight of Loxwood with his head out the window, nickering as he sees me approach with a bucket of feed. It's so cold, but just looking at him wrapped up in his rug makes me feel a little warmer.

I spend all morning helping Rose muck out, after the horses have been put in their paddocks. She insisted that I needn't do any stable but my own, of course, but I'm not going to be here and not help out. It's only half past seven when Paige arrives, the first of the DIYs, shortly followed by Dora/Nora, and the next isn't until nine. It makes me sick, seeing their horses wait that whole time to be fed, and I don't know how Rose can bear it.

By lunchtime, all the horses are back in, groomed, rugged, and munching hay. Loxwood was calm all morning, wandering around the paddock, snatching at tufts of grass. And he settles so quickly in his stable that I have no reservations about leaving him for a few hours to go to the competition. With Paddington and Cinder loaded in the back, and Clara and Hope set to follow with Spirit shortly, we set off.

This venue is beginning to feel like a second home. Make that third - Rose's is my second home. But I still enjoy coming here, and I feel like it will be even more enjoyable this time, knowing that the competitors I'm watching will be my rivals soon.

Cinder rattles an upright on course, and being out of the placings results in floods of tears from Mackenzie. When it doesn't stop after five minutes, Rose banishes her to the lorry. I was upset for Kenzie, seeing her cry like that, but when she trudges into the living compartment, arms crossed and lips in a pout, Rose and I burst into hysterics.

I watch from the sidelines as Clara rides a super clear on Spirit, to finish in fourth place. It's not a very high class, but for her it is a milestone, and we're all ecstatic. After that there's an hour to go until Paddington's class, and in view of the cold weather I decide to watch a few rounds from inside. I take a seat by the window, right up against the glass, and who should be the next rider to ride into the ring but Helena Cullen. Her name hasn't been announced yet, but I know it's her without being told. As always, her turnout is immaculate. White jodhpurs, smart, tailored jacked, expensive hat, and shiny, black leather boots. And I don't need to hear the announcer say her horse's name either to know that it's Lochmere. Even if it didn't sound familiar to *Loxwood*, I would still remember it anyway. Other than the fact that I can remember any horse's name, a trait possibly due in part to the hundreds of horses that pass through Frank's yard, Lochmere is kind of amazing. I think he's the reason I first envied Helena Cullen. I'd seen pictures of them before, but the first time I saw him go cross country was when I was watching some live footage online. He's not very big, probably only fifteen three, but he has a huge stride and scope to match. Watching him is like watching a masterclass. I was glued to the screen during that entire ride, as he cleared every fence with ease. It was one of those cross country rounds that is just flawless. Lochmere never looked strong, he was always flickering his ears backward, asking his rider for instructions. Helena could take tight turns to corners and skinnies, and still he stayed straight, never once thinking to duck out. I remember the commentators talking about how it was without a doubt the best round they had seen all day, and how Lochmere is truly a one in a million horse, and all that. I was in awe during the whole round, and even more so when I saw him in person just a couple months later. I had gone to an event to support Clara, alternating between helping her and Rose, and it so happened that Helena Cullen was riding. I was by the show jumping ring when Lochmere came trotting in, and before I even realised it was him I seriously felt my stomach flip. He's that kind of horse, the kind your eye just goes to. Like Loxwood, I like to think, or at the very least hope. When I realised the all black horse was Lochmere, I actually felt starstruck. I didn't even notice how Helena Cullen was riding, I was too focussed on *him*. It reminds me of what Rose said a couple weeks ago, when I asked her about Sterling. What she said about a horse not having anything wrong with it, and yet not possessing that extra quality. Because in truth, if you were to describe Lochmere on paper (as with Loxwood), there isn't anything obvious that stands out. You'll find plenty of horses that are better made, and with a bigger jump, but they just won't be special. It's not even about beauty, it's about a feeling. Maybe that's the nameless quality I'm always trying to pinpoint - it's not about how a horse looks, it's about how they make you feel. Nobody can put a finger on that.

The little black horse pops into a collected canter, his head carriage high and round, as Helena sits quietly in the saddle, her hands close together and hardly moving. I'm just glad Mackenzie isn't around to point out, once again, what an amazing rider she is. It's true, I know that, but I still remind myself that it's easy to be a good rider when you've got a good horse. And natural talent, to top it off.

Unsurprisingly, Lochmere jumps a clear round, popping over every metre-twenty fence like it's nothing. I feel a pang, seeing him leave the ring, but then I remember that I have a beautiful horse of my own waiting for me, and for the first time, watching Helena Cullen ride doesn't seem like quite the kick in the face that it was before.

There are some really good riders today, far more than usual, and I find myself studying each round so intently that I barely notice the number of people piling into the room, until it's so crowded that every other table is taken, and I hear someone beside me say, 'I'm sorry, do you mind if I sit here?'

I look up from the window, and beside me is simultaneously both the first and last person I expect to see, Helena Cullen. Before replying I glance to my left quickly, seeing that the one chair at my table, next to me, is the only one left in the room.

'No, not at all,' I stammer, frustrated with how polite it sounds.

Helena smiles gratefully, putting a paper cup containing a hot drink down on the table before sitting down. She's still in her jodhpurs and boots, but she's taken her jacket and hat off since her round, so that she's now in a long sleeved white top, and her hair is still pulled back into a hairnet. It only occurs to me once she's seated that she has some fancy lorry with a living compartment even nicer than my house somewhere outside that she could go sit in, but then she seems to be watching the next rounds, so maybe she just wants a front seat view of the ring. I'm not even sure I care anymore, so I go back to staring out the window.

'At least this place has good coffee,' Helena says at some point, stirring her cup with a wooden stick.

I don't know whether she's talking to herself or trying to make conversation, so I hesitate before saying, 'Good doughnuts, too.'

'Really?' she says brightly. And judging by her tone, the previous sentence *was* supposed to be a conversation starter, so at least I got one thing right today.

I nod.

'Arr, I so almost got one.' Helena says, turning to look at the counter where there is now a rather long queue. 'Maybe I'll give it a while,' she adds with a smile, and somehow I find myself smiling back.

The starting bell rings, and we both turn our attention back to the window, where a guy on an ugly bay horse is about to begin his round. He completely misses his distance to the first jump, resulting in him pulling on the reins as they crash over it, and I wince, just as Helena says, 'Oh, God, that was terrible.' I turn to look at her, and immediately her hand goes to her mouth. 'Crap, sorry. I shouldn't have said that. You don't know him, do you?'

'No,' I say, almost laughing. 'I was thinking the same thing, actually.'

She lets out a breath. 'I don't mean it meanly. I just, sometimes, say what's on my mind without thinking. You know?'

*I know.* I think of all the things I've said to teachers without thinking, or my parents, for that matter.

The guy on the ugly horse ends up having three more rails down, and the next rider in the ring is a slim girl with a long blond ponytail, on a grey pony.

'I know her,' Helena says quietly, leaning in towards me. 'I mean, not like "know her know her", but enough to know how much she paid for that pony.'

'Really?' I say despite myself. I still don't know why Helena Cullen is talking to me, or why I'm talking back, but somehow I'm too intrigued to cut it off. At the very least, maybe I can get some gossip.

Helena nods. 'Cough,' she says, 'a hundred and fifty grand, cough.'

My surprise is combined with laughter. 'Seriously?'

'Yep. She's a show jumper, but at the end of last year she decided she wanted to start eventing. Like it's that easy, you can just wake up and decide. Anyway, her parents approached me because they wanted to buy my horse. Obviously, I made it quite clear he wasn't for sale.'

I'm worried Helena and I are about to get into a stump, where we're either completely stuck for conversation, or I'll have to admit that I've probably read every article ever published about her, so I say, 'I saw your round earlier. It was great. I love your horse,'

Helena smiles widely, looking almost, *surprised?* 'Thanks. That's the horse she tried to buy, actually,' she says, nodding at the ring.

'Lochmere?' I say.

Helena nods. 'They were literally shaking a cheque in front of my face. I told them it was never going to happen, though.'

'I don't blame you,' I say. 'He's really lovely.' *Good God!* If someone had told me ten minutes ago that I would be sitting here complimenting Helena Cullen, I'd have suggested they were suffering from brain damage.

'I love him,' she says, with the same kind of grin on her face I reckon I have when I talk about Loxwood.

'What breed is he?' I ask, thinking I had better hurry up and get some facts that I actually want to know.

'Thoroughbred. Ex-racehorse.'

'*Really?*' Possibly the last thing I expected to hear. He looks like he could have a little Thoroughbred in him, sure, but I expected it to be be mixed with Warmblood, or something like that. After all, anyone who's loaded doesn't just buy an ex-racehorse.

'Yeah,' Helena says, clearly unaffected by my shock. 'He was on his way to the knacker's yard. My mum,' she continues, 'runs a riding school, down in Devon, and there's this dealer down the road she often goes to. We used to buy anything that looked half decent, then I'd ride them until they were sane enough to sell on, and it just kept going. Riding schools don't exactly make much money, so that was a good way to earn extra income. Anyway, I was twelve, I think, and we went down to this dealer to look at some Connemara ponies he'd just got in, and he had Lochmere in his barn, locked up in a dark stall. I only saw him because I got bored of Mum and the guy talking, and I could hear some horse brewing up a storm somewhere, so I went looking. He was a complete hat rack, and he had,' she breaks off to shake her head, clearly lost in the memory, 'this red head collar on, and I swear there wasn't a millimetre between it and his skin. It must've been left on for over a year. And there were scars all over him… he was a complete mess. There was only a small window I could look through, and when Olly realised I was standing there he came and put his nose through it. I put my hand up so he could smell, and literally the second I felt his breath on my palm I knew I had to have him. It was just a feeling, you know? So, I run to Mum, and drag her to see him, the dealer following behind, in a complete huff because I'd just interrupted his deal. And when he saw which horse I was taking her to, he said, "Oh, that thing's hopeless. Bag of bones, complete nutcase." I still remember his words exactly. He goes, "I was supposed to take him to the knacker's yard this morning, then I got your call, so I haven't had time yet." Even now, I can't think about how easily things could have not turned out the way they have. Mum *so* nearly didn't call him back that morning. Thinking about it now makes me feel sick. You know how you remember some things so clearly? I just remember being excited about the Connemaras he'd told us about in a voice message, and begging her to ring him right away. Imagine if she hadn't. Anyway, so by this point I'm practically crying, and Mum manages to convince the guy to just lead the horse out for us. He was already seven years old, he said, not worth investing time into anymore. But as soon as we saw him we both crumbled. And,' Helena smiles. 'He came straight to me. He *actually* chose me. I know it sounds pathetic, but he dragged the dealer straight towards me, and buried his nose in my hands, the way he had through the window. We paid two hundred pounds for him, and that was that.'

'Wow,' is all I can manage.

'It wasn't all that simple, obviously,' Helena continues. 'It took ages to get him back to condition, and admittedly he *could* be a bit crazy. But I loved him, I still do. I was obsessed with *Black Beauty* when I was little, and I seriously thought that was what he was.'

'He is,' I say.

Helena smiles again. 'Anyway, that's why I'll never sell him. Despite how much I needed the money.'

As my emotions begin to recover from the powerfulness of the story, my mind starts picking out the odd pieces, the bits of information that throw everything I thought I knew about Helena Cullen right out the window. 'You train with Amanda Walton, right?' I say cautiously.

'Sort of,' Helena says. She looks awkward, and stares at me a moment as if weighing up whether or not to go on. She obviously decides to, because she keeps going. 'I'm a working pupil, which basically means I work all hours to earn my horses' keep.'

'How many do you have?'

'Horses? Three. Well, I ride three, but Lochmere's the only one that belongs to me. The others are rides I've been given by owners. Up to last year I just had Olly, and kept him at home. But then I got offered this opportunity with Amanda after Europeans, and, obviously she's the best of the best, and we don't have anywhere near the kind of facilities and finance needed, so I took it. And it's since being there that I've gained a ton of sponsorship, which I desperately need. But, still, it's a lot of work, to put it mildly.'

'You enjoy it, though,' I say. 'Right?'

Helena hesitates, and then seeing that her apprehension has answered the question, she laughs. 'Amanda's tough. If you've heard of Amanda Walton, you must know that. She's good, she's been doing her job for fifty odd years. She's ridden enough four-stars, and trained enough people to do the same. But when I say she's tough,' she pauses to look over shoulder, 'I mean brutal. Like, miss a stride and she'll yell bloody murder at you. And although I have one day a week off from working for her, I still have to look after my own. I'm not complaining, but it's… exhausting, to say the least. And I've got studies to think about, too. I don't physically go to school anymore, but I'm still doing my A-levels, so I spend all evening working. And I actually enjoy it, even though that sounds really stupid, but I like studying. I live on site, and it gives me something to do in the evening that isn't labour. But between studies, and working for Amanda, and riding, it's hard. It would be all right if I only had to do one or the other - be a rider or be a groom - but I have to do both, and by the time I'm supposed to ride my own, I'm just so tired. The last time we came here, I'd already mucked out ten and ridden six before we left, and… you're almost not in the mood anymore. It takes the fun out of it. And there's pressure from owners, too. Some are nice, too. But others… I have the ride on this grey six year old, Arturo,' (I don't tell her I already know), 'and he's great, but his owner is vile. Seriously. I was in the lead going into cross country at this event with him last year, and the ground was really deep, so I didn't want to push him. He went clear, with just a few time penalties. And those time penalties cost us the win. And his owner went ballistic. She just yelled at me, back at the lorry, in front of Amanda. I managed to keep a straight face, but as soon as she left I just completely burst into tears. But Lochmere's mine, so I don't have to worry about anyone else. I took that for granted before. It sucks not having a say.'

'I know what you mean,' I say. Helena looks up at me, suddenly alert, and I quickly clarify. 'Not pressure from owners, but not having a say. I exercise Thoroughbreds at the track, and I have no control over what happens to them. I'll be riding a horse one day, and then they'll be gone the next.'

'You ride in Newmarket?' Helena says. I nod. 'That's so cool. I'd love to do that if I had time. Do you live there, then?'

'Yeah,' I say. 'My parents aren't into horses, but luckily it's walking distance.'

'Wow, you're lucky. I love it there. I go once a week, on my day off. Once my horses are in, they have a couple hours until evening feeds, and that's when I get away. It's a waste of time, in one way, but I almost feel like if I didn't get out I'd go crazy, you know? And my mum comes up to visit occasionally, but it's a long way, and it's hard to leave the riding school, and my little brother, too. But she still tries.'

'It must be nice,' I say. 'Having your parents involved in horses, too.'

'Just my mum,' Helena says. 'My dad passed away a couple months after my brother was born, which is why it's hard for her to get away. She works hard.'

'I'm sorry.'

'Don't be. It's okay, I was young, I don't remember him.' As if suddenly remembering everything she's said during the past ten minutes, Helena straightens in her seat, looking embarrassed. 'I don't know why I've bored you with all this. Sorry.'

'No, I'm not bored, it's interesting,' I say, and we both laugh.

'So,' Helena says. 'I never actually asked you your name.'

'Georgia.'

'Georgia. Okay. I love that name. Call me Leni, anyway.'

'All right, Leni,' I say.

'So, Georgia,' Leni says. 'Do you compete?'

'Not yet,' I say. 'I only just got a horse. As in, literally, yesterday. I'm planning on it, though. Eventing,' I add, to clarify.

'I didn't think you sounded like a show jumper,' she jokes. 'And we'll be competing together, then, maybe. I'll give you the inside scoop. So, anyway, tell me about your horse. What's he like?'

I smile, as I always do when I'm about to talk about Loxwood. And I go into the story of how I fell in love with a certain chestnut Thoroughbred I worked with, and how he is now mine.

# A PERFECT STRIDE

## BOOK 2

# Chapter 1

The sun is setting beyond the horizon, sending a warm glow across the field. The light shines off Loxwood's coat, catching his chestnut mane with every step he takes, glimmering like gold. I inhale deeply, taking in the newly present smell of spring - freshly mown grass, flowers blossoming on every tree, and the ever constant horse scent. I never want the moment to end.

A pheasant shoots out the long grass on the verge beside us, its wings flapping loudly, accompanied by that awful cry, enough to make you think it's being murdered, when really I am the one who should be fearing for their life. Loxwood leaps forward, his haunches spinning to the left, and takes off at a full out gallop. I throw my weight backwards, pushing my heels down even farther in the stirrups, and shorten my reins, careful not to startle him with a pull in the mouth.

'Easy, boy,' I mutter, Loxwood still fleeing.

We've covered what would have taken three minutes to walk

by the time I've managed to convince Loxwood that the pheasant is long gone, and coaxed him back to a walk. Most of the past month has been spent, on my part, trying to convince him that there are other paces than a flat out gallop.

'If you'd had that same kind of energy at the track,' I say to Loxwood, 'you might actually have been a racehorse.'

He might have come back to a walk, but he's still tense, keeping his neck rigid with every step. I drop my left hand to his withers and keep it there, watching his ears flicker backwards.

'You're okay,' I say.

Loxwood lowers his neck and blows air from his nostrils, his ears flickering back to the comfort of my fingers on his neck each time he startles. Like a child, reaching for a security blanket.

'We've still got some work to do as far as killer pheasants are concerned,' I say to Rose as I ride into the yard. She has her two-star horse, Paddington, in the cross ties of the wash bay as she combs through his tail.

'I swear, they have an agenda!' Rose says.

I take my feet out the stirrups and swing off Loxwood's back, pain shooting through the tendons of my feet, all the way to my ankles, as my boots make contact with the concrete. I turn to run my leathers up, but the sound of something rushing towards us makes Loxwood jump.

'How was he?'

'MACKENZIE!' Rose yells sternly. 'How many times do I have to say it? NO running around the horses!'

Kenzie ignores her mum, instead just looking at me for a response.

'He's not ready yet,' I say, and Mackenzie immediately lets out a moan.

'I'll be fine, Georgia,' she says, pressing her hands together dramatically. 'Please, please, *PLEASE* can I come out riding with you next time?'

Ever since I started hacking Loxwood out a couple weeks ago, Kenzie has been begging to come along on Cinder, but I refuse. Not until I know he isn't going to pull something like he did today. Worrying about my own safety is enough, I don't need the responsibility of preventing my horse from sending an eight year old into a ditch as an added stress. Though it's true that Loxwood's worst spook probably wouldn't affect the elderly Cinder, it's not a risk I'm prepared to take.

'Remember what I said,' I say, walking round to put up the other stirrup.

Mackenzie sighs. 'Three bombproof rides,' she recites.

'Three bombproof rides,' I repeat, finding myself amused by this authority.

She frowns. 'You promise, right?'

I look over at Rose, who gives her blessing with a nod. 'I promise,' I say.

'Okay…' Mackenzie says. 'How long do you think it will take?'

'Ask Loxwood,' I say, clicking my tongue to lead him forward. Mackenzie follows at my side, all the way to the stable. Whenever she is around, she is there like a shadow. In the weeks he has been here, Loxwood has become her idol. I can't even groom him without Kenzie offering to help, and as confident as she is with her own horses, she is cautious with mine. She listened patiently as I explained his dislikes (being patted for one, but what horse does like having his neck slapped?) and likes (having his ears scratched). I knew I was probably being a bore, even going over things Mackenzie has heard zillions of times before, but as little as I care for my own safety, a child's is a different matter. And not only has Kenzie respected every instruction, but Loxwood seems as infatuated with her as she is with him. And seeing her stand beside him, scratching his favourite spot behind his ears, and him lower his head with closed eyes, makes my eyes well. I spent a year dreaming of this moment - not my horse bonding with Mackenzie, but actually having a horse. Some days I take it for granted, having grown used to my new routine, but then I'll be looking through a magazine and there will be an add for a nutritional supplement or some new kind of brushing boot, and the thrill of actually owning a horse to get these things for will come rushing back to me. Some days it still seems surreal that this chestnut Thoroughbred, big and muscular, with a small white star on his forehead, belongs to me. I spent so long riding and dreaming about him, and yet had no say in his day to day life. Sleep used to be clouded by scenes in which Loxwood was mine, and then I'd wake with heavy disappointment in my gut as reality settled. But now I dream that he is still at the track, that something happens that takes him away from me, and I'll open my eyes in a panic, but this time it's reality that is a comfort. Because it's real. Loxwood, the horse of my dreams, is safe in his stable, and I am the only one that cares for him.

Mackenzie puts Loxwood's cooler on while I put his tack away, second hand saddle I bought from a fitter over one arm. A good fitting saddle can be the difference between triumph and defeat, and despite my limited funds it was not something I was going to take a risk on. Rose was more than happy to lend me one, but I still insisted that she give me the number of her fitter. A man arrived the next day, with forty saddles in the back of his van. I tried to only look at the second hand ones, in spite of how luxurious some of the newer models were, but as it turned out I needn't have worried. Loxwood is a classic shape, with good sized withers, and was easy to fit.

'The Thoroughbreds always are,' the saddler said. 'It's the Warmbloods that make you spend thousands.'

The saddle isn't fancy, and it has the odd scratch here and there, but it doesn't matter. What's important is that it fits Loxwood beautifully, and didn't completely break the bank. And I get to call it my own.

One luxury I allowed myself was a nice bridle. I was standing in the tack shop, fully prepared to pick up the cheapest, but I couldn't do it. I let my eyes stray to one of higher quality, and after that there was no turning back. Once he starts competing, Loxwood will need smart tack, and I figured that I'd only end up having to buy a better bridle in time, and therefore was saving money by doing so now. At least it sounded convincing at the time. But when I saw him clad in the supple leather, I knew it had been worth every penny.

Fellow DIY liveries start pitching up while I'm skipping out Loxwood, the first being Paige. Even in the months I've been here every day, she still hasn't spoken more than a couple words. I thought she might start talking to me once I had my own horse, but that has yet to be the case. I don't take it personally - she barely talks to anyone - it just means that she is still somewhat of a mystery.

'I'll see you in the morning,' I say to Loxwood as I slide his evening feed bucket through the door, planting a final kiss against his neck and slipping a hand beneath his rug to check he isn't too warm.

The days are getting longer, and I'm consistently no longer cycling home in the dark, but I'm still eager to get the trip over as quickly as possible. No - forget that - I wish I didn't have to do the trip at all.

There are multiple voices when I push open the door, a bad sign. Warning bells in my head go off straight away, and I almost turn back around. But then I hear my mum's voice.

'Georgia? You're back?'

*Obviously I am back, or else I wouldn't be walking down the corridor.* I thought I would find my parents less annoying since getting the one thing I've always wanted, but somehow the feeling has increased. 'Yep,' I say, forcing glee into my voice as I let the handle bars of my bike fall against the wall.

'Come see who's here!' she calls happily, her voice followed by laughter.

'Do I have to?' I mutter, quietly enough that she can't hear.

Unzipping my chaps, I lean against the wall for balance, head tilted in a bid to hear the conversation in the other room. Who could she have invited? It won't be family, there would have been warning if that were the case. Colleagues? My mother's job of the moment is a receptionist position in a beauty salon - the last thing I need is to spend the evening with a group of stylists pointing out what's wrong with my own appearance. But I haven't met any of her new work colleagues, so doubt it is that.

I kick the final boot off, and my mind continues to whirl through the possibilities as I make my way to the kitchen. There's my dad's voice, accompanied by another male's, so it's obviously a couple. Who -

It hits me as I step over the kitchen threshold, too late to turn around and hide. Even as I see the backs of their heads, I hope that I'm wrong, and that it could be anyone else. But they turn around, and I'm not wrong at all.

'Georgia!' Bethany Payne exclaims. 'It's been so long!'

*Not long enough.* The Paynes, my parents' supposed best friends. I'm still not quite sure how they met, or why they remain friends for that matter, and was kind of hoping they had been forgotten, seeing as how we hadn't seen them in months. The friendship has been going on for about five years, and I wouldn't care if it didn't involve me, but inevitably it does. The daughter, Jasmine, is a similar age to me, and therefore we have always been thrown together, despite the mutual disinterest. It's not that the Paynes themselves are horrid, but Bethany's idea of a nightmare or the worst thing imaginable (both expressions she has used to describe the following) is a supermarket running out of her favourite kind of juice. He - I can't remember his name - is obsessed with golf, and talks of nothing else, and Jasmine is one of the dullest people I've ever met. Like me, she is always forced along to these rendezvous, dragged against her will, and then spends most of the time staring at her nails. Though today her hair is no longer blond, as it has always been, but a deep blue, and I feel a sudden, albeit brief, rush of admiration at the idea of her daring to do such a thing that I know her parents would disapprove of. I remember my own mum's reaction when I came home after letting Clara's sister dye mine, and laugh internally at the thought.

'Isn't it wonderful!' my mother says. 'It's been so long since we all caught up!'

'You're still riding, I see,' Bethany says.

I look down at my dirt stained jodhpurs and nod.

'She looks after her own horse now,' my mum says proudly - you know I'm a disappointment when my horse hating mother resorts to that as the only good thing to say about me. 'You were given a free horse to look after, weren't you, Georgie?'

Oh, kill me now. I almost wish my mum was her ignorant self

when people are round, and not the sympathetic mothering figure she turns into. I avoid having to reply by stretching my lips into a thin smile.

'It will be so nice for you girls to catch up,' Bethany says, nodding at Jasmine who, quite frankly, looks even more fed up with the whole situation than I imagine I do.

'Yes!' my mother agrees. 'Why don't you girls go off!?'

'I need to change first,' I say quickly.

'Well, hurry then,' my mum says.

'I'll just shower quickly,' I say, dragging out each word.

'We have guests, Georgia,' my mum says carefully, her voice walking the fine line from caring to tense.

'And I've been shovelling manure,' I retort, shutting down any future comment, as I turn on my heels to hurry up the stairs.

I let the bath run slowly, and move around at an equal pace. Never before have I even put my clothes away after changing, but now I spend as long as I can folding them until they look acceptable enough to grace the shelves of a window display. I'm in the middle of refolding every single item in my drawers when my mum calls for me to hurry up, and I'm left with no option but to go downstairs.

'What took you so long!?' she says when I walk back into the kitchen. They're all seated at the table, with wine glasses and bowls of crisps in front of them.

'I wasn't that long,' I say, sitting down at the only empty chair and reaching across for a handful of tortilla chips.

My mum keeps her eyes on me a moment longer before turning her attention back to Bethany. '..as I was saying, everyone is really nice, and they treat me with respect, you know? They appreciate my skills.'

'That's so hard to find,' Bethany says.

'I know! And they recognise my talent -' she cuts off abruptly, glancing at me. 'Georgia!' she says, sounding annoyed.

'Yes?' I say tiredly. She looks surprised to see me sitting there, and I'm compelled to point out that she's the one who's insisting I join them.

'You and Jasmine don't want to listen to our boring chat,' she says. 'You don't get to see each other often, make the most of it! Go on! Go hang out on your own.'

My expression is blank, and judging by the stillness beside me, so is Jasmine's. It's painful, but at least sitting at the table we are free to drift to our own worlds, and not forced to make conversation.

'Go on,' my mum says again, nodding her head.

Reluctantly, I rise from the table, my supposed guest doing the same, as our parents resume their chatter.

'Do you wanna watch a movie?' I ask. Jasmine does something midway between a nod and a shrug, and we walk over to the sitting area. I get bored by movies, and never watch them with the exception of an old childhood favourite (featuring horses, of course) but it's the only option.

I find our stack of DVDs from the cupboard beneath the TV, and put them on the floor for Jasmine to choose. For a moment, I think that she's going to refuse to pick one, and leave me with the odious task, but after a quick flick through she hands me a copy of *School of Rock*. It's no wild horse being rescued, and certainly not as good as the *International Velvet* DVD she's ignored, but at least I actually like it.

Jasmine sits down on the sofa silently, and I slide the disc into the DVD player, before hurrying back to the kitchen to get us a bowl of crisps. That one handful earlier is the only thing I've eaten since having a bite of the apple I gave Loxwood when I brought him in from the field before going for a ride, and I'm starving. Between working at the track early in the morning, cycling the four miles there and back to Rose's to care for Loxwood twice a day, riding him, and that nightmarish thing called "school", I'm always hungry.

I take a seat beside Jasmine on the sofa and place the large bowl between us.

'Thanks,' she says, the first thing she's said to me yet, as she takes a few.

'No problem,' I say.

It's clear we've both seen the movie before, but at least it offers a distraction. About a quarter of the way through, Jasmine pulls her phone out of her pocket and begins glancing down at it every so often, presumably to answer messages. In all my time wasting attempts upstairs I forgot to put my own in my pocket, so instead I reach forward onto the coffee table to pick up my latest horsey magazine. I flip straight to the eventing section, where photos from a recent competition's cross country phase are.

'Wow,' Jasmine says, looking over her phone at the pictures. 'That looks terrifying.'

I glance down at the open ditch fence, and a small smile tugs at my face. 'You think?'

'Yeah. That girl doesn't even look that old,' she says, leaning in closer for a better look. 'She can't be much older than us.'

'She isn't,' I say, and hesitate before adding, 'I know her.'

'Really?' Jasmine says, looking more interested than she has since I arrived.

'Yeah, she's a friend.' It sounds weird using that word, seeing as how I've know her name for so long without really knowing her, but that's what Leni is now. Ever since I first saw her ride her gorgeous horse Lochmere, I had been filled with jealousy. I spent hours perusing articles, wishing I were in a position to train with a four-star rider like she is. But then I actually met Leni some months ago, and learned that all my assumptions about her had been false. Her family was not loaded, far from it, and her amazing horse was the product of years of struggling and hard work. Not to mention that the seemingly dream position with retired event rider Amanda Walton made my current workload look light. But even more of a surprise was how easily we got on, and how we actually had things in common. And now I am friends with Helena Cullen, something I never thought I would say. Even though Loxwood isn't competing yet, I still accompany Rose to nearby training outings, and Leni is almost always there. Now there's just the wait until it is my turn to compete. Forget wait, more like agonising hard work. But I love it, and when I do go to my first event, Leni has already pledged to introduce me to every person imaginable.

'So she's, like, famous.' Jasmine says.

I shrug. 'In the horse world, I guess.'

Jasmine nods, still looking down at the picture. 'Is this what you do, then?'

'It's what I'm *going* to do,' I say, staring at Lochmere flying over the massive fence. *It's what I'm going to do.*

# Chapter 2

*Relaxing* isn't a word most people attribute to riding young Thoroughbreds, but it is when that Thoroughbred is Nantucket Winter. Next to Loxwood, he has always been one of my favourite to ride, and of all the horses at the track he has now gained that number one spot. His balance is perfect, and he moves in a collected rhythm. He is built similarly to Loxwood, but unlike my own chestnut Thoroughbred, Nantucket is not overly sensitive. He's the perfect horse on paper, except that he lacks one quality needed on the track. Speed.

'Do you have to go?' Lizzie whines when we get back to the yard, handing her own ride over to one of the grooms as she removes its saddle and pad.

'You know I do,' I say.

'We miss you,' she says, putting the tack down on the floor, and looking over at Graham. 'You're the peacekeeper. It's not the same when it's just the two of us. It's no fun.'

'Don't sugarcoat it,' Graham says, walking over to stand beside us. 'You don't have to hang out with me,' he teases.

'But *then* what am I going to do?' Lizzie exclaims. 'It's so dull without you!' she says to me.

'I'm, like, right here,' Graham interrupts.

'Georgia,' Lizzie says, ignoring him. 'Please. As your friend, I am begging you. Stay a little longer, and then we'll go get something to eat. You can't keep leaving me with Graham - he *doesn't* even eat dessert! I feel like I'm in prison.'

'Seriously,' Graham repeats, 'I'm standing right here.'

Lizzie rolls her eyes, still keeping her attention directed towards me.

'I just…can't.' I say, and she lets out an obvious sigh. 'I'm sorry,' I say quickly. 'But you know I can't. It's not like I have a choice, I have to go look after him.'

'There are other people there!' says Lizzie. 'Surely they can do it every now and then!?'

The truth is, Rose *would* feed and turn out Loxwood for me, and she has even offered to do so, but it's not right, and I'm certainly not about to tell my friends about the proposal.

'Tonight,' I say. 'We'll go get a Chinese or something. I can be ready by half six. Okay? I'll text you details. Or, you text me. Whatever. Deal?'

'Fine,' Lizzie says, trying but failing to hold a grudge. 'I'll speak to you later.'

I practically run the whole way home, grabbing an apple for Loxwood, and for myself a healthy looking smoothie drink and a packet of Maryland cookies (because balance), before hurrying out the door with my bike.

It's almost eight o'clock when I arrive at the stables, and unsurprisingly Rose had already fed. I've had to cut back to exercising only one horse a day at the track now, in order to have time to look after Loxwood before my first class, but on Saturdays I push it to two, reassured that should I ever be running late, like today, Rose wouldn't let my horse starve.

'Thank you. You shouldn't have to.' I say, walking into the clubhouse off the tack room, where Rose and Leah, the full time groom, are pouring themselves cups of tea.

'Of course,' says Rose. 'Don't be silly.'

Leah wordlessly passes me a mug, and I wrap my hands around its warmth. I've got into the habit of having breakfast with the two of them in here most mornings. Make that two breakfasts - one before mucking out, and one after. Mackenzie usually joins us, and if we're lucky she brings out a tray of her latest baked goods.

'Oh, I've got cookies.' I say, taking the packet out of my rucksack. Rose and Leah both politely decline, and I end up stuffing my face on my own.

Our cups are almost empty when Paige appears through the door, as usual looking ready to run away at any time. I reckon she'd have turned away on the spot, but Rose says her name warmly and jumps up to pour her a mug of tea. To be fair on Paige, I have no evidence that she really *is* as flighty and anxious as she looks, but I also have no reason to believe otherwise.

'Maryland cookie?' I say with my mouth full, holding the packet of biscuits out to her. I see her begin to reach for one, only to hesitate, as though she's done something wrong. 'Go on,' I urge, swallowing down my last bite. 'Please, or else I'll end up eating them all myself.'

Paige shoots me a timid smile (an actual smile! I've only ever seen her smile at her horse, whose name I've learnt is Brumby) as she reaches into the packet. 'Thanks,' she says, and it strikes me it's one of the first times she's ever addressed me personally. Her voice isn't how I imagined, wispy and shy, but rather deep and, mature? She looks about ten years old, but I know she's at least six years older, so I shouldn't be surprised that she sounds her age.

After breakfast, I swap Loxwood's rug for a waterproof sheet, put on his tendon and overreach boots, and turn him out in his paddock. I start mucking out his stable, occasionally catching glances of Rose, who is riding Paddington in the school. Next weekend, she and Clara are competing at an event, and I agreed to go along after Leah assured me that she could care for Loxwood should we not be back in time. I'm looking forward to it, though what I'm looking forward to even more a couple weeks later is Rose's Badminton Party, as she's calling it. Basically it's just watching the live cross country footage in her living room, which we did last year too, with an array of drinks and snacks. But giving it a name has brought the occasion great importance, and Rose is inviting everyone on the yard, not that I expect they will all show up. It's on a Saturday, beginning around lunchtime, which means I'll still have time to work in the morning, look after and ride Loxwood, and it will then end just as it's time to do the evening yard chores. The Badminton cross country phase was obviously scheduled with horsey people in mind.

'Do you want to try some more pole work?' Rose asks when she comes back from the school with one of her younger horses.

'Sure,' I say, the excitement tinted with dread. We introduced Loxwood to poles last week, and although he took to it well enough, I'm terrified of doing something that will harm him. Rose put up a cross bar, and after some initial hesitation Loxwood cleared the fence, but I seemed to do everything wrong. It wasn't like riding Sterling, Rose's elderly schoolmaster, but a different matter altogether. I couldn't keep my balance over my heels, or my hands down, or my shoulders out of the way. I felt like a beginner again, and the problem is that Loxwood is, too. He can't make up for my inexperience the way Sterling can. I'm the one who is supposed to be teaching *him*, and I realised just how much I still have to learn. And I'm not afraid for myself, of falling off and getting hurt, but I'm afraid of messing up Loxwood. Of messing up my only chance I have.

As always, Loxwood starts off springy. He has beautiful movement, and a stride that covers the ground. When Thoroughbreds come off the track, some require months of work before they understand that they're not supposed to carry their heads straight up in the air, clacking their teeth. But Loxwood learned to arch his neck and take a contact after only a few sessions, and I can't help but wonder if it had something to do with the fact that I'd been riding him for so long, anyway.

Canter strike-offs, on the other hand, are still an issue. Although he knows the correct leg aids - and this at least I *do* know is thanks to me - Loxwood still throws himself into the transition, taking off with his head all over the place. Once he's in the canter, though, it's lovely. You don't have to fight to hold him together, his balance is perfect, and when he collects his pace through the turns it feels as though he has enough power to sail over anything.

Rose comes to the school and sets a few poles down on the ground. With each one that falls to the sand, Loxwood flickers his ears back and jumps into the next stride with even more spring. His sensitivity makes him both enjoyable and complicated to ride. The feeling of having a horse so in tune with your movements, that he slows his pace when you take a deep breath is something that can't be described, but then one moment of distraction can be crucial. If I lose concentration for a second, Loxwood picks up on it and something is bound to go wrong.

I trot him over each pole in turn, varying the order so that he never knows which one I'm going to turn him to next. It's a simple exercise, but when dealing with a young horse it takes an unexpectedly long time. Rose watches from the sidelines, advising me to add more lower leg, or keep my hands closer to me and slow his pace. In spite of all the things I always feel like I do wrong, the glimmer of hope is that since he started schooling over them, Loxwood has seemed unfazed by poles. Like any young horse, he needs time to understand what is being asked of him, but he is willing, and doesn't back off unfamiliar sights.

By the end of the session, which included more random leaps into the air as a response to a certain noise or movement from elsewhere in the yard, we're both sweaty and tired. Rose is complimentary, but even as she rattles off everything that went right I still feel a bit despondent. Training a horse takes time, I know that, and I certainly never expected to be sailing around a cross country course after a few weeks work, but reality is always harder to stomach when you're faced with it. Being prepared to put the hours in is one thing, but doing so, and realising that even that isn't always enough, is a different thing altogether.

The wind is bitterly sharp, stinging every ounce of exposed skin. Tears appear in the corners of my eyes as I battle my way to the nearest concessions stand, cold air blowing in my face. Clara is riding first, but with an hour to go until she needs to get Spirit warmed up for dressage, she and Rose have gone to walk the cross country course. I offered my services as a groom, whether it be to get the horses ready or collect numbers from administration, but Rose reminded me that I'm here for myself, not to work, and when that didn't work she instructed me to go get myself a warm drink while they were gone. This event is only half an hour away by horse box (less by car), and when it warms up a bit later, Ben will be bringing Mackenzie and Jemima along. I won't exactly have much time to myself once Kenzie arrives, so I might as well make the most of it.

'Cappuccino, please,' I say, pulling loose change out of my coat pocket. The woman behind the counter sets about pouring coffee grinds into the machine, and I peer to my right where the administration tent is. There are a lot of quality riders here today, and a few I'd like to watch. Maybe I'll go look through the start times once I have my drink…

'I knew I'd find you wherever there's coffee.'

I spin around, having not noticed someone approach me, only to see Leni standing to my left. 'Make that two,' I say to the woman. 'You just arrived?' to Leni, now.

'Yeah, a few minutes ago,' Leni says with a smile. She is wearing a tracksuit over the top of her white jodhpurs and shirt, her hair is already pulled back into a hairnet, and small pearl earrings are in her ears. In the short time we've been friends, I've already learnt that from the second Leni's foot steps out of the lorry at a competition, she looks the part. She has an image to uphold, for owners and sponsors, and both she and her horses are turned out to perfection, the embodiment of professional. The rest of the time, however, she is dressed like a laundry basket (her words). 'You?'

'Same,' I say. 'Rose is off walking the course.'

'I've got two to walk,' Leni says with a sigh.

'What classes are you entered in?'

'Arturo's in the novice, and then Olly and Cooper are in the Intermediate.' Leni says. She competes three horses full time, but only one of them actually belongs to her. Known as "Olly", Lochmere is a beautiful black Thoroughbred Leni saved moments before he was due to be sent to the knacker's yard. Their incredible success is a testament to just how hard she's worked, and Lochmere is now the envy of many, myself included. Next to Loxwood, of course, he is one of my favourite event horses. I met him at a show jumping outing a few weeks ago, and he was just as magnificent up close. His condition is beautiful, and he even has a nice, albeit quirky, temperament.

'What time's Arturo's dressage?' I ask, knowing he'll be up first.

'Uhh,' Leni drags the word out as she pulls up her sleeve, revealing skin covered in black marker. 'Ten twenty-six,' she says. And then seeing my amused expression she adds, 'I wouldn't remember if I didn't write it down. I've been doing it since I was little, after I ended up having to ride Olly straight into a test without warm up because I reversed the number. I thought it was nine fifty-three, and not nine thirty-five.'

'I'm not even surprised,' I joke. Leni laughs, and we both turn towards the concessions stand as the woman places our drinks down on the counter.

'Four pounds,' she says.

'On me,' I say, quickly putting change down as Leni begins going through her pockets.

'I'll buy the next round, then,' Leni says defeatedly as I hand her a cup. 'Okay? None negotiable.'

'Uh huh.' I nod before taking a sip. The coffee is warm, but not too hot, and the heat runs down my throat, a little comfort against the cold.

'How's Loxwood, anyway?' Leni says. 'Let me know if you have to go,' she adds hesitantly. 'I need to get my numbers at some point, but I've got a good ten minutes free.'

'Where's Amanda?' I ask, referring to her coach. Amanda Walton retired from eventing decades ago, after a very successful career, and is now a just as successful trainer, not exactly known for her kindness.

'She won't be here for an hour at least. One of the grooms drives the lorry - there are other students' horses in there, too. Sure you're not busy?'

I assure Leni that I'm not, and quickly fill her in on Loxwood's progress since the last time we saw each other, including the last hack he went on.

'Those pheasants are pure evil disguised beneath feathers,' she says. 'I had a pony send me into a ditch once after one shot out the bushes, and we'd just had a load of rainfall, so it was full of water and I was soaked to the skin. The pony buggered off, leaving me to traipse two miles in drenched clothes. Anyway, when do you think he'll be ready to go out?'

'Loxwood? Once he can get over something more than a cross pole.'

'He looks great in all the pictures I've seen,' Leni says sincerely. 'He's so flashy, I bet he'll lead the dressage. And you said he doesn't seems phased by anything - well, other than pheasants.'

I laugh. 'Too bad for him he's stuck with me as a rider.' I say, and before Leni can say anything I add, 'I can't wait, though. To be competing.'

'It's great,' Leni agrees. 'And, I mean, I know there are *some* people who are ridiculously competitive, but on the whole there's a pretty great bunch of people. There are still some I wouldn't go near with a ten foot bargepole, but the good ones make up for it. Remember, I can introduce you to everyone, if you like?'

'Okay.'

'By everyone,' she clarifies, 'I mean the other juniors and young riders. In fact.' She starts looking around. 'I can start today.'

'Don't be silly,' I stammer. 'I'm not even riding, why would anyone want to meet me?'

'It'll give you an in,' Leni says. 'That way, when you *do* start competing, everyone will already know who you are. It always helps to have people on your side.'

Leni starts walking quickly, and I jog a few steps to catch up with her, nerves rising. Telling Lizzie and Graham I want to be a professional rider is one thing, but others who aspire to the same thing is a different matter. They actually have what it takes, and have been competing for a decade. I'm just some random person with a horse, who thinks she's going to go round Badminton.

'Oh,' Leni says excitedly. 'There's Alex. Blue trousers?'

I glance where she's staring, where a girl is standing in turquoise tracksuit bottoms, an older woman beside her. There's something about her, both of them, that rings a bell.

'Wait,' I say. 'You don't mean Alexandra Evans?'

Leni laughs. 'Yeah.'

'As in Ridley and Joan Evans' daughter?'

'See! I don't even need to introduce you! Though quick bit of advice, don't bring that up. I'll explain later.'

'Leni,' I say, but she's already stepped forward.

'ALEX!' Leni yells, and the girl turns, and upon recognition begins walking towards us, leaving her mother to chat to a group of passers-by, with a scruffy terrier-like dog following at her heels.

The Evans family are close to eventing royalty. Both Ridley and Joan came from horsey backgrounds, and are one of the longest standing "eventing power couples", as they are always referred to as. Their only child, Alexandra (or Alex, apparently), has followed in their footsteps, with four team appearances already under her belt aged eighteen. It's hard not to envy her perfect life.

'Hey!' Alex says happily, smiling at Leni and then glancing towards me.

'This is Georgia,' Leni says quickly. 'We met a couple months back. She's got a four year old with Rose Holloway, who's set to make his competition debut any minute.' How does she manage to make my almost non-existent event training sound professional?

'Nice to meet you,' says Alex, the dog sitting at her feet. 'I've seen Rose ride a load of times, she's great. She's got such a nice cross country position. She's supposed to be really nice, too.' And I warm to her instantly.

'She is,' I agree, hoping I won't have to come up with the next part of the conversation.

'How many have you got today?' Leni asks, and I'm instantly grateful.

'Um.' Alex hesitates. I still can't imagine a life in which I could actually lose count of how many horses I'm competing. I wonder if she needs it written on her arm, like Leni. 'Five. No - six! Yeah, six.' I notice that unlike Leni, who looks the picture of a competition rider, Alex looks as though she's just tumbled out of bed. The clothes she wears over her dressage kit are mismatched and colourful, unlike Leni's traditional black equestrian brands, and her dark hair hangs loose and unbrushed at her shoulders. If I walked out like that people would assume I was homeless, but somehow Alex gets away with it. She's tall and slim, with dark blue eyes, and high, protruding cheekbones.

'ALEX!' a shrill voice yells. We all turn round to see her

mother, *the* Joan Evans, waving an arm. 'Come on! You've got three courses to walk!'

'ONE SECOND!' Alex calls before turning back to us, the pleasant expression she put on for her mum vanished. 'She's driving me crazy,' she mutters. 'Seriously. I can't stand it when she isn't riding herself, because she spends the whole time getting after me.' She sighs. 'Do you hate your mother?' she asks me.

The question catches me off guard, but I quickly recover. 'Most of the time.'

'Oh, good.' Alex smiles. 'It's not just me, then. You're outnumbered, Leni. Anyway, I'd better go before she has a hernia. See you both round. Come on, Winnie.' She turns on the spot, the dog trotting alongside her as she starts walking back towards the lorry park, and I'm left in shock. Maybe Leni's right, and getting to know the right people really isn't a bad idea.

'Well, that's Alex,' she says.

'She seems nice,' I say. 'Though she was probably just saying that stuff about Rose.'

'Oh, she meant it. Alex doesn't know how to be polite.' Leni says. 'Seriously, you saw the last thing she said. She says what's on her mind, and that's that. That's what's great about Alex, she never beats around the bush.'

We begin walking again, stopping to toss our empty cups into a nearby bin, and I remember what Leni said before Alex came up. 'So, what's the deal with her parents? You said not to mention..'

'She hates being referred to as their daughter. People say it like it's the only reason she's successful, and it really bugs her. Alex works her butt off, and her parents… don't. I mean, obviously they ride, but that's about it. They've got loads of grooms, and while her parents do no mucking out or anything,

Alex is expected to do everything. I'm not saying you *shouldn't* look after your own horses, obviously, but she rides eight to ten a day, and her mum expects her to chip in twenty-four seven. It's just hypocritical, because Joan is always saying things like, "Alex, honey, you can lend a hand, can't you?", yet she herself does nothing. My workload is nothing compared to Alex's. Not to mention the pressure she's under. Ridley's the same, and the two of them coach her every day. I don't think she's even allowed to ride on her own, with the two of them on her back. Think Amanda, except that she's your mum, and therefore speaks to you the same way a parent does. I don't exactly envy Alex. She's got it tough.'

'You'd never guess,' I say.

'That's the problem,' Leni says. 'Too many people do, and they guess wrong.'

Those words are only too true, I think, remembering how just a few months ago I'd thought Leni too had a perfect life of luxury, unaware that she works full time and gets by on a shoestring. 'You know everyone here, then?' I say, changing the subject.

'All the pros.' Leni corrects. 'I don't really know any of the people who just ride as a hobby.'

I think about the friends Clara has made riding, all of them riding a few times a week between school and other hobbies, and then competing on weekends, and I understand what she means.

We're walking back towards the lorry park, the warmth the hot coffee offered long vanished, when somebody cries, '*Leni!*' and suddenly there is a figure crashing into her. 'You're here!' He releases her then looks around. 'Where's the devil?' he says loudly.

'Shush!' Leni yells, but he's just laughing. He must be about our age, and he has an almost geeky appearance. His limbs look too long for his body, and his face is covered in freckles. 'Georgia,' Leni says. 'This is Ryan. As you can see, he thinks he's hilarious.'

'What!?' Ryan says innocently before turning to me. 'Have you met Amanda? Surely you can back me up here?'

'I don't really know her,' I say cautiously. 'But from what I've heard I'm not sure that's a bad thing.'

'It's not,' Ryan agrees.

'You only hate her because of that one time she completely scolded you.' Leni points out. 'You see,' she says to me, 'Ryan and I have been riding against each other since we were on ponies-'

'-What she means is that I've been beating her since we were on ponies,' Ryan interrupts, and Leni waves an arm at him.

'And this *genius*,' she enunciates the word as she shoots him a glance. 'Decided to start a water fight in the lorry park after cross country one day.'

'I was just trying to have some fun,' says Ryan, defence creeping into his voice. 'It was a few years ago.. The course was so huge I think we'd all spent the day being sick, so we needed to celebrate somehow.'

'Naturally,' I say, and he shoots me a smile.

'Anyway,' Leni continues, 'he starts throwing buckets of water over us all, and soon we're all involved. Alex was there, too, and Ryan was trying to get his own back after she threw a sponge at his face-'

'-For the record, this *isn't* the only reason I can't stand Amanda.'

'-And so he's running towards Alex's lorry with a full bucket of water, hiding round the side so that he can throw it over her head without her seeing-'

'-And I saw Alex go round there to hide-'

'-AND,' Leni drags out the word. 'Who should be the person that walks out from behind the lorry but Amanda Walton!'

I could sense where this conversation was going, but I'm still surprised at it being true. 'No,' I say, raising a hand to my mouth.

'Unfortunately, yes,' Ryan says with a smile. 'When you think about it, it's pretty funny.'

Leni grins. 'Amanda Walton soaked to the skin in the middle of a lorry park, and you standing there, helpless, while she tears you to shreds.'

'See? *Funny.*'

'Come to think of it,' says Leni. 'She probably doesn't even know I was involved that day, or else she'd never have hired me.'

'Tough luck,' Ryan says sarcastically. 'You know, she still remembers me.'

'I doubt the list of kids who've throw buckets of water over her is very long,' I suggest, and Leni laughs.

'Fair point,' Ryan concedes. 'She's still not over it, though. No matter how polite I try to be she just gives me the stink eye. Anyway, I've got to go get Twist ready for dressage, and I'm sure Jade will have something she wants to yell at me about. Or for. '

'Jade's his sister,' Leni adds for my benefit.

'Older or younger?' I ask Ryan.

'Twins,' he says despairingly.

'Not that you can tell,' says Leni. 'Ignoring the fact she comes up to your waist, you're complete opposites.'

'Let's put it this way,' Ryan says to me. 'If Jade had been part of the water fight, she'd have been the one urging Amanda to file a complaint. Anyway, I'll catch you guys later.'

I accompany Leni to collect her numbers, and then we part ways at the lorry park. Rose and Clara still aren't back, so I start filling water buckets for the horses, by the end of which my hands are pink raw. But as I look around, at all the people united here by a common goal, I feel like I belong.

# Chapter 3

I sit deep in the saddle, keeping my knees open as my weight falls down into my heels, and push my shoulders back. Loxwood canters forward, ears pricked, towards the small fence. It's only small, but it's an upright, and he seems ready to take it on. I try to focus on what Rose told me - soft seat, shoulders back, hands together, keep lower leg on. The fence is coming closer, and I try not to think about the take-off stride, but rather the quality of the canter. But as we approach I think I can see the right one, and afraid to lose it I push Loxwood forward, his neck going rigid at my demand, but it's too late to do anything about it. The stride would have been perfect, but I interfered with the pace out of panic, and now we're too close to get it right, and he has to chip in a small one, resulting in a less than comfortable jump. I am furious with myself.

'Try again,' Rose says gently. 'Don't worry, just wait for the fence to come to you.'

I fight back tears as I turn Loxwood back to the jump. A few strides out, he anticipates a demand for acceleration, as I asked last time, and goes for it himself. The jump isn't awkward, but it's far too long, and if the upright were any higher we would be in trouble.

'That's okay. Go again, and remember that you want to take off as close to the fence as you can.'

This time I'm prepared for Loxwwod to fire, and I do my best to keep him between hand and leg. It's not perfect, but we take off at a reasonable distance, and jump a normal jump.

'Good!' Rose calls as I bring Loxwood back to trot, letting the reins out as I rest a hand on his neck.

'Why do I keep messing it up!?' I say frustratingly. 'He's great, but *I* keep ruining him!'

'You got it right that last time,' Rose says, and I bring Loxwood back to a walk, in circles around her.

'Yeah, but I shouldn't have got it wrong in the first place. It's just,' I pause as I struggle to get the right words out with tears appearing in my eyes. 'When I get in front of the fence and I don't see the right stride… I just panic.'

'It will come with practice. You've just got to stop thinking, and react the way that feels right.'

'I don't see that happening any time soon,' I scoff. 'But Loxwood's good, right?' I say.

I come to a halt, and Rose walks up to lay a hand against his neck. 'Loxwood's *great*. You both are. Now, go get him cooled off, Badminton starts in twenty minutes.'

A feast has already been laid out on the coffee table when Rose and I walk into the sitting room. I took my boots and chaps off at the door, and am now just in hole-filled socks. The room is like the rest of the house - modest and cozy, with an easy atmosphere in which it is hard not to feel at home. All the walls are white stone, some striped with dark beams, the same kind that run across the ceiling. It's the kind of room made to live in, and not just look nice. Comfy-looking sofas laden with tartan blankets and embroidered cushions, well thumbed equestrian magazines on side tables complete with mug rings. There are a couple low cupboards on which balance photographs in old silver frames, featuring horses and dogs and country houses and tweed jackets. Alfred, the elderly Westie, is curled up in a ball on his bed, a white ball of fluff on a tartan cushion.

Jemima is sitting in an armchair, with her knees drawn up to her chest, and a colouring book resting against them. As much as she enjoys ponies and riding, unlike her sister she spends just as much time doing indoor activities. The competitive streak seems to not have reached Jemima - not yet, anyway - and she would choose plaiting Pheasant's mane over going to a show any day.

'*Georgia!*' Mackenzie yells, her voice following the sound of her feet running down the stairs. She's wearing purple jodhpurs, with pink and turquoise striped socks pulled up to her knees, and a long-sleeved top on which there's a drawing of a horse head.

'You're colourful,' I say.

Rose laughs beside me. 'I can't believe I let her talk me into those purple jods!'

Kenzie glares at her before turning back to me. 'What do you think?' she says, gesturing at the table of food. 'I set it out myself! Mummy said we didn't need popcorn as well, but I told her she was wrong.'

'Of course she was,' I say, shooting Rose a quick glance to make sure she knows I'm joking. One look at the table is enough to know that we'll never make it through all that food even without the popcorn. There are bowls of crisps, with side dishes of humous, tzatziki and salsa, garlic bread, plates of Mackenzie's cupcakes, cheese sandwiches, bottles of iced tea and lemonade, and piles of paper plates and cups. In fact, I'm already anticipating how ill I'm going to feel later when Ben walks into the room, carrying trays of homemade pizza. Tomato sauce peaks out along the edges of the crispy dough, mozzarella has bubbled until dotted with brown, and each pizza has a sprinkling of olive oil and rocket. No wonder Rose never cooks - why would she when her husband is capable of that?

'You didn't put pineapple on them!' Mackenzie complains sulkily as her dad makes space for the trays by moving one bowl of popcorn onto the sofa and handing the other one to Jemima.

'There are two more in the oven,' Ben says calmly.

'With pineapple?' says Mackenzie.

'With pineapple.'

When I'm with Rose, I always wonder what it would be like to have a mother who's interested in horses, and now I try to imagine what it would be like to come home to dinner on the table. Between the three of us, my parents and I can just about open a can of soup. You would think one of us would have learnt to cook by now, but my mum is hopeless, my dad has no inclination, and I'm certainly not about to. One day, maybe, when I have my own place, or am old and have nothing better to do. I think the only thing I've ever made is flapjacks.

'Sit with me, Georgia,' Kenzie says, taking hold of my hand and dragging me towards one of the sofas. Rose takes a seat in the one running the other way, and Jemima is still colouring in attentively, one hand methodically shovelling popcorn into her mouth.

I'm just wondering how long it will be until Clara gets here (she said early afternoon, but knowing her that could mean anything), when I hear Ben say the words, 'They're just through here,', and another figure steps into the doorway.

'Hello, Paige,' Rose says warmly. 'Come! Take a seat. We've got so much food…'

I'm slightly surprised to see her, but quickly push the emotion away. Paige looks just as unnerved, almost as if she had expected to find the room empty and is scared at having found it occupied. Rose always seems to speak to her easily, and nobody else seems to find her as intimidated as I do, so perhaps she finds *me* worrying, for some reason. I highly doubt it, but just to be sure I try and think of something to say that will make her look less like she wants to run away.

'I hope you're hungry,' I say.

Rose laughs. 'Ben and Kenzie went a bit overboard, didn't they?' she says. 'Sit down, Paige,' she repeats lightly, as Paige is still standing near the doorway. 'I don't know how we're going to get through all of this… Did you hack Brumby? How was he?'

Paige walks unsurely to the nearest armchair, also wearing socks and jodhpurs, both with even more holes in them than my own, and clears her throat before speaking. 'He was good.' Again, I'm struck by the seriousness of her tone. 'I took him down to the water, and he didn't hesitate at all this time.'

'I'm not surprised,' Rose says, nodding her head as she lifts a slice or pizza onto a paper plate. 'He's brave. And he trusts you enough to go over anything. Have you seen the work Paige does bareback and bridleless with him, Georgia?'

Mackenzie pours me a cup of iced tea, and I thank her quickly before replying. 'Yeah, I've seen him in the school,' I say, turning to Paige. 'It's amazing, seriously. I wish I could do that.'

Paige shrugs as she looks down nervously at her hands, and

then hesitates before reaching to take a single crisp from the bowl on the table. 'I don't know. It's not much.. I probably haven't taught him properly, or anything.'

'That's even more impressive,' says Rose. 'You've done it all on instinct.'

'Two pineapple pizzas!' Ben announces, walking into the room before Paige can say anything more.

'SHUSH!' Mackenzie cries. 'IT'S STARTING!'

We all look towards the TV screen to see the first horse coming out of the box, and as Rose turns up the volume with the remote control, the sound of cheers floods the room. An Olympic horse, the first of his rider's two rides today, is serving as trailblazer, and the whole crowd is behind him.

'Go on!' Rose yells, and Mackenzie starts cheering.

The horse clears the first fence, and we all let out a whoop, eyes glued to the TV.

We barely move during the next four hours. You would think that watching the same fences over and over again for that amount of time would get old, but it doesn't. That's the thing about cross country, because every horse and rider is different, and each combination has their own way of going. And it's the rounds where the horse is paying complete attention to its rider, whose position is perfect and instinctive, and there isn't a single jump that leaves you gasping or cringing, that are magical.

Clara showed up sometime during the second hour, and as she always does when we watch this kind of footage, she spent a good amount of time bewitched by the fact that some people can possibly be brave enough to do this.

I think we all ended up on our knees around the coffee table to avoid getting up to serve ourselves snacks every few minutes, because when the last horse jumps the final fence I am on the floor, feeling too full to move.

'That's it for another year,' Rose says as the provisional scoreboard comes up, and we then proceed to spend another twenty minutes discussing the rounds before going back out to the horses.

Loxwood whinnies when he sees me coming round the corner, golden ears pricked and nostrils flared. The sun is shining directly into his stable, and his coat is glowing. I left him without a rug this afternoon, in view of the warm(ish) day, and he beams quality. With off the track Thoroughbreds, it's normally considered a given that they need a good couple months of gaining condition before they can begin their new careers, but thanks to the quality of Frank's yard I never had that worry. Loxwood was in good health when he arrived, and he is in good health now.

'Hey, rabbit,' I say quietly, running my hands along his delicately curved ears as he lowers his head over the door. 'What do you think, is that going to be you someday?' Loxwood is clueless to my question, having grown bored of the attention and turned back to his hay.

I spend the next hour doing all the things I do every evening - skip out, refill water bucket, more hay, groom, rug, feed.. Hope arrives to collect Clara just as I'm finishing up, and I'm more than happy to accept her offer of a lift home, my mind still whirling with all the horses and riders I watched today.

# Chapter 4

As I wheel my bike through the door, waving goodbye to Hope and Clara behind me, I want nothing more than to collapse into bed. As always, I was up at four this morning, and the excitement of the afternoon, in addition to many hours riding, has left me wiped out. I pull my boots off in the hallway, and as I come into the living area I find my parents dressed up for going out, and my mood brightens at the thought of being able to have the house to myself.

'Where are you going?' I ask, just as my mother says, 'Hurry up, or we'll be late.'

'It's only half six,' my dad comments from where he's watching TV, probably the only thing he'll contribute to the disagreement I sense is about to take place.

'What?' I say, looking at my mum.

'Don't pull that face,' she says quickly. 'I told you.'

'Told me what? No you didn't.'

'Georgia,' she says despairingly. 'I told you weeks ago that we were having dinner with your father's parents tonight.'

'How did you expect me to remember if you told me weeks ago,' I snap. 'Obviously I've forgotten by now.'

'There's no need to discuss this,' she says, keeping her voice light and calm. 'Just go get changed so we can go.'

'No,' I say quickly, before adding, 'Why do I have to go? You'll only complain that I don't join in with the conversation, or whatever, so there's no point, really.'

'It's your grandparents! It's *you* they want to see.'

'Then take them a photograph,' I retort, walking past her to get a glass of water from the kitchen.

'Why do you make everything so difficult?' my mum says, in a hopeless bid to make me feel bad.

'I didn't know we were going out tonight!' I cry. 'I wasn't prepared for it, therefore I do not want to go.'

'It's dinner with your family, Georgia, how much preparation do you need!?'

'Look,' I say as calmly as I can, 'I don't want to go, you don't want me being moody all evening, so the way I see it, it's a win win situation.'

My mother obviously doesn't see it the same way, because half an hour later I'm trailing behind my parents into the restaurant, as they gush over the plates of food we're walking past. I only have to look at the portions to feel as though I'm about to be sick.

'There they are!' my mum says, pointing to a table where a couple is taking a first sip of wine, a waiter standing with the bottle in his hand, waiting to see if it has been deemed satisfactory. I literally do not think I could be any more bored as I watch my grandfather swirl the alcohol around the glass and spend far too long smelling it before swallowing it down. I have a sudden admiration for the waiters in this place, having to witness performances like this on such a regular basis.

They see us before we get to the table, and my mum is the first to reach them, smiling and laughing as they hug. She's always got on with her in-laws, and they with her. I don't get it, and frankly, it's sickening. The way they all gush just confirms that there is no reason for me to be here.

My grandmother has hair no longer than an inch and dyed red, areas of grey visible at the roots. And every time I see him, I always think that my grandfather looks like the villain in a children's movie, the kind who always ends up stepping on a snare, or being carried away by some giant bird. They don't actually live that far away, which is partly why I manage to see them so rarely, because they don't have to come and stay the night if they visit, and my dad pops by their house regularly.

'Isn't this a nice place,' my grandmother says, looking around at the dark lights and tacky decor. I don't even need to look at the menu to know that none of us can afford to be here, and that the amount that will be spent tonight is nothing but a waste of money.

'We should do this more often,' my mum says. *Please no.*

A waiter comes to take our drinks order and bring menus. I'm still not very hungry from my earlier feast, but even if I was I wouldn't order much. I pick the least filling dish on the menu, ignoring my family trying to get me to choose something different, and try to zone out of the conversation. They're talking about a reality series, which is tedious, so I stare down at my hands and think about Loxwood. He would have been good today if I hadn't kept messing up, but what can I do to fix it? Rose said we can jump him again tomorrow, so maybe if I work on just focussing on the canter, as she is always saying.

'…So, what are you up to at the moment, Georgie?' my grandmother's voice cuts into my thoughts.

'Riding,' I say blankly.

'Oh, those racehorses?'

'And my own.'

Her eyebrows go up. 'Really?' she says, lifting a ring covered hand to run it through her hair before returning it to her lap. 'Horses are very expensive.'

'It was free,' my mum says quickly from across the table, before glancing at my dad, but he's in a deep sports conversation with his own.

'But horses still cost a lot to keep,' my grandmother continues. 'Food and vet bills…' her eyes go to me for confirmation. *Shut up,* I think. *Please, just shut up.*

'They don't cost that much to keep,' I say. 'And I work, so…'

'Still,' my grandmother says, her voice having gone to the pitch of a four year old's. 'There are much better things you could spend the money on. Horses aren't going to come to anything in the long run.'

I open my mouth to reply, to say that she's wrong, and that all I want to do is ride, and that horses are my life, but then my grandfather asks a question, and as my grandmother turns to answer him, going off into another conversation, I really can't be bothered.

His ears prick when he locks on to the fence, and I sit still to steady him. *Just think about the canter,* that's what Rose said. *Just think about the rhythm.* I count the beats in my head - *one two, one two, one two* - and try not to think about the upcoming fence. *One two, one two.* We're a few strides out when I realise that the distance isn't going to be right, and there won't be room to add another one. Panicked, I kick Loxwood on, and he takes off five feet from the small upright. My heart sicks, not because there was anything particularly wrong with the jump, but because yet again I made the same mistake.

'Do it again,' Rose says calmly. 'All's fine.'

I replay instructions in my head, thinking of all the ways Rose has tried to explain this to me. *Think of it as trying to get as close to the fence as you can with enough momentum. You move forward and build up energy, but you don't push the horse out of his stride - you can move forward and still wait for a stride. It's better to add a stride than take a flyer.*

Even though my mind knows all the right things to do, I still don't do the right thing when faced with a jump. Out of fear of missing my stride, I choose the wrong one, anyway. I always warm Loxwood up over poles, Rose setting them between wings to pretend they're fences, and I only have to think about the rhythm of the canter. I have no problem getting my stride right then, but the poles in the show jumping ring at Badminton are hardly going to be on the floor.

I turn Loxwood to the fence again and again, until we finally get a jump that is somewhat acceptable. I should be reassured that my horse is so willing and jumps over anything, but my own failures override that.

'It's not as bad as you think,' Rose says when I walk over to her at the end of the lesson, trying desperately to blink away the tears in my eyes.

'I'm useless,' I mutter. 'I've never seen other people struggle this much,'

'Most people your age have horses who know their job,' Rose says. 'You've never had a problem on Sterling - *that's* what other people are dealing with. The Sterlings of the world. But the

Sterlings are never going to be as successful as the Loxwoods in the long run.'

'I dunno,' I say, wiping my eyes with one hand and resting the other against Loxwood's neck.

'Hey, remember the saying. Blood, sweat and tears.' Rose pauses. 'Though, actually, let's try to avoid the blood part.'

Mondays are Loxwood's days off, and so after school, instead of rushing to the yard to have enough time to ride, I go into town and order drinks at a cafe. I've only just put the tray down on a table when Leni walks through the door.

'You shouldn't have done that,' she says, reaching for change in her coat pocket.

'Give over. You know I won't accept it.'

We bicker over who's paying for what a while longer, until finally sitting down with warm cups of coffee and slices of cake. I never have to worry about getting caught up because, like me, Leni also has horses she needs to get back to and take care of. But it's nice to be able to talk about riding with someone who actually understands. Leni fills me in on how the weekend's competition went, including the names of people I now know, and I listen to all with interest.

'Anyway, how's Loxwood?'

I begin saying how he's well and whatnot, but as I start talking about his jumping I find that I want to lay my problems down on the table.

'I struggled with that a bit when I started riding bigger horses, like Cooper, but I found watching other people helped. It just reminded me that you still have to keep the stride short, but while pushing towards the fence.'

'That's the thing,' I say. 'I *know* it in my head, and I can see and explain exactly what I'm supposed to do, but then when I'm actually in front of a fence I just panic.'

Leni doesn't look horrified by my incompetence as I thought she might, but is instead thoughtful. She swallows another mouthful of coffee before saying, 'Do you not think that maybe that's what's wrong? You know exactly what you're supposed to do, so you're thinking too much. You're thinking about how your horse *should* be going, and so you stop actually focussing on how he *is*. Like, maybe,' She shuffles in her seat. 'Don't think of it as seeing a stride, so much as reacting to a stride!? Don't try to think about what you're supposed to do, and instead just do what feels right? Get the horse moving forward and responsive to your leg, and then just react to what you've got in front of a fence. If you've got impulsion, then it shouldn't really matter where you take off from, anyway, because he should be able to do it from anywhere.' She takes another sip of her coffee, and I swallow down a forkful of cake.

'You're good at that,' I say.

Leni shrugs. 'My mum runs a riding school, I'm used to having to explain things.'

I don't know how things will go next time I jump Loxwood, or if there will be any change from before, of if I'll just end up pushing him hopelessly into the fences again. But I do know that it's ridiculous how twenty-six letters, arranged in a slightly different order, can say the same thing in such a different way.

# Chapter 5

The next jumping session isn't until a few days after my talk with Leni, and I walk into the yard feeling both confident and anxious. It's late afternoon, having just finished school, and I go straight to bring Loxwood in from the paddock. I rode Nantucket this morning, and both Lizzie and Graham were in a good mood, partly because Cookiemoon, one of the crazier horses (to put it mildly), had gone. It didn't seem right to me to be happy about a horse being sent away, but to be fair I probably would have felt the same way if I were the one who'd had to ride her.

I've just brought Loxwood in when Rose comes to the stable door. 'Before we work him,' she says, 'can you ride someone else?'

'Uh, sure,' I say, not knowing where she's going with this. 'Who?'

'Cinder.'

'What?' I say, only out of surprise. 'Why? Won't Kenzie mind?'

'Of course not,' Rose laughs. 'I have an idea. Humour me.'

I pick out Loxwood's feet before leaving his stable, and follow Rose to the tack room where she hands me all of Cinder's kit, and tells me to meet her in the school when I'm ready. The bay Connemara mare is easy to do in all ways, and within minutes I'm swinging up into the saddle. A small laugh escapes me when I settle onto her back.

'Feel close to the ground?' Rose says knowingly.

'Just a tad,' I joke. 'I never really got to ride ponies,' I say. 'I wish I had, though.'

'That's why you struggle,' Rose says, and I sense she's edging towards whatever it is she's planning. 'Most people spend years as kids kicking ponies into anything and everything, because you don't have to see a stride the way you do with horses.' *Yep, here we go.* She walks to the middle of the school and takes a seat on a plastic filler. A small course of jumps is set up, and what Rose is expecting me to do clicks.

'You want me to jump?'

'Yep. Warm her up, and then when you're ready we'll pop the cross bar a couple times.'

I glance down at the pony beneath me, then back at the course of jumps. The fences aren't exactly big, seventy centimetres at most, but still. 'I'll squash her,' I say to Rose.

'Nonsense!' she laughs. 'Even I ride her. Anyway, get her going, or else we won't have time to do Loxwood.'

Still not knowing quite how this is all going to go, I push Cinder forward and walk her a few circles before asking for a trot. As soon as she springs into the pace, I smile. No wonder kids get to ride ponies. Her head carriage is still, her neck arched and mouth responsive to the bit, and she moves off my leg. Getting used to the short stride is easy, in view of the fact that there are plenty of youngsters at the track that move in a similar fashion.

'Piece of cake, isn't it!' Rose calls.

I laugh. 'I should've got one!'

'Why do we bother with horses!?' she agrees.

Cinder's canter is just as flawless, and as I bring her back to trot and continue circling and changing rein, I realise something that I haven't thought about in the past couple months. Right now, riding this little Connemara is *fun*. *Fun*.. I don't know when I last associated that word with riding. You don't when it becomes your job, but in this moment I'm reminded that it can be.

At Rose's instruction, I canter Cinder towards the cross pole, sitting lightly in the saddle and letting her do her job. I'm not really thinking about what she'll do, and she plods over effortlessly. I pat the pony on landing, as Rose calls for me to keep going. Again and again I canter Cinder over the low fences, keeping my body still on the approach, sitting her steady stride. She always remains on the contact without any fuss, the weight in the reins nice and light.

I pop over every fence Rose asks, thinking about the ponies that have climbed to the top level in equestrian sport and wondering if it's too late to get one. *I don't mean it*, I think immediately after, as though I'm worried Loxwood is going to hear my thoughts.

When we've been over every fence in the ring, Rose lists directions for a course. Cinder is happy to oblige, and clears every fence with ease. I'm patting her when she comes back to walk, and glance over at Rose. I'm not quite sure what her master plan was, seeing as she's only spoken up to tell me which fences to jump. She hasn't corrected by position, or any of the things she usually does. In a lesson, Rose is normally talking throughout, but today it's been minimal.

'So?' she says when I walk Cinder toward her in the middle of the school.

'So..' I repeat, not sure where this is going.

'That was all right, wasn't it?'

'I think so..'

'Just tell me one thing,' Rose says, her voice almost humorous. 'How come you hit a perfect stride every time.'

Instinct tells me to protest that I didn't, but then I realise I can't. I wasn't thinking about the stride, because this is a small pony we're talking about, but it's true that there weren't any awkward jumps. 'I dunno..'

'You don't know?' says Rose. 'How come you don't know?'

I know where she's going with this. I know what she's waiting for me to say. 'I wasn't thinking about it.'

Rose nods, and without warning walks to the nearest fence. 'You kept moving through the turns, while keeping her steady and not rushing.' She stands a good three paces away from the upright. 'Why didn't you ask her to take off from here?'

I frown. 'It's too far out. She wouldn't make it - or, she might, but it would be too long.'

Rose nods again. 'You see, if you get to this point.' She takes a step back. 'And realise the distance isn't quite right, then you can push for a longer stride, but you get nearer the base of the jump. But you wouldn't expect Cinder to take off from here.' She steps forward again. 'Right?'

It's a pretty obvious question. 'Right.'

'Then, tell me, why do you expect Loxwood to?'

I stare at where Rose is standing, a few paces from the fence, and picture a horse taking off from there. I know I've been riding him badly, and that I was making mistakes, but seeing it like this just makes it more obvious.

'I panic,' I stammer.

'You didn't on her, though,' Rose says, nodding at Cinder. 'You rode her on instinct and she went beautifully. I know horses are different and more difficult, but at this height you shouldn't treat Loxwood any differently. It goes wrong because you push him out of his stride and you're no longer in a good canter. With her, you focussed on keeping the rhythm consistent throughout, and as a consequence you always met the fences right. Remember, there's always going to be another stride. If you just focus on the canter up to the last one, instinct should tell you what to do, and if you've got the right impulsion then a "wrong" jump won't feel that bad, either.'

I nod, not sure what to say.

'So, go get this one away,' Rose says, patting Cinder on the neck. 'And let's practice with that firecracker of yours.'

It's easy to override the fear of making a mistake when you realise that you've already screwed up anyway, and there's nothing left to lose. I try to blank out my mind, and just think about the horse beneath me. It's not like jumping is supposed to be maths - if it were I'd be done for. I only think about having Loxwood between my hand and leg, with the feeling that the power and impulsion he builds is enough to sail over a Land Rover. His stride covers the ground, and as I bottle the energy it also goes upward. *All I have to do is think about keeping him in this rhythm,* I think. *NO! STOP THINKING!*

'When you're ready,' Rose says, and I look for the fence out of the corner of my eye.

Keeping the momentum in the canter, I circle Loxwood once to check his attention is with me before turning towards the fence. His ears swivel forward, the tips almost touching, and I do my best to stay calm. He hurries a little a few strides out, anticipating the demand that he do so, but I sit still. We're getting closer to the fence, and there's a moment when I feel like we're hovering, almost like wind gathering beneath wings to power into the air. Loxwood swings upwards, his neck and back round and soft, and his knees snapped. A smile of relief comes over me when we land, and Rose cheers.

'Yes! That's it - keep going! Go over anything!'

I bring Loxwood back to trot to change rein, and he rushes into a left canter lead. As we turn round to the fence, I clear my mind again, focussed only on how my horse is feeling. We approach the fence, and one stride out I realise it's going to be a bit long. There's not room to add another one, so I push him slightly, getting closer to the obstacle. I expect Rose to scorn me, to say I've just undone the work I did before, but she doesn't.

'Good decision!' she yells. 'There's a big difference between taking a slightly long one and firing a horse at a fence,' she adds, seeing my confused expression. 'Go on, keep going.'

Every fence we meet, we meet right. Loxwood is jumping beautifully, and when he collects himself in the last stride before take off, the feeling of power I get as he prepares to swing over the fence is unreal.

The yard is buzzing with the regular onslaught of DIY liveries when I lead Loxwood back to his stable, unable to hide the smile of relief on my face. And I can tell he knows he's done well by the way he walks with his head at my waist and his ears pricked forward, happy to be fussed over. I don't know what it is that made the difference, whether Leni's pep talk was all I needed, or if riding Cinder gave me extra confidence, or maybe it was neither of those things. Maybe it's something I've slowly been working towards this whole time and it's taken this long to see the difference. Maybe it's like a fallen tree - it weakens and weakens over time, but you don't notice the change until it's toppled over.

It's still light when I head for my bike, a perk of daylight savings time. Loxwood is rugged and fed, but I always worry about the possibility that I've forgotten to do something whenever I'm about to leave. Gravel crunches behind me as I lean down to take hold of the handlebars, and I turn to see which livery it is.

'Hey.' It's Paige.

'Hi,' I say, pulling my bike up towards me. Paige also cycles here, but I don't think we've ever left at precisely the same time before. 'You heading home?'

'Yeah,' Paige says, reaching for the rusty pink bike that leans against a railing. 'You?'

I nod, not sure how long I can keep this conversation going. Since watching Badminton, she's been quicker to say hello in the mornings, and things like that. Though, I realised with shame, I hadn't exactly made the biggest effort to start a chat before that. 'Which way are you?' I ask, looking down the road.

Paige points in the direction leading to town. 'About a mile that way.'

'Me too. That way, I mean. In town.'

'That's a long way to cycle,' Paige says, swinging one leg over her bike seat.

'Not too bad,' I say, also getting on my bike. 'If my legs are up to it I can do it in twenty minutes.'

'You do it four times though, right? There and back in the morning, and same again in the evening.'

'Yeah,' I say. We turn onto the road, and as from this direction the first stretch is slightly downhill, I stay still on my bike. 'Sometimes I think I'm crazy for wanting to do it, but it's worth it to have Loxwood.'

'I know what you mean,' Paige says.

'How did you get Brumby?' I ask, seeing a conversation topic present itself.

'I saw a flyer for him in town,' she says. 'Somebody rescued him from the track because he was going to be sent to slaughter, but they just kept him in a garden for a few months. He was so thin.'

'I remember,' I say, thinking back to when I first saw the scrawny horse at the yard.

'I'm lucky, really,' Paige says after a moment. 'That he's so kind. I didn't really know much about horses, I just loved them, and he's just so gentle.'

'He's a sweetie.'

Paige smiles. 'I know he's not beautiful, like Loxwood or Rose's horses, but I love him.'

'He will be, though,' I say. 'It just takes time for them to get back to condition.'

'Yeah,' Paige says thoughtfully. 'I don't mind if he doesn't, though. If he never is, I mean. He's still the best to me.'

We cycle on, passing country houses and studs, until the next village is in view, and the smaller houses scattered around it.

'I live over here,' says Paige, nodding to the left. I can faintly see a small bungalow, built of dark bricks and with an overgrown lawn around it.

'Okay,' I say. Although it's little, it seems like a nice enough house, and suddenly I wonder why I've always thought that there's something of a mystery surrounding Paige. Why have I always assumed that there's something in her life that goes unsaid?

The closer we get, the more run-down the house appears. I'm not exactly a gardening enthusiast, but the lawn is seriously scruffy, with weeds and brambles covering the majority of it. I cycle past here every day, but I've never particularly paid the home much attention before now. The windows are dusty, lined with blinds dotted with mould. The front door is over ten feet from the road, but even from here we can hear the sound of the TV, loud voices creeping into the countryside.

'I'd better go in,' Paige says, sounding almost regretful.

'Okay,' I repeat, not sure what else to say.

She's just about to swing her leg over the bike when a sudden cry comes from inside the house. I don't even have time to ask questions before Paige is running towards the front door. I yell her name, but she either doesn't hear me or chooses not to. She hasn't exactly invited me in, but I don't feel like I can just sit here without offering *some* sort of assistance, so I run after her.

'What's wrong?' I ask as Paige fumbles for a key in her pocket.

'Carrie,' she says shakily, turning the key in the lock and slamming her body weight against it for the door to give way.

Immediately I'm greeted by clouds of cigarette smoke and the booming sound of the TV, even louder than it was outside. The door opens into the sitting room, where two ripped-up sofas face a television set, and a small kitchen is at the back of the room. Everything's a mess, with dirty plates and beer cans seeming to cover every surface, and the smoke in the air rising from cigarette butts in an ashtray, so much so that I almost don't see the woman on the sofa. She's not asleep, but she looks close to, with her head back and her body limp. I wonder whether I should say hello, but Paige seems to have ignored her, and is instead walking towards a door on the right, so I follow her.

'Carrie,' Paige says again as she opens the door. We're in a bedroom, painted a pale pink that's pealing off the walls in the corners, with one open window, and two single beds. What appears to be a wheelchair is beside one of them, and there, on the floor, is a young girl.

'I fell,' she says through tears.

'Hey, it's okay,' Paige says quickly, reaching past me to close the door as I step into the room, before hurrying to the floor to help. Skilfully, she picks the child up and sits her in the chair. She can't be much older than Mackenzie, and she has her sister's colouring and pale features. 'What were you doing?'

Carrie begins to cry again. 'I just wanted a drink,' she says. 'I tried calling Mum, but she didn't hear.'

'It's okay,' Paige says, running through more words of comfort before Carrie looks up at me, standing nervously against the door.

'Who are you?' she says.

'I'm Georgia,' I say, not sure what else I can offer.

'Georgia rides,' Paige says to her sister. 'She has her own horse with Brumby.'

'Really?' Carrie sniffles, still looking at me.

'Yeah,' I say, and something about the way Paige is looking at me makes me think, I realise quickly, that she wants me to keep talking. To offer her sister a distraction. 'Do you want to see a picture?'

Carrie nods shyly, and I pull my phone out of my pocket, finding a photo I took of Loxwood a couple weeks ago, on a day when the weather was warm enough for him to be turned out without a rug. He's looking straight into the camera, ears forward, and the sun makes his coat look golden. I hand the phone to Carrie, and she takes hold of it in her right hand.

'He's lovely,' she says whimsically, looking down at the photograph.

'Not, as nice as Brumby, though,' I say, to which Paige smiles.

'Do you have a picture of them both together?' Carrie asks.

'No..' I say. 'But we could take one, if you like?'

'Paige, will you remember?' Carrie says seriously to her sister.

'Of course,' says Paige.

Carrie is looking more settled now, tears no longer flooding her eyes, and her face generally brighter. 'I'd better be going, then,' I say to Paige. 'If you're all right,' I add.

'Yeah.' She smiles. 'We'll be fine. I'll walk you out.'

'It was nice meeting you,' I say to Carrie.

'Will you come back?' she says quickly. 'Georgia can come and visit again, can't she, Paigey?'

'Of course she can,' says Paige.

'I'd love to,' I tell Carrie. 'And I'll bring you more photos.'

Carrie smiles widely, calling goodbye as Paige and I walk out of the room. Their mother is still passed out on the sofa, and judging by how Paige isn't thinking to close the door quietly, I reckon she knows she's not going to wake up.

'Thank you,' Paige says when we're out the front door.

'I didn't do anything,' I say, a hundred questions burning at my tongue.

'We haven't always lived here,' Paige says, seeming to read my mind. 'Our old house had stairs, and Carrie fell down them when she was little. Hasn't been able to walk since. Our parents weren't exactly the best before then, but since… They just haven't coped.'

'You look after her,' I say.

'And everyone else.' Paige pauses. 'That's why I have Brumby, in one way. He's the one thing I have for me, you know? And Carrie likes hearing about him.'

'Is it not hard, having to go to the yard twice a day when

you've already got so much to deal with?'

We've reached our bikes, where they were left on the side of the road, and I lean mine up while Paige just moves hers onto the grass. She's still contemplating my question, trying to find the right words. 'That's the thing, I never look at it as *having* to go to the yard, no matter how tiring. I *get* to. I'd always be with him if I could.'

'I guess you're right,' I say, swinging one leg over my bicycle seat. There are more things I want to ask, but I feel like there have already been enough revelations for the day, and I'm conscious of the three miles I have left to go and the darkening sky. 'I'll see you tomorrow. And maybe we'll try to get that picture for Carrie?'

Paige smiles. 'Yeah. I'll see you tomorrow. And, Georgia? Thanks.'

I make it back before nightfall, with my usual evening routine of propping my bike up in the hallway and removing my chaps and boots.

'Georgia?' my mum calls.

'Yep,' I reply, walking into the kitchen where she's seated at the table.

'You're later than usual,' she says.

'I... got caught up in something. Sorry.'

She nods, eyes on her computer screen, and the matter seems to have been dropped. Usually, I'd be annoyed by now. At her for sitting here, doing nothing, and my dad for reclining in front of crap TV, but today I'm not. How can I complain when people like Paige and Carrie have the parents they have? Not long ago I thought my family was making my life miserable by dragging me to a restaurant. How stupid can I be? The fact that I even have a mother who notices when I get home late is something. Paige could possibly be missing for a week without her own realising it.

I take a glass from the cupboard and pour myself a serving of pomegranate juice, watching my mum as I gulp it down. I'm not even sure *how* to start a conversation with her anymore. It's kind of something I usually try to avoid at all costs.

'So…' I say, drawing out the word to see if I get a reaction. I don't. 'How's work?'

Her eyes flicker from the computer screen for a moment, checking that I am actually asking this question, before looking down again. 'Work's fine. I had a half day today. How's the horse?'

'He's good,' I say, 'He's jumping really well.'

'Good.'

'Anyway, I'm gonna go have a bath.'

'Okay.'

As I walk up the stairs, I decide that that conversation was a huge success.

# Chapter 6

It's almost four months to the day after his arrival that I find myself loading Loxwood onto the lorry again. Cinder's already been loaded, and as their noses make contact over the partition, Loxwood crests his neck and lets out a snort.

'It's a pony,' I tell him good-humoredly, watching his attempt at showing off.

'You little flirt, Cinder!' Rose laughs, stepping up the ramp behind me to close the partitions as I tie Loxwood up. Despite his interest in the Connemara mare, he is far more interested in his haynet, snatching mouthfuls wildly.

I lift the ramp with Rose, and then run round to check every bolt and door before jumping up to the cab. Mackenzie sits in the middle, with a bag of chocolate balanced on her lap. I take one when she offers, but it takes a lot to swallow it down. It's ridiculous to be nervous, I shouldn't be, but I am. It's an eighty centimetre training round, not even an event, but my mind has been turning for days, ever since Rose suggested the outing. It's what I've been waiting for, I should be thrilled. And I am, but I'm also terrified that I'm going to mess up. We're not exactly expecting Loxwood to go out there and be foot perfect, that's why we're calling it a training round, but I don't want either of us making some stupid mistake.

It's beautiful weather, and the sun is shining when we arrive. Loxwood comes down the ramp like a firecracker, while Cinder plods along, looking positively bored.

'I'll go check times,' says Rose, 'You girls take their boots off and walk them round. You all right?'

I think the last question is for my benefit, and I reply in the affirmative.

'Are you excited?' Kenzie asks as we walk the horses round, grinning widely. While Cinder is trailing behind her handler, Loxwood seems to have grown ten inches, holding his head as high as he can as I struggle to keep control at his shoulder.

'Not really,' I say, trying to pull Loxwood's attention away from a group of horses tied to a very fancy-looking lorry.

Mackenzie's round is first, and I wait with Loxwood while Rose goes to help her. He starts whinnying as soon as Cinder disappears from sight, and to try and distract him I take him for some grass, and while it works, he still follows up every other mouthful with a piercing neigh.

It's been the longest thirty minutes imaginable by the time a familiar bay pony comes back this way, a rosette hanging from her bridle.

Mackenzie takes care of Cinder while Rose and I run to walk the course, before coming back to get Loxwood ready. Rose holds him and puts on his boots as I find my saddle and bridle, adjusting each as he is used to. This only being an unaffiliated round, I'm not in white jodhpurs or a jacket, but the jodhpurs and top I'm wearing are clean.

For all the fuss he made when Cinder went off, Loxwood clearly has no loyalty, because when we lead *him* away, he doesn't let out so much as a nicker.

The ring is crowded, horses cantering every which direction, and as the horse beneath me stops at the sight, I feel panic rise in my chest.

'Georgia,' Rose says beside me. For a moment I had forgotten she was there. 'Remind me again how many horses you rode him out with in the mornings?'

My mind flashes back to the constant flow of racehorses around the track, barely room to breath between them all, and for a second my body relaxes. 'Right,' I say.

'If anything's going to bother him,' Rose says, 'it's not going to be that.'

I ride pass a steward into the warm up ring, Loxwood looking as though he's expecting a dragon to swoop down out of nowhere and swallow us whole.

'You're fine,' I mutter to him, placing a hand in front of his withers.

I do as Rose suggests, and spend ten minutes walking circles and serpentines, until Loxwood is paying attention and is responsive on the other end of the rein. I find myself relaxing slightly, but the feeling disappears when I ask for a trot and he hurls himself forward the way he should have done at the start of a race. It's only a few strides of no control before I have him back at an acceptable pace, trotting in circles. The only comfort I get from his craziness is the fact that I know he looks impressive, his strides round and with more elevation than he can bother to maintain at home.

As I did in walk, I keep working Loxwood until I feel that his trot is controlled, and when I look at Rose to ask if I should canter him yet, I find Kenzie beside her, having finished looking after Cinder, and now sipping a carton of apple juice.

'Sure,' Rose says when I ask her. 'Keep him on a circle if he takes off. You're doing really well, don't worry. You're doing everything right, and you both look like a million dollars.'

The thought of Rose's latter statement almost makes me laugh out loud when Loxwood goes into a canter strike-off with a massive buck, earning us a few looks of disapproval. Despite the hiccup, he goes on to canter nicely. To be fair, most of his work so far has been nice, he just needs to turn down the enthusiasm a little.

I canter him over the cross twice, before jumping both the upright and the oxer the same number of times. As soon as his ears lock on to the fence, Loxwood forgets all about what's going on around him, and focusses solely on soaring over the obstacle. He loves to jump. And that seems to be something a lot of people who aren't involved with the sport seem to forget. So many of the horses have the same drive and adrenalin as their riders. You might be able to force a horse round a course of small uprights, or over a lone log, but the same cannot be said when the fences get bigger. A great horse jumps with the same passion and determination as the person in the saddle.

When I trot Loxwood into the indoor arena, I can feel his heart beating beneath me. I slow him back to a walk as I await the starting bell, moving a hand forward to his neck. *I trust you,* I think, as though I can telepathically send him the message. *I trust you. You'll be all right. You just need to trust* me.

As soon as the bell sounds, I push Loxwood into a canter, and this time his neck stays round as he strikes onto the right leg with much more enthusiasm than I was expecting after his hesitant entrance. I thought my mind would be buzzing, but I realise, upon the discovery that I'm attentive enough to hear someone in the seats by the entrance mutter, 'That's a lovely horse,' that any reservations I had disappeared as soon as I rode into the ring. My horse *is* lovely, even if that is an understatement, and I've waited a long time for this - I've *worked* for this - and if I fail for any reason, it sure as hell isn't going to be fear.

I don't think about anything other than the rhythm of Loxwood's canter, keeping my shoulders back as my hands follow the movement. His ears flicker every time we pass a fence, asking me for instructions. *Which one? Which one?* When we come round to the first obstacle, an upright down the long side, and my legs guide him towards it, he locks onto the fence, the tips of his ears swivelling forward as though they're metal and the fence a magnet. I wait for my stride, and it comes easily. Loxwood tucks his knees, and I lean forward through the air, my eyes already searching for the next fence. It's an oxer, and the Thoroughbred clears it with the same exuberance. The next three fences come as easily, and as we have a galloping stretch back round to the other side of the arena, I allow myself to truly think about this moment. Competing my horse, my own horse, a horse that actually stands out. Suddenly everything seems possible. Because that's the thing, the first step is always the hardest. The hard part is dipping your toe in the water, or fastening a bungee cord and taking that leap. But once it's done, and you're falling into the decision, the possibilities are endless. The reassurance that comes with the courage to start is enough to fuel the bravery needed to follow.

We turn to the combination from the curve, and Loxwood doesn't even slow his pace as we sail through. There are only three fences left, and I think we're going to go clear, but then his front feet just brush the next upright, and the thud of it hitting the ground echoes behind us. I prepare myself for disappointment rather than feel it, but then the emotion doesn't follow. How important is a single pole, one jump needing to be no more than an inch higher, when I have everything I've ever wanted?

Loxwood is clearly not quite as unaffected by the fact he's knocked a pole, and clears the next two fences with far more air than necessary. I hold on to his mane when he launches over the final one, and as we land I hear Rose and Mackenzie clap and cheer from the entrance gate. Everyone else must think they're crazy to show so much enthusiasm for a simple training round, but I'm thrilled. I run my left hand up and down Loxwood's neck, ruffling his short mane and leaning forward to mutter praise. One pole doesn't matter, because that's not what any of this is about. Because right now, everything seems possible.

# Chapter 7

A few days later, I introduce Loxwood to the few cross country fences Rose has in the field behind the paddocks. They're neither immaculate nor huge, some simple logs and palisades, but it's all I need to start. Rose is there, and under her watchful eye I take Loxwood over the obstacles. He's hesitant at first, unsure of what he's doing in this field, and why he's being pointed at random objects, but once he figures out that he's supposed to jump them he sails over. The way he takes on the fences with a steady stride and enthusiasm sends a grin straight to my face.

The week after, Rose drives Loxwood and Cinder to a bigger cross country course nearby, where I teach him to go through water and over ditches. The previous session is still fresh in his mind, and he happily takes on every challenge I put in front of him. His ears are pricked the whole time, and more exciting than the fact that he jumps everything is the joy at seeing how much he loves it.

'You know,' Rose says to me as we're driving back, Mackenzie asleep on the sofa in the living compartment. 'There's a four year old class coming up in a few weeks, where Clara and I are competing. It's on the second, I think.' She names the event, and the thought of riding there makes my fingertips tingle.

'You think we'll be ready?' I say.

'Absolutely. You've got to register yourself online, and make sure entries are still open and all that, but I don't see why not. What do you think?'

'I *want* to,' I say cautiously.

Rose smiles. 'Then it's settled.'

The whole process of registering both myself and Loxwood leaves me with a headache, and my bank account with an even bigger one. Between the many payments, and having to work out how to use our printer to scan his passport, I can't imagine the actual competition being any more tiring than the process of getting there. But once it's done, it's done. And I feel a rush of excitement when I look at the entries online, and see the names *Georgia James, Loxwood.*

If I thought membership and entry fees were a hit to my bank account, then I was completely unprepared for the price of just about everything else. Buying a competition jacket, pale jodhpurs, and the many other things needed sets me back another small fortune, but it's necessary. I keep reminding myself that I won't have to do it again, and at least the money I earn at the track is always enough for Loxwood's feed and bedding. I'll just have to think of other ways to help fund the competition side.

Some days before the event, after running through our test for the second time that week in the arena set up in the field - Loxwood finally convinced that the white boards aren't snakes out to get him - I'm beginning to go over all the details of the competition day with Rose. It's been a tiring afternoon for her, having had another DIY livery leave as a result of Rose giving their horse some hay at ten o'clock in the morning. That a person can be angry about the fact their horse is getting fed, and actually rather that they remain without anything, is beyond me. Rose agrees, having said that losing one client like that is good riddance, and is now wanting to talk about other things. She's already adamant that Leah will muck out the day of the event, so that there's not that added worry early before we leave, and we're just trying to work out times.

'I reckon we should leave at half five,' Rose says. 'We don't want to be in a rush the other end.'

'Okay,' I say. 'Does Clara need to be here at the same time? I can see if I can stay over there, so she can drop me off in the morning.'

'Just stay here,' Rose says easily. 'Ben and I were saying just the other evening that you should stay over on weekends to avoid constantly cycling back and forth. We have a spare room, you even get your own bathroom.'

'You sure?' I say. I'm both nervous that Rose has only offered because she feels the need to be polite, and also excited at the prospect of spending the night here.

'Of course. Though Kenzie will probably freak out when she finds out. So long as you're prepared to deal with that it's the least I can do. Goodness,' She shakes her head to herself. 'You do too much as it is, if I know you're at least cycling eight miles less in a day, *I* will sleep better.'

Getting through school feels impossible. My mind is going through everything that needs to be done, and wishing I could get a head start. As soon as the bell rings, I'm off, running home for my bag, and heading back out the door with my bike. To think that this time tomorrow, I'll be finishing up my first event.

It's really warm, and I find myself cycling the whole way to the stables in a t-shirt. Knowing the predicted weather for today, I put Loxwood out without a rug this morning, even though the decision to do so worried me throughout my first lessons, but I'm glad I did. The sun is shining directly over his paddock when I go to get him in, his chestnut goat gleaming.

'Hey, beauty,' I mutter, fastening the head collar round his head. 'You ready to get scrubbed up?'

I throw his tack on quickly, flicking only the worst of the dust off with a body brush, and set off down the lane. I ran through the dressage test with him again yesterday, confident that I'm not going to achieve much better, and so a hack seems like the reward for the workload, not to mention a rest before tomorrow. *Tomorrow.* The idea of competing sends tingles to my limbs, and I'm glad no one else is around to see my grin. I'm not expecting to win, or even place for that matter, but just being able to have the chance, finally, to ride myself and not be the supporter on the ground while everyone else competes is all I've ever wanted.

I walk Loxwood on a long rein, before both trotting and cantering in the same manner, all the while hoping not to be surprised by a rogue pheasant. He was good to hack out from the beginning, mostly to do with the fact that he was used to doing so in town, and the fact that I was usually the one riding him didn't hurt much either, but when I think about it, his improvement is massive. I'm not on my guard when we go down the tracks, confident in the knowledge that should Loxwood spook, it won't do much in the manner of unseating me.

Back at the yard, competition mode is truly in full swing. Clara is scrubbing Spirit's tail, Rose is balanced on a grooming box to plait Paddington's mane, while Leah is filling haynets for the lorry. Equipment is piled up outside the tack room door - bridles, martingales, saddle pads, boots… You would think ten horses were competing at a glance.

'How was he?' Rose asks through the elastic bands she's holding between her teeth.

'Perfect,' I say, sliding down from the saddle.

'YES!'

I jump at the cry, as does Loxwood, and Rose swears as Paddington fidgets right as she's in the middle of tying up a plait.

'KENZIE!' she mumbles through gritted teeth.

'That's the third time you've said that,' Mackenzie says, hurrying to my side, still in her school uniform. My mind is so full with the to-do list I have to complete by the evening that it takes me a while to get her point. *'THAT'S IT!* We can go hacking together now!'

I look towards Rose, who is refolding a plait, and she shrugs in a way that suggests she has no control over the matter. 'Okay,' I say. 'We can try taking them out next week.'

After prying Mackenzie's arms from Loxwood's neck, I lead him to a free tying point and start untacking. I leave my things in a pile with the rest of the mess nearby, knowing that as soon as I'm done with him I'm going to have to clean everything and load it into the lorry.

It's funny how plaiting always looks so easy when somebody else is doing it. Section off strands of mane, plait, roll up tightly - how hard can it be? The three simple steps go through my mind as I pull an elastic band from a bunched-up plait for the fifth time, my fingers so sore that I barely feel when it breaks against them. I have been determined not to ask for help, as tears of frustration threaten to cloud my vision, but apparently I'm not doing a very good job at hiding my struggles, because Rose comes to my shoulder to offer assistance, It turns out that my mistake was trying to roll the plaits, when really I should be thinking of it as folding. After Rose redoes a couple of them herself, I manage to follow suit and finish the rest. Loxwood is rather patient during the whole ordeal, and when I'm done I think he looks even more magnificent than he usually does, if that's possible.

Leather is polished, every piece of it stored neatly in the lorry. I go through everything I'm going to need (boots, hat, saddle pads, more elastic bands...), seeing where every item is packed in my mind until my head hurts and daylight has faded. Loxwood is plaited and rugged, having finished his evening feed and returned his attention to the pile of hay. The horses' travel boots are piled up and ready to go for the morning. I've been working nonstop all evening, between caring for Loxwood, cleaning tack, and organising, that the rhythm had settled over me, and I was reluctant to stop for fear that I would forget something. Now that I have, though, I'm overcome with a wave of exhaustion, and suddenly every part of my body seems to ache. With a final glance at Loxwood, I switch off his light and follow Rose to the house.

On the one hand, the warmth and comfort of the old farm dwelling only accentuates my fatigue, but then it also has the opposite effect by lifting my spirits. The familiarity pushes the notion of sleep from my mind, making me want to make the most of every second.

'Finally,' Mackenzie says when we walk into the kitchen. She and Jemima are both in their pyjamas, playing a card game at the table, while Ben is alternating between reading a novel and stirring whatever sauce it is he has boiling in a saucepan, on top of the Aga that heats the room.

'It's not like we had any help from you,' Rose says to Kenzie with raised eyebrows. Mackenzie offered to help when she came out earlier, but when Rose happily accepted and asked that she start washing buckets to take with us, her daughter was suddenly hit by a headache.

Jemima gets up from the table to walk over to me, her arms not even reaching my waist as she gives me a hug. She hasn't said a word yet, so I just put one arm around her shoulders silently. That's the thing with Jemima, she doesn't really chat that much, rather she shows sudden and random gestures of affection.

'How long have we got?' Rose asks Ben, walking up behind him to peer into the saucepans. I don't know what he's making, but whatever it is, I can smell it from here and my mouth is watering.

'Fifteen all right?' he says, and Rose nods.

'I'll show you your room, Georgia, and if you'd like to change or have a bath before we eat you can. Or after - whichever you prefer. I just know I hate eating before I have a bath. I only notice the dirt once I'm inside.'

'I'm the same,' I say, following Rose back to the entrance where I left my bag, and then up the stairs. Every step creaks, each one worn with age. I've never been upstairs before, although Mackenzie has tried to drag me to her room a handful of times, but I'm not surprised by what I see. It has the same feel as downstairs, with off-white walls and wooden floors - the bare boards being enough to make me think of my own carpeted room with hatred. It isn't all straight lines and cornered edges, but everything seems to work together, as though whoever designed the house just added one room at a time, not thinking about the overall plan until it was finished, and then making sure each nook serves its purpose. Every alcove is shelved, and framed photographs hang on the pieces of wall flat enough to accommodate them. The age and history of the house is preserved, with the one modern exception of good lighting.

'I love your house,' I say as I trail behind Rose past bedroom doors. I think it every time I step foot inside, but I wonder how often, if ever, I say it aloud.

'It's not everyone's cup of tea, but I wouldn't trade it,' she says. 'You're just through here - mind the step.'

I follow Rose through a low doorway at one end of the house, anticipating the drop as I see her head lower a foot. Dropping down behind her, I almost feel giddy at the thought of spending a night here.

The room isn't massive, but far bigger than my own at home. The lights are dimmer than they are on the landing, which only adds to its charm. A large seagrass rug covers most of the floor, reaching all the way under the canopy double bed. The windows are small, with diamond panes. There's a desk in one corner of the room, and a wardrobe in the other. A bookshelf runs around the top of the wall above the bed, complete with large volumes that I don't recognise at a glance.

'The bathroom's through here,' Rose says, stepping forward to open the wooden door on our left, between the wardrobe and the desk. She switches on the light, which this time is bright again, revealing a bathroom far more modern than I was expecting. 'We redid this room a couple years back,' she says. 'It keeps the in-laws happy,' she adds with a laugh.

Rose points out every tap and switch before leaving, making sure I know where everything is. Once she's gone, I wash and change at top speed, pulling on tracksuit bottoms and an oversized jumper, before heading back downstairs.

I'm relieved to find Ben still doubled over the pages of his book, while Mackenzie and Jemima are setting the table. Alfred is sound asleep in his basket, his white fur rising and falling with his breathing, and I'm about to ask what I can do to help when Rose walks in, wearing checkered pyjama bottoms and a chunky cable-knit jumper, dark hair loose for a change, and says, 'What, it's not ready yet?'

Dinner tastes just as good as it smelled, a combination of pasta and a cheesy vegetable sauce. Ben keeps insisting that Rose and I eat more, saying we need out strength for tomorrow, and something as simple as being somewhere where the physical demands of riding is valued makes me feel at ease. I end up eating two bowls, and wish I hadn't when he pulls a tiramisu out the fridge for dessert.

I get talked into watching a movie after dinner by Mackenzie and Jemima. Rose insists that I don't have to, and not to hesitate to say if I want to go to bed early in view of tomorrow, but I accept. I doubt I'll sleep much tonight, anyway. It's a Disney animation featuring animals, which is enough to know that it will meet my idea of *good*. Though Kenzie and Jemima are horrified to hear I've never seen it before.

Ben brings out bowls of popcorn, and as full as I feel, the buttery smell is too hard to pass up on, and I join the girls in stuffing my face.

I think the best thing about watching a movie with kids is that you're allowed to laugh. Every joke, no matter how obvious, is met with loud giggles you don't have to hold back. It seems to be something you're not supposed to do as you age.

It's only just gone nine o'clock when the movie ends, and when I'm met by eager questions from Mackenzie and Jemima, I honestly concede that they were right, and it was fantastic. That earns just about as many cheers as the film ending, and Kenzie jumps up to look though their DVD collection again, set on continuing my movie education, when Rose walks in and informs them it's time to bed.

'What? NO!' Mackenzie whines, but Rose insists, even though I'm pretty sure it's for my benefit.

'You know you don't actually have to go to sleep,' Rose says despairingly. Then to me, 'That's their rule. I don't care how long they stay up reading, or drawing, or whatever they want to do, but they do so quietly in bed.'

'That sounds very fair,' I say to Kenzie, pulling a face as she rolls her eyes at me siding with her mother.

'But I can't believe you haven't seen that film,' Mackenzie continues, holding up another DVD. 'It's sooo good! It's about these wild horses-'

'Another time, Kenz,' Rose says.

'Can Georgia come stay again!?' she perks up.

'Georgia can come stay whenever she likes,' says Rose. 'But not unless you get to bed.'

'Okay,' Mackenzie says. 'But how about next weekend?' She hurries over to me. 'Can you stay next weekend? You could come Friday night, and then you could stay *two* nights! Or you could just stay tomorrow!'

'We'll see,' I say, just as Rose repeats, 'Bed!'

I change into pyjamas quickly, my eyes looking around the room as I do so. The wall through which the door opens is covered in framed paintings and prints I hadn't paid much attention to earlier. They're a mixture of landscapes and horses, and landscapes *featuring* horses. One of my favourites is a painting of Thoroughbreds going up Warren Hill, which I'd recognise even if it weren't written at the bottom of the picture. I run my eyes over each individual horse, thinking about how it wasn't so long ago that one of them was Loxwood. There's a chestnut horse in the picture, with the same small star and white socks, and I imagine it is him. At the beginning of the year it still was, and the fact that I'm eventing him tomorrow would have seemed surreal to me however many months ago.

I stare at the horse in the picture until my vision blurs, before brushing my teeth and climbing into bed.

# Chapter 8

I barely slept all night, but when my alarm goes off I find myself fighting slumber to silence it, and turn on the bedside lamp. My phone reads four-thirty, which is pretty much a standard time to get up at for me. Rose said I'd be fine setting it at quarter to, but I didn't want to take the risk.

Stifling a yawn, I sit up in the bed and look around. The comfort of the room, the same that is present throughout the rest of the house, wraps around me, and despite my nerves about today, I instantly feel a little more relaxed.

Without wasting any time, I put on my new jodhpurs and shirt, pulling tracksuit bottoms and a sweatshirt on over the top. I wrestle a brush through my hair before tying it back into a bun at the nape of my neck, using three hair-ties to be safe. When I look at my reflection in the bathroom mirror, a rush of excitement passes through me at the concept of being dressed for a competition. There are thick bags beneath my eyes, but I know with confidence that I won't be the only one. Four-thirty is probably getting off lightly compared to some.

I have five minutes left until the time Rose said she was getting up at, so I pick up one of the books on the nightstand by the far side of the bed. It only draws my attention because of the horse on the cover, and I find that it's an old manual on horse care. The pages are dog-eared, and when I turn to the first page I find Rose's name scrawled in a child's handwriting on the back of the cover. It makes me smile, to think of Rose being a pony-mad child of Jemima's age. I sit back down on the bed with the book in my hands, allowing it to open to a random page. One passage must be much more read than others, because the book opens as if of its own will, but before I can see what's written on the pages my attention is diverted to what falls out. For a second I'm afraid that it's a section of pages and that I've just broken Rose's childhood book, but my heartbeat slows when I see that it's in fact a handful of photographs. I glance over my shoulder, as if afraid I've stumbled upon a secret, before inspecting the first picture in my hand. At first I think it's of Mackenzie, but as I look closer in an attempt to identify the pony beside her, I realise the girl in the photograph is Rose. Her dark hair is long and divided into two plaits, and she's staring into the camera with a toothy grin. She's wearing a bashed-up looking riding hat and a pair of beige jodhpurs that are too small, at least two inches of bare skin visible above her ankles. The pony beside her, being held by his reins, is in no way a beauty to look at. He's a dull bay, with a mane that looks like it's been affected by sweet itch. But if Rose's face is anything to go by, she thinks he's wonderful. The next picture was obviously taken a few years later, and it takes me a moment to realise it's of the same pony. His coat is shiny and his body muscular, and he appears to be working correctly as

Rose is taking him around a dressage test, wearing one of those green tweed jackets. She's getting too big for him, her feet falling below his stomach, and her face is full of determination. It makes me smile as I turn to the next one, the last picture, which leaves me puzzled for a moment. It's more recent than the previous two, and I wonder if Rose is closer to my age, if not a couple years older. It's a cross country picture, captured mid-air over a large table. The horse is beautiful, a silver grey with pricked ears and high knee carriage. It has to be an Intermediate fence, at least, and the picture is clouded by a curtain of rainfall. I flip the photograph over absentmindedly as I try to think of the horse's identity, and the name comes to my lips just before my eyes settle on it scrawled on the back. *Orion*. Rose's one in a million horse, the one she was forced to sell. I've never seen a photograph of him before, and I feel a pang. Rose had a good, country upbringing, being allowed to keep a pony and ride, but I know her family was neither well-off nor seriously into horses. People always say you need one or the other (preferably both) to succeed in the sport, neither of which I have, and nor did Rose. But she had Orion, that horse of a lifetime, and she sacrificed him for the life she has now. She never made it to Badminton or the Olympics, but that doesn't change the fact that Rose has been successful, *is* successful. I wonder if she regrets it, though. She must do, for her eyes to glisten with sadness the way they did the only time I've ever seen her mention him. But it allowed her to defy the odds and build herself a successful career.

All three pictures are still in my hand, and I force myself to look away from Orion and turn my attention back to the first photograph, the one where Rose is youngest. She's one of those people who wasn't supposed to succeed, and you wouldn't think she would have looking at this, but she did. She beat the odds.

I hear a door open on the landing, and I slide the pictures back into the book, placing it on the nightstand. Thinking of Rose now and how she was once just a little girl with a scruffy pony makes me smile. I bet nobody took her seriously when she said she wanted to ride professionally. And she ended up doing it.

As I get up and head towards the door, there's a single phrase in my mind. And it's exactly what I need to think of today.

*Why not me?*

Rose and Ben are in the kitchen, the latter spooning pancake mixture into a frying pan over the stove. When I walk into the room, Rose is sitting on a pulled-out chair at the table, sliding her feet into boots. She's dressed the same way I am, old clothes covering up her whites.

'I'll go feed the horses now,' she says, and I insist on going to help before she can say any more.

It's dark outside, and there's something so peaceful about it. Moonlight shines down on the stables, a canopy of stars overhead. There's the noise of shuffling straw as horses hurry to stand at the sound of our footsteps, followed by blinking eyes when Rose turns on the lights. The feeds were prepared the evening before, and we work out a system where I start at one end of the yard and she at another. Loxwood nickers loudly when I open the door to slip his bucket through, and only then does it occur to me how much of a relief it is to be sleeping where he is, and not however many miles away. Maybe that's why I feel so at ease in Rose's house.

Plates of pancakes have already been laid out on the table, as Ben urges me and Rose to eat. I'm not really hungry, feeling too nervous to swallow, but I don't want to refuse him, and I find that once I wash a few mouthfuls down with some coffee the nausea begins to disappear. Rose seems unaffected by the looming competition, and it's when she reaches her third pancake that she says to me, 'I never used to be able to eat before an event. But Ben kept insisting, cooking up a feast every morning, and now I don't like competing *without* stuffing my face first.'

I expected at least Mackenzie to be up and ready to leave, but she has yet to make an appearance when Rose and I start heading out the door, and when I bring it up she says, 'I told Ben not to wake her. I figured you have enough to deal with today without having an eight year old following your every move.' I laugh when she says it, but then I realise gratefully just how right she is. I love Kenzie, but today I need to focus on nothing but Loxwood.

Hope and Clara pull up just as I'm leading Loxwood, who is wearing the new travel boots I got him, to the lorry. Paddington is already loaded, and Rose is ready to close the partitions when I lead my chestnut up the ramp. There's only time for a brief hello before Rose and I drive off, horses pulling at haynets in the back.

An hour and a half later, we're rolling up into the venue, and I'm feeling extremely grateful for the large breakfast I ate, because even with a full stomach I feel rather faint.

After offering the horses a bucket of water in the lorry, Rose proposes that we go walk the cross country course before unloading them. She walks mine with me once, and I then do it a second time on my own while she goes round the Intermediate track. The bonus of the event holding bigger classes is that my own fences look pretty miniature next to the Advanced ones. There's nothing neither I nor Loxwood haven't seen before in training, but I'm still nervous.

When we get back to the lorry, we unload Paddington and

Loxwood. While Rose's horse is laid back and content, mine is all eyes popping out of his head and flared nostrils. I'm nervous about leaving him, but Hope and Clara have pulled up not far along from us, and with Rose they all assure me they'll keep an eye on him while I go to collect my number and have my hat inspected. Thankfully it doesn't take long, and when I get back to the horse box, Loxwood has completely mellowed, tugging at wisps of his haynet beside Paddington.

The plan was to walk calmly to the dressage warm up, but Loxwood practically jogs the whole way, leaving me no choice but to hang on and call out warnings to clueless passers-by. At least he looks like he's on the bridle when he does. Rose has a fair amount of time free until she needs to start warming up Paddington, and her mere presence beside me is a comfort.

I get on forty minutes before I'm set to go in the ring, leaving me with plenty of time to work Loxwood until he's calm. The sight of so many other horses around him actually makes him relax, whether out of fear or a desire to show off I don't know. But once we're in the warm-up area he lowers his head into a contact, accepting the pressure of my legs against his sides. His ears flicker backwards as he listens to my commands and searches for the next. Within five minutes I have him walking perfect circles, and when I dare look up around me I realise with pride that not only does my horse belong with these other four year olds, but he stands out. Judges mark based on accuracy, though, which I'm sure the other combinations will be far better at than we are, but Loxwood looks smarter than most of them. A few people shoot me glances when they ride past, and for once I think it's actually for the right reasons. I didn't pay too close attention to the entry list, knowing that doing so would only increase my nerves, but I recognise some of the riders around me, and already I'm counting five Olympic medals between them. But their horses aren't any nicer than Loxwood.

'Hey, Georgia!'

I glance to my left, where a girl about my age is looking at me from the back of a flighty-looking grey with an elegant head. I'm wondering why she knows my name, or if she's possibly confusing me with another Georgia, but I realise she's familiar. It takes me a beat, but finally it comes to me.

'Hi, Alex,' I say, surprised that she not only remembered my name and actually recognises me both wearing a hat and being on horseback, but that she should choose to address me. I almost didn't recognise her, the well turned out figure she is now, with pinned back hair and stock a far cry from the pyjama-clad one she was when we met.

'He's lovely,' Alex says, nodding at Loxwood. Her own horse suddenly spooks for no apparent reason, chucking his head and scooting to the side, but she seems unaffected by the outburst. 'Who's he by?'

I tell her the name, and when she doesn't recognise it I add, 'He's not an eventing sire. I got Loxwood from the track.'

'Really?' Alex says, looking surprised but not judgemental. I suddenly remember what Leni said about her always saying what's on her mind. 'You'd never guess!' she adds, and I know it's a compliment. Thoroughbred go for millions in racing, but once they leave the track they're almost worthless. 'I thought for sure he had some Holsteiner in him,' Alex continues, 'he's so chunky for a Thoroughbred. In a good way. Most of them are so spindly now, but he's gorgeous.'

I hope my cheeks don't show the redness I feel. 'Not bad for a free horse,' I say cautiously. Leni said Alex isn't snotty, but I'm sure she's still used to paying large sums for horses, and I don't know how she'd feel about someone who only got one because it was free.

'You're kidding!?' she says, the smile on her face looking impressed as opposed to amused. 'Wow. And I thought this guy was cheap at eight hundred.'

'Seriously?' I say, feeling pretty impressed myself. From what I've gathered, today's riders seem to find a ten thousand pound starting price for a youngster acceptable. 'That's a bargain.'

Alex laughs, lifting her shoulders in a small shrug. 'Not really, he's completely stir crazy. Most people wouldn't pay a penny for him.' As if to reinforce the point, the grey chooses this moment to spook again, this time kicking out behind as a bird flies overhead. Alex gives him a kick in the side, only to laugh again. 'See what I mean? His name's Tightrope Act, go figures. I chose "Waffles" as a stable name, because I thought that something cute and pathetic might stop him thinking's he so tough.' She smiles. 'It's working wonders, as you can see,' she adds sarcastically.

'At least he's nice to look at,' I venture.

'Ha! That's what I tell myself.'

'ALEX!' I recognise the voice immediately as that of her mother's, famous rider Joan Evans. 'Get him trotting, you've only got twenty minutes!'

'It'll take a helluva lot more than that to work the crazy out of him,' Alex mutters in my direction, and I laugh. 'Anyway, catch up with you later.'

'Good luck,' I say as she pushes the horse forward into a loose trot, only to be met with two argumentative bucks.

Wasting time chatting isn't exactly what I should be prioritising when I'm about to go into both mine and my horse's first ever dressage test, but as I push Loxwood into a long rein trot I realise that a couple minutes of distraction, including a good laugh, was actually the best thing I could do, as I suddenly feel a lot more relaxed, a feeling he only reciprocates.

I repeat the exercise in canter, standing in my stirrups to allow him to stretch his nose down, curving through his neck, before stopping to talk to Rose. She's as optimistic as I am, saying that Loxwood is looking as good as ever, and gives me some exercises to work on before I collect my reins and push him back into a rising trot. He's happy to allow me to keep my legs on him, and I feel him come through from behind when I steady his pace and ask for smaller movements. The fear I've tried not to acknowledge up to now that I'm attempting to break into a world in which I have no place begins to evaporate, and the longer we warm up for, the more hopeful I feel. Out the corner of my eye, I see Waffles let out another fly buck, and when Alex rides past me a few seconds later she looks completely undisturbed, merely muttering, 'Someone's springy today.'

In spite of how well the warm up is going, when my number is called to the ring I feel dread. My mind searches for anything I could have forgotten to work on, while also trying to remember the test. When I utter my concern to Rose as I walk Loxwood to the arena, she tells me to just ride down the centre line and it will all come back to me. I don't have much time to question this logic, because the bell rings and it's time to go.

When we come to the final halt, I'm not sure whether I'm more relieved at having remembered the test, or about the fact that it's over. I expected to be paralysed by nerves, the way some people are when they step foot on stage, but I felt unexpectedly calm when I turned down the centre line. I was anxious to do well, but I didn't find it interfering with my riding ability. Even if there is something slightly worrying about knowing that your every movement is being scrutinised. But Loxwood was a champ. Obviously, he still has the paces of a gangly four year old still trying to find his balance, but that goes for everyone. And he certainly faired better than Alex's horse, who finally succeeded in bucking her off during the first canter strike-off, only for her to keep hold of the reins and remount after a few words from the judges, coming out of the ring in a fit of laughter, calling, 'Who knew that a fall in dressage wasn't eliminatory!?' Admittedly, I didn't.

Rose helps Clara warm up Spirit for dressage while I take Loxwood back to the lorry for a quick change of equipment before heading to the show jumping ring. I only have one saddle, so at least I don't need to change that, only shorten the stirrups, add boots, and grab a whip. I consider pulling his plaits out, but decide to leave it for later. Loxwood stands perfectly still beside Paddington, without me even having to tie him up, and I offer him a drink from a bucket quickly before getting back on and riding off.

I have a fair amount of time until my round, during which I'll have to walk the course, but for now I stay in the warm up ring. There are only a couple other horses here, both of which I recognise from the dressage, and Loxwood is happy to be with them. I walk him on a loose rein, occasionally collecting him to trot a few circles before coming down a gait again. The course is announced open to all riders just moments after Rose and Hope come into view. I swing off Loxwood's back, bending my knees to lessen the blow to my ankles, and run up my stirrups. I've barely had time to worry about the obvious problem of what to do with him when Hope comes forward, offering to walk him round while I learn the course. I happily hand over the reins, confident that not only is Loxwood easy to do in hand, but in Hope's own ability, before climbing between the railings to join Rose at the first fence. Not only is the course not intimidating, but it's less difficult then the one we went round a few weeks ago, giving me exactly the confidence boost I need to get back on.

There are three fences in the middle of the warm-up ring, and Rose has sent me over all of them by the time my turn comes to enter the ring. Alex has already gone, and if I thought Tightrope Act was difficult in the dressage warm-up then he was positively easy compared to how he is to jump. He has talent, sure, but it wouldn't be obvious if he didn't have a rider as good as Alex to bring it out in him. I can't believe she actually stayed on, let alone got him over all the fences clear.

Loxwood is jumping even better than he was at his last outing, clearing the fences but without over-jumping them. The point of eventing isn't who jumps highest - I don't want a horse that is afraid of the obstacles. You need a horse that gets over everything without fear.

The bell rings, and I don't even ask Loxwood for a canter transition before he's off. It's an open, grass ring, not like the indoor arena in which we last jumped, and much bigger. Loxwood's stride seems to cover more ground out here, and with the quicker pace comes less time to think. Each fence comes to me, and I barely need to interfere with the distances. He might not have been a successful racehorse, but it certainly had nothing to do with lacking competitiveness because Loxwood is one hundred percent game on, keeping his ears pricked the whole time as he searches for the next fence, knowing all eyes are on him.

It all happens quickly, and while I was wishing it would be over already, when it actually is I find myself wishing it hadn't. I almost don't believe it until I hear a muffled voice over the speakers say, '*Nothing to add for Georgia James and Loxwood. They go through to the cross country phase on their dressage score.*'

Rose is waiting for me when I trot Loxwood out the ring, all smiles. 'That was super!' she says, looking almost as ecstatic as I feel. 'I've got to go,' she says quickly. 'But I'll do everything I can to get to the cross country on time.'

'Don't worry, we'll be fine.' I say. Ever since the times went live, Rose has been worrying about having time to help me warm up for cross country, when her dressage test is just minutes before we're set to start. I was nervous too, granted, but after that round I realise that it's down to Loxwood and me, and at the end of the day it's my responsibility to get it right. Plus, Rose has done enough for me as it is, she doesn't need to be worrying when Paddington should be her sole focus.

'If I don't make it,' she says nervously. 'Just keep riding like that. You did great, and he only needs to pop a couple fences before the course. You can do this.'

I nod, and Rose wishes me luck as she hurries to get Paddington ready. The cross country is straight after show jumping, with just enough time to swap boots and bits as needed.

Rose's figure retreats towards the lorry park, and I'm ready to follow when another one, hurrying my direction, catches my attention.

'Great round!' Leni calls, giving me a thumbs up. She's kitted out in white jodhpurs and a jacket, wearing knee high boots, and a riding hat over her tidy hair. 'I ran to watch. He's awesome! You'd never guess he's only four - then again, I suppose he's got two years under saddle on all these others.'

'I can't believe you saw,' I say, both embarrassed by how awful my riding must seem compared to Leni's standard, and touched that she should actually bother to watch.

She appears undisturbed by my reaction. 'You've got to take him to the four year old finals in autumn. He'll win if he goes like that, the others don't even come close! I don't think you need to qualify or anything. Just watch you don't exceed your entry limit before it comes around.'

'I'll look into it,' I say, my fingers tingling at the thought of competing in a championship of any sort.

Leni steps forward to run a hand down Loxwood's head, smiling as he tries to use her as a scratching post. I turn his head hurriedly, horrified at the thought of my horse ruining a jacket that must cost three figures. I scorn him, but Leni shrugs it off. 'Don't worry,' she says, 'they're pretty indestructible. One of my sponsors gave it to me, anyway - I've got two more identical in the lorry. Anyway, Olly goes in half an hour, so I've got to go. I just wanted to catch your round. Good luck cross country if I don't see you before then.'

'Bye!' I call as she turns away, before adding, 'I'll come watch later.'

Back at the lorry, I swap Loxwood's open front tendon boots for sturdier cross country ones, as well as a pair of overreach boots, and shorten my stirrups another couple holes. I pull the plaits out of his mane, not worrying about saving the elastics to reuse, laughing as it goes into tight curls. Hope comes by to offer her help, holding Loxwood for me while I remove my show jacket and put on a body protector, and then insists on me drinking a carton of apple juice before getting back on.

I'm glad I haven't been to see if dressage results are up yet, because if by some chance I'm not terribly placed, the knowledge would only make me more nervous, and I feel sick enough as it is. I remember what Rose said about how to warm up, and I focus on collecting Loxwood through the turns and then asking him to lengthen his pace as we canter down the long sides, varying the exercise. The one upside to an off the track Thoroughbred is that they know how to gallop.

There are three fences to warm up over - an upright, a log, and a chest. I pop the pole once to get Loxwood back into the rhythm before turning to one of the natural fences. His ears lock on to the log without him rushing, and being on a forward, cross country stride, the fence comes easily. I turn on to the next for the sake of it, but I know it won't be a problem. And it isn't. Loxwood jumps it beautifully, and I bring him back to a trot as the steward calls our number. We're up.

All the time he spent training as a racehorse comes back to him as he sets off out the start box with the same kind of burst of the speed he would starting a race. The galloping distances between fences are nothing for us. We've both spent enough time going up Warren Hill for this to be minor in comparison, so that only leaves the jumps. I stop thinking when we come to the first, squeezing my legs to guide Loxwood over it. There's no time for thinking, only riding.

It's an easy track, what you'd expect for a young horse, but Loxwood's no ordinary four year old. The plan was to nurse him round gently, but right now he's the one taking me over everything. My heart swells with pride as he guides me towards each fence, going forward with such pure joy, that I figure all the hard work is worth it. Thoroughbreds are bred to have speed and adrenalin, and as Loxwood gallops beneath me with only the slightest instructions and guidance, for possibly the first time in my life I feel like I've done something right. No matter what happens and where we get to, I've given a horse a second chance at life. That's something you can't put a prize on.

The more difficult the fence, the more game on Loxwood is.

Any that is a little higher or a little spookier, he approaches with even more determination, bringing me along for the ride. I always knew it, from the moment I set my eyes on him, that chestnut three year old arriving at Frank's, looking out of place. He's a cross country horse.

Any worries I had disappeared as soon as we jumped the first fence, and when we reach the last I'm wishing it could go on forever. Loxwood takes me over the last fence, and as we go through the finish line the reality sinks in. *We're clear.*

I collapse onto his neck, wrapping my arms around it, until I realise that he isn't stopping on his own, and I have to grab hold of the reins again to convince him to slow to a walk. Loxwood seems disappointed, like he too wanted to keep going.

'Don't worry,' I whisper, after checking his breathing, and however many more hugs. 'Badminton will be ten minutes longer than that.'

# Chapter 9

I walk him round for a good ten minutes, reins slack and girth loose, before heading back to the lorry. Rose is riding back when I get to the entrance to the lorry park, smiling at me widely, and before I can tell her how it went she yells, 'I heard over the speakers! I almost cheered right in the middle of my test!'

There's no rest for the wicked. As soon as Rose has untacked Paddington she's off to help Clara warm up for show jumping, and I'm left to care for Loxwood. I take my time hosing him off, feeding him an apple every time the reality of today goes through my mind. Part of me wants to stay here forever, stroking his neck and admiring his chestnut coat, but I'm also eager to look at the scoreboards and offer a hand to Clara, seeing as everyone else has been helping me today.

As I walk to the results tent, pulling a hoodie on along the way, I see Leni running between stalls, whip in hand, presumably to catch her next ride. She's looking straight ahead, but as she glances me she slows her pace slightly, and calls, 'How did it go?'

I know she clearly doesn't have time to stop, so I just smile and hold up my thumbs, to which she responds by grinning and letting out a mini fist pump, and I wish her good luck as she goes past.

Groups of people crowd the large results boards, only half of them dressed to ride. I squeeze past where I can as I search for the four year old section. There aren't any cross country results yet, but dressage and show jumping are up, and the sight of mine and Loxwood's names up there makes me just as excited as the result. I can't believe it. We're lying fourth after show jumping. I refrain from jumping straight into the air, and look around at everyone else's composure. How can they be so calm when I myself am ready to burst!? Because they haven't just ridden Loxwood, that's why.

I go back to check on my horse at the lorry, having retrieved my dressage test and read it while I walked, where he is happily munching from his haynet, already dry beneath his cooler. I tell him that we're guaranteed a placing, and that he's the most amazing horse in the world, before getting my wallet from the cab and going in search of the photography stand.

I'm shaking while I wait for the pictures to come up on the screen, worried that there won't be a single one worth printing, but the feeling completely vanishes when they do.

It's a show jumping shot first, and clearly I am mistaken to think that Loxwood doesn't over jump the fences. He's way above the oxer, all four feet tucked, and I… don't look too terrible, actually. My heels could be a little further down, and my back straighter, but other than that my hands are halfway up his neck, allowing him to stretch out, elbows bent as I lean forward, my seat staying a couple inches above the saddle. Loxwood's ears are pricked, both of us searching for the next fence. Most importantly, we both look professional.

There are show jumping shots to chose from, but I go with that first one as the cross country pictures are searched for. A photograph taken over a brush fence comes up, taken head on, and the determination in both of our eyes is enough for me to select it, let alone the fact that Loxwood's knees are around his chin.

Rose is back at the lorry, getting Paddington ready for show jumping. It turns out I missed Clara's round, in all the excitement of seeing my results, which transpired into a catastrophe, and an elimination.

'She got herself worked up about a filler,' says Rose. 'Kept trying to pull up, and Spirit did what was expected. They've gone, anyway. Just left.'

I feel a rush of sympathy for Clara, disappointed that we can't be celebrating triumphs together, but then Rose asks to see the photos in my hand, and the worry vanishes as I'm reminded of Loxwood's success.

'Wow, Georgia! He looks amazing!' she gushes, admiring the two pictures. 'He's so tidy in front, isn't he!?'

'I know,' I say, glancing again at how effortlessly Loxwood snaps his knees right up around his chin.

Rose rides off on Paddington, and I stay with Loxwood a few minutes to make sure he settles before following. In the show jumping ring, the Intermediate class is underway, and I can make out Paddington's chestnut figure in the warm-up.

Staying where I can still see Rose, I make my way to the edge of the arena, and contently watch the competitors. I couldn't have timed it any better, because after only one round a familiar black horse comes into the ring, the number announced followed by the words, 'Helena Cullen riding Lochmere,' as the bell rings.

As always, Lochmere looks magnificent. Before I knew Leni, I saw him as a finely bred horse only money could buy, who looked as well as he did because of the expert training he had always experienced. But now I see Olly, an average Thoroughbred with a bigger than average heart, with old scrapes and scars along his legs, the picture of beauty because of all the hours of hard work and care that have been devoted to him. It just goes to show that we see what we want to.

Leni and Lochmere go clear, as does the combination after them, a young guy on an impeccably turned out dark bay. Outside the ring, Leni is still walking Olly off, and when the guy rides out past her, he holds out a hand in something midway between a high five and a handshake, a gesture that she returns. The next few riders are quite clearly not professionals, all with horses lacking muscle, and it's a quick run of clattering poles before I see Alex, cantering into the ring on a small grey I recognise as her three time European horse, Anchor Lane. The start bell has only just gone when Leni appears at my side, having now removed her hat and jacket.

'Good round,' I say.

'Sorry I was in a hurry earlier, I've got some time now until cross country.' she says, both of us keeping our eyes on Alex as we speak. 'But you went clear, right?'

'Yeah,' I say, watching Anchor Lane power over a spread from a short stride, with scope you wouldn't think possible at a glance. 'He didn't look at anything.'

'Really? That's amazing!' Leni beams. 'Not that I'm surprised. So many of the four year olds are so weedy, I bet he left them all for dead.'

Alex makes a right rein turn towards the upright directly

along the fence line opposite us, and the closer he gets, the smaller Anchor Lane seems. 'How big is he?' I ask Leni quietly once the grey has cleared the fence and carried on towards the next.

'Fifteen-one,' she says. 'I know, right?' she continues, seeing my surprise. 'Alex never thought he'd get this far. He was only supposed to be a resale project, to wean her off ponies, but she completely fell for him, and he just climbed the ranks. I'm surprised she's managed to hold on to him this long, what with all the offers they've had for him. But,' Leni looks over her shoulder quickly before speaking, lowering her voice further. 'If there's anything Joan can't resist more than a large cheque, it's being in a position to repeatedly turn them down.'

Anchor Lane clears the last fence, completing on a clear. 'I think that's only the third decent round I've seen,' I say. 'Including yours, obviously,' I add with a grin.

'Who was the other one?'

'The guy after you. On the dark bay?'

'Oh, Thomas.' Leni nods in acknowledgement. 'Thomas Donnelly? Biggest ego you've ever seen, but unfortunately he's entitled to it. I swear, he barely even has lessons. He does have good horses, though. His parents own hotels in the Caribbean, something like that. Absolutely loaded.'

'You looked like you were friends,' I say, somewhat confused.

'Oh, we are,' Leni says, pausing to wince as the next horse in the ring completely misses his stride to the first fence. 'He's super nice, and he knows full well how smug he is. I'm not saying anything he wouldn't say himself, it would probably only take two minutes talking to him for him to tell you that he's rich.'

While we're watching the following rounds, me waiting to see Rose's, a blonde girl wearing a coat so thick I feel hot just looking at her comes up to us, clearly another friend of Leni's. She's skinny, with very pale hair, poker straight, a freckly, tan face, and dark brown eyes.

'Georgia, this is Erin,' she says, and the girl smiles widely and politely. I haven't time to say anything before Alex is suddenly beside us, wearing just her white under jacket t-shirt, cheeks flushed red, and hair no longer in a hairnet but pulled back messily into a ponytail.

'God, it's so hot,' Alex says, leaning her arms onto the railings.

'Are you joking?' Erin cries, and there's a slight accent to her voice that I can't place. 'It's…' she pulls her phone out of her pocket. 'Twelve degrees!' she confirms. 'That's not *so hot*.'

'Erin isn't crazy,' Leni says to me, humour seeping into her voice. 'She's just still acclimatising.'

'Where are you from?' I ask.

'Johannesburg,' she says, pulling the zipper of her coat up tighter. 'And let me tell you, twelve degrees is most definitely *not* warm.' She shakes her head. 'Definitely not warm.'

'What's going on!?' It's Ryan, charging up to us as if this particular spot by the show jumping ring is the cool place to hang out, and I have a sudden image of being in a comedy skit, where all the characters seamlessly bump into each other. 'And by the way.' He turns to Alex. 'How the heck does somebody fall off in dressage!?'

'It's not my fault,' Alex says. 'Ask Georgia, she'll back me up on this one. She saw.' I nod in agreement. 'Anyway,' Alex continues. 'We were just talking about how Erin's freezing,'

'Oh, so, the usual, then?' Ryan says.

'Seriously, how do you guys do it!?' exclaims Erin, gesturing at both Ryan's and Alex's bare arms. 'It's too cold in this country!'

'Hey,' Leni interrupts, nodding toward the ring. 'Zach's up.'

'And looking as jolly as ever,' Alex finishes, which I'm guessing is supposed to be sarcasm, because the guy riding into the ring looks anything but jolly. I notice his horse, however - a gorgeous dark brown gelding, with a tan muzzle. The voice of the commentator comes out fuzzily through the speakers, but I make out *Zach Hastings and Arthur's Flight.*

'Smile!' Alex calls out as he canters past, prompting the rest of the group to giggle, but the feeling doesn't seem to reach the rider.

'Always so serious,' Leni mutters as the dark brown horse pops over the first fence.

'He puts himself under so much pressure,' Ryan says, and I realise a beat later that he's talking to me. 'He's a working pupil,' he continues, naming a rider whose pictures I've hung on my wall before. 'Let's just say he makes Amanda Walton look like a saint,' Ryan says with a laugh, glancing at Leni.

'I'm not even going to debate that,' she says. 'I have it easy compared to Zach.'

I'm not in a position to comment, so I merely say, 'He rides well.' Because it's true.

'He works hard,' says Leni. 'Remember how I described Thomas? Well, just picture the opposite.'

'His parents are evil,' Alex confirms.

Leni sighs. 'They're not *evil*-'

'-*EVIL!*'

'Alex-'

'Aww, Leni,' Ryan says mockingly, putting a brotherly arm around her shoulders. 'Always wanting to see the best in people,'

'You're too nice, Leni,' says Alex. 'Anyway,' She turns back to me. 'His parents are somewhat evil. Dad's a drunk, and his mum - well, I don't really know what she does, but Zach doesn't like her.'

'His grandparents were farmers,' Leni continues, seeming more concerned with facts than Alex. I sneak a glance at the ring, seeing the brown gelding fly through a combination. 'And they had a couple hunters, and Zach literally got one of them to Novice by working at a pub all hours to pay the entry fees. He was always last after dressage, but he never gave up, and kept working until he was at the top. Then - a couple years ago, was it?' She looks at Ryan for confirmation. 'He left home and got a job as a working pupil, bought an ex-racehorse with a pulled suspensory for a hundred quid, and spent a year rehabilitating it.'

The word "suspensory" is enough to terrify any rider. It's right up there with "colic" and "navicular". 'Did it recover?' I ask, my question being overshadowed by the modest cheering that comes from around the ring as Zach and Arthur's Flight clear the final fence.

Leni nods at the brown gelding. 'You're looking at him.'

As quickly as everyone seemed to migrate to this spot, they all disappear. Ryan sees the time and hurries off to get ready for cross country, his doing so reminding Erin that she still has a phase to ride, and they head to the lorry park. Only a minute later, Joan Evans sees Alex standing around and flips out.

'What are you doing, Alex?' she calls. 'Goji goes cross country in fifteen minutes, and Fruitloop's right after.'

Alex sighs loudly. 'And?' she says, much calmer than I would have expected under the circumstances. 'I've got fifteen minutes!'

Joan holds her arms out, letting them fall back to her side despairingly. 'Go get Goji, and I'll start leading Fruitloop to the warm-up.'

'Fruitloop,' I repeat, amused by the name.

'Right?' Alex laughs.

'Wait 'til you hear his show name,' Leni says with a smile.

'Okay,' Alex says, taking her cue, and unaffected by her tight schedule. 'He didn't have a name when I got him a few years ago, and he was screwball crazy, and weedy, so for ages I referred to him as Crazy Youngster, until we ended up calling him such. Fruitloop's just a nickname. A fitting one, though.'

'Keep going,' Leni says, showing that there's more to the story.

Alex laughs again. 'Yeah, okay, so the only problem is that, like, a year after I got him, he completely mellowed out, and gained a ton of weight. So now he looks like a cob, and I have to practically kick him round a course. People think the name's supposed to be ironic.'

'Fatloop?' I suggest, and Alex laughs.

I thought Joan had gone away, but I'm clearly wrong because there comes a sudden, loud cry of, 'ALEX!', and finally she relents by running off to get ready.

'I've got to go, too,' says Leni, pulling up her sleeve to look at the times written on her arm. 'I have to get Olly tacked up. We'll catch up later though, yeah? Let me know when your results are up.'

'Later,' I call as she hurries away, realising I forgot to say that we were guaranteed fourth, and I'm left alone as Paddington canters into the ring. He's not as flashy as some of the horses we've seen, but he and Rose can certainly hold their own.

Paddington rattles an unfortunate pole, but Rose rides beautifully, and I'm overcome with a sudden pride at being associated with her. She doesn't have the greatest horses, or expensive kit, but she has good horsemanship and a work ethic, two things you can't buy. Her seat is natural, and her hands soft.

I jog to meet Rose as she comes out of the ring. 'Unlucky,' I say, resting a hand against Paddington's neck.

'My fault,' Rose says, always blaming herself.

I follow her back to the lorry, where I swap Paddington's show jumping boots for cross country ones while Rose gets changed. There are tacked up horses walking past every second, some primed and polished to perfection, their manes up in plaits and their riders in white jodhpurs and spotless jackets, while others are drenched in sweat, coming back from the cross country course, with curls instead of plaits, and exhausted-looking riders beside them. Determination is in the air, coupled with the sound of a commentator's voice, echoing through speakers. Everybody walks with a short-term purpose and a long-term goal, and the atmosphere is oxygen to my lungs.

When Rose comes back out the lorry, I have pulled all the elastics out of Paddington's mane, and he is patiently standing. Loxwood has grown tired of his haynet, and is instead dozing, resting one leg and keeping his eyes closed.

'You've worn him out,' Rose says good-naturedly as she gathers her reins in one hand and swings onto Paddington's back.

'About time,' I say, laughing to myself as I think of his usual bottomless supply of energy.

Loxwood doesn't even neigh when we walk off, which I take as a sign that he too is enjoying the competition environment. I find a spot at the edge of the warm up ring, where I am in time to see Alex pop who I can only presume is Goji over a log, approaching it from an angle. The horse is gorgeous, a black Warmblood-like gelding, with natural balance, and a thick white stripe down his face, perfectly even. And he couldn't be any more different from Alex's other horses I have seen today, which only goes as proof that she can ride anything.

Rose begins trotting Paddington round, just as Leni appears on Lochmere, and a short moment after Alex rides out the ring I hear the commentator announce, '*And our next starter is Alexandra Evans, riding the first of her three horses in this Intermediate class, Goji Berry.*'

*Three horses.* Forgetting Tightrope Act, which brings the total to four. Riding one horse in three phases has just about stressed me to breaking point, let alone three more, and around bigger tracks, too. Just thinking about it makes me sick with nerves. But then it also prompts another feeling, from the part of me that claims to be fearless. Because this is the life I want. I made that decision a long time ago, and the thought of running around, jumping from horse to horse, and the challenge of training and succeeding, ignites a fire deep in my gut that only makes me more determined. I'll do it, I think, the words quiet in the cacophony that is all my doubts. But the sun is shining, and my horse is tied up a stone's throw away, having performed to the same level as some of the best four year old prospects in the country, and I'm standing here, surrounded by people with the same hunger and passion. The metaphorical fish in a wide, wide sea. And yet I believe the words, the whisper creeping through all the cries. *I'll do it.*

# Chapter 10

I'm running to catch up with Paddington as he and Rose come flying through the finish line, home clear. It's nothing they haven't achieved before, but I cheer, and we're both smiling from ear to ear, as if both of our successes have rolled into one. The day's work is done, and now we can just enjoy it.

Loxwood is still dozing when we get back to the lorry, and while Rose cools off Paddington, I excuse myself to head to the results tent. There's a more relaxed atmosphere, now. Instead of riders rushing every which way, fully kitted out and ready to jump on their horses, everybody is now hanging about and laughing, wearing zip-up hoodies over white shirts, faces showing the exhaustion of the day, now that adrenalin is no longer there to cover it up.

The scoreboards are even more crowded than they were earlier. There is a volunteer copying out results with a marker pen, glancing down at her clipboard each she time she notes a cross county time. I can't get to the four year old board yet, there being too many people in the way, but I can see the scores for the Intermediate sections. Paddington is well schooled on the flat, but he doesn't have a flashy quality that makes him stand out, and I know that Rose will be thrilled with the fact that he's tenth after dressage. A well known rider is in the lead, and Alex is both second and third, with Anchor Lane and Goji Berry respectively. Leni and Lochmere are fifth.

A group of people move away, and I waste no time in scooting toward the four year old results. There's just something about a giant, handwritten scoreboard that makes me happy. Especially when I see Loxwood's name on it. I move my eyes to the right, running them across the grid. There's our dressage score of 33.6, and all the zeros where any show jumping and cross country penalties incurred are to be written down… I reach the last box, the one where each horse's overall standing is written, where the number *3* has been scrawled. I can't believe it. I count all the other horses' positions in the section, just to be sure there's no mistake, and after adding up all the points myself, I find myself hurrying out the tent, not caring who's looking as I prance along like an idiot.

'We're third!' I yell to Rose, running toward the lorry where she is running a sweat scraper across Paddington's back, a bucket and a sponge at her feet.

'*NO!?*' she says, her face spreading into a wide smile.

I nod, the excitement in my chest bubbling to reality. 'Two points from the lead.'

Rose lets the sweat scraper in her hand fall to the grass as she draws me into a hug, looking almost as ecstatic as I feel.

'When's the prize giving?' she asks, composing herself and bending down to retrieve the sweat scraper.

'I don't know…I came straight here,' I say, staggering over to Loxwood and throwing my arms around his neck, burying my face in his familiar scent.

'Check,' Rose says, as drops of excess water fly from Paddington's back. 'Make sure you don't miss it. You get prize money, too.'

For the umpteenth time today, I whisper to Loxwood that he's the greatest horse in the world, before heading back towards the heart of the venue. I didn't think it was possible to feel any happier than I did when I came off that cross country course, but I do.

I've barely eaten anything since swallowing down Ben's extravagant breakfast this morning, and seeing that there isn't a queue in front of one of the food vans, I stop to buy a cheese toastie, fishing for change at the bottom of my pocket. I don't realise just how hungry I am until the first mouthful, and proceed to finish the whole thing by the time I reach the results tent. After some enquiring, I find out that the prize giving for the four year old section is in fifteen minutes time, so I resort to hanging about outside so as not to miss it. I turn my head to watch the last show jumping rounds of the day, all experienced riders, when someone addresses me, and I look round to see Leni approaching.

'I heard you went clear,' I say, remembering hearing the commentator announce it shortly before Rose started her round.

'Yeah,' She smiles. 'He was great. I don't know where we were after dressage, though.'

For once, I have an answer to something. 'Fifth. I saw.'

'Really? Oh, I suppose that's not too bad. I bet Alex has at least one horse ahead of us?'

'Two,' I say, and Leni laughs. 'She's second and third.'

'Ha, figures. Goji's only just moved up to Intermediate, but the judges love him. And Anchor and Olly are always swapping places between them. They were actually on the exact same dressage score at Europeans last year. We couldn't stop laughing! Anyway, do you know your results yet?'

'Yeah,' I say, smiling to myself at the thought of saying the words out loud again. 'We're third.'

'What!?' Leni exclaims, looking surprised. But I'm the one left shocked when she continues by saying, 'Is that all? I thought for sure you were going to win when I saw you!'

I let a breath out through my nose. 'I'm not complaining,' I say good-naturedly.

'No, that's amazing,' she says quickly. 'But I seriously didn't think anyone else would even come close.'

'It'll be my fault. I think they said most of my circles looked like ovals.'

'Ugh,' Leni sighs. 'I like dressage and schooling, don't get me wrong, but accuracy is the worst. Like, just because someone rides a perfect circle, they'll get a better mark than somebody who's actually working their horse correctly. The judges used to slam me for it. Like I could think about the shape of a circle when I was trying to stop Olly from exploding!'

'How did you fix it?' I say, thinking of the perfection with which she rides in a dressage test now.

'Well,' Leni says, shrugging as she thinks. 'It's easy to think about movements when you're no longer worrying about your horse rearing or jumping out of the ring, *and* trying to keep him soft and round that whole time too.'

'Fair point,' I say, and as somebody Leni knows walks past, a woman I get the feeling is somebody's mother, I excuse myself to go back inside to the results test, where I wait to collect mine and Loxwood's first rosette.

Anyone would have thought that Rose and I were playing a game of seeing how much we could eat in the shortest time on the drive back. The kitchen cupboards in the living compartment are raided, until we have three large bags of crisps, two bottles of iced tea, packets of red liquorice, and some of Mackenzie's leftover Easter chocolate. But with the amount of exercise we've done today, we've probably burnt off everything we eat three times over.

'If you think your parents won't mind,' Rose says when we're about five minutes away from the yard, 'you're welcome to stay the night again. Don't feel like you have to say yes,' she adds quickly. 'The choice is yours, but you're more than welcome. It would give you a chance to have a lie-in. You could even stay in your pyjamas all day.' She laughs. 'When I only had my own horses, I always used to have one day week when I'd have a pyjama day, even if I had one to ride.'

'You sure you don't mind?' I say, wanting nothing more than to spend another night a stone's throw from Loxwood, with some of the people I care most about in the world.

'Don't be ridiculous. Consider the room yours whenever you want it.'

We get back at a reasonable time (by which I mean that it's still light), to find that Leah already has everything ready, and Mackenzie is clearly over the sulking I'm sure will have taken place when she awoke to find us gone, and bouncing about for news.

'How did you do?' she yells, bouncing all over the place. 'Did you place? You didn't get eliminated, did you?'

I respond by handing Kenzie the large rosette we won, and her face widens with excitement.

'Third! You came THIRD!?' she says, jumping up and down some more before admiring the rosette again and throwing her arms around me. 'Loxwood's the best horse ever, isn't he?'

'Yes,' I say. 'Loxwood's the best horse ever.'

It's actually daylight when I wake up the next morning. My phone shows the time seven-thirty, which I'm sure any other event rider will agree is a lie-in. As the realisation of yesterday's events settle, I can't stop grinning. It wasn't a dream. Actually, it kind of is, but I'm waking up to it.

Remembering Rose's words yesterday, I pull a large, oversized jumper on over my pyjama top, and a pair of thick socks. The photos I bought are sitting on the nightstand, in their envelope, and I pull them out to look at one more time before going downstairs.

Rose is standing with her back against the Aga, a coffee cup in her hands. She immediately gets me a mug out a cupboard, pouring me my own drink. I take it happily, and with the cups in our hands we go out to feed the horses, pyjama bottoms tucked into boots. I can't help but think that this is what happiness is - pyjamas, wellington boots, hot drinks, and a barn full of horses.

It goes without saying that Loxwood is getting the day off, and I take Rose's advice and both turn and muck out in my pyjamas, before Mackenzie comes out to ride Cinder. Paige arrived a little earlier, and I'm chatting to her when Kenzie runs up.

'I just had the best idea!' she says.

'I'm not sure I like the sound of that,' Rose says, overhearing as she walks past.

'It's true.'

'Okay,' says Rose, laughing. 'Enlighten us.'

Mackenzie smiles. 'We should all,' she drags out the last

word, reaching both me and Paige. 'take it in turns to ride Cinder bareback.'

Rose looks down at her pyjama-clad self, and smiles. 'That actually sounds like fun.'

So unsuspecting Cinder is led to the school, wearing only a bridle, as Rose gives Kenzie a leg up. She walks and trots her around for a while, until coming to a stop to offer somebody else a turn, and we encourage Paige to go next. The time she has spent riding her own horse bareback shows, and her seat is effortlessly still as she goes round. It's my go next, and I can't stop laughing as the pony bounces along, me struggling to stay with her. Messing around bareback is the best reminder that riding doesn't ever have to stop being fun.

Paige and I both got on by jumping to lean over Cinder's back, and then swinging our right leg over to shuffle towards the withers. But when Rose steps up to take the reins, she says, 'Let's see if I can get on without jumping.' She slides her right leg over, but as she does so, Cinder takes a step forward. Rose lets out a small cry, unable to keep her footing, and is already laughing before she falls, still holding the reins as she hits the sand. She's laughing so hard that she can't even bring herself to get up, as are we. We laugh until tears run down our faces, and we're holding on to our sides as we gasp for breath. And just when we think we've recovered, it starts again, and it's impossible to keep a straight face. It's amazing how something so simple, the humour of which nobody would grasp when told the story, can leave you laughing until your body aches, and when it's over you feel nothing but elation.

The afternoon is spent in the living room, watching the movie about wild horses that Mackenzie was so adamant I must see. And I must admit, it's amazing.

Hope and Clara show up towards the end of the afternoon to see Spirit, just as we're mixing the evening feeds, and offer to drop me off at home to avoid me having to cycle back. I accept, happy about being spared doing so, and yet the fact of having to leave upsets me far more than it should, considering it's hardly news. And yet, as always, being separated from Loxwood makes me feel as though part of me is missing.

# Chapter 11

When my alarm goes off, I instinctively squeeze my eyes shut even tighter, wanting to remain in the dream. I'm dreaming that Loxwood is about to clear the final Badminton cross country fence, but since the clock started beeping my eyes have gone out of focus, and no matter how hard I try to concentrate, the obstacle becomes a blur, until vanishing completely. And as the feeling of loss begins to settle, I remember this weekend, competing Loxwood, and that's better than any dream.

    I sit up groggily, hitting the top of the alarm clock before switching on the bedside light. Trying to keep my eyes open feels like trying to ward off a streak of tigers with a stick, enough to make you want to give up and lie down. Instead, I lean forward to rest my head in my hands, trying to remember the details of the dream. It's nothing new - I've dreamt of riding around large competitions plenty of times before - but this time, something feels different. *Off,* even. And it's a nagging sensation I can't place, until it hits me just as I walk out the door half an hour later, dressed to ride and stepping out into the pouring rain.

Because dreaming, in both senses of the word, feels ridiculous right now. I competed my horse at an event two days ago, and it certainly wasn't imagining and wishing about it that got me there. Sitting around and hoping that something will happen won't get you anywhere. The only way to make your dreams a reality is to get up, get out of bed, and go outside and work for it. I just wish I'd known, or at least acknowledged, that, all the times I sat around wishing I had natural talent (if that even means anything). Because it's irrelevant if you don't actually work. Hard work and determination inevitably lead to success, and no matter how hard you want something, you'll never get there without that.

If I want to get to Badminton, if I *really* want to ride around that cross country course more than anything else in the world, and not just be one more person who had unbelievable dreams when they were little, which remain just that, then I have to work for it. Talented people aren't the most successful, hard-working people are. And picturing me and Loxwood flying over huge fences isn't going to get me anywhere. I'm going to succeed because I'm never going to accept that there is any other option.

As I traipse along the pavement, getting more and more soaked with every step, I finally feel as though everything is coming together, and nothing short of an apocalypse can change that.

I doubt I have slept more than ten hours across the past three nights combined, but yet I feel particularly jolly as I walk into Frank's yard, even if the English rain has decided to use me as a punching bag. Thoroughbreds are already being walked in circles on the concrete around which the stables run, most looking less than pleased at being out in this weather. Lizzie and Graham are both already riding, and I raise a hand in acknowledgement as each of them shoot me a smile. Frank is standing nearby, still holding the clipboard on which he tracks his schedule in his hand. He suddenly becomes alert when he notices my presence.

'James,' Frank calls. 'Nantucket's not going out, can you take the Believer colt?'

It's not a question. 'Okay, boss.' I say. And then, because I'm both too curious for my own good, and too invested in all the horses here. 'Has Nantucket pulled a shoe?'

Frank has already turned his attention back to his clipboard, and he doesn't look up as he speaks. 'No, owner's ditching him.'

'What?'

'Came to see him run this weekend, and told me straight up to ditch him. You know who it is, don't you?' I nod, knowing Nantucket's owner is about as rich and evil as they come. 'He wants him gone yesterday. I'll call a dealer later, I don't have time to advertise him.'

My blood runs cold with nausea and disgust. I understand what people mean when they see they feel their heart in their mouth, and I wish there were something next to me to hold on to. But there isn't, and before taking the risk of having my legs give way, I say the only thing I can. They come out on their own, the words, and I almost don't hear them until they've been spoken.

'I'll take him.'

# BETWEEN THE FLAGS

BOOK 3

*'Success is not final, failure is not fatal. It is the courage to continue that counts.'*

Winston Churchill

# Chapter 1

The words escape me without thinking. *I'll take him.* Three words - or is it four? Three, I think. Spoken so recklessly, without a thought for anything else. No warning, no planning, and certainly no realism. And I'm terrified. But isn't it the moments that terrify us the most, the situations that result from impulse, from an instant reaction, that sometimes end up being the most beneficial? If there's anything I've learnt from my seventeen years, it's that you can usually trace back the important things to one fleeting moment. A single word, or action, that proves to be the catalyst of your life. On the other hand, planning often gets you nowhere. You can think, and overthink, and write a pros and cons list, or whatever it is you do when trying to make an important decision. But it's not the same. Those actions will never live up to the fate and spontaneity of events like this. When your life can make a complete U turn in under sixty seconds. You think everything is clear, but then one word, or one encounter, throws the whole thing out of orbit, and all you know is that there's no going back. Once the thought enters your head, a different future is unimaginable.

As I stare at the grey horse in the stable, his head hanging over the door, I see two outcomes. The easier one, where I backtrack and laugh off the matter, remembering how difficult things are as it is, and that throwing another spanner into the mix will only result in chaos. But that is not an outcome I can even begin to stomach as I look more closely. The Thoroughbred's ears pricked forward, his dark eyes shining with the same kindness they always do, unbeknown to him that his whole life is about to turn upside down. All I need to do is look at him, and think of the uncertainty that first outcome would offer, to know that there is only one thing I can do.

*  *  *

The afternoon light is casting shadows across the paddocks, and the air is warm. I unzip my hoodie as I walk, and raise a hand to shield my eyes from the sun. There are two figures grazing in the paddock opposite me, both facing the same way, and as they come into view, I find myself stopping to stare. My eyes run over the arch of their backs. One gold, the other silver. Tails swishing at the ever-present flies, not letting it affect them as they snatch away at tufts of grass. Both horses boast well-muscled frames, and coats that shine with a vitality only obtained by care.

Nantucket spots me first, his head shooting up as he sees my figure approach the gate. His friend's reaction rouses Loxwood, and he follows suit, ears swivelling forward as he searches for the commotion. He lets out a nicker as his eyes settle on me, dark nostrils fluttering, looking as beautiful as ever.

'Hey, boys,' I say, their acknowledgement putting me at ease like nothing else can.

Despite his initial enthusiasm at seeing me, Loxwood quickly decides that grass is far more interesting, and lowers his head again, once more pulling at the green blades. On the other hand, Nantucket is walking straight towards me, his eyes shining with the same unconditional trust responsible for him being here in the first place.

If I thought telling Rose about Loxwood was hard, it was nothing compared to having to confess that I'd just done the same thing again. At this rate, "instinctively gets horses without any forward planning" is the only thing I'll ever have to put on a résumé. In contrast, Rose found the whole thing hilarious, and spent the rest of the day bursting into laughter whenever the concept popped into her head. Thankfully, the vacant stable left by a DIY livery not long before meant that we weren't stuck trying to materialise a stable again.

We picked Nantucket up that evening, my nerves about the whole situation coupled with the worry of what would await me at home, where my parents had undoubtably been contacted by the college to know why I hadn't been in any classes that day. But that was unimportant as soon as I focussed on caring for the grey gelding. Loxwood had been uptight when I picked him up, anxious at having spent a couple of days cooped up, but Nantucket was completely laid-back. He stood still while I put on his travel boots, and calmly walked out of the stable, and up the lorry ramp. It didn't pass my attention that Rose was very quiet during the whole process, and I had a horrible feeling that she was truly fed up with me now that this situation had come about and was no longer just a funny story. There was a strange look in her eyes when she saw Nantucket, and I felt my stomach sink with the realisation that she mustn't like him. Even as we drove off Rose remained silent, until I could bear it no more.

'I'm really sorry,' I said, for the umpteenth time that day. 'If you don't like him I'll sort something out. I know it was stupid of me to say I'd take him-'

'Sorry?' Rose said, looking distracted as her eyes flickered to me, as though she had only just noticed I was sitting there.

'If you don't like him,' I stammered, only in that moment realising how much I cared for Nantucket as I acknowledged the feeling of nausea brought on by saying the words.

'Don't like him?' Rose repeated.

'Nantucket,' I said, wondering if she remembered his name.

'Why do you think that?' she cried, which momentarily reassured me.

'I'm sorry,' I said again. 'You looked like you were maybe not too keen on him…'

Rose shook her head quickly, a sad smile on her face. 'Georgia,' she said. 'He's lovely. That's not what's wrong.'

'What is?' I said.

We came to a stop sign, and as the horse box slowed to a halt, Rose let her eyes turn away from the road, looking straight at me. 'He reminds me of Orion.' And with that I knew that she felt as strongly about him as I did.

Everything was easy from the moment Nantucket stepped foot in the yard. Loxwood had been relatively laid-back compared to most racehorses, but Nantucket was a different ball game altogether. He had none of the sensitivity. He didn't prance on the spot, nor did he walk around with the expectation that everyone keep their eyes on him. If he were a person, he would wear his heart on his sleeve. It was as though he was so trusting in people that he couldn't imagine that anyone would ever do him harm. Seeing him, safe in Rose's yard, made the thought of him being sent to a dealer even more appalling. I was proud of my decision, and thankfully Rose was just as besotted.

The discovery that he would have to share me didn't go down so well with Loxwood, though. They weren't stabled next to each other, but whenever he saw me go to Nantucket he would neigh, kicking out at the door in frustration. But he soon got over it.

I was apprehensive about turning them out together, for fear that they would become too attached to one another, and as a consequence make my life hell, but I needn't have worried. Loxwood tried to provoke Nantucket, squealing and snorting as he tried to coax him to play, but the grey Thoroughbred couldn't have cared less. Grass was far more interesting.

In the five weeks he's been here, Nantucket hasn't done a single thing I can reproach him for. I thought I got lucky with Loxwood, but he's like a Mustang in comparison. Rose agrees that he's the easiest four year old she's ever come across. I'd been prepared for having a second horse being a difficulty, but so far it's a walk in the park. Well, this part is, anyway. The financial side is another matter.

'You all right, Tuck?' I say, running my hand down the grey's wide forehead as he lowers his head towards me. Naturally, the sight of Nantucket getting attention attracts Loxwood even more than food, and he abandons the grass to walk over, ears pinned back in jealousy. '*Now* you care about me, do you?' I say to him, keeping one hand against Nantucket's head as I reach out the other to run it down Loxwood's chestnut coat. 'Spoilt, much? You're both lucky, do you realise that? If it weren't for me, God knows where you'd both be right now. A little appreciation would be nice. Huh?'

Loxwood's clearly not hearing a word I say, because he pushes straight past Nantucket to nudge my pockets with enough force that I stumble back a step.

'Grateful as ever,' I mutter, pulling the apple they both know I have out of my hoodie pocket, twisting it with both hands until it gives in the middle, separating into two halves. 'One each,' I say sternly as Loxwood immediately tries to push Nantucket out of the way, but the grey is unperturbed.

I bring them in together, a lead rope in each hand, making Nantucket wait as I spin Loxwood into his stable, before continuing round the yard to his own.

'Is the school free?' I ask Rose once I've put my two horses away. I find her in Sterling's stable, grooming the elderly horse's coat.

'Go for it,' she says. 'You doing flatwork?'

I nod. 'I hacked them both yesterday, so..'

'Okay. Has Clara told you I'm taking her cross country schooling next week? Do you want to bring Nantucket along?'

In the time he's been here, Nantucket has achieved in weeks what took Loxwood months. He's more unbalanced, granted, and I have to work hard to steady him through the turns, but he doesn't resist. His unsteadiness is overpowered by his willingness, and his dressage was test-worthy after only a week. Jumping came even more easily, though that could be because I knew what I was doing this time around. Already he is clearing a small eighty centimetre course, and one afternoon I even rode him down to the few cross country fences in the field to see how he would react. He popped a log the first time I trotted him up to it, and I was thrilled. Everything seems to be coming easily, too easily, and my cynical side can't help but feel that it won't last. Though I keep reminding myself that things would probably have been the same with Loxwood had I had more of a clue, which only makes me feel guilty.

'You think I should?' I say.

Rose shrugs, leaning over the stable door to rub two brushes together. 'Why not? Might as well get him out. You never know, he might even make the next event if entries are still open.'

'Really?' I've entered Loxwood in another four year old class in a few weeks time, and am bursting with excitement at the thought of taking him out again. At our last event, our first, we finished third. And I'm quietly confident that if we ride the test right, we might have a chance of winning next time around. To ride two horses in the class would be even more amazing.

'You might as well enter him anyway. Check that the withdrawal deadline falls after the day we're taking them schooling, and if it goes badly you can just pull. That's what I would do.'

'Okay,' I say, not voicing the maths I'm doing in my head, trying to work out whether I can afford another entry fee. I'll find a way, though. I have to.

I ride Nantucket first, after knocking dirt from his legs. As if this horse doesn't have enough going for him, he also never rolls in the field. As in ever. I can spend the same amount of time trying to brush mud from Loxwood's coat as I do riding him, and I have to say that I slightly resent him for it when I look at Nantucket's shiny, silver body.

After forty-five minutes of flatwork, coaxing Nantucket to soften through his back and neck, we're both exhausted. He's still learning to use muscles that up until this point have been idle, and due to his instability, my own balance has to be as perfect as it can be, so that I'm not doing anything to interfere with his. But he's also light in the hands, and willing to work in a correct outline even if he can't sustain it for that long. It's just about repetition, and building up those muscles little by little, every day, until it becomes as effortless as breathing.

'You star,' I say, scratching Nantucket's forehead as I lead him back to the stable.

It's a further twenty minutes until I'm standing beside Loxwood, ready to tack him up. I should do flatwork with him too, really, because I've been taking dressage a bit lightly these past few weeks, due in part to the fact that I've been devoting so much of my time with Nantucket to it, that when Loxwood's turn comes I just don't want to know. Of course, I ride him first some days, too, yet flatwork seems to elude us. Though I'm not greatly concerned, because he knows how to go soft and round in a nice outline, and eventing isn't really a discipline for the detail-obsessed.

I could lunge him, allowing me to stand back and watch while *he* improves his flatwork, but I find lungeing the most tedious of all tasks, and only resort to it when I'm too tired to make my legs function.

'How about another hack?' I say to Loxwood, running a hand down his chestnut neck. 'You'd like that, wouldn't you? Make the most of the weather,'

He swishes his tail at a fly, which I take as a "yes", and I feel jollier than I did a couple minutes ago as I lift my saddle from the ground, where it is leaning beside the stable door, and swing it onto my hip. A hack is definitely more appealing. What event rider needs dressage, anyway?

# Chapter 2

At least I know I'm not going to be bringing my current morning ride back to Rose's any time soon. Mackerel Cloud, a three year old colt, is one of the stars of Frank's yard at the moment, and it's a wonder I get to ride him at all. And not only is he a beast on the racetrack, but he's a lamb to handle. A racehorse possessing those two qualities is about as rare as an event rider saying "I love show jumping and dressage". He's nothing much to look at - small, fine, and bay - but when he hits the track, he seems to have an infinite number of gears.

As much as I love that feeling of connection I get when riding Loxwood and Nantucket, that sensation of being in control of their every movement, riding a horse with Mackerel Cloud's turn of speed is something else. The exhilaration I feel is indescribable, how I imagine it must feel to fly, and when we reach the top of the hill, coming back to a trot, I can't help but grin.

'He felt amazing,' I say to Frank as I pass him on the way down. He stands close enough to hear feedback from each jockey as we ride back, only a sentence or two, while deciding which ones to send back up for a second run.

'Good,' Frank says, his brow furrowed in thought. 'Looked it, too. Take him in, he's done for the day.'

I'm not even halfway to Rose's yet, pedalling like mad, and I'm already exhausted. Getting up early every day is one thing, but combining it with a crazy amount of physical commitment is another. I've been getting up at four, five o'clock for so long now, that not doing so isn't a lifestyle I can envisage. But every night when I pull my duvet back to go to bed, or when my eyes open in the morning, and it goes without saying that in both cases I am exhausted, there is almost always a moment, when I remember the number of horses I have to ride and the number of miles I have to cycle, that I feel physically ill, as though all four of my limbs are being weighed down by bricks. It's not even eight o'clock yet, and soon I'll be forking straw and wheeling barrows, which if I'm perfectly honest is probably the easiest part of my day. But after that, I'll be loading my horse onto the lorry, away to go cross country schooling. Loxwood will stay behind, because besides the fact that I don't think he really needs the training outing, I also don't want to dish out another thirty pounds on venue hire. What money I did have saved up before getting Loxwood is as good as gone, and what I earn at the track is spent just as quickly, whether it be on feed or on entry fees. But it doesn't matter, I remind myself, because I am going cross country training today, and if that goes well I will have not one, but two horses competing next weekend. A real event, against fellow eventers. The saying goes that you're supposed to train until your idols become your rivals, and that's what I'm doing. Already my four year old horse has battled it out against others belonging to riders that have been round Badminton and Burghley more times than I can count, and not only did he hold his own, but he beat them. And now I actually have *two* horses in a position to do so. Finally, everything is coming together, and if that means I'm a little exhausted from time to time, so be it.

Monday it's so hot we're all going around in shorts, Wednesday there's a hail storm, and Friday it rains, so when Saturday morning rolls around I have no idea what to expect of the weather anymore. And when we pull up at the competition venue to a drizzly grey sky, I count my lucky stars.

While the fences are supposedly the same size as the ones I jumped with Loxwood at our last event, they look enormous. The atmosphere is larger here than it was there - the course rolling, each fence kitted out to the nines, a large country house in the background, not to mention the calibre of the horses and riders here today. And the overall image only adds intimidation to the obstacles. If I'm perfectly honest, I've been quietly confident coming into today. Nantucket's a blank canvas, but Loxwood's last time out was a triumph. We finished third, much to my amazement, and now the only way is up. I haven't told anyone this, but I reckon we're in with a chance of clinching the class this time. When I entered, I was given the choice to say which order I wanted my horses to go, and I opted to have Loxwood up first. That way I can use him as a trailblazer and then rely on the experience to help get Nantucket round. It all sounds so simple. Though I wasn't expecting the course to look quite so professional when I thought of all that.

The weather I considered decent clearly has other things in mind, because when I walk Loxwood to the dressage warm-up, the greyness of the sky has only increased, and the slow rainfall is now accompanied by random gusts of wind. Not that it should affect him. After all, this is England, and unpredictable weather isn't exactly unusual.

It suddenly occurs to me that my thoughts are being projected above my head in a bubble, because no later is something crossing my mind before the reverse happening. As the misty rain continues to fall, Loxwood begins jittering, shaking his head angrily against the drops, and refusing to listen to my command that he soften his neck and reach his nose to the floor. It's only the sight of Alex riding into the ring on her four year old Tightrope Act that calms my nerves slightly. Waffles is certifiably crazy, and while the last thing I want is for him to cause Alex any trouble, I also know that I won't be the only one struggling to control their horse.

I don't even have time to say hello to Alex as she passes me before she begins rattling on.

'Bloody weather,' she says loudly. 'What the heck is wrong with this country!? It's summer! I was sunbathing a few days ago! Stupid England! At least if it were raining all the time I'd be used to it, but no, we have to be tricked into thinking it's going to be nice, and then *BAM.N!*' Waffles spooks as Alex enunciates that last word with venom. But she's unperturbed. 'And now we've got to spend the whole day getting absolutely soaked to the skin! I'm riding five, and I've only got three pairs of jodhpurs with me, so you do the maths. I'm gonna be drenched for at least half my rides. Five horses - that's fifteen phases, and I don't know how many jumps. And now I get to be carted around by this idiot,' she adds, nodding at the grey horse beneath her. 'Anyway. Other than that, all good. Right?'

'Right,' I agree, because what else can you respond to that?

'I saw you've got two rides down,' Alex says. 'One of Rose's?'

'Nope. I've just got to learn to stop putting my hand up every time racing yards chuck them out.'

Alex laughs. 'I'll look out for him. Anyway, I'd better hurry. I'm up in three numbers! Catch up later - actually, swing by the lorry whenever. You know which one it is? It's only got our name printed across the side of it, which reminds me-' I don't find out what that reminds Alex, because one of the stewards calls another horse forward, leaving only one more before her, and she swears under her breath before clicking her tongue and sending Waffles into a trot. As his wet, grey body moves farther away, down a long side, I can't help but notice his improvement since I last saw him. I'm sure he's still screwball nuts, but his scrawny figure has filled out, and he certainly looks more like a contender and less like a lost cause. Though even a lost cause looks pretty half-decent with Alex in the saddle.

My horse, on the other hand, is beginning to look like a laughing stock. I don't know what's got into him, but Loxwood is being pathetic. He's jittery, spooking at every sudden movement around him. Apparently, each gust of wind that builds up behind us is the ghost of a murderer, out to get him. Rose is getting ready to ride herself, a catch ride for some friends of hers, so I can't even go up to her and ask for advice. Everything that normally works isn't - instead of stretching down and engaging his hind quarters when I squeeze each of my calves simultaneously and play gently with the reins, Loxwood takes advantage of the freedom to prance. When I try the opposite - shortening the contact and riding him up to the hand from the leg, he goes rigid. After over twenty minutes of absolutely no improvement, I'm at a loss. I almost went up to Alex, seeing as not only is she the only person in this ring I know, but an amazing rider, but she rode out of her test in such a hurry, presumably to hop onto another horse, that I didn't want to disturb her. Not to mention the humiliation. Just some weeks ago, Loxwood left Waffles for dead in the standings. And not only are the odds of that happening today non-existent at this rate, but Alex's horse has improved leaps and bounds, while mine has regressed if anything. I know I haven't done much real dressage lately, but should his progress really be going backwards? It's with relief that I see Rose ride into the warm-up area three minutes before I'm supposed to be up. I go into some frazzled description of how catastrophically everything's going so far, and she does her best to calm me, repeating the word *breathe* over and over again (and, I mean, I love Rose, but does that ever really help!? If a person needs to be told to breathe, then they're obviously too flustered to do so), and telling me to work on smaller movements, never the same one twice. I work in as she tells me to for the time I have left, also changing direction and incorporating loads of transitions, and I just about feel like it could possibly begin to work when I'm called into the ring.

I'm still convinced that we could have pulled off a decent test if I'd had another ten minutes to warm up with Rose, but considering the disaster it was before she arrived I can't really complain with what I got. At least I didn't completely humiliate myself, though I doubt we'll do much better than top twenty. At least Loxwood stayed on the bridle for the most part, but I was so preoccupied with keeping him calm that I completely neglected my shapes, and once again I'm sure the judges' comments will feature the word *oval*.

I leave Rose warming up who she has been referring to as Fender, a lean bay, as I walk Loxwood back to the lorry, disappointment hanging heavy in my stomach. But I remind myself that this is an event, not a dressage competition, and the day is far from over. Loxwood is a Thoroughbred, after all, built for speed and endurance, not prancing around in some tiny ring. He's good at jumping, it's what he lives for, and I highly doubt everyone will be going clear over this course, let alone in this weather.

Having Paddington beside him, Loxwood doesn't fret when I take Nantucket away from him. I threw a cooler over his back, and he's now happily pulling at a haynet. And I now need to completely forget about him, because Nantucket is the one about to go into his first ever dressage test.

Rose is finishing up her test in one of the other rings when I start warming up. Fender's nice enough, but nothing special. *Not like mine*, I think, because I know that at the end of the day, I have two pretty special horses.

I spot Alex warming up for the Novice, on a pretty chestnut with four white socks I haven't seen before. There are three dressage arenas, and as a consequence there are loads of riders from various classes scattered across the large working-in area. I pat Nantucket reassuringly as we navigate our way through the madness, but he doesn't seem particularly bothered. I remember what Rose said to me the first time I took Loxwood out, about how ex-racehorses are used to havoc, and agree that she is definitely right .

Nantucket has walked a couple circuits when I recognise Leni making her way to a steward, announcing her arrival. She's riding Arturo, a lovely grey Warmblood of a different calibre to most. Not that he's hers - an owner gives Leni the ride - because I'm not the only one who'll probably never be able to afford a horse like that. I love Thoroughbreds, mine in particular, but I still envy those who get the advantage of going into a dressage test on a horse like that. Leni deserves it, though. The only reason she gets to ride horses of that quality is *because* she's spent years getting the best out of rejects, and now few horses hold a candle to her own ex-racehorse. I just hope I can get Loxwood to the same level. *And Nantucket*, I add as an afterthought. I dreamed of owning and competing Loxwood for so long that it's still surreal to think that I actually have the opportunity of producing two eventing stars.

It takes Leni a moment to recognise me. Her eyes look absently over other horses and riders, face closed and expressionless, something I mistook for arrogance before I knew her, when really it's nerves that send her into competition mode, game face on. When she does meet my eyes, though, she smiles widely, trotting Arturo to my side.

'Oh my god, he's gorgeous!' Leni says, looking at Nantucket admiringly. I told her about him the day he arrived, and her initial reaction had been the same as Rose's when I announced that I'd managed to pick up another free horse. 'How's he doing so far?'

'Don't know yet,' I say. 'He seems calm enough. Lox was full of it, though. It will be a miracle if we're not last.'

Leni smiles compassionately. 'Bummer. I'm saving Olly until the team's announced,' she says, referring to the fact that she and Lochmere have been long listed for the Junior European Eventing Championships, as have Alex and Thomas. 'So just him and Cooper here today. Only two to ride - almost feels like a holiday!' She laughs. 'Good luck, see you later!'

'You too!' I call as Leni starts circling Arturo.

The weather is easing up, but thankfully Nantucket doesn't seem as bothered by the rain as Loxwood was. He's a little anxious, but nothing I wouldn't expect from a four year old. And soon Rose reappears, having handed Fender back to his owners, and with her help I feel as prepared as I can be when I ride into the ring. Nantucket's balance isn't naturally as good as Loxwood's, and it takes strength to keep him stable through the turns, but overall he does a good job, and it's certainly an improvement on my first ride. And while it's completely stopped raining by the end of it, I'm freezing. Alex might have thought that three spare pairs of jodhpurs wasn't enough, but I don't even have one, and there's nothing to do but suck it up for the rest of the day, and hope that the sun makes an appearance. I have some tracksuit bottoms with me, so I'll at least be able to change into those once I'm done riding.

In spite of the amount of rain that has already fallen, the show jumping ring seems to be in reasonably good nick. The ground is good, thankfully not too affected by the water. I'm not sure if and when I'll be able to walk the course, so I stand by the edge of the ring to watch a few rounds, which is all it takes for the track to be in my mind. Again the jumps are surely the same height as they were some weeks ago, because the four year old classes are all supposed to meet the same standards and requirements, but they seem bigger. Colourful fillers, bright poles, not to mention the facade of the estate house in the background. It's the kind of place most people dream about riding at, and I remind myself how lucky I am to have such an opportunity. Now all I need to do is go out there and show everyone what I've got.

Rose has time between her next rounds, and I'm grateful to have her standing in the middle of the warm-up ring, calling out advice, and adjusting fences as needed. I had hoped that Loxwood's mood earlier was weather-related, and that now that the sun is coming out he would get over it, but I'm proved wrong. He's just as unresponsive as before, trying to rush around as he ignores my aids, and as more horses and riders fill the ring I want to die with embarrassment. Anyone who heard me say I want to get to Badminton one day would think I'm not right in the head, and those who've seen him before will most likely be wondering what the heck I've done to screw him up in such a short amount of time. I was nervous about messing up in front of Alex, but Waffles came into the warm-up on springs, and she was pretty preoccupied right up until the moment they entered the ring, after which she was hurrying off again. Some of the other riders are far more prestigious, but at least they don't know me.

When Loxwood and I canter into the ring, I try to think back to my confidence coming into today. After our last competition, I thought for sure we would be here to win. I know Loxwood isn't going to stop, so all I needed was to nail the dressage. But we didn't, and now I need a double clear more than anything if we're going to have any shot of climbing back up the leaderboard.

The starting bell rings, and Loxwood takes off of his own accord. I'm unprepared, but there isn't exactly much I can do, other than watch that we don't cross the start line before we're ready to turn to the first fence. He's pulling at my hands, which is unlike him, my attempts at sitting down and collecting him are futile, so for now I'll just have to go with it.

We clear the first with more than enough speed, and I have a job to turn towards the second. I try to steady him with my leg, but Loxwood couldn't care less, and scampers over the jump. The next few are on a curving line, and I desperately attempt to gather more control before confronting them. I'm taking checks on the reins as we come into the first one, and it almost seems like it's going to work, but then Loxwood fights for his head, and I realise that my hands are way too strong to allow him to jump well, and we're forced to chip in a small stride, so close to the fence that for a moment I think he is going to stop. But somehow he scampers over it, and I'm pushing to the next, now afraid of interfering in any way, and resigning myself to merely being a passenger.

When we jump the last fence, I have tears in my eyes, but the commentator is either clueless or very polite or both, as he congratulates me on a "super clear". But I don't care about going clear. Okay, maybe a little, but I care about riding well. About a round that fills me with so much pride, in a way that almost no result can.

'You got round,' Rose says when I ride out of the ring, like it's supposed to make me feel better.

'I don't understand,' I say, fighting hard to keep my expression neutral. 'He was so perfect last time. What's changed?'

Rose shrugs. 'That's horses for you. Some days are better than others, you've just got to learn to control it. The second time out is often worse than the first, because the first time everything's new and exciting. Same with everything - you don't fight unless you know what you're fighting against.'

I feel completely frazzled when I ride Nantucket into the ring some thirty minutes later. He warmed up well enough, though he slipped more than once coming through a turn, and I wondered if I had made a big mistake in not replying affirmatively when the farrier asked if I wanted stud holes the last time he came. But stud holes cost more money, and I didn't really see the point in using them on four year olds. But now I'm wishing I had that extra grip.

Nantucket is naturally cautious, unlike Loxwood who is all about speed and courage, and he takes his time round the course. Every fence he jumps as though someone were standing beside it, marking him out of ten, and he moves steadily through the turns, much to my relief. And the fact that he goes clear is nothing compared to the feeling of elation I experience at having redeemed myself for earlier's catastrophe.

'*Clear jumping, with just one time fault for Georgia James and Nantucket Winter.*'

My heart sinks slightly when I hear that, but I quickly shake the notion away. I said I wanted nothing more than a round I could be proud of, and that is what I've got.

Rose is pretty jam-packed for the rest of the day, so I set off with Loxwood to the cross country course alone, both of us suited and booted. I'll only jump him a couple times, and focus more on getting control. So long as I make sure I can get my leg on him, and brake when needed, the rest should come easy.

After a few circuits, I've managed to slow Loxwood's pace. He no longer feels like the racehorse he once was, and more as though he's collected enough to go back into the dressage ring. Remembering how Rose told me not to over jump him in the warm up last time, I point him at the smallest log, which he pops over, before heading to the start box.

'Ready?' the steward asks. I nod, and prepare to hear the words. 'Three, two, one, GO - Good luck!'

Loxwood tries to take off when we plunge forward, and immediately I sit in the saddle, doing my best to steady him. The last thing I need is a flyer over the first fence. Reluctantly he slows his pace, allowing my legs to balance him, and I let myself relax as we come to the obstacle. *Sit and wait,* I think. His ears go forward, and I take a check on one rein to make sure he isn't going to take off.

In the last three strides before the fence, Loxwood fights to accelerate, but I hold my ground. Unwillingly, he complies, slowing his pace, and I count down the take off in my head. Three, two, one… But the feeling of Loxwood pushing off his hindquarters, propelling into the air, doesn't come, and instead I'm thrown onto his neck as he grinds to a halt.

# Chapter 3

I feel like my entire body turns to ice. As soon as his feet make contact with the base of the fence, Loxwood leaps backwards with a snort. Tears prickle my eyes as I regain my balance, and I wonder whether I should just pull up now. I don't understand what's happening. I was in perfect control, and Loxwood was collected, so what is going wrong?

No matter what, I'm not letting him get away with not jumping that fence, so I slide my left leg back as I ask for a canter lead, going wide so that I can turn back to the fence from the right. I work at keeping him steady again, but Loxwood seems just as frazzled by that stop as I am, which inadvertently sends him forward. My legs are trembling as we approach, fighting to keep in control, and for an awful moment in the last stride, I think he's going to stop again. But somehow we scamper over, though not a pleasurable experience for either of us, and I'm pushing him on to the next. My brain feels like it's gone into overdrive, and I don't know whether I should be fighting to put what just happened behind us, or if it should be at the very front of my mind. I feel helpless.

Loxwood's shoulder comes up in front of me, uncertain, and if I were a horse I'm pretty sure my emotions right now would translate the same way. I don't know what's been going on today, why everything seems to be spiralling out of control, and I'm at a loss. So instead of holding the chestnut Thoroughbred back until the base of the jump, or firing him forward, pushing him out of his stride to take a flyer, I do nothing. I don't trust myself to make decisions anymore, and so I sit there, paralysed. A couple of strides out and I'm still clueless. One more and we're at a safe distance to take off from, and I sense Loxwood hesitate, ears flickering back for instructions, but I think it's too long, so I do nothing. I realise it's a mistake as soon as I commit myself to it, because there's barely room for another stride, and he goes to take off, only to decide that it's impossible, front legs falling down onto the gentle slope of the palisade. My gut twists, and I want nothing more than to take my feet out of the stirrups and swing to the floor, running off to go hide somewhere. I would also settle for a time machine, so that I can backtrack the past two hours and start over, but neither of those things are a possibility. I could retire, but I don't want to leave Loxwood refusing a fence, so I do the only thing I can and represent. This time we get over, but we're both shaken, and we're eliminated a few fences later.

'*Sadly, three refusals means an elimination for Georgia James and Loxwood,*' a voice announces through the loud speakers, and it feels as though somebody has ripped into my chest, gathered all my dreams from within it, and set fire to the lot, the smoke and ash drowning me as we head back.

I didn't think I could feel any worse, but I'm proven wrong

when I catch sight of Rose in the middle of the track, her face enough to tell me that she has seen at least some of the past three minutes. I want to calmly ask her what I did wrong, to explain how I felt, and how Loxwood and I reacted to each fence, but as soon as I part my lips to speak I find myself weighed down by tears, unable to get a word out. My teeth are clenched as I fight to restrain them, furiously hating myself for showing such weakness, but the plug has been pulled and there's no going back.

Rose walks back to the lorry with me as I try to form sentences, and it's only once we get there, and I spot a familiar grey horse, that I remember my day is far from over.

'I just don't understand,' I manage once Loxwood is untacked, and I'm sitting on the steps to the living compartment. I'm seriously cutting it fine, and really should have Nantucket tacked up by now, but I'm not even sure I can face going back on the course again.

'I know he's a bit uptight today,' Rose says cautiously, 'but I was running to watch you start, and..' She pauses, and I know she's going to say what I did wrong, and is hesitant to add to my disappointment, but it's necessary. 'You had no pace, sweetie.'

Not what I was expecting to hear. 'I was trying to keep him steady,' I choke.

'I know,' Rose says quickly. 'And that would have been fine in the dressage ring, and the show jumping, even, but this is *cross country*. You're supposed to charge out there like you're riding into battle. Nobody cares if it looks nice.'

'But,' I squeeze my eyes shut as try to remember what I did. Forcing myself to relive those awful few minutes, recalling every click of the tongue and check on a rein. 'It wasn't any different than last time, was it?'

'It looked a lot slower to me. And you weren't thinking so

much the first time. All you thought about was getting round - you weren't exactly trying to hold him back.'

'He didn't want to jump,' I stammer, blinking away a fresh load of tears. 'He didn't want to jump just then. He would've gone over if I had made him...But I shouldn't have to hit a horse to get over a fence. That's the whole point! A cross country horse should *want* to jump! I shouldn't have to *make* him!'

'No, you don't have to make him,' Rose says, 'but you've still got to *ride*. You stopped riding out there. You sat still, expecting him to sort it out. Trust me, I get what you're saying about a cross country horse jumping of his own accord, and trusting you enough to do it, but if that was all it took, then we'd all be riding at Badminton.'

I collapse into my hands, my entire face feeling raw from the saltiness of tears. 'I've messed him up.'

'No, you haven't.'

'I have!' I cry. 'He'd never refused a fence up to today!'

Rose sighs, standing up from the overturned bucket she'd been sitting on, and placing her hands on her lower back. 'Okay, so what if you have?'

'What?' I say.

'What if you have screwed him up? What if he was a ready-made event horse, and you've just ruined him?'

Hearing someone else say the words is even worse. 'Have I?'

Rose shrugs. 'I dunno. Let's say for argument's sake that you have - what are you going to do about it?'

'I don't know.'

'You going to sell him?' she continues. 'Give up? Turn him out? Switch to dressage?'

'I don't know,' I repeat, wanting to stuff my face into a pillow and scream for all I'm worth.

'Well,' Rose says. 'Let's say - again, hypothetically - that you've messed him up. There's nothing stopping you from fixing him.'

I look up, keeping my hands crossed against my knees. 'Do you really think I've ruined him?'

'Truthfully? No, I don't. I think you were both a bit distracted, and you forgot to attack the fences, and perhaps he was testing you a little bit, and you gave each other a fright. Big whoop! These things happen. Sure, you didn't help matters much,' (trust Rose for honesty), 'but for all you know it would have happened even if you hadn't done anything wrong. They're horses! These things happen! The only thing you can do is practice, and come out fighting next time.'

'I don't know what to do,' I say, straining my eyes to look at the chestnut Thoroughbred tied to the side of the lorry, pulling absent-mindedly at a haynet.

'Right now,' Rose says. 'You've got a second shot.' She turns to Nantucket. 'So hurry up and get him tacked up, and I'll come warm you in.'

This time, I make sure Nantucket is covering ground, doing as Rose says as she instructs me to push him forward. We go over the practice fences a couple times before heading to the start box, a lump in my throat.

'Just keep moving,' Rose says. 'This is cross country, remember.'

I nod, and before I know it we're off. Instead of focussing on a short and collected pace, I push Nantucket towards the first fence, as though we are charging into battle. His rhythm slows of his own accord, still uncertain as to what he's doing, but instead of holding him back I squeeze him on. My confidence translates to him, and we clear the fence. *We can't exactly do much worse than the first round.*

Nantucket is more cautious than Loxwood was on his first outing, but while he looks at the jumps, he doesn't think to refuse. I keep encouraging him round the course, feeling more and more dazed with each fence we come to, until I realise we're already halfway around clear. The thought of being able to redeem myself with a placing on my second ride fills me with hope, and I feel my confidence increase with each jump.

When we come to the final combination, the second part three strides away on a curving line, I only realise too late that I haven't thought about turning until a stride after the first. Instinctively I pull my right hand out, sitting up, but Nantucket is inexperienced and unaccustomed to sudden turns, and unaware of what I'm asking we fly straight past the fence. *Idiot,* I think to myself. *Serves you right for losing concentration.*

The second approach is uneventful, as is the rest of the course. I'm furious with myself for those twenty penalties, but twenty minutes ago I didn't think I would even make it this far. I pat Nantucket madly through the finish, and find Rose there waiting for me, and I smile at her.

'That's more like it!' she says.

'The run out was my fault,' I say quickly. 'I lost concentration, and forgot to turn early enough,'

In all her helping me out, Rose is well and truly behind her own schedule, and she hurries off to get ready again while I walk off Nantucket. He seems happy enough with his efforts, and I tell him again and again what a good job he did. The mistake I made at that fence plays through my mind again, and I wonder in some ways if that's what went wrong with Loxwood. I was so confident coming into today that it didn't really occur to me to ride into each fence, or that I would have to help him out. I almost assumed he was just going to get me out of trouble. I rode each fence on Loxwood the way I did that second part of the combination on Nantucket. Coupled with the lack of pace, we were doomed. But I shake the thoughts from my mind again to stop an onrush of tears, because what's to say that I haven't now ruined him beyond repair. I'll think about it later.

It's warming up by the time I'm walking toward the show jumping ring, having left the horses with haynets at the lorry. I sponged and dried Nantucket off, throwing a cooler over his back, and brushed out Loxwood's earlier sweat marks which had now dried, trying to keep my body language calm as tears blurred my vision each time I looked into his eyes. I didn't want to resent him, and I don't, but looking at that familiar head I know so well was like acid to a wound, thinking about how anything can seem possible one minute, only to have reality slap you in the face.

I offered to help Rose between rounds, seeing as she's juggling two horses and all, but she insisted that Fender's owner was keen to be hands on, and told me to get some rest. Personally, I'm pretty sure she does need the help, but I'm such a useless lump in this state that she didn't see the point. Can't exactly blame her.

Beneath the guilt and worry, there's a heavy hunger in my stomach, but just the thought of swallowing down food makes me feel queasy, and I decide to give the concessions stands a miss. Horses are far better therapy.

I always find watching the warm-up more interesting than the actual rounds. On course, you're not thinking so much about working the horse as you are getting the best you can out of it, whatever the cost. But it's behind the scenes that you see riders' true colours.

Rose is trotting Fender round, the bay looking nice enough in comparison to the others. But there's one horse my eye is immediately drawn to. It's a bay again, but dark, as though he started out with that bright mahogany coat, but the colour faded into black at the extremities. He has no white socks, his legs dark, but there's a diamond-shaped marking on his head. It isn't often that a bay stands out from the crowd, but he does. It doesn't hurt matters that he's got to be over seventeen hands tall.

'Gorgeous, isn't he?' a voice says in my ear.

The amount of people around means the voice doesn't catch me off guard, and even before I turn I recognise it as Leni's. 'You can say that again,' I say.

She stands next to me with her arms crossed, her white jodhpurs now covered in black marks from a wet saddle, eyes only on the horse. 'Can you believe Alex bought him online without even seeing him?'

I do a double take at the mention of Alex's name, but as I look up at the rider I realise, stupidly, that it's her. I was too busy admiring the horse to pay any attention to whomever was on top. 'Sounds like something she'd do.'

'Right?' Leni laughs. 'She got him for a bargain price from the Netherlands, and he arrived on a lorry a few days later. Then again, I don't see why anyone would need to go through that kind of trouble when you know someone who gives away quality horses by the bucketload.'

I pull a face. 'Not so sure about.'

Leni's expression falls. 'Err. What happened?'

I take a deep breath, bracing myself to say the words out loud without my voice breaking. 'Nantucket got round with twenty, but Loxwood was eliminated.'

'You're joking!? What happened?'

I calmly do my best to explain what took place, starting with the less than stellar show jumping round, and trying to make light of the idea of stopping at the first fence, while also not hiding the fact that I didn't help matters, because I'm past even being ashamed. The whole time, Leni looks thoughtful, listening intently without ever trying to interrupt.

'It could just be a one time thing,' she says reassuringly when I'm done.

'But he's learnt to stop!' I say, almost wishing everyone could blame me so that I can get what I deserve. 'A cross country horse can't stop over eight or ninety!'

'It doesn't mean anything,' Leni says dismissively. 'I mean, God, if you'd seen Olly when he started out you would have been horrified! He jumped anything and everything at home in training, but it took me three events to actually get him round a course! And it wasn't because he was scared, or couldn't do it or anything like that. He was just playing up.'

'And what did you do?'

'I had to get tough,' she says. 'I told him off once, let him know that I meant business, and from then on he was fine.'

'Seriously?' I say. Leni nods. I've always thought of Lochmere as the sort of horse that has always jumped no matter what, not one that ever had to be told to. 'But, I just,' I pause, trying to make sure the next words don't sound offensive. 'Shouldn't Loxwood want to do it on his own, without me telling him to?'

'I know what you mean,' Leni says. 'But at the end of the day, they're horses. It's not about telling them off, but you've still got to be in charge. I mean,' She looks around the warm-up. 'Like, do you think Alex would hesitate to give Anchor a tap if he tried to stop at a fence? That's what makes a cross country rider. Of course horses are going to hesitate every now and then, you've just got to tell them it's all right. Besides, he jumped clear last time, didn't he? He probably just got a bit starstruck, and wanted to see what he could get away with.'

'I hope so,' I say, watching as Alex rides the beautiful dark bay into the ring, and the commentator names the horse as *Veni Vidi Amavi*. 'Bit of a mouthful,' I comment.

'It's Latin,' Leni says causally. She probably knows what it means, too, but I don't ask for fear of sounding stupid, and we stay around to watch Alex jump clear, walking up to congratulate her afterwards.

'You guys free?' Alex says brightly. 'I've got an hour until my next ride, and I need a break.' Her eyes turn to me. 'How did it go?'

'Train wreck,' I say quickly.

Alex laughs. Not exactly the reaction I was expecting. 'Ha, tell me about it! That bloody horse,' By the way she's saying it, I'm assuming she means Waffles. 'Jumped me off in the water, and then I couldn't even get back on 'cause he buggered off! Ran all the way back to the lorry, the little sod. I didn't even have time to change for my next ride, so I was drenched, and only managed to before getting on this guy. Quit laughing, Leni!' she adds. 'Just because you went clear,'

'With six fences down show jumping between the two of them,' Leni says.

'Whatever,' Alex says, getting off the beautiful dark bay horse as one of her grooms hurries forward to take him. 'I need to buy something to eat, I'm starving! Either of you want anything?'

When Leni and I decline, Alex tells us to feel free to go wait in her lorry, and that she'll meet us there. It seems weird to walk into the living compartment of somebody's horse box without them being there, and I hope we're not going to run into Joan, because while I have yet to properly meet her she doesn't come across as someone who would be on board for that, but the couple grooms that are caring for the horses tied to the lorry are unperturbed by our going inside it.

Alex wasn't joking when she said the thing was hard to miss - regardless of fact that the words *EVANS EVENTING* are printed along both sides, the horse box stands out for its size alone. At a glance, it looks like it has space for eight horses, not to mention the enormous living compartment, part of which extends out one side of the lorry.

The interior looks like the inside of a modern apartment. Black leather sofas run in an L shape, around a pop up table, facing a TV that is mounted on the wall. We walked past a bathroom on our way in, and to the left of the seating area is a mini kitchen, complete with microwave and coffee machine. There's a double bed above the cab, on which blankets and duvets are piled up miscellaneously.

Leni has clearly been in here many a time before, and looks right at home as she walks over to the sink to fill a kettle, switching it on effortlessly.

'This is nicer than my house,' I say, unable to stop myself from looking around as I tentatively take a seat. Just in time I stop myself from sitting on a black cat that is camouflaged against the sofa, and I look up at Leni to see if she is at all disturbed by this, which she doesn't appear to be.

'Right?' she says. 'We always hang out in here.'

'You've got a lorry, though, haven't you?' I say, looking nervously at the cat again as I sit beside it. The way Leni is looking at it suggests that its presence is a normal thing.

'Yeah, but other riders at Amanda's use it, and most of the time it's just full of owners. Remember Arturo's owner, the one I don't like? She practically lives in it at events.'

'They're allowed to go inside?'

Leni almost laughs. 'Are you joking? Owners think they have a free pass to do whatever the hell they want, which I suppose they do. You can come back from a round to find them sitting in there making tea for a bunch of friends you don't even know!'

Sounds a bit like what we're doing now, minus the owner part. At least it would be to Joan, though I'm sure she does at least know Leni.

'What kind of tea do you want?' she asks, opening a cupboard that reveals a larger selection than I have at home, and I can't help but comment on it. 'Alex's rule,' Leni says in response. 'She thinks a cup of tea solves everything.'

There are two cups of steaming tea on the table when we hear somebody step up onto the steps leading to the door, followed by Alex's voice calling, 'Watch out, Leni. It's the F word!'

I have no idea what she's getting at, but Leni clearly does, as she screws up her face in disgust, and a second later we're greeted by the smell of fried batter.

'That's so disgusting,' Leni mutters.

'Fish and chips!' Alex announces proudly, shoving a greasy potato wedge into her mouth, and the thought of eating anything like that right now makes me gag. 'You're the only person I know who doesn't like this,' she continues, speaking to Leni with her mouth full.

'Not liking it is one thing,' Leni says. 'But how can you actually eat that *now?* You're about to ride cross country.'

'Exactly, I need fuel,' Alex says before holding the paper tray out towards me. 'Chip?'

I feel my stomach turn. 'No, thanks.'

'You guys don't know what you're missing,' she says happily. 'Shove over, Evie,' she adds, pushing the cat off the sofa so that she can sit down. 'Hey,' she continues, looking at the table. 'Where's my cup of tea?'

'Sorry,' Leni says, jumping up to make another one.

'So,' Alex says to me as Leni sets about finding another mug, dunking a chip in ketchup. 'Why was your day a train wreck?'

The sinking in my stomach I have been ignoring for the past few minutes returns, heavier than ever. 'Loxwood basically stopped at every fence,'

'Oh well. Just one of those days,'

I frown. How does everyone else seem to think that this isn't a big deal? 'What about Waffles?' I ask, remembering that Alex looks particularly relaxed for someone who was dumped in a water complex not long ago.

To my surprise, she laughs. 'Man, that horse. I swear, I don't know why I keep riding it!'

'What are you going to do about it?' I ask, hoping it sounds sincere and not patronising, because I'm genuinely interested to know what somebody like Alex's reaction is to these kind of situations.

Leni places another cup of tea down on the table, and Alex points at it while she swallows down a mouthful of fish. 'I'm already doing it,' she says. 'Sit down and have a cup of tea.'

'That's Alex's solution to everything,' Leni chimes in.

'Because it's the only thing there is to do,' Alex says. 'I used to try to analyse everything, but there's just no point! They're horses, these things happen, end of. You'll drive yourself mad if you keep thinking about it. Just have a hot drink and move on. Even if part of me does want to strangle Waffles,' she adds with a smile.

'Are you going to keep riding him?' I ask.

'He's not exactly saleable, is he? Even so, yeah. Because although he's nuts, and a pain, he isn't really dangerous.' I'm not sure what she means by this, and she continues. 'He's smart, and quick with his feet. The only time I refuse to ride a horse is if they have dangly legs, because that's what puts you in danger. Like last year, I had this lovely gelding, but he was just so careless with his front legs, and I didn't feel safe anymore. He was lovely to ride, though, and I kept telling Mum and Dad to sell him as a show jumper, because he had no problem jumping high to make up for his hanging forelegs, but they didn't. It doesn't matter if he hits a fence show jumping, but cross country's too dangerous, and we had one massive fall. But an event rider bought him anyway, and there's nothing I can do about it, even if I think it's ridiculous.'

'Why would someone want to take the risk?'

'Because when he doesn't fall, he wins. Basically.' Alex says. 'But riding a horse like that is way more dangerous than all the Waffles-like horses in the world.'

'And that completes this week's episode of *Life Lessons with Alex*,' Leni mutters.

'I'm not even offended,' Alex says, before suddenly leaning forward. 'Wait! Shh!' She tilts her head. 'Do you hear that?'

I look over my shoulder. 'Hear what?'

'Nothing!' Alex cries triumphantly. 'That's the point! Mum's not here today. It's so much more peaceful.'

Leni closes her eyes despairingly, and Alex looks like she's about to go on, just as the steps make the sound they do when someone steps onto them, and Ryan appears round the doorway.

'Alexandra. Helena.' He pauses as he looks over at me. 'Georgina?'

I shake my head. 'Sorry.'

'Oh well. Two out of three,' he says with a shrug, before his eyes go to the TV on the wall. 'EVANS!' Ryan yells, taking a running leap to the sofa. 'Time for a Mario Kart rematch.' He reaches down the side of the seat, pulling out two video game steering wheels.

'Ha! You're on!' Alex says, happily taking one and switching the TV on with the remote. I'm not surprised by the fact that the lorry has a games console in it, so much as I am by the fact that anyone could be relaxed enough to play between rides.

'What were you guys talking about?' Ryan says as the game loads.

'Crap horses,' Alex says. 'Not that you'd know anything about that. It must be hard, buying ready-made horses.'

She must have said this to him before, because Ryan doesn't seem in the least bit offended. 'You underestimate just how much,' he says.

'Arrg, that reminds me, did you guys see that Lottie Gallagher-Smith has bought another horse? It's gone three-star.'

'I'm pretty sure she buys a new horse every week,' Leni says. And to me she adds, 'Lottie has three horses - well, four now - but the three she had have all been on European teams. And won medals, for that matter.'

'She competes in a ponytail,' Alex says to me with disgust, as though that should tell me everything I need to know. 'She has lessons with Amanda, and worships the ground at her feet,'

'Who's she bought?' says Leni, never good at dissing her coach, no matter how much of a nightmare she is supposed to be. 'What's it called?'

'It's got some stupid name,' Alex continues. 'Something Butler. Met? No! Rhett Butler, that's it! What's that even supposed to mean.'

'It's a character from Gone With The Wind,' Leni says, sounding fed up, but not meanly, by Alex's ignorance. 'It's only one of my favourite books-'

'You've lost me, Leni,' says Alex. 'You know I don't read.'

'Not to mention the fact it's about a thousand pages long,' Ryan says.

'It's also a movie,' Leni points out.

'Actually, I think I've seen parts of it, and it would take you less time to read the book!' Ryan says.

Leni starts launching into a debate on why it's such a great story, but Alex tells her to stop being so intellectual, and resumes talking about the horse at question. 'The thing's pushbutton,' she says. 'God, it must be nice to be rich and buy your rides.'

'Marry a millionaire,' Ryan says to her, both of them keeping their eyes firmly on the video game that has now started.

'I'm not getting married!' she yells. 'I don't want to die!'

Ryan laughs despairingly at the seemingly random statement, but Leni pulls a face that suggests she somehow knows where it came from.

'Care to elaborate?' Ryan says.

'I listen to the news! Every day there's another story about a woman burying her husband in the backyard, or a guy shooting his wife because she told him she didn't like his tie, or something like that. Please! Why would you get married when the odds are your spouse will end up killing you?'

'You could always kill him first,' I say.

'Hey, there's an idea!' Alex perks up.

'And spend the rest of your life in jail,' Leni points out.

'I could stage it to look like an accident,' Alex says. 'But maybe it's not worth the risk.' I'm slightly concerned by the amount of thought she appears to be putting in to this, but she continues. 'I'll only get married if it's to a millionaire like you said,' she says to Ryan. 'And spend the money on horses.'

'You know,' Ryan says a few beats later. 'Thomas is a millionaire.'

'That much ego under one roof?' says Leni with a grin. 'The world would end.'

Alex doesn't have time to reply to the statement, because before the last word is out, she has launched a bomb at Ryan's character, and the two of them start yelling at each other.

'Anyone in there?' someone says, as a blonde figure appears round the door, and I recognise the girl as Erin.

'You all right?' Leni says.

'No!' she huffs, falling onto a seat. 'Excalibur ran out at a corner, and I fell off.'

'Leni!' Alex calls, still focussed on her game.

But Leni is already jumping up. 'Yeah, cup of tea. I'm on it!'

A lot of shouting goes on after Alex beats Ryan to the finish line, as he tries to claim that she cheated by trying to knock the controller out of his hand, and they're still at each other's throats when Thomas, whom Ryan mentioned just a couple minutes ago, walks in, though it takes me a moment to recognise him.

'Hey, Alexander,' he says smugly. 'The photographer just got the *best* shot of you flailing about in the lake. Fancy a swim, did you?'

Alex stares at Thomas in horror, before turning to Ryan, as though the former isn't standing there, and says, 'I'm sorry, but no number of ready-made horses is worth putting up with *that* for.'

# Chapter 4

Three days later, I take Loxwood cross country training with Rose, and frankly the only good thing I take from any of it is that he at least jumped every fence at some point, though rarely on first approach. I'm sure some of it was my fault - or if I'm being honest with myself, I'm sure it was *all* my fault - but that doesn't change the fact that he's lost his confidence. But we managed. So why do I feel this shattered?

'It just takes time,' Rose says to me on the drive back. She brought Spirit along to ride, because Clara is either too scared or too disinterested or both. Though that's one horse I don't know will ever find his bottle. I love Clara, and at school we're still as close as we've always been, but it's getting increasingly hard to stand back and watch her ruin that horse. Then again, she's probably thinking the same thing about me now, too.

'I don't have time,' I say, staring out the window at the darkening sky. At least the weather gods waited until *after* our cross country session to unleash a truckload of downpour. 'I have a few weeks. And I can't even enter him anywhere before the finals, because everything's full up. I checked.'

Rose waits a moment, nothing but the sound of the windscreen wipers filling the cab, before speaking again. 'You know,' she says, and from her tone I already know what she's going to say. 'You don't *have* to ride him in the finals.'

While the Four Year Old Event Horse Championships isn't exactly something I've spent my entire life aspiring to (not like Badminton), it has been the focus of my attention since the notion first entered my mind. It's all the most promising young event horses in the country coming together. It's where top event horses start out. Where there are a special few that stand out, and people will point and whisper things like "That one's going to make it all the way". Too many four-star riders to name will be there, as will I, competing as an equal. And after our first event together, I really thought Loxwood would have a chance of winning.

'I've already entered and paid stabling fees,' I say. A weak excuse, but also a true one, which my bank account is more than aware of. Rose is competing Paddington in the two-star, and I will therefore be there longer than I need to be, which means additional stabling costs. Not that I can even begin to complain when she is doing so much for me. But the three days will set me back more than a few hundred, and I really need something good to come out of it.

'You could always just do the dressage,' Rose says. 'Get him out, let him see a big atmosphere, but with none of the pressure. There's no reason you can't still ride Nantucket in all three phases.'

'Maybe,' I say, because what else can I say to that? The thing is, I know she's right. Rose is always right, as far as horses are concerned. I can't exactly compare my own experience to hers. But I don't want her to be right. I want the confident horse I had a few months ago back, and with him the comfort I had of knowing that my life plan isn't so crazy, and not destined to remain a childhood dream. But dreams are irrelevant, I remind myself. You can't just wish for something and hope that it becomes a reality. You work your way to the top, you don't dream it. Which I am more than prepared to do, and have done up to now.

So why does it feel like nothing is going to come right?

The rare occasions I did still go get coffee and cake with Lizzie and Graham are now extinct, and it's not even my fault. I was eating a bagel at the kitchen table one evening when my mum looked at what is referred to as the food jar, which is where spare notes and change are put for me to use to buy groceries, officially letting everyone in the house off the hook as far as cooking an evening meal is concerned.

'Georgia,' she said. 'I put five pounds in here just this morning. And I put ten in a couple days ago, and it's all gone already! What did you spend it all on?'

After various mumbles about the cost of milk and cereal, and some back and forth bickering, I *mentioned* the fact that I *might* have bought a coffee or two, which launched an argument.

'That money is for essentials. A category that coffee and cake do not fall into!'

I beg to differ, but my days of ending the afternoon with a slice of red velvet are over so long as I don't pay for it myself, which I can't exactly afford right now. So cake-less I remain, with only instant coffee to drink. And I can't say that it's improving my general mood at all.

'Wait, Georgia,' Lizzie says to me now, as I'm getting ready to leave Frank's yard. She's hurrying towards me, having carelessly dumped her exercise saddle on the ground in the courtyard. 'I keep meaning to ask. You're still coming to the races, right?'

Next week, there's a race on at Newmarket racecourse, and Graham has a ride. A horse in training with Frank that nobody thinks much of, with an owner that doesn't seem to even care about winning, but still. A big deal for Graham, and naturally he's asked me and Lizzie to come along.

'Umm,' As fun as a day at the races can be, it's not exactly high on my list of priorities. And I know I'm being a useless friend at the moment, but it doesn't matter when I compare it to Loxwood. The fact that he is going through a tough patch, to put it mildly, takes up just about all of my concern, leaving none for anything, or anyone, else. I don't resent Graham and Lizzie for being the way they are, and I love them for it, but neither Leni nor Alex would ever expect me to go to *anything* that didn't link directly to eventing. It's such a crazy world, full of early mornings and a kind of dedication you wouldn't think achievable, that it's impossible for anyone that doesn't live the life to fully comprehend it. But it is everything, and social gatherings most definitely do not come into consideration.

'Are you kidding me?' Lizzie says, too loudly, though pretty subdued compare to how she can sound. 'I know you're busy, but that doesn't mean you *never* do anything else.'

'Actually, it does,' I say.

'You know what,' says Lizzie, throwing her arms up. 'I'm not even gonna stand here and argue with you. I shouldn't have to tell you how to be a friend,'

'Don't be like that. It's not like I don't *want* to go-'

'Really?' she says, raising her eyebrows in a way that makes her look like she should be on a soap opera. 'You could've fooled me!'

'Lizzie,' I call as she turns and walks away. I should go after her, and I would if I could. But it's already gone seven, and I'm late. So I do the only thing I can, and break into a run, ready to swing onto a bike and cycle the first of many miles I have yet to do today.

All I can think the next day is that there is such a thing as karma. Not that I ever *didn't* believe in karma, but it's not so funny when it aims its arrow at you.

Even if I hadn't behaved like a rubbish friend the other day, I had it coming. I knew, last week, when Rose asked if I wanted the farrier to book me into his session, that I should have said yes. But he's coming again next week, and I thought I would be able to push it until then. Loxwood's feet were long, and one of Nantucket's shoes had some movement to it, in addition to clinking when we went on the roads, but they weren't *terrible*. And regardless of the fact that I didn't even *have* the money to pay for the farrier last week, pushing it even further would benefit me in the long run. It's a heck of a bill to pay every six weeks, and I thought if only I could get it to eight…

But I see it straight away - or, more to the point, it's what I don't see, which is a shoe on Nantucket's right fore. Whenever I bring the horses in, my eyes instinctively flick over each of their feet, reassured by the silver of a toe clip. Great.

'Hey, boy,' I say, holding out a hand to Nantucket's nose as I lean down to check his foot for nails. As I lift his overreach boot up, I wince at how much hoof the shoe has pulled off.

A warm breath blows into the back of my head as I'm holding up Nantucket's foot, and I put it down with a start. 'Get back,' I snap at Loxwood, pushing his shoulder. 'Go on! You'd better not have lost a shoe, too.' But one glance reassures me, and I push him back again. Which, I realise too late, is completely stupid of me, because I need to catch Loxwood, and having taken offence he is now walking away.

'Fine,' I mutter, reaching under the fence for the two head collars in the grass. Because, of course, the best way to catch a horse is to make him feel jealous, and as soon as Loxwood sees me throw a rope around Nantucket's neck, he comes right back up to me.

'And you think you're so clever,' I say, his long chestnut ears swivelling forward.

I'm concentrating only on getting both horses past the gate, so I'm completely unprepared to see Nantucket stumble, as though he were completely lame, when he hits a stone.

'I'm sorry,' I say, the words coming out in a panic. He's halted, now, and I can feel my heart thumping against my chest as I ask the grey to step forward again. It's most likely just one unlucky stone, I think. Thoroughbreds are notorious for having bad feet, especially when they've come from the racetrack, and it's not uncommon for them to be unable to walk on hard ground without front shoes on when they're not used to it. 'Come on,' I say, clicking my tongue as I ask Nantucket to walk again, while also trying to pull Loxwood's head up from the grass with my other hand.

Never one to disagree, Nantucket steps forward, this time with me making sure that he's staying to the grass, and to my relief he walks normally. 'You're okay,' I say, putting a hand against his neck as we walk. 'You're fine. It's my fault, it always is.

I'll get the farrier out, and he'll put some new shoes on you, and you'll be as good as new. And you're going to go and show those other four year olds what you're made of, aren't you? You're going to go show them how amazing you are.' Saying the words to him, even if I don't believe them, is all I can do to calm the butterflies in my chest. It would be typical, wouldn't it? To miss out on the Championships because I tried to save a little money. The worst thing is that I know feet aren't something you ever take a gamble on. No feet, no horse. It's one of those mantras I store alongside *Stable management is everything*. And in a perfect world I would have my horses re-shod every four weeks, but I can't. No wonder it's so easy to succeed in this sport when you have money. To have parents that pay for all your horses' running costs and then some. I can't even imagine what it would be like to only have to focus on riding, and not on where the next cheque is going to come from, or how much it costs to hire a cross country course.

'Is everything all right?'

I look up from my daydream of pity to see Paige, bucket in hand, looking right at me as I come into the yard. I've really got to get a poker face. But her words do bring me back to reality, and as I always do when I'm around Paige, I feel guilty for feeling sorry for myself, when my life is a bowl of cherries compared to hers.

'Nantucket's lost a shoe,' I say, nodding at his bare foot.

'I can come help you look for it,' Paige says, setting the bucket of water down at her feet.

I shake my head. 'Don't worry, I've got it.'

Right, I thought when I stepped to the gate, I'm going to walk back and forth across the paddock, as though I were mowing it. It sounded so simple. It's only a two acre paddock, after all. But forty-five minutes later, and I've walked across the whole thing twice, and am now wandering about without a game plan, since that hasn't exactly worked. Nantucket will need a new set of shoes, anyway, but I can't leave this one lying around in case the nails are pointing upwards, and with the luck I'm having Loxwood will most likely stand on it tomorrow. It's a good thing I chose to ride them both this morning, because there's no way I would have had time for anything else now.

My phone vibrates in my pocket, and I pull it out, keeping my eyes on the grass. I texted the farrier as soon as I got the horses in their stables, and it's taken this long for him to reply. *Tuesday*, the message says. Today is Sunday, which means that Nantucket has to go a full day without a shoe on.

Sliding my phone back in my pocket, I look up from the ground, feeling the relief in my neck that comes from no longer being hunched over. That means Nantucket can't be turned out tomorrow. Or ridden, for that matter. Just what I need. I raise my hands to my neck, digging my fingers into my tired muscles, when a glimmer of silver catches my attention along the fence line. I hurry towards it, my heart leaping at having finally found the shoe. The nails are sticking out, too, so I was at least right to keep looking. But how many times have I passed this spot? Three? Without spotting the shoe.

'When you win Badminton, I'm investing in a metal detector,' I inform Nantucket later that evening.

Loxwood neighs when he realises that his friend isn't joining him in the field, while Nantucket couldn't care less, happy to continue munching his hay. I muck out Loxwood's stable at top speed, before moving Nantucket to it in order to do his. Rose is around, as is Leah, and she gives me a lesson in the importance of duct tape.

'It's a life saver,' Rose says, securing pieces around the outside of Nantucket's hoof to avoid any more of it breaking off. I'm inclined to agree.

My mum's been recommending a book to me for a while now, which I've declined because A) Her taste in books is terrible, B) There are smiling people on the cover, which is enough to make me gag, and C) I haven't exactly had much time to read recently. But as my plans for today consist of holding Nantucket to graze, it only occurred to me while I was rushing out the front door this morning that I needed something to occupy myself, and the paperback was the first thing I laid eyes on. So I grabbed it, and am now sitting in the grass, scorching sun bearing down against my bare arms, fully entranced while Nantucket grazes, occasionally going a step too far and pulling me sideways.

I lose track of how many hours I remain like this, but I know that one character has died by the time Mackenzie comes rushing towards me with a plate of homemade cookies, and I have a sunburn by the time I've finished the book. I'm at least satisfied that Nantucket has had enough time out when I put him away and bring Loxwood in to ride. And after an enjoyable hack, I cycle home feeling content.

The feeling doesn't last. I wake up at three o'clock in the morning, shivering, my entire body aching. I have a thumping headache, and I lie there, suffering, until my alarm goes off. Everything hurts, and I feel ill, but I can't miss out on a day's pay, so I get dressed anyway. The thought of food turns my stomach, and I manage only a few mouthfuls of coffee before giving up and heading out the door.

I'm feeling no better by the time I make it to Rose's, and I'm not sure how I cycled all the way here, let alone rode three-year-old racehorses before doing so. The pain and sickness I feel is clearly obvious, because when I see Rose, the first thing she says to me is, 'You look like death.'

'I feel like it,' I say, staggering onto a chair in the clubhouse. She asks me what's wrong, and when I list the symptoms she does one of those sighs - the mum sigh, I call it - as though whatever is wrong with me is obvious, and most likely my own fault.

'Sunstroke,' she says. 'I almost said something to you yesterday, sitting out there without a hat on,'

'I wouldn't have worn one even if you'd said,' I say.

'I know.'

'I don't even own a hat,' I mutter, each sentence I say a chore. I can't keep my eyes focussed on anything, instead letting my vision go out of focus as my eyes settle on a chair leg.

'Go home,' says Rose.

'I can't. I've got to muck out, and the farrier-'

'We can do that. You're sick.'

'I'm fine,' I mutter.

I most definitely am not fine, but I'm not about to let Rose and Leah pick up my slack. The farrier shows up at eleven, which at least allows me to spend the next hour leaning against Nantucket's neck for support, and then repeat the process with Loxwood, because I'm not waiting for him to lose a shoe too.

My teeth are actually chattering when evening feeds come about, and no matter what I do I can't get them to stop. I have a feeling that as soon as I've cycled home, I'm going to collapse into bed, though whether or not I'll actually get any sleep is doubtable.

'Get your bike in the back of my car,' Rose says when I walk back round from Loxwood's stable.

'I'm fine,' I say.

'I'm driving into Newmarket with or without you,' Rose says, walking towards her jeep. 'So whenever you're ready.'

I don't even have the energy to argue, and as we cruise along the road, minutes later, I can't imagine having to do the journey on a bike right now. My headache is still present, combined with pains in my limbs, and trying to stop my body from shivering, even though I'm hot.

'Thanks. You didn't have to,' I say as Rose pulls up in front of my house. In all the time I've known her, she's never been to where I live. Which, though logical, is strange seeing as she is such a huge part of my life. And as I directed her down the street - a street she has probably been down many times before - I couldn't help but try to see my home through her eyes, comparing it to the white farmhouse and stable yard she gets to call her own.

'Just do me a favour and go to bed for at least a day,' Rose says, climbing out the car to help me lift my bike from the boot.

'I'll be fine by morning,' I say, though as I've just wheeled by bike straight into the edge of the pavement, I'm sure my words aren't very convincing.

'Whether you're at the yard or not, I'll feed, turn out, and muck out Lox and Tuck myself. Okay? So, if you do show up I'll only make you go to sleep on my sofa. Seriously, you need to rest. When have you ever had a day off?'

'I don't need a day off-'

'And how are you going to ride next week if you're in hospital with sunstroke?'

That I don't have a reply to, and my headache isn't helping with my ability to form sentences, so I keep quiet.

'Get some rest,' Rose says again. 'Okay?'

Maybe it's the fact that she is standing in front of my house, looking at me with concern, or because I've suddenly been hit with another wave of nausea that makes me want to curl up right here on the pavement, but I nod. 'Okay.' I pause, my eyes scanning the still-light sky. There are only about six hours of darkness a day now, which only makes sleeping seem even more irrelevant. Should I be asking Rose to come in? I'm not sure she's even met my parents before, and I don't know that I even want her to. But she's driven me here. 'Do you want to come in?'

She shakes her head, smiling. 'I'd better run. Thanks, though. Another time.' She climbs back into the car, pausing her hand on the door as she sits in the driver's seat. 'I don't want to see you tomorrow, remember.'

I have no intention of not cycling to the yard tomorrow morning, even if it kills me, but I nod. 'See you later.'

# Chapter 5

My head is thumping, my mind a fuzz from waking up every hour to throw my duvet to the floor, drenched in sweat, until being cold rouses me again. And then my alarm goes off, beeping for all it's worth, and I feel ill just thinking about fighting sleep to get out of bed, my arm flailing to silence it, but then I remember Rose's offer, the knowledge that my horses are being fed and cared for sinking into my brain, and as the beeping ceases, I allow myself to fall back into a slumber.

When I open my eyes again, I feel as though I have just woken from a heavy spell. It starts getting bright at four now, meaning that I'm always getting up to light shining into the room, but today something's different. It's… brighter. And there are sounds - cars, people, a general busyness. I turn my gaze to the clock by my bed, blinking until the hands come into focus, and I throw myself forward with panic. Quarter to ten. *Frank, Loxwood, Nantucket…* each name coming with a solution. *I'm not working today. Rose is feeding the horses.* Slowly, my normal breathing resumes, and I lean back against my headboard. *Quarter to ten.* When did I last sleep in that late? If ever, for that matter. Since working at the track, the latest I've ever woken up is half-seven, and even that is only recently, the day after a competition. But I need to go now, I think, swinging my legs to the carpeted floor. I've barely tried to stand before being hit with another wave of dizziness, and I lie back down just as quickly. On any other day, I would push through it. Even if it meant passing out once I reached the bottom of the stairs. But of course Rose said one thing that stood out to me - I need to ride next week. Actually, I need to ride today, and every day, until the Championship comes about. Which even I know is impossible right now. I'll stay in bed today, so that tomorrow I'll be able to lunge the horses at the very least, and take it from there. As much as I want to fight being ill, maybe I just need to accept the help I have been offered for one day.

As it turns out, my body picked the right time to come down with sunstroke, because it just so happens that today coincides with the cross country phase of the Junior European Championships. Alex, Leni, and Thomas are in Italy, with the other half of the squad. Not only were all three of them selected for Europeans, which is amazing, but they are all riding as part of the team and not as individuals. Already Great Britain is in silver medal position after dressage, due greatly to the fact that Thomas and Tenerife are lying in second. Both Alex and Leni are just outside the top ten, only a few marks from the lead, which means it's all to play for today. I only recall all this after I've been awake for about an hour, glancing through old magazines on my nightstand, already remembering why I choose to have horses, because I loathe being idle. But the idea of live cross country footage is more than enough to make me appreciate the fact that I have nothing else to do. After a good twenty minutes of searching online, trying to make sense of foreign websites, I find the live stream, which comes with an Italian commentary that I end up silencing for the sake of my headache. I also find a page of start times, around which I plan my trips downstairs to the kitchen, so that I have half a bagel in hand each time a British rider is about to go. I feel more nervous than I do when I'm riding myself. Maybe this is how football fanatics feel where their team is playing? No, I push the thought away, because comparing eventing to football is, quite frankly, insulting.

After hours of feeling nauseous for a different reason, I'm elated. Every single British rider went clear, most of them very close to the optimum time, including Leni, whose round was the standout one for me. Alex and Anchor had some scrappy moments, including a jump into water that left her without stirrups, reins at the buckle, but there's a reason Alex is a cross country rider and that's because she can ride by the seat of her pants, somehow managing to keep kicking to the upcoming log, getting them both out of a sticky situation. And Thomas made the course look effortless. Too easy, almost. There's no doubt in my mind - Lochmere stole the show. But of course my opinion doesn't mean anything, and the leaderboard that flashed across the screen showed Thomas, Leni, and Alex to be in second, fourth, and fifth positions respectively, with the other team rider in ninth place. It goes without saying that Great Britain took the lead.

The thrill of watching the horses for hours has made me feel better in a way that nothing else can and I'm ecstatic as I walk down the stairs, but apparently it's only my mind that is feeling better, because my mum is in the kitchen and when she sees me she says, 'Please don't tell me you're about to try cycling eight miles like that.'

Of course, that is exactly what I'm about to do. Upon hearing which my mum is so horrified that she grabs her car keys from the kitchen counter and offers to drive me herself. In other words, to quote Rose, I really, really do look like death.

Because I'm grateful to my mum for driving me, or because I'm bored, I don't know, I bring up the fact that I read the book she recommended to me in the car, and the fact that I didn't totally hate it, which seems to make her far happier than it should, and we discuss the characters the whole way to Rose's.

'Wait,' my mum says, as we pull into the car park, snapping out of our book discussion. 'This is where you cycle to and from every day.'

I nod. 'Yeah.'

'It's a long way,' she says. 'I know it's four miles, but…' her voice is quiet, thoughtful. 'It's a lot every day.'

She's looking right at me, almost with concern, and I push away any and all snide remarks that enter my head. 'It's not so bad. Do you want to meet Loxwood?'

To my surprise, she's already unbuckling her belt, and I feel a sort of pride as I walk her round the yard, staggering to my horses' respective stables, where they are both more than happy without me. I introduce my mum to each of them, even though I'm sure she can't distinguish one horse from another, as well as whomever we pass. I can tell from her face that she's taking in how familiar I am with the yard and the people, not caring that I'm wearing my pyjamas. And when Rose appears, she introduces herself before I even have a chance to, immediately praising my work ethic to my mum, which I can see surprises her, though she seems pleased. Soon Mackenzie is with us too, arms around my waist, frantically wanting to know if I watched the Europeans cross country footage and discuss it with me. And every time I look up at my mum, talking to Rose, she seems to have her eyes on me, taking in the whole scene, in a way that almost makes me feel uneasy.

'You'd better be getting back to bed,' Rose says to me finally. 'And I thought I had succeeded in getting you to take a day off.'

I grin. 'Never.'

Rose pulls a face. 'It'd do you some good to have a break every now and then. Trust me.'

I know she's right, because already having had to be away a day has only made me more determined to come back tomorrow and get ready for next weekend, but I'm not about to admit that. 'Thank you so much for looking after them today,' I say instead. 'You have to let me give *you* a day off next.'

Rose laughs. 'Dream on.'

'They were all very nice,' my mum says after the first mile. We climbed into the car in silence, and it has been that way up to now.

'They are,' I agree. 'Rose has helped me out loads.'

'You look very happy there.'

I glance over ay my mum, her eyes firmly on the road. 'I am.'

'And Rose says you work very hard,' my mum continues, her voice tight, but not with frustration.

I shrug. 'Only as hard as anyone else.'

She nods. 'I know I've never really got this whole horse thing, but I can see why you like it there. And you look like you belong, too. I'm glad you've found something that makes you that happy.'

Her words shock me for a moment, which isn't helped by the fact that my mind is still finding it hard to function from the drowsiness I feel. But somehow that last sentence hits me like a heart attack. Something I've forgotten recently, in all my struggles. Because horses and riding do make me happy, or they *did*, anyway. But that hasn't been the case lately. And it's easy to forget why you ever started. But between that reminder and the fact that a day away from Loxwood and Nantucket makes me feel like I'm missing my soul - which, credit to Rose, is a good thing to be reminded of every now and then - I remember that horses always made me happy. I didn't start riding because I wanted to win, that came later, but I started riding because I loved horses, and being in the saddle was when I felt happiest. Maybe I do need to slow things down a little and not take everything so seriously.

'Yes,' I say. 'I am happy.'

'How come your horse is so well behaved?'

'Really? You think?' Paige says, looking down at the supposed ex-racehorse who is plodding along happily, while mine seems to have caught word that a dragon is going to burst out of the bushes any moment now.

'Look at Brumby, Loxwood,' I say teasingly. 'See how nice and quiet he is? Do you see him trying to put Paige on the floor?'

A butterfly shoots out the brambles beside us, and Loxwood snorts, letting his hindquarters skid beneath him as he jumps forward. He's only going for a couple strides, and once I have him back at a walk, one glance at Paige is all it takes for the two of us to collapse in a fit of laughter.

'To be fair,' she says. 'It was a pretty scary butterfly.'

'Great! My event horse is scared of butterflies.' I stand in my stirrups to lean over his neck and look down at him. 'This doesn't bode well for the future, Loxwood. I hope you know that.'

Loxwood flickers his ears backwards, before the slight wind picks up behind him, and he takes off for a stride again, sending me unceremoniously to the back of the saddle, arms flailing, which only makes Paige laugh more.

'Seriously,' I say once I've regained my balance. 'What's up with your horse. It's like a saint.'

'It's just his nature,' Paige says with a shrug, looking down lovingly at the plain bay gelding, walking on a long rein, completely unaffected by Loxwood's random outbursts. 'It's nothing I did. He's always been like this.'

'Is that supposed to make me feel better?' I say, as Loxwood walks into Brumby's side to avoid going near a suspicious-looking branch, looking as though his eyes are about to pop out of his head as he turns his neck to snort at it.

'Well, yeah. If you were on Brumby, he'd be the same way. And if I had got a horse like Loxwood then I'd have already fallen off about a hundred times. But Brumby is never going to be able to jump the kind of fences Loxwood will.'

We trot along a flat section of the bridle path, side by side, Brumby relaxed as Loxwood tries to hold his head high and overtake. Paige slows back to a walk first when we come to the foot of what we refer to as a hill, though it isn't much more than an incline by most people's standards. Even if they have never been here before, horses seem to naturally associate the sloping track with the word *gallop*.

'Do you want to walk up it so he doesn't take off?' Paige says, looking down at Loxwood as he chomps the bit angrily, chucking his head every few strides.

'Brumby doesn't mind when he takes off, does he?' I check. Paige shakes her head. 'It's fine,' I continue. 'He needs to blow off some steam. He'll be worse if we don't.'

'Do you want to go ahead?' Paige says, halting Brumby. 'He might be calmer if there's nobody to overtake.'

I might also never be able to stop him, but I know it makes more sense. Allowing Loxwood to walk past Brumby, I shorten my reins in a bid to have some sort of contact, before sliding my outside leg back, and preparing myself to go.

Loxwood powers forward, as though this is what he's been waiting for the entire hack, which is probably true. I glance back at Paige quickly, making sure she's all right, and am comforted to see Brumby going at a leisurely pace, clearly not worried about keeping up appearances. This stretch of path uphill is a mile long, and as Loxwood fights for his head, before my own can override my actions, I push my hands further up his neck.

'Go on,' I say, clicking my tongue. Loxwood flickers one of his long, golden ears in my direction, questioning, and I click my tongue again. 'Go on.'

The chestnut Thoroughbred lengthens his stride, and I can feel his muscles bunching beneath me. I know the ground is good here from having ridden the track so many times, but I still keep an eye out, occasionally steering away from an odd stone, or hollow in the dirt resulting from a dried-up puddle.

'Good boy,' I say, entwining my fingers through his short mane. He isn't pulling anymore, just going forward. 'You're a racehorse, you know that?' I yell against the wind in my face, satisfied that the words will reach only Loxwood. 'I know the past few months have been confusing enough, and I haven't exactly helped matters. But we're going to work it out, okay? We're going to work as a team. You listen to me, and I'll listen to you. Deal?'

The wind echoes in my ears, hollow cackles and silent whispers. And in the sound of rushing, met with the rhythm of Loxwood's breathing, the feeling of mane between my fingers, I hear my answer.

*\*\*\**

It's like walking into a freak show. Smiling figures in suits, adorned with wealth and arrogance, and clueless heads shaded by oversized hats. There's cheering going on somewhere, accompanied by a fuzzy voice booming out of speakers. Everywhere there seems to be laugher, the type you can't help but turn your head and stare at, and I'm immediately sceptical of anyone who could possibly be that happy.

I glance down at the schedule in my hands, even though I already know the particulars, before looking back up and heading towards the parade ring. It isn't crowded at this moment in time, with people preferring to buy drinks than stare at one or two horses while waiting for others to arrive, and it doesn't take me long to spot her.

'See any you like?' I say.

Lizzie spins round, and I can't tell whether she's more overcome with surprise or shock. 'You're here!'

'And you're in a dress,' I say, looking down at the floral frock that is so very un-Lizzie-ish.

Her cheeks go red. 'Shut up.'

'You're in a dress,' I say again, laughing.

'Why are you *not*?' Lizzie retorts, eyeing up my jeans and shirt. 'We're at the races!'

'You only have to dress up for the VIP area,' I say, laughing. 'You, in a dress.'

'You're being ridiculous.'

'You look like a *girl*,' I sing the last word, and Lizzie responds by stomping and walking off, and I can only just contain my laughter enough to catch up with her.

'Have you placed a bet yet?' Lizzie asks finally. Sticking to silent treatment isn't exactly one of her strengths.

'No, I need to!'

'Let's go,' she says, holding on to my arm to steer us through the crowds.

The betting stands are all set up in a row, near the track, with giant boards up above each one, proclaiming the odds.

'Five pounds on number two, to win,' Lizzie says boldly, rummaging in her bag for her purse.

'Wait, Lizzie,' I say, glancing down at my schedule again to make sure I'm right. 'Graham's horse is number five.'

'You think I don't know that?' she says loudly. 'But number two's the favourite, and I want to win!'

We manage to spot Graham before the race starts, walking to the parade ring as he prepares to get on his ride.

'Why are you in a dress?' is the first thing he says.

'I asked that,' I say cheerily.

'It's the races!' Lizzie yells. 'Everyone knows you're supposed to dress up!'

Graham glances back over his shoulder at the horses in the ring. 'Well, wish me luck.'

'Go. Good luck!'

'Break a leg, or whatever you're supposed to say,' Lizzie says.

'And you'd better win!' I call. 'I've got two quid riding on this!'

Graham doesn't win, but he does come second. Lizzie and I are both happy for him, and as the horse she bet on came first, drinks are on her.

# Chapter 6

If it weren't for nerves, I would be quite ready to go back to sleep by the time we pull into the venue at six o'clock on Friday morning. I spent the night at Rose's in view of the early start, but the biggest surprise is that my parents didn't even pick a fight about me missing school today, especially when the term has only just started. Ben wasn't up when we left, meaning no giant breakfast feast, which was a good thing because there was no way I would have been able to swallow down anything. I drank the cup of coffee that Rose made me, but other than that I haven't managed more than two bites of the apple I split between the horses.

The butterflies in my stomach only increased when we drove past the first sign indicating the *Young Event Horse Championships*, and now the huge lorries with their accomplished riders beside them are only making the feeling worse. The last time I pulled into an event, I was expecting a top three finish. It's crazy to think, when right now I would give anything to just complete.

The sun is shining down when I ride Nantucket into the dressage warm-up. Rose has Paddington in the two-star, with only one dressage test to perform later this afternoon. After the disaster of the last event, it's a relief to have her presence today, and I'm not sure I've ever been so grateful to have help.

We're second to go, and there are only a few other horses already here. While Nantucket copes well in busy environments, I can't think of better circumstances to warm up in. No worries of bumping into anyone and having to constantly be on the lookout.

Nantucket is feeling the best he has ever felt. His head carriage is soft and round, the contact in the reins light but present, and the dry ground was made for him. In contrast to Loxwood, Tuck's main difficulty has been finding his balance through the turns. Circles aren't exactly something most racehorses are accustomed to, much less having to do so while bending through their body and engaging their hindquarters. But Nantucket has never fought my insistence that he learn to keep his balance - the opposite, in fact. He tries his heart out, uncomplicated in every way, giving every task his all. And like a slap in the face, something you don't plan or see coming, I feel an onrush of emotion as I think of how far he's come. How far *we* have come. Earlier this year, Loxwood himself was just a dream, calling him mine just a fragment of my imagination, a fantasy. And now not only do I have two horses, but they're competing against some of the best in the country.

Rose gives me a thumbs up when I ride over to her, as the horse before me goes into its final canter transition. 'He's looking great,' she says. 'Just keep riding as you're riding. Remember to keep your hands still through the turns, and don't rush the halt.

You're doing great, just keep going. You've got this. Blank slate, remember? Just focus on what's in front of you.'

I nod, glancing over at the ring to see the first horse turn down the centre line for the final halt, the rider saluting the judges. Once she begins walking out the ring, I push Nantucket into a trot. We go round the edge of the arena, taking in the spookiness of the small white railing surrounding it, and I bring him back to a walk as we go past the judges' car, giving them a nod of acknowledgment. They smile in response, and I continue working in around the ring, halting once to let Nantucket look at a flower pot, putting my hand against his silver neck, then continue circling near the boards, until the car horn beeps, and I carry on straight towards the entrance. Nantucket hears it too, flickering an ear back towards me, and I squeeze my legs more firmly around his sides. And immediately I know that the sudden increase of anticipation hasn't made him any less rideable, but prompted him on even more. He accepts my leg readily, shifting his balance onto his hocks, and coming up through the withers. I think of all of Rose's words of advice, last minute tips she gives before going into a ring or out on course, and two phrases stand out above others. *Breathe. You've got this.*

When I bring Nantucket down the centre line for the final halt, keeping the contact until I feel him square up, I can barely keep myself from throwing my arms around his neck long enough to salute the judges. Not only was it better than his last test, but I feel like it's the best he's ever gone, and the best I've ever ridden, too. I know there's a possibility that I'm the only one that thinks this, or that my standards have lowered, but one look at Rose is enough to put all that to rest. She looks as ecstatic as I feel, fist pumping her arm triumphantly, and I bite my lips to stop my smile from stretching even wider.

'That was the best you've ever ridden,' she says, stepping forward to pat Nantucket enthusiastically. 'He really is something special. You know that?'

'I know,' I say, throwing my own arms around him.

Somebody Rose knows calls her name, and she hurries over to say hello, while I pat Nantucket some more before preparing to walk back to the stables.

'Lovely horse,' someone says. I look to my right to see a woman on a beautiful chestnut, smiling admiringly at Nantucket. I don't recognise her face, but the small Union Jack embroidered on her hat-silk is enough for me to narrow her identity down to a handful of people.

'Thank you,' I say, wondering too late if I should have said the same thing to her.

'Good luck for the rest of the day. He looks like something special,'

'Thank you. You too,' I say, pushing Nantucket into a long rein walk. I didn't need to hear it from someone else, but it's still nice to. Because that woman's right. He is something special.

Loxwood seems to approve of this whole being stabled on site thing. There's so much going on around him, in his line of vision, that he's looking through the railings as though it were his own personal television, munching on hay happily as he does.

'None of that, now. Sorry,' I say as I slip his head collar on over his head, pulling him away from the forage. Along with Nantucket, he was showered and scrubbed yesterday until I was certain that not two specks of dust had escaped my attention, and plaited afterwards. Nanucket's mane is naturally thin, the small braids that result from it giving him an elegant look, while Loxwood's are larger, accentuating the muscle line of his neck. It's no wonder people find it hard to believe that he's a pure

Thoroughbred, let alone an ex-racehorse.

'We're putting everything behind us, remember?' I say once his bridle is on, leading him out of the stable, and stopping to adjust the girth. 'We're here to do our best. I've messed up, but I won't this time. We're working together, okay?' I pause as a woman walking past gives me a suspicious look, as though talking to your horse at a competition isn't normal (which it is). Loxwood's ears are pricked as he takes in the surroundings, holding his head high the way he does in public. He likes all eyes on him.

I raise my left foot to the stirrup, which is much more difficult in restrictive competition gear than it usually is, and swing into the saddle. 'You'll do great,' I say to Loxwood, resting a hand against his neck. 'We've just got to show everyone why we belong here.'

It's getting busier when I ride into the warm-up for the second time. The nice weather is attracting spectators, standing in small groups - some laughing, others watching intently and discussing the horses they see.

Farther down the warm up ring, trotting a fifteen metre circle, I make out Alex and Waffles. I do a double take for a moment, because the gelding looks even less like the scrawny thing he had first been when he came out. He's not slight anymore, but lean and muscular, with a curving top line, and a still head carriage. His dapple grey coat seems to be getting lighter by the day, and his plaits have been executed by someone who has surely had many years practice. Alex is also well turned out, having actually polished her boots (or, knowing her, got someone else to do so), and wearing her smartest navy blue jacket. Even from here I can see Joan Evans, in the middle of the ring, quietly uttering instructions which, judging by Alex's body language each time I see her mother's lips move, are not welcome. But Waffles, a name that seems even more ridiculous now, really does look amazing. I can't believe he's the same horse she started the season with, and it really does make me wonder what Loxwood would be like if he'd had someone as competent as Alex riding him. What happened last time wouldn't have, that's for sure. And his flatwork hasn't improved much, though it was naturally pretty good. But if Alex can turn Waffles into that, then she would probably have Loxwood doing half-passes and flying changes by now.

Picking up on my distraction, Loxwood breaks into a prance, shying away from my leg. So much for my optimistic mood. It would almost be easier if Alex were horrid, because then I could dislike her, and put her success down to her parents. But nothing could be further from the truth, and I feel my cheeks flush with guilt at the thought of my horses having to put up with my incompetence.

I've got plenty of time, so I walk Loxwood round on a long rein, encouraging him to relax and stretch his nose to the floor. Alex is now cantering a twenty metre circle, her seat barely moving in the saddle, and as I walk past I hear Joan say, 'He's sitting on your right hand.'

'You think I don't know that,' Alex snaps through clenched teeth.

'Get him off it, then. Lift him up!'

'If I could I would.' Alex says, able to maintain a perfect rhythm while speaking. 'You get on and do it then, if you think it's that easy.'

I continue walking past, and only glance back once Alex and her mum are out of earshot. Waffles still looks great to me, stepping under with his hindquarters and holding himself upward. But then, I guess the whole point of being a competitive rider is getting your horse to look good in the ring, and that doesn't betray the hours of work and suffering that go on behind the scenes. *Stop comparing yourself to everyone else,* a voice in my head scolds. That's the problem with competition, it leads you to compare your struggling with everyone else's finished result.

Loxwood starts rushing, running away from my leg and holding his head high with a rigid neck. I don't have time to start panicking before Rose is at my side, instructing me to ride smaller movements. After some ten metre circles, she has me ask for a few strides of shoulder-in, something he's been learning, and I feel the progress almost immediately. Asking Loxwood to move his hindquarters means he has to start listening to that thing called "leg" that he's been ignoring since we started warming up, and once he accepts the pressure, everything changes. His balance and carriage is naturally very good, but that doesn't change the fact that it's far easier to rush around with his head in the air, ignoring my demands. But once he understands that there's no getting out of working, Loxwood is lovely to ride, feeling again like the horse he was a few months ago. His balance shifts to his hocks, and he comes up into the hand. Finally I get that feeling, the one that makes such rare appearances that it's hard to believe that some people experience it all the time. And it makes up for all the struggling, and the heartache, because if only for a few seconds, your horse is working *with* you, both completely at one.

And… it's gone again. The sound of a nearby car horn sends Loxwood shooting forward again, evading the contact. It does eventually get better, though. More smaller movements, and shoulder-ins, and the chestnut Thoroughbred settles, but he doesn't feel as great as he did for those few strides when we go into the ring. The test isn't terrible, and certainly better than last time, but he doesn't track up down the long side, and throws his head above the bit for each canter transition, and I'm so concentrated on keeping Loxwood going correctly that I neglect the movements, and end up with seventeen metre ovals. But it's okay, I think as I drop my hand to salute the judges, letting Loxwood out onto a long rein. *Because I'm* here. I don't know where all this bright side optimism has come from, maybe I've been spending too much time around Leni, but it really is unbelievable to be riding here. And considering what a disaster the last outing was, I'll take what I'm given. *And there's still Nantucket,* I remember suddenly. That little grey horse that came into my life completely unexpectedly, without warning, and has claimed part of my heart. Before, I thought Loxwood, the horse of my dreams, left no room for another. Even though I rode Nantucket every day, it wasn't the same. And I would have pledged to that, up until the day that he suddenly wasn't wanted anymore, a forgotten toy, simply discarded. Seeing the kindness in his eyes, and knowing that he had nowhere to go, was enough to break my heart a little. I spent so long imagining life with Loxwood that the thought of sharing myself with another horse was unimaginable, but now I wouldn't have it any other way.

'You're something special, you know that?' I say to Nantucket, running a hand down his neck before tightening the girth. He is standing perfectly still, though his eyes are alert with interest.

It's a big show jumping ring, with plenty of space between the fences to either get into a rhythm or lose it. I walked the course earlier, when I went to the secretary's tent to collect my numbers and pay starting fees, and while it isn't complicated, it's bold. If Nantucket jumps the way he has been at home, he should be fine. It's Loxwood I'm more worried about.

The warm-up ring is set up with three fences - a cross bar to be jumped going upward, and both an upright and a parallel coming down. There are only four other horses trotting round, one of which I recognise as the chestnut that the woman who complimented Nantucket was riding. I didn't get much of a look at him earlier, only enough to know that he's nice, but seeing him move now confirms that the woman really is a pro. He's built uphill, with a high head carriage, and overtracks by a foot. If any part of me thought I stood a chance today, it's been knocked down by watching this. It I didn't know any better, I would never believe that the horse is only four years old. I can only imagine what it must be like to ride a horse like that... Or to ride as well as the woman on top, for that matter. That's what I dream of - to be able to get on a horse, any horse, and get the best out of them. Every movement being second nature, not having to think about what to do. To be the kind of rider that makes people stop and stare, because the harmony between you and the horse you're riding is so magical that it leaves people in awe. A kind of genuine trust and dedication that is near impossible to find in this day and age, that anyone just wants to witness it, if even for a few seconds. Through all the struggling, and failures, and moments of feeling like I'm kidding myself if I think that I'm ever going to achieve anything, that's what keeps me going. Because I witness something like that, and my heart catches in my throat, because all I've ever wanted is to experience that with a horse. Competing is great - being fuelled by adrenalin to soar over things that no ordinary person would consider jumping, and proving that women can finish ahead of men when competing on equal terms... but this is what motivates me. Just having that relationship with a horse, an animal capable of killing you should they so desire, is what makes me keep fighting.

I've been trotting Nantucket round the ring this whole time, and can see Rose approaching, walking to stand by the practice fences, but I hold him to a halt, releasing the pressure when I feel all four of his legs square up.

'You really are special,' I say quietly, leaning forward to wrap an arm around his neck. 'Now, you ready?'

# Chapter 7

I'm smiling before we even land. I knew from three strides out that we were going to hit a perfect one, and we have. Nantucket's ears are pricked forward, his whole body rounding through the air.

*'And that is a clear round for Georgia James and Nantucket Winter. They go through to the cross country phase on their dressage score of twenty-eight point three..'*

*What?* The score cuts through the relief, and I search for Rose as Nantucket trots out of the ring. Surely there's a mistake... But she's smiling, holding her hands up above her head to give me a thumbs up, and I almost laugh as I lean forward to pat Nantucket again.

'We got twenty-eight in the dressage?' I say, unable to even believe the words.

Rose nods. 'Not sure where that puts you. I think somebody got a twenty-seven, but you're right up there!"

It seems too good to be true. I thought Nantucket did a good test, but it never occurred to me, in the lead up to today, that I would get a sub thirty dressage.

'You really are amazing,' I say, squeezing my right arm tightly around his neck. Nantucket doesn't fuss about receiving attention, but he seems to almost ignore it, standing happily with his ears pricked, as though he is watching the other horses jump.

The day's getting hotter now, and I'm officially envying everyone walking round in shorts by the time I get back to the stables. I tell Nantucket he's amazing every other second as I untack him, leaving only his boots on since he has just the one pair, and give him an apple without Loxwood seeing. I think one of the main differences between the two of them is that Loxwood loves to have a crowd's attention, he knows when all eyes are on him, and when he's done well you can almost see the smugness on his face. In comparison, Nantucket is humble, like he doesn't know how to not do his best, because he thinks it's normal, and doesn't see that there's anything special in that. And while the horses like Nantucket are a heck of a lot easier to deal with, I can't shake the feeling that it's Loxwood who will end up being extraordinary.

The warm-up ring isn't nearly as empty as it was just a short while ago, and I feel Loxwood come up in front of the withers, ears swivelling forwards. The glaring sun is shining off all the poles, making the impeccable paintwork and imposing fillers look more intimidating than ever. That's another difference between my two horses - Nantucket likes to make you feel at ease, as though he's holding your hand when things get scary, while Loxwood plays up just to see how *you* are going to reassure him.

I give him a kick in the side when he baulks at a discarded filler by the side of the ring, and he walks around it as though it were a dragon. *Great*, I think, *this is a good start.*

Rose is here again, her dressage test not being until this afternoon, and she sets me exercises to get Loxwood listening and responding to my leg. But even as he responds to me asking him to alter his pace, lengthening his stride down the long side and then collecting himself again through the turns, it still doesn't feel right. Nothing I can pinpoint, because there isn't really anything to fault, but he feels... *off.* Like we aren't truly working together, rather he's putting up with me. And that's not how anyone wants to feel going into a ring. But I'm not going to tell Rose that, otherwise she will have me withdraw.

'When you're ready, come down the cross pole,' she says.

I nod, glancing over my shoulder just in time to see two horses almost collide as the riders both turn to the fence at once. First thing to remember before I start jumping - keep your eyes up.

Loxwood drops back from my leg when I get him into a canter, and I push him forward, keeping my hands low and together. He reacts by lengthening his stride, and when I turn him to the fence his ears prick, and he takes off. I do my best to sit still, but he's going to take a flyer, so I hold him back, releasing on take-off.

'Good girl,' Rose calls.

Because he lands on the wrong canter lead, I bring Loxwood back to trot before asking for another strike-off, and collect him for the cross bar again. I need to keep him steady, because he bolted last time, and he obliges. The feeling that I don't have him completely between hand and leg is still present, but at least I'm in control.

I have to turn wide, because a horse that has just jumped the upright from the other way has decided to throw himself into a bucking fit on landing, the rider not looking where she's going as a consequence, which means I'm farther out than I would like. But at least I have more time to prepare Loxwood for the fence, and avoid being dragged to it. He's even listening, and slowing his pace. I can see two strides - one might be a bit close, but the other is far too long, and would require me to ask for a sudden turn of speed, which defeats what I've been doing. So I wait, making sure my legs are on, allowing with my seat, and ready to give with the reins on take-off. I hesitate for a second, though only a second, wondering if I should have gone for the other stride, but I quickly push the thought away. Besides, this fence is low enough to jump from a standstill. I add more pressure with my calves, making sure Loxwood knows I mean it, before preparing to push my hands forward. But as I lift my seat from the saddle, I feel him baulk beneath me, and before I know it, I'm falling.

Hard as I fight to keep hold of the reins, they slip from my grasp. I don't think twice as I lift myself from the ground, and hurry to Loxwood, who seems as confused as I am by the turn of events, and is standing still, a few feet away, blowing heavily.

'Hey, you're all right,' I say, ignoring the shake in my voice. Shortening the reins into my left hand, I swing straight back into the saddle, before Rose, and certainly any of the stewards, can reach me. My shoulder is aching from hitting the pole, and the breath in my chest feels tight, but none of that matters.

'You okay?' Rose says as she comes to my side, glancing over her shoulder at the steward that is now waving me over. Hard as I try to ignore her, she isn't having any of it, and forces me to keep Loxwood still at the edge of the ring as a paramedic comes over. He asks me pointless questions, and finally cottons on to the fact that I'm not going to admit to anything that could make him stop me from riding. When the guy turns back to the steward, the two of them exchange an aggravated glance at my short temper. I don't know what they're so annoyed about - I'm the one that just fell into a fence, and has now lost two minutes of precious warm up time. There's nothing more annoying than people that don't ride giving you horse advice, and certainly not when it's in a riding environment.

I push Loxwood back into a canter before I can have time to second guess myself, and at Rose's nod I re-present at the cross bar. This time I make sure my riding is attacking, and he jumps as though the earlier blip never happened. I'm flooded with relief, and I bring him back to a trot, and then pop into a canter on the other lead, towards the upright with the flags on the opposite sides. To my relief, Loxwood's pace stays consistent, and we meet the fence on an easy stride. I push my hand forward to touch his withers, before stopping to talk to Rose.

'How's he feeling?' she asks, looking concerned.

'I think he's all right,' I say with more confidence than I feel. 'That was my fault,' I add, referring to the fall.

But Rose doesn't look convinced. 'You're the one on him. But I don't want either of you having another bad experience. It will only hurt both of your confidences. You can still scratch,'

No. No. *No.* 'I'll take him over the spread,' I say quickly. 'And if he jumps that all right then I'll go in the ring, and if it's a disaster then I can withdraw before cross country.' I in fact have no intention of withdrawing at all, despite what everybody thinks, but I'll deal with that later.

'Okay,' Rose says, resuming the role of confident coach. 'Get him moving, then. Don't let the engine die - even on a short stride, you still need fuel in the tank. The canter needs to be bouncy, remember? Feel like you could pop over anything.'

I nod, interpreting her instructions the best that I can under the circumstances, and Loxwood's jump over the parallel is acceptable. There's no time to do it again even if I wanted to, because the steward is calling me into the ring.

'Good luck,' Rose calls as I trot past the steward, hoping I haven't just made some huge mistake.

If I hadn't already been around this course clear once, I don't know that I would be able to hold myself together. Loxwood felt like a loose cannon earlier, but it has now been fired, and I'm already regretting my decision. But the starting bell has sounded, and I have about forty seconds to pull myself together.

As soon as I ask for a canter, Loxwood rushes away from my leg, shaking his head away from the contact. I almost wonder if I should raise a hand and retire now, but quickly push the thought away. Too late now.

By some miracle, we jump the first fence cleanly, and he tanks to the second. I try to sit still and let Loxwood find his stride, but my body isn't listening to my brain, and insists on holding him back. He gets in deep, the way he did in the practice ring, but I'm not taking any chances, and hold both reins in my left hand as I bring the whip down behind my leg. Loxwood isn't expecting that, and it's only surprise that makes him jump - if it can even be called that. All I know is that we make it to the other side, though the sound of crashing poles follows us. Great. That's four faults already added to our score, and there are still nine jumping efforts to go.

Everything I'm doing is just making matters worse, and it's only upsetting Loxwood, so I resolve to doing nothing. I stay in a two point position, only lowering my seat a few strides out from a fence, and allow him to gather speed. I'm appalled by my riding, and even more so by the fact that people I respect are watching this and probably horrified, but at least Loxwood is jumping now. Even if he is taking flyers.

Somehow, even as one terrible jump follows another, we make it to the end of the course, and as worried and as disappointed as I am, I'm also relieved as we make our way through the finish flags. I drop my hand to pat Loxwood's neck, remembering too late that he isn't Nantucket, and am greeted by a sudden leap to the side as he pins his ears back in response to my pat.

'Sorry, sorry, sorry,' I say, my voice cracking each time I repeat the word. I run my hand up and down his neck, softly, and gradually Loxwood's neck loses its rigidity, and he lowers his head. 'I'm sorry,' I say again. Through the speakers, I'm vaguely aware of a voice announcing that Georgia James and Loxwood add four faults to their dressage mark of thirty-six, meaning that they shall move forward to the cross country phase on a score of forty.

*I'm sorry.* The words keep running through my head like a scratched CD. *Sorry. Sorry. Sorry.* I've imagined this for so long. *Sorry. Sorry. Sorry.* For years Loxwood has been the only thing on my mind. *Sorry. Sorry. Sorry.* I promised I would take care of him. I promised him - Loxwood. I promised Frank. I promised myself. *Sorry. Sorry. Sorry.* And something went right at some point, because we finished on the podium a few months back. *Sorry. Sorry. Sorry.* But everything has unravelled into a pile of threads, and right now they seem tangled beyond salvation. *Sorry. Sorry. Sorry.* Among the mess lies Loxwood's confidence, his trust in me, and the stupid belief I'd once had that anything was possible. *Sorry. Sorry. Sorry.* But my dreams right now don't even matter, because never achieving them is one thing, but having wrecked the one thing I care about in the process is another.

'I'm sorry,' I say, leaning over Loxwood's neck as he trots out of the ring. I've turned back the way I came in, and now the voice over the speakers is yelling at me to please exit the ring at the other end, thank you, and I want to cry, because I can't get anything right. Loxwood throws his head as I abruptly turn him in the other direction, because of course, once again, I've just made another mistake that affects him. *Sorry. Sorry. Sorry.* I'm furious with myself, and I'm also furious with that stupid voice coming across the speakers, because what difference does it really make which end of the ring I come out of? They both lead to the same place. And now my horse is suffering, again, because they couldn't just let me trot the few extra strides needed.

Once we're out of the ring, Loxwood comes back to a walk, and I lean forward again to rub my hands up and down his neck, his coat silky against my bare fingers. *Stupid.* The word replaces "sorry" now. *Stupid. Stupid. Stupid.* I have everything I've ever wanted. *Stupid. Stupid. Stupid.* I always thought all I needed was Loxwood, because then the rest would be up to me. Loxwood was the golden ticket. He was my chance to escape my stupid little life, and break into a world where I could dare to imagine a different life for myself, one that just doesn't happen to people like me. And I got the ticket. I stepped foot across the threshold. I was welcomed with open arms. But now my foot has slipped on the shiny tiles, and I'm falling, limbs flailing, and I don't know how to get myself back up. And I can see Loxwood, standing just out of reach, and hard as I try, I can't get to him. And my soul feels like it's being ripped to shreds, watching the chestnut horse slip from my grasp, and nothing that I'm doing is making the slightest difference.

*Loxwood.* This word is worst of all. *Loxwood. Loxwood. Loxwood.* I can feel each letter burning my throat like acid, and it's all my fault.

    Wrecking my own life I can deal with. But his is what kills me.

    A few months ago, the world felt like a sea of possibilities. But now I'm gasping for breath, fighting a moving current, as Loxwood drifts further and further away from me. His golden body being eaten up by the waves, pulled towards the precipice. And I'm utterly powerless, fighting against the salt that is drowning me, and catch a glance of him being pulled off the edge of the Earth, before the sea pulls me under.

# Chapter 8

I didn't know it was possible to feel so low when you're about to go into the final phase of an event on a sub-thirty score. When I got back to the stables twenty minutes ago, I untacked Loxwood robotically. Every moment was a chore, and I felt just about ready to topple over when I swung the saddle off his back, the weight an anchor to my arms. Rose tried to talk to me, her voice calm and comforting, as she repeated things I've now heard too many times to count. *It wasn't that bad. You've both just lost your confidence. It can be fixed. You don't have to do the cross country.* If I had a pound for the number of times each of those sentences have been repeated to me (well-meaningly, I know) then I might actually be able to afford my current lifestyle, and not be wondering how I'm going to pay for my horses' feed when we get back, let alone the next farrier bill. And having these things on my mind really isn't helping right now.

'Think about the horse you've got under you,' Rose says from the edge of the ring, once again confirming that my mind is not even a mere open book, but a flashing billboard for the whole world to see. The only problem is that I'm not quite sure how to hide it anymore.

A sunny day was predicted, and Mother Nature did not disappoint. The sky is the colour of the rosette I most definitely won't be leaving with, not a fragment of a cloud to obscure it, and shadows follow all of the horses around the large warm-up ring. How misleading they are - when I look down into ours, I see the outline of an event horse, the shape of a rider on top. No worry, no heartbreak, no sign that I feel like I'm going to shatter to thousands of tiny pieces. None of it shows. Only a girl and a horse.

'Georgia!' Rose calls after who knows how many circuits of canter, her voice offering no hint as to what mood she's in. She's probably going to tell me to withdraw, before I mess up another horse. And by this point, despite the fact that I'm inclined to agree, my body and mind feel so numb that I'm not sure those words will even cut through.

I bring Nantucket to a halt in front of Rose, who is standing far enough away from the gate steward that he can't hear us, and drop the reins. The only pain equal to that of knowing I've let my horses down is the knowledge that I have disappointed Rose. Rose, without who none of any of this would even be possible, who believed in me when she had absolutely no reason to, who not only welcomed me into her home but made me feel like family. And now I brace myself to hear the words I've already prepared myself for in my head.

As Rose steps round to Nantucket's right side, I keep a hand on his neck. My arms are so limp that I barely register her pulling the short whip I'm holding from my grasp, and watch as she brings it down on my thigh. Not hard enough to make a sound that would scare Nantucket, whom is happily standing as though he is being admired by a dressage judge, but hard enough that my whole upper leg stings.

'That was actually quite fun,' Rose says, eyeing the whip up and down. 'Now pull yourself together!' She speaks the words boldly, confidently, an order not a request, but not unkindly. 'Forget about everything else that has happened! It's done, nothing can change that, and he,' She points at Nantucket, 'certainly couldn't care less about the fact that you rode a bad show jumping round. Because - let's face it, you did - nothing's going to change unless you get some grit, put it all behind you, and get out there and ride. You think you're the only one that's ever messed up? You think that once you become successful that's it? You've made it, job done? You *never* stop learning. And it *never* gets easier. You just get up and get on with it! Success isn't a destination, it's something that has to be repeated every single day.'

Tears prickle my eyes, and I will them not to fall. 'What if I'm not good enough?' I slur.

Rose frowns, not making sense of my mumbles. 'What?'

I force myself to repeat the words, hating how weak I sound.

'No more of that!' Rose says decisively, finally comprehending what I'm saying. 'Stop moaning about talent, or lack of, or whatever it is you keep going on about! Actually, I'd quite like to ban the word "talent" as far as equestrian disciplines are concerned. Some people might find it easier than others at the beginning, but nobody's born with the ability to get round Badminton. How do you *get* good? You practise, end of. You don't succeed because something comes easily to you. You succeed because you fight back at every curveball. Nobody is born being the best. You get up and you train and practise until you are. Talent isn't what makes you drag your butt out of bed every morning. Now stop crying, stop moaning, stop making excuses. Do you seriously think Alex and Leni don't fail sometimes?' The mention of my friends, names I'm always referring to in conversation, uttering wistful remarks of wishing I rode as well as they do, fires my eyes up. 'Do you think they've alway been that good?' Rose continues, my thoughts clearly still on display, because the expression on her face shows that she knows this is working. 'That black horse of Leni's was a train wreck when he started out. And do you think they don't still screw up sometimes now, for that matter? Alex fell off in your class last time, and I saw her have a stop at a first fence last week. And do you see her proclaiming that the world is ending and that she should give up riding and become a recluse and take up knitting!? No! She gets her butt back in the saddle - granted, yelling profanities I'm not going to repeat - and keeps riding.' Rose pauses to look at the whip in her hand. 'Now, are you going to get going, or am I going to have to use this again?'

This time, when we come out of the start box, the words, '… one, GO! Good luck!' echoing behind us, I mean business. Nantucket shoots forward of his own will, but I push him on more, clicking my tongue and riding my hands up his neck. And Rose's last words, the ones she said before we went into the start box, play in my head. *It's cross country - ride as if you're going into battle.*

Nantucket eyes up the first fence, framing it with his ears, and I push him forward. No pulling, no adjusting, just going, plain and simple. *Jump the first fence as you mean to go on. The first fence is supposed to give them confidence. Mean business.* The grey

Thoroughbred meets it on a forward stride, and I click my tongue again on landing, urging him forward.

When I'm on course, I don't think about the disappointment. I don't think about Loxwood, or the fact that I'm not sure I have enough money to get by the next week, or this issue that I probably completely suck at this whole eventing thing. Because when I'm riding cross country, that's the only thing on my mind. I focus on Nantucket, galloping beneath me, and ride him into every fence as though a sinkhole would open up and swallow us whole if we didn't get to the other side.

And it works. And we come through the finish line, between the red and white flags, clear. And I'm thrilled, patting him again and again, but then I remember Loxwood, and my stomach sinks. This day is far from over.

'Well done!' someone says, and I recognise the rider as the person who spoke to me earlier. This time I make a mental note to memorise her number. 577.

'Thank you,' I say. 'Good luck.'

I don't know whether or not she wanted to keep talking, but I haven't got time. Rose comes up to me, ecstatic, and I almost want to climb out the saddle and throw my arms around her for all she's done.

Nantucket is untacked, sponged down, and put back in his stable with fresh water and a net of hay. Rose talks again about how I don't have to run Loxwood, but I shake my head. At the very least I have to try.

Soon we're off again, Loxwood walking purposely, and I glance down a second time to check that I remembered to swap the numbers in my bib round. Anything to think of something else. The fact that Nantucket has gone clear, and will most likely be placed, has barely increased my confidence. Because they're different horses, and right now I feel as though Loxwood and I have taken several wrong turns that we can't find our way back from.

I see Alex warming up, knees bent as she stands in the stirrups, encouraging Waffles to lengthen his stride down one of the long sides. A quick glance around the ring is enough to locate Joan Evans, talking to a woman with short hair, both of them standing with their arms crossed, faces giving nothing away. The typical body language of support crew. But true to from, Alex seems to be ignoring her mother, quite clearly warming up as she sees fit. And whatever she's doing is working, because Waffles looks great, jumping boldly and neatly.

Tightrope Act is announced as the next horse to go, and I begin trotting Loxwood as Alex gallops out of the start box, building speed straight away. I think about the first fence being jumped the way you wish to go on, and if the forward manner with which they clear it effortlessly is anything to go by, they are going to do great.

Rose is at the edge of the ring again, watching as I canter Loxwood round, and as I pass her she tells me to encourage him on more. I click my tongue, riding my hands further up his neck, and squeeze with my legs. Trying to make sure that my body language translates to "we mean business". The sun is beating down, and I can feel myself sweating beneath the tightness of my body protector. I'm sure many riders here are thrilled with the weather, seeing as it seems that sunshine rarely makes an appearance on cross country day, but the heat is doing nothing to help with the fuzziness that is my mind.

'When you're ready, pop him over the small log,' Rose says the next time I trot by her, and I push Loxwood back into a canter. He doesn't fall back behind my leg, or rush away from it, but instead feels like he's responding to it. Moving forward, while also allowing me to remain in control. My heart soars, because while it's easy to sometimes mistake a bad rhythm as okay, when the canter really is good you know.

I circle Loxwood once, checking that he really is between hand and leg, and moving forward with enough power and pace, before turning to the log. Coming out of the turn, when his ears swivel forward as he locks on to the fence, his entire attitude changes. His balance remains on his hocks, but his stride shortens, all momentum lost, and I feel his neck go rigid. I don't want to circle, because if this happens on course then we'll both just have to get over it, so instead I add more pressure with my lower leg, and use the whip to tap him on the shoulder. Loxwood reacts as though I've set a bomb off beneath him, flattening out his stride as he shoots forward, taking an ugly flyer over the fence, which leaves me thrown behind the movement and hanging on to the reins. Without wasting any time, I put him straight back onto a circle, and turn to the log again as soon as I feel in control. This time I'm prepared for him to take off and stay still, waiting and waiting, but we get too close to the fence, and I'm sure he's going to stop, but somehow Loxwood chips in a short stride, but the jump is even uglier than the flyer before. And just like that I feel myself panic again.

'Take him over it again,' Rose says. 'Just try and get a nice jump over it.'

I brought Loxwood back to a walk beside her, a timeout for the two of us, and before I trot off again I catch site of a grey horse flying over the last jump, whizzing across the finish line.

'*Alexandra Evans and Tightrope Act are home clear, and in good time, so they remain on their score of thirty-three point four.*'

The hairs on the back of my neck rise at the sight of Alex's joy. If ever I'm being held hostage, or being interrogated, and whoever is doing so is trying to make me break down, all they have to do is show a clip of a horse jumping the final cross country fence, accompanied by the rider's words of praise, and the yell of pure joy as they cross the finish line, and that would do it. Even now, watching Alex, who I wouldn't have pegged as the type to get overly excited by a clear round, and certainly not at this height, yell 'Good boy!' as they gallop the final stretch, patting Waffles as she does, makes me feel emotional.

Loxwood breaks into a canter as soon as I move my outside leg back, and I work on getting him into a forward rhythm. Get him confident, I think. There are only a few horses left to go before us, and he needs to trust me again. Like Rose said, he's just lost his bottle, and it's my job to help him find it.

We turn back to the log, and I think about keeping my body light and soft. Soft hands, soft seat, soft mind. There are more horses coming to the warm up ring now, and it's harder to focus on the fence when you're also trying to dodge people. But we're approaching it, and I make sure Loxwood knows so by channelling him with my legs. I only know he has once his ears line it up, and I feel his attitude change. I click my tongue at his hesitation, willing myself to remain still and let him choose the stride he wants. I count them in my head - three, two, one... It would have been perfect, but Loxwood's slowed his pace on approach, and is now too far off, so instead I squeeze my legs again, telling him it's all right to add another. But between both of our hesitations, I know the attempt is futile, and I'm prepared enough to not fall off as he slides to a halt, front legs colliding with the log so that it makes a sound loud enough to be heard across the whole warm up ring.

There are horses coming up behind us, wanting to go over

the same jump, so I quickly move Loxwood to the side, running a hand down his neck. I feel like my own breaths are choking me and I try to focus on inhaling and exhaling in a rhythm, like Rose has had me do before. I should probably go over to her, talk to her, but my mind is made up, and I ease Loxwood back into a canter before I can change my mind.

This time I really do make sure he is moving forward, knowing that the log is small enough to clear without much impulsion, just so that he can have a confidence-giving jump. He's worried, and I can feel the hesitation in his stride as we approach, but I'm insistent, clicking my tongue and willing him forward with everything I have, and Loxwood jumps. I reward him straight away on the other side, making sure he knows he's done the right thing, wanting to give him confidence. And before Rose tells me the same thing, or I change my mind, I raise my hand at the gate steward, who is looking in my direction, and shake my head.

'Withdraw,' I yell. I meet Rose's eyes, farther along from the board where numbers are written up, and she nods in agreement. I should have listened to her in the first place, but I needed to make this decision for myself.

Loxwood has lost his confidence, I know that, and going out on course now isn't going to do anything to help. I shouldn't even have jumped earlier. Because confidence isn't something you can make up for with one good jump in the space of thirty seconds, though it's that easy to lose. It has to be built up, gradually, like a jar of loose change. One penny isn't going to go far, because it doesn't count until there are loads of them. And there's no magic formula, either. It just takes time.

'Withdraw?' the steward repeats.

I feel myself hesitate for a second. I've been round this course once already, clear at that, and it was great. I want to know what Loxwood would think of that brush nestled between trees in the wood, and if he would even look at the coffin fence. And there comes a point when you have to try if you want to stand a chance at gaining anything. But I know that right now he's not ready. A bad round will only make things worse, and I'm acknowledging that. Because this isn't a movie where everything comes together for the big championship, or whatever. I need to go away, repair what has been broken, and hope I can do so enough to render the cracks invisible.

And I've got Nantucket, I remember, the thought of that clear round suddenly much more exciting now that I'm not worrying about getting another. This may not be the outcome I had planned when I got Loxwood earlier this year, but since when does life go the way you expect it to?

I run a hand down Loxwood's neck again, a horse that has lost his way, and I'm confident that I'm doing the right thing. Even if it feels cowardly, it's putting him first.

'Withdraw,' I say back, letting my reins out as proof.

The steward erases a number from the whiteboard, and begins speaking into his walkie-talkie, a crackling sound, followed by a beep, coming before his voice. 'Georgia James and Loxwood withdraw.'

# Chapter 9

By the time I've untacked and cooled off Loxwood, refilled both his and Nantucket's water buckets, skipped out the stables, brushed out sweat marks, picked out feet, and covered the small matter of carrying all my belongings back to the lorry, I'm boiling. It seems all anyone in this country ever does is complain about bad weather, but if it were as hot as this every day then I don't think any of us would bear it. And for once I have no shortage of clothes with me, seeing as I've packed for a few nights, so before going off to do anything else I swap my jodhpurs for shorts, leaving my white competition t-shirt on top. And it's only now, my head able to take a breather for the first time today, that I remember the fact that Nantucket is pretty much guaranteed a placing. The thought sends tingles down my arms, and I almost want to jump around. Because even if this event hasn't gone the way I had planned, nothing ever does, and to have achieved anything at all is unbelievable.

I stop at the stables again to check that Rose doesn't need my help, where I find her scrubbing at Paddington's not-so-white socks, before heading to see if there are any results up. It's only one o'clock, and while my day may be done, a lot of people are just beginning.

As I stand in front of the results boards, my eye first goes to the number *577*, followed by the name *Imogen Hollis-Rye*. Oh my god. Ohmygod. *Ohmygod*. Imogen Hollis-Rye. I knew there was a possibility it was her, that she was competing in the same class, but I still don't believe it. She isn't the most prolific of riders, but she came seventh at Badminton this year, and has made her fair share of European team appearances. And she congratulated *me*.

I've never disliked Imogen Hollis-Rye, but right now I vow to becomes her biggest fan and supporter as I look through the numbers for my own. I find Nantucket, and across from his name is that low dressage score of 28.3, followed by zeros where penalties should be, and then I see a *2*. I'm pretty sure it must represent time penalties, even though I know that makes no sense in a four year old class, but then I see a scribble at the top of the number, to the right, and all I can think is *No*. This isn't possible… But I look through the other placings, and feel the reality settle. We're second. More importantly, Nantucket is the second best four year old event horse in the country. I glance up at who got first, and my eyes fall on the number *577* again. Oh. My. God. Not only are we second, but we're second to none other than four star rider Imogen Hollis-Rye.

Suddenly all the heartache of the past few weeks, and months even, disappears. It seems horses are more lows than highs, but one good result, hard work finally being rewarded, one single triumph, is enough to make up for it all. A smile spreads across my face, and I think, *Now I can relax*. There's still the small issue of having to restore Loxwood's confidence, something I'm sure will keep my up at night, every night, for the foreseeable future, but right now, I just want to pretend that everything is okay. I've got two more days here, among friends and horses, and I plan on enjoying them.

I read through the results a few more times in search of anything interesting, and am happy to find that Alex and Tightrope Act are sixth, which I'm sure isn't a result Alex would usually get excited about, but considering what Waffles looked like when he first came out this season, I think it's a heck of an accomplishment.

The heat is unbearable as I sit in the grass to watch Rose warm up. I'll have to make sure Loxwood and Nantucket get out to graze in the shade later, or else they will boil. Not to mention the fact that Tuck and I have a prize giving to attend - the idea of which still doesn't seem real.

The competition in this class is high, but Paddington looks more than up to the other horses' standards. Rose rides him beautifully, and while he isn't the flashiest of horses, I still find that my eye is drawn to him, even though I'm trying to watch others. And my attention keeps being caught by a woman sitting farther along from me, intently watching the horses, while a kid I presume is her son is looking down at his games console. The woman, who looks to be going on forty, is familiar, but I can't think why. It would probably come to me if I looked at her long enough, but you can only blatantly stare at a person so many times without coming across as a psychopath.

Trying to work out why I know the woman is soon pushed from my mind as Rose pulls Paddington to a halt in front of me, and I jump up to remove his brushing boots.

'Thank you,' she says appreciatively, looking red in the face from the heat. 'You don't have to hang about, remember. I don't want you being late for the prize giving..'

'I've got plenty of time. And I want to watch.'

Rose smiles, before easing Paddington forward again, walking three strides before perfecting a canter transition, and I watch him swish his gleaming chestnut tail. *That's how Loxwood should look*, the self-hating voice in my head that won't shut up no matter how many times I tell it to murmurs. *Loxwood will be better in the long run*, the other super-optimistic one says. To be honest, I'm sick to death of them both.

I turn my attention back to the horses, where it is drawn to a nice, chunky bay, and it only takes me a beat to recognise him as Flintstone Cooper, one of Leni's. He doesn't belong to her, only Lochmere does, but his owner is one of the nicer ones, and I know that Cooper's future with Leni is pretty secure. The other horse she has a ride on, Arturo (who is the nicer of the two, if I'm being honest) is the one with the nightmare owner. *At least you own both of your horses*, that annoyingly perky voice says now, though this time I'm not quite so quick to tell myself to shut up. It's true, being in control of my own horses is something I've quickly taken for granted. If Loxwood weren't mine, than his owner would have most likely taken him away from any rider that succeeded in producing the two back-to-back performances we have.

Leni's position is perfect as Cooper trots around. Her seat both soft and secure, barely rising from the saddle, her hands still and close together, and her lower leg directly in line with her shoulders. The two voices in my head launch into a debate again - *you'll never ride as well as that*, says one, *Leni built her way up from nowhere*, the other reminds me. *Shut up*, I yell at them, then remind myself that I'm the one talking. *Get a grip, Georgia!*

Rose is asking Paddington for a half-pass when Leni trots Cooper in my direction. For a moment, I think she's coming towards me, but it's only when her head snaps back in surprise, and she calls the word "Hi" that I realise she hadn't even noticed me yet. Instead she's heading for the woman farther along from me, and it clicks.

'How's he feeling?' says Leni's mum.

Leni shrugs. 'All right, I guess. Where's Amanda?'

'Looking at a horse with Lottie. She said she'll be back in a second.'

'Okay,' says Leni, shooting her brother a brief glance before looking over at me. 'How did you do?' she calls, and I feel my throat tighten as her mum looks my way too.

'I withdrew Loxwood before cross country,' I say, with a lot of calmness considering what the voices in my head say about my current mental state. 'But Nantucket is second!'

'That's amazing!' says Leni, at the same time as her mother, who doesn't even know me, says, 'Wow! Well done!'

I see Amanda walking in our direction, which is enough to know that this conversation is over. 'Good luck,' I say, nodding at the approaching figure.

Leni glances over shoulder. 'Oops. Better get going. Georgia - mum. Mum - Georgia.' And with that she pushes Cooper back into a trot, and our ears are instantly filled by Amanda's voice as she says, 'He's on the forehand, Leni. Come on, shorten him up!' And the three of them move farther away.

'So nice to meet you, Georgia,' Leni's mum says, and when I look back at her I realise that she's moving closer towards me, leaving her son with his games console. 'We haven't met before, have we?'

I shake my head. 'I don't think so. I haven't been competing long.'

'I think Leni's mentioned you. You have the Thoroughbreds, right? From Newmarket.'

'That's me.'

'So lovely we have a chance to catch up! My name's Poppy, by the way, and that antisocial squirt over there,' She nods at her son, 'is Rufus.'

'It's nice to meet you,' I say, hoping I haven't already said that. But what else is there to say?

'Well, second! That's amazing! What class is that in? The four year olds?' Poppy says, saving me from having to come up with the next conversation topic. It's hard to say whether she was familiar because I have caught glimpses of her in the past, or because of the resemblance to her daughter. While Leni is taller, and leaner, with a slightly different colouring, and generally has a more serious air to her, there's also something so similar between the two of them. Leni's dark blond hair is thick and wavy, while Poppy's is both redder and thinner, and where her daughter's eyes are green, her own are icy blue. But their features are the same, and the way they smile, and the tones of their voices. And like Leni, Poppy makes me feel at ease, and not as though she's only asking me questions with the intention of being polite, but because she is actually interested.

I nod. 'Yes, the four year old class. It's only his second event, so I really wasn't expecting to be placed, but he did a really nice test. My other horse didn't do so well, though.'

'What happened?'

'Well - he's four, too - his first outing he went double clear, and then last month he lost confidence, and then today the same thing happened again, so I withdrew before the cross country.' I glance over at the area where Rose was warming up earlier, the sight of Paddington practicing halts reassuring me that I haven't missed their round.

'That's very good of you,' says Poppy. 'Better safe than sorry. That's what I always tell Leni. It's better to wonder what might have happened than to have it go badly. Competition is supposed to be fun, it's all about doing your best. The end result doesn't matter.'

'That doesn't sound like something Amanda would say,' I say before I can help myself. To my relief, Poppy seems to share the same sense of humour as her daughter, and she laughs loudly.

'No, it doesn't, does it? We don't share the same philosophy, but I trust her to keep my daughter safe. She's tough, and I don't necessarily agree with all her ways, but I know Leni's as well prepared as she can be going out on that course. You lot don't know how terrifying it is as a parent to see your child go cross country. I can't even watch! How does your mum hold up?'

'She doesn't come to events.' I say. 'My parents aren't really into horses, so they kind of let me do my own thing. I come with Rose. Holloway,' I add, and Poppy pulls a delighted face.

'Oh, I know Rose. Such a sweet girl! So lovely. She's always been so nice to Leni whenever their paths have crossed.'

'She is,' I agree. 'If it weren't for her, I wouldn't even be able to compete.'

'Is she riding?' says Poppy, looking round the warm up field, and I point out Paddington's chestnut body in the distance. As she gushes over him, I feel like it's my turn to return some of the compliments.

'I'm completely in love with Lochmere,' I say, thinking back to the time, before I got Loxwood, when I used to be glued to the screen whenever I watched him go cross country. Saying that, I still am. 'He's amazing.'

Poppy smiles, and I'm suddenly reminded of Leni's reaction the first time we met, when I said something similar. A genuine smile, seeming surprised by praise even though it's more than merited. 'He's a funny one, isn't he? But we love him. Leni's told you how we found him? Gosh, it took so long to get him doing descent flatwork. We were despairing. Show jumping wasn't much better, he just crashed through everything. He loved cross country, though. Mind you, he still tested Leni more than a few times, but once she put him in his place it was all right.'

'I can't imagine him crashing through a fence,' I say, thinking of all the times I've seen him show jump beautiful clears.

Poppy nods. 'I've still got videos, somewhere. Oh, he'd jump anything solid no problem, but he didn't make an effort with poles, because he knew they would just fall down. Of course, Leni insisted that was precisely *why* he would make a good event horse, because he wasn't afraid to touch anything. She still doesn't like show jumping, though.' I find that hard to believe, but I don't have time to ask anything else because Poppy points suddenly and says, 'Is that Rose going in?'

I glance over towards the dressage rings, and sure enough I see Rose and Paddington circling near one of the judge's cars, awaiting the bell.

'I'd better go,' I say, pushing myself up off the grass. 'Nice to meet you,' I say again.

'You too, dear. We'll be at the truck after Leni's done - come by! She always says I make too much food, we've got loads to spare!'

I thank Poppy again, reassuring her that I will make an appearance at some point, before going off to watch Rose.

Nantucket stands proudly, neck arched, ears forward, and biting my lower lip is all I can do to stop from smiling. I may not be on Loxwood, but I'm standing in a prize giving, beside none other than Imogen Hollis-Rye, on a horse I have produced myself. I can barely believe it.

A rosette is attached to Nantucket's bridle, and a sponsor or an organiser or both (who really knows?) shakes my hand, and I finally feel as though maybe, just maybe, this dream I have always had of making eventing my life isn't so crazy.

Rose smiles and claps from the sidelines as we canter the lap of honour, and my eyes fill with tears at the sound of music and cheers. No matter what happens in the future, with Loxwood, or any problem I should encounter with horses, I will always be able to close my eyes and come back to this moment. When we come out of the ring, I'm so proud of Nantucket that I fear my heart will explode from my chest.

'You did that,' Rose says emotionally, coming up to my side, clapping one hand on Nantucket's neck and the other on my thigh. 'Don't forget that, okay? No matter what has or hasn't happened with Loxwood, *you* made all this happen.'

I'm very grateful for the acquaintance of Rose's that chooses this moment to call her name, because if she hadn't walked away I'm afraid I probably wouldn't have been able to hold back tears any longer. Instead I take my feet out of the stirrups and slide from Nantucket's back, wrapping my arms around his thick, silver neck.

'You're amazing,' I say. 'You know that? You really are. Thank you for making my dreams come true.'

'Excuse me?' someone says, and I look up from Nantucket, not even caring that whoever is standing beside me probably overheard me talking to my horse.

'Hello,' I say to the woman. At a guess, I would say she's in her fifties. Her hair is blond, pushed back with a pair of sunglasses, and her face made up. While she isn't dressed in a particularly fancy way, money seems to ooze off her.

'Well done today,' she says, running a hand down Nantucket's neck.

'Thank you,' I say, thinking I just might get used to having people come up and congratulate me.

'You're Georgia? My name is Liz Woodley,' she continues. The name rings a small bell, which she confirms when she says, 'I own quite a few event horses.' She names a couple, and I try not to gawk at the mention of horses so notorious to all event riders. 'I also own the horse Imogen just won on,' she says, nodding at the spectacular-looking chestnut that is being cared for by a groom a few paces away.

'Congratulations,' I say, trying to be polite, and still not knowing what any of this has to do with me. 'He's lovely.'

'Yes, he is rather. But here's the thing. I've been keen to find another horse for Imogen, and we've been looking this past month to no avail. But Immy spotted your fellow here in the dressage, and asked me to have a look at him. We saw him jump earlier, and he really does have talent. He's exactly the kind of horse Imogen likes. A real nice stamp of a horse. They're few and far between these days.'

'He's not for sale,' I say, sensing exactly where this conversation is going.

Liz smiles, a smile that makes me feel rather uneasy. 'Every horse has a price.'

'He isn't for sale,' I say again, tightening my hold on the reins.

Swinging her handbag off her shoulder, she reaches in and

pulls out a chequebook. 'Name your price,'

Is this woman deaf or stupid or both? *She's rich,* I remind myself. Lulled into a false sense of security and conviction that money can buy you anything. Though in the world we live in, maybe the idea isn't so crazy.

'I'm not interested in selling him. You said so yourself - he has the potential to go all the way.' I force myself to hold Liz's gaze as her eyes meet mine, hoping to show her that I can be neither bought nor swayed. It obviously doesn't work, because she laughs.

'You're a smart girl, I daresay.' She opens up her chequebook, pulling a pen out of her bag with the other hand. 'Okay, since you clearly aren't stupid, I won't try to play around and negotiate.'

I want to tell her just where she can put that chequebook, but I'm too dumbstruck to do so. Instead I watch her perfectly manicured nails move with the expensive-looking pen, as the black ink spreads into a *3*. It's not enough for a top level prospect, I know that much, not that I would even consider it if it were, but for a fleeting moment, I imagine what I could do with three thousand pounds. No worrying about shoeing bills, or entry fees, or paying for overnight stabling. It wouldn't last forever, but it would be a weight off my mind for a while. But certainly not worth sacrificing Nantucket for, and I push the thought away as quickly as it appeared, watching Liz add three zeroes after the number three. But then she adds one more. And once again, the look on her face is enough to tell me that I have in no way succeeded in hiding my reaction.

'As I said, Miss James, you are a smart girl.' Liz pulls the piece of paper - which is all it is, at the end of the day - from the chequebook, and holds it out to me. 'And so I do not need to tell you that this is a very generous offer. Subject to vet, of course.'

'He's not for sale,' I say, the only thing I can think of, but there is an air of doubt to my voice.

Liz smiles as she runs a hand down Nantucket's neck, and I fight the urge to swat it away. 'He could be a four-star horse, you know, and Imogen could make him into one.' Her other hand, the one holding the cheque, is still held toward me, and I can't stop my eyes from looking at it, feeling very much, as I did that day I spoke those three fateful words some months ago, that what I choose to do next will alter my entire life. 'Take it,' says Liz, and I look up to see that she has been watching me. 'I don't expect you to decide right away, but why don't you hold on to this for the time being. How long are you here for?'

I force myself to speak. 'Until Sunday.'

'There you go. So are we. Perfect! I'll give you until the morning to think about it, and then if you do decide to accept my offer, which I think you will, then I'll organise to have him vetted before then, and if he passes we will take him straight back.'

I glance down at my hand, and somehow the cheque has found its way to my fingers. 'I don't want to sell him,' I say, my voice shaking. Earlier, I said that he wasn't for sale, and now the phrase has changed to merely say that I do not want to, and Liz knows it.

'Take the rest of the day to think about it. Nobody *wants* to sell a horse, but it doesn't work that way, does it? And I couldn't help but notice that chestnut you were riding..'

'Loxwood is not for sale,' I say, and I suddenly feel as though I am betraying Nantucket with the contrasting bitterness of my tone.

Liz laughs. 'I don't want to buy him! All I saw him do was

stop! But clearly he isn't going quite so well as this one,' She nods at Nantucket. 'And I would hate to see him end up refusing to jump like that chestnut. He's a good horse, and I'm sure you don't want to stand in the way of his future.' She pauses, taking in the anger on my face, and I just hope that she can't see the tears I am struggling to hold back, like trying to divert a river with a matchstick. 'People are already bringing up "that nice grey horse", and if I buy him, I promise you that I will be the first to tell people who I got him from, and how well he was produced. Not to mention the fact that you've got enough money there to find help with that Loxwood of yours. Anyway, I'll let you get on. I'm always around, and I'm sure Imogen would like a word with you at some point.' She smiles again, the way one does at a cute dog in the street, and walks away.

Only when I think Liz isn't going to turn back do I look down at the cheque. How can one flimsy piece of paper hold such value? I stare at the handwriting, each letter and number traced in a confident, accentuated movement. Why couldn't she have just offered me a few grand, and I could have refused on the spot. But *thirty thousand.*

Bored of no longer having my full attention, Nantucket nudges my shoulder, bringing me back to my surroundings. I look up from the cheque, panicked, as though I've been caught doing something I shouldn't.

'Hey, buddy,' I say, rubbing that spot between his eyes that makes him bob his head up and down. He smears foam across my white jodhpurs, but I don't even care.

Keeping a hand on Nantucket's head, I look down at what is held in the other. I feel like I'm in a nightmare - two options laid out before me, and I can only choose one. Yes or no? Left or right? On the one hand, Nantucket is a living, breathing thing, and how can a piece of paper match up to that? But when I think of the value written on said piece of paper, tens of thousands of pounds, it also seems ridiculous to consider refusing it, when the money can be mine if I only say the word.

Nantucket nudges me again, with enough force to send me back a step, and I feel my face give way. 'I don't want to sell you,' I say through quiet sobs, leaning forward to rest my head against his. Self-pity won't get me anywhere, but still I find myself thinking, *it's not fair.* I'm playing a rich man's sport, I've always known that, but still I find myself getting angry with the many people around me who won't have to sacrifice one of their horses because they can barely afford to feed it. Others my age who probably go to fancy boarding schools, home only at weekends to compete horses that are kept fit by a team of grooms, and who never even think twice of the cost of it all.

Ever since I was little, I've never been able to comprehend how somebody could actually sell their top horse. Even when Rose, not all that long ago, said those famous words. *I was made an offer I couldn't refuse.* And still I thought, *What? Of course you can! Just say no. I wouldn't sell a horse I loved for millions...* Yet here I am, feeling my chest tighten and tighten at the thought of losing Nantucket, but also not knowing what else to do.

'I don't want to sell you,' I say again, my whole face contracting as I speak the words. I don't want to, but I know, as inevitable as death is to life, that I have to.

# Chapter 10

By evening, I feel as though I have spent the day being thrown around like a volleyball. I spoke to Rose. I cried. She cried. I spoke to Liz. She most definitely did not cry. I spoke to Imogen, at least reassured that if Nantucket has to go anywhere, he's going to the best place he can. If he passes the vet, of course, which has been organised to take place tomorrow, so that Imogen can take him straight back to hers on Sunday if all goes well. For a moment, I thought, *What if he fails? The deal will be off,* and there was a flash of hope, but I pushed the notion aside, because as much as I would love to have this whole ordeal taken away from me, there no longer being a choice to be made, I can't wish Nantucket ill. What's all that rubbish movies and songs are always going on about? If you love someone you put their happiness above yours, or you let them go, or get out of their life to make it better, or something like that. The kind of things you spend your whole childhood being told, and ponder over for hours, because you just can't make any sense of it. And then one day, without even being conscious of the change, you realise that every word is true.

It's warm but cool as I walk across the lorry park, coming from the stables. The horses were fed a while ago, and Rose took up one of the many dinner invitations she received, not forcing me to tag along when I said that I wasn't up to it, and finally accepting my insistence that she still go, despite her offering to stay with me. I then spent another hour sitting in Nantucket's stable, watching idly as he munched on his hay. But as sick as I felt, my body was also shaking with hunger, so I got up, gave him a hug, and left.

Horse boxes I pass are abuzz with laughter and voices, riders and supporters blowing off steam after a busy day, reunited with those they only see at events. Some I recognise as people whose pictures once hung on my bedroom walls, and yet the day has left me completely immune to the joy I should feel at being part of it all. I just need to get back to the lorry, grab myself a cup of tea and a packet of biscuits, and crawl into bed…

'Georgia! Over here!'

I look to my right, where a noisy party is gathered around a camping table and make-shift chairs, and recognise the lorry as Leni's. Around the bowls of crisps and platters of pasta salad are the people I've come to know during the past few months, looking the way I probably did before Liz had to come and ruin everything. Even Amanda Walton, nickname Cruella, is sitting back laughing, drink in hand, as she talks to Poppy.

'Have you eaten?' says Leni, a few Pringles in her hand.

I shake my head.

'Come help yourself,' calls Poppy. 'We've got plenty.'

'Mum always makes too much,' says Leni as I walk towards

the table, wondering if I look as rotten as I feel.

'Not when Lexie and Ryan are here, I haven't,' she says, and I realise by Lexie she means Alex as I catch sight of the huge mound of pasta on her plate.

'My parents can't cook,' Alex says in her defence, the words barely audible through the mouthful of pasta she is chewing.

'I'd still take parents that have been round Badminton over parents that can cook,' says Ryan.

'No wonder your horses get fed up with having you on their backs,' says Thomas, who looks as clean as the rest of us do grubby, his feet perched on an ice cooler.

This is obviously some sort of follow up to an earlier conversation, because Alex sighs loudly, launching into an argument for what I'm guessing is not the first time this evening. 'Those stupid fences judges!' she shrieks, having swallowed down her last mouthful.

Leni slides her chair along to make room for another, and as I sit down she hands me a paper plate and says, 'Alex got a warning for excessive whip use,' which gives me enough context to understand the next part of her rant.

'...If you don't attack the first fence, it stops! I only have to do it once, and then he's fine. I didn't hit it a few weeks ago, and we slammed right into it! I'd like to see that stupid judge get Monkey over that fence without giving him a slap. I didn't even hit him that hard! If he wants to know what excessive use of the whip is, I'll show him.. I mean, what do they expect me to do? Sit back and wait for it to jump the fence itself? Idiots. At least Mum gave him an earful - that should be enough to make him wish he'd never said anything!'

Leni's little brother, Rufus, gets up from where he was sitting on the cab steps, and hands the games console he is holding to

Thomas. Without skipping a beat, Thomas looks down and begins flicking a few buttons, handing it back over to Rufus before saying, 'So, have you bought any horses yet?' to Alex. Meanwhile, Rufus returns to his seat on the step, enthralled by the game, and I can only assume that Thomas has unblocked a level for him, and that it is not the first time it's ever happened.

Since last speaking, Alex has reloaded her plate - how there was room for more I do not know - and is now chewing another mouthful. She nods, speaking once the food is down. 'Got my eye on one. French name - Chevalier des Lauriers? Is that the name of a horse? I think that's it.'

Leni nods, pushing the pieces of avocado in her salad to one side of the plate. 'There's a horse called that. I saw him - he's nice. Bright bay with a white face?'

'That's him,' Alex says, putting her plate down in favour of the ice cream cone that Thomas has just pulled out of a cooler.

'What about that mare James McDaniels is selling?' Thomas interrupts, referring to buying a horse from a four-star rider with such ease it makes my stomach flip. 'The one that beat you in the four year olds.'

'I hate mares,' says Alex, at the same time as both Leni and Ryan say, 'Alex hates mares.'

'Combine my stubbornness with a mare's and you'll never get anywhere. Anyway, as I was saying before I was so rudely interrupted,' she continues, glaring at Thomas. 'Chevalier, they don't want much for it, and I'm thinking I can wing it if Frosty's sale goes through next week.'

'You really should stop referring to horses as "its",' says Ryan, smiling in a mocking way.

'Says the person with the perfect horses who has no reason to. Try riding Monkey, and you'll call him an "it", too,' says Alex, taking such a big bite of her ice cream that I can't believe she isn't going to spit it out again.

I help myself to a slice of quiche, thinking the flow of the conversation might distract me from the sickness in my stomach enough to eat, while Leni puts her own paper plate down on the table. 'You know,' she says to Alex. 'You really don't need another horse.'

'I don't *need* another ice cream either, but what do you think I'm going to do as soon as I've finished this one?' Alex replies, licking a drop that has landed on her finger.

Seeming to be reminded of something, Leni turns in her chair to look in a plastic shopping bag leaning against the lorry behind her. 'There's chocolate as well, by the way.'

'Oh, well, chocolate I *need.*'

Rufus gets up again, stumbling back over to Thomas, who frowns at the screen. 'There's a hidden cube,' he says finally, and after a few clicks the console is handed back to a satisfied Rufus. 'Didn't you just buy another horse last week?'

'That's right!' says Leni. 'You went to Pompadour after Euros, didn't you?'

'What's in Pompadour?' I ask, swallowing down a delicious mouthful of cheesy leek tart.

'The French young event horse final,' says Alex. 'Pompadour is the venue - picture a bowl, with a racetrack running around the edge of it, and the cross country course is set in the middle..'

'Not to mention the fact that a castle runs alongside it,' says Ryan.

'We go down almost every year,' Alex continues, 'because everyone there wants to sell, and it basically just turns into a game of who can get first dibs. And you should see the tracks they jump, it's ridiculous! The four year old track might as well be twice as difficult as ours. More, even. Though they don't really have a set dressage test, which is odd, and most of the horses can't do flatwork to save their lives.'

'Neither can the riders,' mutters Leni.

'Ha! So true! Anyway, I bought a four year old Anglo, though I'm already regretting it. I mean, I've only had it a few days, and the thing's been going round these crazy tracks in France, and it doesn't even go on the bridle. It's never hacked, either. I thought it was going to pass out with fear when I took it down the tracks. It's a good thing it's pretty.'

'And your logical response to that is "I need another horse"?' says Thomas, leaning back further in his chair, ice cream in hand.

In response, Alex grabs hold of his feet that are resting on the ice box, and in one movement she sends him toppling backwards, his chair falling over until the back of it hits the ground, the ice cream colliding with his face.

Ryan doubles over with laughter, as does Rufus, and Leni turns to Alex. 'Does that make you feel better?'

Alex finishes the final mouthful of her ice cream cone. 'It does, actually.'

Poppy jumps up from her end of the table, in time to see Thomas sit up. 'What happened? Are you okay? These chairs are so unstable,'

'There's nothing wrong with the chair,' says Thomas, not unkindly, as he reaches across the table for a paper napkin to wipe his face. 'It's perfectly stable. Alex's head, on the other hand...'

This remark earns him a handful of crisps in the face, at which point Poppy decides that there is nothing to be concerned over, and returns to her conversation with Amanda.

'Are you done?' says Thomas, sitting back down, and staring

half-heartedly at what's left of his ice cream.

'For now,' says Alex. 'Messing with you is too easy. But for the record, getting another horse is a perfect response to almost every situation. That and a cup of tea. And chocolate. You always need chocolate.'

This prompts a debate over what kind of chocolate is the best chocolate, and Leni makes the most of the loud discussion to lean over to me. 'You okay? You don't look as happy as someone who's just come second should. Is it because of Loxwood?'

I shake my head, though it's partly that. 'Someone wants to buy Nantucket.'

Leni barely reacts. 'Not surprising. There'll be more people where they came from. You're not selling him though. Right?'

'No, I mean someone's really serious.' Not sure I can even say the figure out loud, I pull the cheque from my pocket and hand it to her.

'Ho-lyyyy,' She stops herself, the surprise on her face softening to concern. 'You've accepted, then.'

I glance over my shoulder to check that the rest of our party are still distracted by their own discussion. 'I don't know what else to do,' I say. On the one hand, I don't want to discuss just how difficult I'm finding things, because the last thing I want is to cause anyone to worry, but Leni's one of the few people who actually understands what it's like. 'Right now, if I don't cash that cheque, I don't know how I'm even going to feed my horses next week, let alone what I'll do when they need shoeing next. I could try and find another job, but…' I shake my head, letting out a breath. 'I just don't know how I could do it. I get up at four every day as it is, and between going to the yard, riding, and that stupid thing called school.'

'I get it,' says Leni, and we pause as the group next to us

erupts in laughter.

I look down at my plate, and speak aloud the words that have been playing through my head ever since Liz came up to me. 'I don't want to sell him,'

'I know.'

'And, apart from the fact that I love him, and the thought of not having him is unbearable,' I say, my voice surprisingly steady. 'It also feels like I'm giving up my one shot right now. All the progress I'd made with Loxwood has just… fallen apart, but I thought, "At least I've got Nantucket," and now not only will I not have him, but I'm left trying to get Loxwood's confidence back, and any chance of doing well next season looks about as likely as acing my A Levels.'

Leni looks thoughtful, and I feel guilty about the concern on her face. 'Selling horses isn't fun,' she says. 'It never is. I've done it too many times to count, and it breaks your heart every time. I don't have to at the moment, but for a long time it was the only way to get by. Alex still sells almost every horse that goes through her barn, because that's the only way she can fund the others. And Zach - know who I mean? I'm not sure if you've met him before? Anyway, he's obviously got a working pupil position now, but he still has to sell anything he's given to ride.'

'Is this supposed to make me feel better?' I say in a bid to lighten the mood.

'I'm getting there. Okay, here's the "but". Alex has never sold Anchor, and Zach has never sold Arthur, just like I've never sold Olly. If you had to choose between Loxwood and Nantucket, right now, you'd still choose Loxwood, right?'

It's like being asked to pick a favourite child. But we still both know that I can answer that. 'Yeah.'

Leni nods. 'Have you ever seen pictures of the pony I took to

Euros? Battersea? Chestnut, small white star - like Loxwood in pony form, come to think of it.'

'I saw the pictures of him in the prize giving,' I say, smiling as I remember the pony's appearance when the article about the Pony European Eventing Championships appeared in *Horse and Hound* that year.

'His stable name was Leo. Anyway, I loved him. He hadn't even been eventing two years when we got selected. He was only nine. He would have jumped a car if you'd pointed him at it. And I truly thought he would be one of those wonder ponies that went all the way. I mean, I know we all dream of taking our ponies round Badminton when we're little, but I truly believed it. But, as you can imagine, offers just came pouring in after Euros. And I mean ridiculous money.'

'And you sold him,' I say, knowing that Battersea is still competing today.

Leni takes a deep breath, and I realise that talking about it still isn't easy. 'Olly was just starting to go right. I'd already had him quite a while, and we were finally getting somewhere. But it cost a lot, because he needed so many osteo sessions, and ulcer treatments, and things like that. Not to mention running costs and entry fees. Once you get to one-star, you're talking hundreds and hundreds for one weekend of competition. And it came to the point that I - *we*,' she rectifies, glancing over at her mum. 'Couldn't afford to keep going without some serious cash injection. It was give up Leo, or give up on Olly. And it absolutely broke my heart. Even though he went to the best home imaginable, and I still get to see him to this day. But when it came down to it, when I had to choose...'

'It was Olly,' I finish for her.

'Yeah,' Leni says shakily. 'The thing is, sometimes you have to give up something you love in order to keep the thing you can't live without.'

I look down at my plate, all the sadness of today coming back to me. 'I guess so.'

'Who's he going to?' says Leni, lightening her voice as she sits up straighter in her seat. 'A pro?'

I nod. 'Yeah. You know Imogen Hollis-Rye?'

'Oh, she's so nice. And amazing, obviously. Actually, that's who-'

I don't get to find out the end of that sentence, because Ryan and Alex call both mine and Leni's names, asking us to judge their "which ice cream flavour is the best" contest, and for a short moment, everything else is forgotten.

# Chapter 11

No horse has perfect x-rays. Ever. Whether it be one front foot with slight damage to the navicular bone, or the hint of arthritis in a joint, or vertebrae close enough that you could potentially have a kissing spine problem later in life. Not to mention things like heart murmurs, or muscle tears, or any number of conformation faults that could lead to issues down the line. No horse is ever perfect, but Nantucket is pretty darn close.

'Imogen's thinking of taking him back tonight,' Liz announces to me, after sharing the news that he passed the vet.

'Excuse me?' I say, feeling like I've just been hit by a bus. Sunday, that's what we said. I thought I had one more day...

'She's taking some of the horses back tonight,' Liz continues, either clueless or simply not caring now that she's got what she wants. 'So we figured he might as well go back today. No point in him standing about here, is there?'

But he's with *me*, I want to say. In fact, I want to scream it.

But these people are professionals, and when you pay thirty grand for a horse, you don't expect to be made to wait for a seventeen year old girl to spend a few extra hours with said horse before you can claim him. Maybe it's for the better, less time for me to be around Nantucket and regret my decision even more.

'Okay,' I say.

'Excellent. They're looking to leave around four, so we'll send a groom to get him then, or do you want to bring him round yourself?'

We both know the answer to that question, and I think she's only asking to feel self-worth, so that she can praise herself for being so kind as to give me the chance to say goodbye to my horse. I'm filled with loathing for Liz at the moment, but I remember that her money is what's going to pay for Loxwood to eat, and that Nantucket is going to Imogen, regardless of whose name is on the paperwork.

Half an hour before I'm supposed to meet Liz and Imogen at the lorry, after Rose has already bid Nantucket a tearful goodbye, a groom comes by the stable, laden with travel boots. They're expensive-looking, far sturdier than the ones I've been using, and through the tears I force myself to remember that this is why I'm doing this. Nantucket is going to have access to the best tack and feed money can buy, and have the best shot at success. With each velcro strap I secure, I feel my insides collapse further and further. Nantucket and Loxwood should have always had access to items of this quality. And it's my fault that they haven't.

Nantucket stands still while I adjust his head collar, ears forward but not particularly attentive. I've brushed him to perfection, his coat shining like a newly-polished silver coin. His dark mane is even, and his tail flows like silk. His eyes look the way they did that day at Frank's - kind, trusting, showing no hint of him suspecting what lies ahead. My chest tightens again at the sight of him, something that has happened so many times during the past couple of days that I've probably seized some of my muscles beyond repair. *You did this,* Rose's words, come into my head. I try to repeat them to myself, try to ease away the pain. I've produced this horse. I've given him a shot at a better life.

'I love you so much,' I say, running my hand along his neck. I'm supposed to be at the lorry in two minutes, and if I start saying my goodbyes now I fear that I will break down, unable to recover in time to face Liz and Imogen. I'll have to do it once I'm there.

I lead Nantucket out of the stable, watching as he lifts each of his hind legs up high at the unfamiliar constraint from the travel boots. I was hoping to slip away quietly, but Loxwood has heard us walk out, pressing his nose against the railings of his stable with a whicker.

'Say goodbye to your brother,' I say, addressing both horses at once. Nantucket raises his head to Loxwood's, the grill separating them, only to look away with boredom.

The other horses are being loaded when we walk up to the massive horse box, Imogen closing a partition as a groom climbs back past it. 'There you are!' she says. 'Perfect timing. Do you want to lead him up?'

I nod, afraid that to speak would cause me to fall apart. At least Liz, whom I gave *her* horse's passport to earlier, isn't around, Clicking my tongue, I walk Nantucket to the ramp, and he follows me straight up, without hesitation. Every step farther into the lorry makes the pain in my chest grow bigger, knowing there's no turning back. And as I clip him onto the lead rope already in place, I want to yell that I've changed my mind, and rip up Liz's stupid cheque right here, but it's too late for that.

'Would you like a minute?' a voice says, and I look to see Imogen standing on the other side of the partition, with a smile that is both kind and compassionate.

I nod, too choked up to say anything, and she steps back down, leaving me with Nantucket, who is happily pulling at a haynet. 'See that woman?' I say quietly. 'She seems nice, doesn't she? Well, she's going to look after you now.' Still eating hay. 'I don't want to do this, believe me, I really, really don't. But,' Now the ugly crying has started. 'I don't know what else to do. You're going to be so well looked after, better than you ever have been. Okay?' He turns his head to me, probably wondering why I'm still standing here, and I collapse into his forelock. 'You made my dreams come true, you know that? And you are going to be a star one day - you already are. You're going to go to the Olympics, and win medals, and live the life of a champion. I know it.' I suck in a breath again, knowing that I've probably extended my timeframe, but I can't bring myself to turn around, because then it will be real. 'This is what's best for you.' I stammer. 'But I promise, one day, I will buy you back. I'll do everything I can, you have my word. If I win Badminton, you are what the prize money will be spent on. Though at this rate, winning the lottery seems more likely. I would have had a shot at Badminton with you, though. And I know you're going to make it.' I take another breath, glancing over my shoulder at the group waiting at the bottom of the ramp. 'I love you,' I say, kissing Nantucket's wide forehead. 'And... you deserve to be with someone who can afford to change your shoes.' And now I know I'm never going to walk away if I don't just do it, quick and painful, so I turn around, making no effort to hide my puffy face as I come down the ramp, handing a groom the lead rope I unclipped from his head collar.

'I've got your email address and number,' Imogen says. 'I'll send you a message to let you know he's settling in well. And we'll see each other on the circuit next season.'

I nod, struggling to stop a fresh onrush of tears as two grooms lift the lorry ramp, bolting it shut.

'You've done a great job with him,' Imogen says. 'You should be proud of that.'

And then, everyone starts getting in the lorry, and I'm left standing in the middle of the field as it drives away, regret increasing with every roll of the tires. I'm almost prepared to hear Nantucket neigh, his humble whinny calling out to me, but of course it doesn't. That's almost the worst part. If he'd looked back at me when I came back down the ramp, or neighed, or even flat-out refused to load, I could have borne it. I deserve to feel pain. But he didn't. His blind faith and trust, accepting what I ask, is what destroys me.

Loxwood's dark lips tug at the grass, and I focus my eyes on the movement. He's obliviously happy, in the evening sun, and I almost want to yell at him, *Nantucket's gone, don't you care? He's gone so that I can afford to look after you!* But I don't feel that way, because my anger at having to be in this situation is overridden by the pain.

'That horse stands out from a mile away.'

I look up to see Leni walking towards me, wearing blue jodhpurs and a polo shirt. 'For good reasons, I hope.'

'Oh, definitely,' Leni says, ruffling Loxwood's forehead as he lifts his head from the grass to nudge her, before sitting beside me. 'You all right?'

Might as well go for honesty. 'No,' I say, laughing with the word.

Leni smiles. 'You're rich, remember. It's not going to last

long, make the most of it.'

I laugh again, because if I don't I'll cry. 'That's true. What could I buy?'

'I saw some five hundred pound whips. Fancy one?'

'Seriously? There's such a thing?'

'The worst part is that they obviously sell, or else they wouldn't keep producing them,' She breaks off as a couple people start walking toward us, coming from the rows of temporary stables, one of whom is Alex, dressed in terry-cloth shorts and an over-stretched zip-up hoodie, and the person beside her I'm pretty sure is Zach, though I don't really know him. The closer they get, I know it's him, though, because Leni once said something about him having a scar across his face from when a horse threw him into a fence, which this guy does.

'What are you guys talking about?' Alex calls.

'Five hundred pound whips,' says Leni.

'I saw those,' says Zach, who like Leni is also wearing dirty jodhpurs.

'What? For real?' says Alex, sitting down next to Leni. 'Man, at the rate I lose them I would be in debt after one month.'

'You know,' says Leni. 'I don't get how you can lose whips so easily. I've had the same one for about five years.'

'So have I, come to think of it,' says Zach, looking at Loxwood as he speaks.

'Well aren't you two perfect,' Alex scoffs. Her eyes fall on me and she frowns. 'Who died?'

'Alex,' Leni says, not surprised so much as despairing.

'What?' says Alex.

'It's okay,' I say, almost relieved to have somebody openly acknowledge the fact that I look terrible. 'Nantucket's just gone. He's sold.'

'Sorry,' says Zach, before shooting Alex a look.

I shrug. 'It's life, I guess.'

'You know,' Alex says, addressing all of us. 'Someday, we'll all win the Grand Slam, and have so many sponsorship deals that we'll never have to sell another horse,'

'That'll be the day,' says Leni.

'No mucking out,' I supply.

'Yes!' says Leni. 'No mucking out. A team of grooms to do it all.'

'No riding other people's horses,' says Zach.

'None of that,' Alex says happily, and at the sound of voices our eyes fall on three people walking in this direction, not that they've noticed us. Erin, Ryan and Thomas, either laughing or fighting, who can tell? None of them will ever have to give up a horse to get by, I think, and Alex reads my thoughts. 'They don't realise how lucky they have it, do they? I mean, I love them, but come on! They have the easiest lives in the world!'

Leni laughs. 'One day. Right?'

I look at Loxwood, who has lifted his head to watch the approaching group. My heart feels ready to crumble, but I have friends beside me. I have Loxwood. Maybe someday everything will be okay.

# ROAD TO SUCCESS

## BOOK 4

# Chapter 1

I shouldn't have sold Nantucket. I thought - or at least hoped - that it would get easier. I never expected the hole in my chest to fully disappear, but I thought maybe, after some weeks, the pain would subside. But it didn't. It *hasn't*. Not that I want to forget about him, either. But every evening, when I'm sitting in bed and my eyes fall on the crumpled rosette on my desk, and the pictures I got from the photographer, of a grey Thoroughbred jumping each fence with tucked knees, I feel my eyes waver, as though the whole ordeal had only happened yesterday. Even when I see pictures online of him at Imogen's, accompanied by a caption about how well he's doing, or that he's going to be special, or whatever it is she decides to write this time, and I see those familiar eyes on a well-conditioned frame, I want to jump in a car, drive to her yard, and yell, 'He's mine! He'll always be mine!' But that's not how these things work. *A car.* That's what I got out of this, used a fraction of the money to pay for my test and an old jeep I saw advertised by the side of a road. Now I drive to the yard, saving me masses of time. But does that make up for not having Nantucket? On the way back from the championships, when I was too exhausted and depressed to even make conversation with Rose during the journey, my mind decided to go into overdrive and produce a list of everything I could have done to earn extra money. *You turn eighteen in February,* it said. *You could have found a way to manage until then, at which point you could leave school and work full-time.* It was like I'd had two doors in front of me, both identical on the outside, but beyond I could see that one offered a supposed life of luxury, and I stepped across the threshold, only to see that it was not where I wanted to be, but when I turned back around the door had blown shut, and all the pounding in the world would not get it open again. I made a choice, and now I am stuck with it.

My limbs are like ice as I climb into the driver's seat of the green jeep. Tucker, that's his name. And as much as I've come to appreciate his presence, he's still nothing on my other Tuck. I swallow hard, pushing away the lump in my throat that appears whenever I think of Nantucket. It's been almost two months exactly, but the thought still chokes me up. Even if I do have a car to face these December temperatures with. The weather in England changes so quickly - at the Four Year Old Championships, we were burnt to a crisp. But then the sunshine faded, leaving a grey sky in its wake, and winds began to blow through, bringing with them winter's sharp chill.

'I probably wouldn't love Nantucket so much if I didn't have a car to get me there. Hey, Tuck?' I say to my steering wheel. To think that if I hadn't sold him, I would be getting ready to cycle four miles now - or, more to the point, I would already be pedalling like mad, because I would be seriously late. I can see it in my mind, the image of Loxwood standing with his chest pushed against the stable door, giving it a kick every so often, head high and ears alert. The thought of him has always sent butterflies straight to my stomach, but since selling Nantucket, it comes with a pang. I love Loxwood more than I can put into words, and yet we've failed each other. He lost confidence in me, and I've struggled to rebuild it. The competition season doesn't start again for a few months yet, and I'm taking December slowly in view of the upcoming holidays. In other words, we hack if there isn't too much ice on the roads. If I'm desperate, maybe I'll do a small dressage session, working only on suppleness and self-carriage, but seeing a sand school kind of defeats the purpose of a break. Not to mention the fact that now that winter is approaching, the few DIY liveries that did ride out have now stopped doing so for reasons mentioned above, and are now crowding the school every evening, yanking cobs' mouths into submission. Which means that I could quite easily tack Loxwood up with a schooling session in mind, only to find that the arena is occupied, and I know better than to dare interrupt those precious sessions. Mothers giving me the evil eyes as their daughter seesaws on some helpless pony's mouth, obviously thinking that what she's doing is dressage. I wouldn't even care if they rode every day, and actually worked their ponies properly even if they didn't have any ambition to compete, but watching them take charge of the yard when they only ride once a week makes me want to scream. I practically never skip a day's riding, keeping Loxwood to his event horse schedule, and then these people leave me stuck, waiting in the courtyard with Loxwood's reins in hand, looking around me as though another sand school might suddenly materialise.

If possible, it's even colder when I climb out of Tucker at Rose's. I didn't notice the temperatures too much while I was riding earlier, because there's something about trying to keep young Thoroughbreds under control that stops you from doing so, and *they* definitely notice the chill in the air. But now I'm freezing, zipping my coat right up to my chin, pushing my tattered scarf up higher round my face. Good thing I put Loxwood's thick rug on last night. I need to clip him soon, but first I need to buy another cover - an even thicker one. According to the weather app on my phone, tomorrow's temperatures are set to plummet to minus-six degrees celsius. *Minus-six.* My head already aches from breathing in the cold weather we've had so far, but three degrees is still getting off lightly compared to what's in store. Not that I actually mind the cold, if I'm being honest. With sun comes flies, and when flies are around, horses seems to lose half their brain cells. I still remember the last couple of times it was hot - one because I was so ill that I could barely walk, and the other because I lost my best friend. As a consequence, hot weather and I aren't really on good terms at the moment. But below-freezing temperatures are enough to make me consider a reconciliation.

Even though it's been two months, I still have to fight the instinct to walk to the familiar stable in the courtyard. I've learnt to prepare myself for it now, from way back in the car park, but I don't always remember. If I'm distracted, lost in thought, or if I'm not thinking about anything at all, just moving around on autopilot, my feet take me to the stable door on their own. Only once did it happen that badly, that I wasn't even thinking of where I was going and ended up staring into the dark stable, trying to figure out what was out of place. In that moment it was like every effort I had gone through to bury the pain of losing

Nantucket, every shovel of earth I'd piled on top, had been for nothing, and it all climbed back to the surface, discarding my work. I turned around quickly from the empty stable, which still hasn't been filled, and managed to make it to Loxwood's before my face gave way to tears, pressing my eyes against his neck.

Now the safe thing to do is to keep my head down until I'm safely past the courtyard, walking round to what was once a log shed. Loxwood's nostrils flutter as he sees me, accentuating the angles of his face that come from good breeding, and I feel guilty about the fact that he looks at me like I'm the greatest thing since sliced bread, when really I'm a terrible person. *You should hate me*, I think. *Not only have I failed you, but I sold your best friend.* It would be easier if everyone could just hate me, which is what I deserve, and then I could go round like a ghost, never having to speak or make eye contact.

After feeding and haying Loxwood, I sit in the clubhouse with Paige, the two of us warming our hands around steaming cups of tea and fuelling our bodies with cookies. We don't say much because we don't need to, instead listening to the radio that plays in the background. And when enough time has passed, we turn our horses out in their respective paddocks and muck out. The methodical movements of forking straw and turning over the banks are second nature, too easily allowing my thoughts to drift. My fingers go numb when I clean out and refill the water bucket, which is nothing compared to the coldness I feel when I succeed in splashing half the bucket across my legs, soaking my jodhpurs. I swear under my breath, fighting the urge to tip the whole bucket over and throw in a kick for good measure. Stupid bucket. Stupid weather. Stupid socks with holes in them that are making my toes cold. Stupid *horses*. As soon as I've dragged the bucket to the door, settling it in its regular spot in Loxwood's stable, I climb up onto the deep straw bed and lean my back against the wall, my breath coming in heavy bursts. It feels like all the thoughts in my head are fighting for attention, each one getting louder and louder to the point that my mind is going to crumple under the pressure. I squeeze my eyes shut and lift my hands to cover my face, pleading with my mind to block the thoughts out. Just one moment of not feeling like a complete failure. Of not missing my friend so much that I can't bring myself to move. And I know I shouldn't be feeling like this, that I have no right to be this broken up, because I have Loxwood, and a very large sum of money in my bank account for someone my age, or anyone for that matter. But Loxwood is part of it, because things started to fall apart, and now I can't find it in me to piece everything back together when I feel like I am breaking. And the rest was my choice. I chose to sell Nantucket, even if only because it seemed like the only option at the time, so I have no right to feel like this. People sell horses all the time. Leni's given up more than she can remember, and Alex seems to buy and sell on a weekly basis. This is how it goes. This is what happens when you event. If you don't sell horses, you can't afford to ride them. But like Leni said, there are some that you just cannot sell, because to do so would destroy you. For her, that horse is Lochmere. Just like Alex's is Anchor Lane. And mine is Loxwood, so how can I justify feeling the same way about Nantucket? The thought of being parted from Loxwood used to make me feel sick, something I could barely fathom to imagine, which was one of the only comforts in selling Nantucket. Yet this is everything I imagined and worse. Does it always feel like this? Or did it really so happen that I found the two horses of my soul, and have parted with one that I never should have? I don't know anymore. I just know that I can't take much more of feeling like this, but I have no idea when it's going to stop.

The water that spilled across my jodhpurs has me frozen by the time I get home, ready to change for school. Wearing many jumpers, I fill a flask with instant coffee before heading back out the door, mobile phone in the other hand. I'm not quite sure what classes I have today, or what those classes are even about, because sitting at a desk for hours right now just gives my brain free will to ponder over every mistake I've ever made. Or more to the point, the same few mistakes over and over again.

I scroll through social media feed as I walk, barely looking up as I navigate a route so familiar that I can - and sometimes do - wander it with my eyes closed. As I scroll through various horse photos and articles, something jumps out at me, and even as I stand still to move back up the screen, I know what I will see.

*Nantucket.* Same eyes. Same laid-back expression. My chest swells, like my heart is expanding, only to have my ribs tighten and begin choking it. Imogen actively shares training photographs and videos of all of her horses, something about which my feelings are undecided at the moment. What's worse, never knowing what Nantucket is up to and being left wondering, or seeing updates every other day? I'm not sure either is easy, but at least I know he's okay. He's with a professional rider, I always remind myself. But that doesn't stop me searching the photos for any sign of him being in distress. I zoom in on his body, checking he isn't as thin as most competition horses are nowadays. I'll zoom in on his head, wanting to make sure he's still in a snaffle, and examine the tightness of his flash noseband. I can't stop myself from doing these things, even if I know that Imogen takes far better care of him than I ever could.

In today's photo, Nantucket is standing in front of a grid. Cross bars with bounce distances, leading to a larger vertical.

Beneath the visor of her riding hat, I can make out a smile on Imogen's face. The reins are loose against Nantucket's neck, his winter coat already clipped. I bite my lip in response to the feeling of nausea that comes over me whenever I see him, that feeling of disillusionment when I think about how that horse was once mine, but now he's not.

There's a caption below the photograph, which I read silently. **Early morning grid work session with Tuck. Makes light work of it, such an awesome horse! This is one special 4yo. Real one to watch for the future!**

The words make tears spring to my eyes, and I start walking again before I can allow them to fall. At least Imogen's right about one thing. Nantucket really is special.

# Chapter 2

'IT'S THE MOST WONDERFUL TIME OF THE YEAR!'

'Stop.'

'WITH THE KIDS JINGLE BELLING, AND EVERYONE TELLING YOU BE OF GOOD CHEER-'

'-Seriously.'

'IT'S THE MOST WONDERFUL TIME OF THE YEAR! Oh, come on!' says Clara, breaking off from her singing. 'Don't be a Scrooge!'

'I *am* Scrooge!' I say, wrestling my hair into a bun. Clara might have stopped singing, but the Christmas song is still playing from the speakers of the CD player that is mounted on the wall.

'What does that make me?'

I eye up Clara as she lays cookies onto a plate. 'Buddy the elf!' This makes us both crack up with laughter, and we're doubled over for far longer than we should be considering how pathetic the joke was.

'What's so funny?' says Lois as she walks in the room. Clara's older sister is home for the holidays, and in the three minutes I've been here she has already tried to come near me with a pair of scissors. She's training as a hairdresser, which means I've often found myself being a guinea pig. The first thing Lois said when I walked through the door was that the ends of my hair looked like they had been gnawed off by mice, hence why I hurriedly pulled the strands up as soon as she left the room. I don't have the patience to sit still for a haircut, however much I need one, not to mention the fact that my hair is still not back to my natural colour since I last let Lois anywhere near it.

'Your sister's Buddy the elf,' I say, which makes me and Clara laugh again.

'Georgia's Scrooge,' says Clara.

Lois pretends to look shocked. 'Georgia! Don't tell me you don't like Christmas!?'

'Funny,' I say, just as Clara joins in with the track in the background to belt, 'THERE'LL BE MUCH MISTLETOEING, AND HEARTS WILL BE GLOWING WHEN LOVED ONES ARE NEAR!'

And seeing my look of horror, Lois clears her throat to join in with the final lyric, both of them screaming at the top of their lungs, 'IT'S THE MOST WONDERFUL TIME OF THE YEAR!'

'You lot sound happy,' says Hope, walking into the kitchen with what I came here for in the first place in her arms. 'Here you go, good as new,' she says, placing the folded-up fleece on my lap. I was despairing when I found Loxwood had ripped his cooler a few days ago, prepared to throw it away, when Hope showed up at the yard and declared that she would have it repaired in seconds. Which was obviously true, because the fleece is perfect.

'Thank you so much,' I say, admiring the fact that the rug is no longer in two pieces. 'You didn't have to.'

'Of course. It was easy to do,' says Hope, putting a hand on the back of my chair to lean across the table for one of the many decorated cookies Clara has laid out. 'What's this one?'

'Cranberry and cinnamon.'

'Hmmm, yum,' says Hope, walking away with one in her hand.

Clara places a glass of milk down in front of me, and I help myself to a double chocolate chip cookie. 'Okay, so this part of Christmas isn't so bad. You know, you baking me loads of biscuits and stuff. But that's about it,' I say before biting into the baked good. 'Wow, that's good,' I say with my mouth full.

'See,' says Clara, sitting down. 'Christmas isn't *all* bad!'

'Uh huh,' I say, helping myself to another biscuit, this time one heavily decorated with icing. 'The only good thing about Christmas this year is that I have Loxwood, ergo I will not have time to actually celebrate it because I'll be at the yard.'

'You don't need to be there all day-'

'Shhh!' I interrupt, raising a finger as though I'm listening out for something. 'My parents might hear you, this town isn't that big. I have to be at the stables all day, therefore I will be unavailable to help with the Christmas meal. Got it?'

'That's...' Clara hesitates. 'Genius, actually.'

'Right?' I say, glancing back down at the fleece on my knees again. 'I've got to get going in a minute. It gets dark so early now.'

After dunking some more cookies in the glass of milk, I leave Clara's (with more biscuits in hand) and get in Tucker to drive to Rose's. It's only three o'clock in the afternoon, but already that feeling of nighttime being just round the corner is present. It starts getting dark at four, and you only have to be distracted for ten minutes before you find yourself beneath a black sky. And a small voice in my mind reminds me that I would be stuck right now without a car, which is only some small comfort for the pain. This is my first ever Christmas as a horse owner, something I imagined for a long time. I always thought about how I would hang Loxwood a stocking if ever he were mine, filled with carrots and apples, and how I would spend Christmas Eve with him in his stable, warming my numb fingers beneath his rug. How I would be wrapped in so many coats and scarves that I could scarcely move, but none of it would matter because I would be surrounded by horses and friends, all of us laughing about how we spend the day, while others are inside. Eating baked goods, warming our hands around cups of mulled wine. And I have all of that this year, yet none of the magic is there.

'DASHING THROUGH THE SNOW, IN A ONE HORSE OPEN SLEIGH!' The voice comes with Mackenzie's approaching figure, and she comes to a stop, clearly expecting me to finish the lyrics.

I shake my head.

'What? You must know the next bit. *Everyone* knows it!'

'I'm not a big fan of Christmas-'

'WHAT!?' Mackenzie cries, looking outraged. 'How can you not like Christmas! Don't you like presents?'

I shake my head. 'Not really.'

'Georgia!' She rushes towards me, grabbing hold of my arms. 'Christmas is the best thing ever! Come on, you'll see. I'll make you love Christmas, okay?'

Not likely. 'Knock yourself out.'

Mackenzie seems to find those words encouraging, and she lets out a squeal before throwing her arms around my waist, and continuing to sing *Jingle Bells* as she runs about the yard.

Christmas day, as I do every morning, I awake before the sun. Condensation has formed across the window panes, and no sooner have I swung my feet out of bed am I pulling on an extra jumper. And the fact that said item of clothing is red carries no significance as to my feelings about the holiday. Or maybe it could stand as a warning - *Run, run as fast as you can! Yuletide spirit is everywhere!* Perhaps that's why people wear red today. I could be on to something here…

It's still dark when I dodge sheets of ice to reach Tucker. There's the odd bedroom light on in other houses along the street, presumably those of parents being subjected to kids jumping on their bed and opening stockings. I can't even relate to it on any part, because even though I never particularly disliked Christmas when I was little, I never understood the excitement of it. My parents and family always got me presents of some sort (they're not *that* mean), but there was no joy to it. A plastic tree was always put up, and my mum would buy into any sort of decorations that shops were promoting at the time, but there was nothing to look forward to. I've always been an early riser, and I would wait for my parents to get up, and grandparents to arrive, before sitting stiffly by the tree, in a dress I hated wearing, to unwrap gifts and try to show that I was appreciative. There would be a meal, not that I particularly cared for a roast, and then everyone would sit on the sofa to watch whatever TV was showing for the day. Meanwhile I would countdown the hours until I could retreat to my room, where I'd return to my daydreams of owning a horse. And in the years since, nothing has really changed. Except that today, for the first time, I do have that horse.

It's starting to get light when I pull into the yard. I expect I'll be the only one here - except for Rose, obviously. Somehow, I don't imagine DIY liveries that often leave their horses until eleven o'clock without being fed treating Christmas day any differently.

'Morning, buddy,' I say, leaning over Loxwood's door. Even he wasn't expecting me this early, remaining still for a moment before taking a step towards me. I press my head against his, taking in the smell of horse coupled with that of the early morning winter air. When Nantucket enters my thoughts, I push the image away. The pain is still there, and ignoring it won't make it go away, but if I try I can allow another emotion to settle over the ever-present feeling of sadness. And today, I just want to spend Christmas the way I have always imagined - in my pyjamas (and a few jumpers), out in the cold, caring for my horse.

I've barely put Loxwood's feed bucket through the door when Rose appears in the yard. Checkered pyjama bottoms are tucked into boots, with a huge waterproof coat on over the top.

'Morning,' I say.

Rose smiles. 'Have you put the kettle on yet? The kids have already had me up for an hour and I need a break!'

'I'm on it,' I say, walking into the clubhouse as Rose goes off towards the feed room.

'Merry Christmas,' she calls back over her shoulder, laughing as she says the words.

I laugh, too. 'Merry Christmas.'

It turns out I was completely wrong in thinking that people would be awol on Christmas day, because it's not even nine o'clock and the clubhouse is already overflowing. Everyone views having horses as a way to get out of family celebrations, apparently. Paige and an elderly woman named Dora are here, the only DIYs that are ever on time, as is Leah, who wanted an excuse to leave the house, and Hope and Clara have already rocked up, because Hope's mum has already started prepping the meal and is driving them both insane. Mackenzie has already made an appearance, dressed in a onesie, to hand out personalised hand drawn Christmas cards. Mine features a chestnut horse looking out over a stable door decorated with tinsel, the name *Loxwood* written beneath it. It will go next to the one I got from Carrie, Paige's sister, of Loxwood and Brumby pulling a sleigh in the snow.

Ben is next to make an appearance, bringing with him a tray of paper cups filled with mulled wine, and plates of minced pies. The radio station in the background is playing nothing but carols, and everyone is either in their pyjamas or a ridiculous Christmas jumper featuring at least one reindeer of some sort or both. And we're all chatting and laughing, swapping stories of bad presents and annoying relatives and family members fussing over preparing a meal. And just for a day, or a moment, we all have something in common, and we're all on the same page. If this is what Christmas is supposed to be, then maybe I could get used to it.

At eleven o'clock, having brought Loxwood in early from the field, I decide that I've pushed my luck enough for now, and make for home. There I find waiting grandparents, all less outraged by the fact that I've been missing for so long and more so by the fact that I was out - and I quote - "dressed like *that!*" I personally think they look far more ridiculous in impractical clothes, ugly shoes, and ridiculous amounts of jewellery, but unlike them I am polite enough not to say so. Geez.

Just as everyone rises from their seats to begin washing up, after a painfully dull meal, I announce that I have to return to the yard, and run out of the door with a grin on my face. Seriously, getting out of these kinds of situations alone is reason enough to have a horse.

Loxwood nickers when he sees me walking towards him, and I slip straight into his stable, gliding a hand beneath his rug to check he's warm enough. His coat is clipped now, and I'll add a neck cover over the top for the night. Because it really is so unbelievably cold right now.

Soon I'll have to refill Loxwood's water bucket, and skip out, and top up hay and prepare his feed. But for now, when no one else is around, I just want to sit for a moment. Walking to the back of the stable, I collapse into a corner, landing in the deep straw. I'm still in my pyjamas, strands of hay are stuck to the jumper I'm wearing over the top, and I wouldn't have it any other way. This is how I like to live my life - outside, not caring how I look, focussed on what really matters, and putting my trust in something, or someone, I love. Horses are hard, tiring, more lows than highs, and generally don't seem worth the hassle when you try to explain it to somebody. But this life, among nature and wilderness, communicating with an animal so extraordinary that we almost shouldn't be allowed to tame them, whose presence we are not worthy of, is magical. This is the good life, and all other examples fall short in comparison.

Loxwood turns round to face me, stretching his neck out to nudge my knees with his nose. I laugh, putting a hand out, which startles him, and he takes a step back, only to realise his own foolishness and come back towards me. This time he doesn't shy away when I lift a hand to run it down his head.

'I really love you, you know,' I say, and Loxwood steps forward another step, his head hovering right above mine. 'You're the best thing that's ever happened to me, and all I ever wished for. But these past months have really sucked. And it's not your fault. And I know I've been angry, but it's only because I care so much. Everything I do is for you, you know that? Absolutely everything. I promise. You're the first thing I think about in the morning, and the last when I go to sleep.' He lowers his nose to my lap, and I trace the outline of his head with my fingers. 'I really miss Tuck,' I continue, pushing past the lump in my throat that usually has me hyperventilating with panic by now. 'I really, really miss him. And I'm sure you do too. We both lost our friend... But he's okay. He's living a better life than either of us are, and we need to stop thinking about him. Not forget - that'll never happen, and I don't want it to. But we, *I*, need to move on. Because I've got you, and you're the reason any of this happened in the first place. This time last year, you were still a racehorse, and I was sitting at home, wishing you were mine. When things get tough, it's so easy to forget all the good that's happened. But in a week, it'll be a brand new year. And it's going to be our year. You hear that? Next year is our year. We're going to go out there, all guns blazing, and show them all how it's done. What do you think, next Olympics? Maybe?' Loxwood nudges my chest, as if even he knows how stupid that sounds. 'Probably not,' I concede. 'But we should still try. Aim for the moon and the worst that will happen is we'll land on a star. Right? We've just got to do our best. I know you can do it, I believe in you so much. And I know you'll do anything to look after me, and I'm sorry I've made you doubt yourself. But we've got to try, Lox. I'm gonna give it my all, and I know you'll do the same. If you were with someone like Imogen, I know you'd succeed no problem. But I really don't want that. I really want us to make it together, and I know you're more than capable. I'm the problem, so maybe you can put up with me for just a little while longer, and I promise I'll learn to do better. And I know I've said this a lot of times, but please trust me. Please, please just trust me once more. I know we need to find our way again, so please trust me and let us do it together. Just put your heart on the line for me a little while longer, because mine lives there. I trust you so much, you have no idea. And everyone thinks we - *I* - am crazy, because I am basically resting my entire future on your shoulders, and I don't want you to feel pressurised by that because that's my choice to make, but it's only because I believe in you. So please, just bear with me a little while longer, and I promise we'll crack this. What's passed is passed, and from now on we'll start afresh. I know I'm a pain, and I complain a lot, and generally look miserable most of the time, but I mean it when I say you're the best thing that's ever happened to me. I care about you more than I do anything else, and that's really scary. Especially when I know you don't feel the same... And I know all this blabbering isn't going to help me convince you that I'm not crazy, but I love you so much. I'd sacrifice everything I own before seeing you suffer, I promise. Let's just work together, because I believe that we could have something really great. You already *are* great, but I want everyone else to know that. So let's work together, because we've got less than four years to make it to the Olympics. What do you say?'

Loxwood has grown bored of my monologue, and is now turning back to munch on what is left of his hay.

I smile, feeling the most peace I have since watching a certain horse box drive away a few months ago. 'Merry Christmas to you, too.'

# Chapter 3

I spend New Year's Eve the way any sensible person does - in bed. And I open my eyes early the next morning to a new year. Frank has given me the day off work, because apparently I look like the type to spend last night partying, which I actually find quite amusing, when in reality I was asleep by nine, and am now up at five to go see my own horse.

'How do you fancy another horse?'

I turn around from the straw, pitchfork in hand, to see Rose standing at the stable door, behind the wheelbarrow. 'I don't like horses.'

She laughs. 'I'm not sure I do today, either.' I smile, and she goes on. 'Anyway, the farmer that cuts the tracks for me has just called because one of his neighbours has had a horse living in their garden for a few months, and he's just seen that the thing's a hatrack. He confronted them, apparently, and they claim they can't afford it, and have told him he can have it in exchange for not calling the RSPCA. And when Greg tried to think of someone to call, I'm the first sucker that came to mind.'

I frown. 'That sounds dodgy. Do you actually know anything about the horse?'

'It has four legs?' Rose says. 'Actually, I don't even know that. But it's a Thoroughbred. So they say, anyway. It's not far away. Wanna come?'

Who ever says no to going to see a free horse?

Despite the freezing temperatures, the sun is bright as we roll along the narrow country lanes. Hay has found its way into every cranny and nook of Rose's car, and a thick layer of dust covers the dashboard. There are buckets and lead ropes on the floor in the back, and various coats are flung over the car seats. A working, horse person's car.

'You don't know how old it is, do you?' I say when Rose makes a right hand turn to go down a driveway.

She shakes her head. 'I don't think it's that old, though, because the people seem to think it raced last year. But I don't know for sure, no.'

We drive past a couple of shabby bungalows before pulling onto an expanse of concrete, surrounded by tin hangars stocked with thousands and thousands of bales of hay and straw. I'm not sure where we're supposed to be going, but Rose pulls the key from the ignition and climbs straight out, so I follow.

'Hi, Greg,' she calls, and I look over her shoulder to see a man with a short, stocky figure approaching us. At a guess, I'd say he's in his fifties, and he's wearing a big tweed coat, jeans tucked into wellington boots.

Giving me a brief but warm hello, Greg begins asking Rose about her Christmas and New Year, and I let my eyes scan the surrounding fields for sign of the horse as the two of them exchange pleasantries.

'Right, let's go see that mare,' Greg says finally, taking a step forward.

'Where is she?' I ask, walking beside Rose as she follows Greg.

'At the neighbours' - the second bungalow you went past coming in.'

'There's a horse there!?' I say, craning my neck to look down the driveway as I remember how it looked coming down. I didn't exactly pay that close attention, but I certainly didn't see a horse, and there were no fenced fields.

Greg makes a sound somewhere between a grunt and a laugh. 'Why do you think I called you?'

How I remember the bungalow being is pretty much accurate as I glance it for the second time today. The house itself is nice enough, but the lawn surrounding it is scattered with log piles and pieces of discarded metal. It's under an acre for sure, the garden bordering harrowed farmland. As the hopelessness of the situation reveals itself, I feel my heart sink slightly. I wasn't even aware it had lifted before now, but I can't deny it. What I was thinking about this horse I do not know - it's Rose's to save, anyway - except that I'm now conscious of the fact that for a moment, I wasn't thinking about Nantucket. Loxwood I spent a year pining for, while Nantucket came into my life completely unexpectedly, like it was meant to be. And while I'm not sure if I do believe in fate anymore, I thought maybe this horse was coming at the right time. But one look at this lawn assures me that any animal living here must be nothing more than a pet - definitely not a potential event horse. But Rose said it was a Thoroughbred...

As we walk round the back of the house, a small shed comes

into view, white wire fencing a pen the size of a stable from its door. A Thoroughbred living in that? I highly doubt it.

'It's in there,' says Greg, tilting his head to peer through the narrow doorway. 'Come on,' he says, to whatever horse is inside, clicking his tongue. For a moment, I don't believe a horse is really going to step out, but then it does.

Rose gasps, and I feel my stomach twist like a towel being wrung out. It doesn't even look like a whole horse, more like a shell of one. Her coat is bay, covered in scrapes and scars, and it looks like all her bones are fighting to escape her body, every ridge showing through skin. My first instinct is to unzip my many coats and throw them over her, because a normal horse facing temperatures this low without a rug is one thing, but a Thoroughbred that looks like *that* is another. I hear Rose mumble something beneath her breath, Greg replying with a similar remark, but I don't listen closely as my eyes drift to the mare's face. The angles that come from fine breeding are what give her away as a Thoroughbred, but that's not what's concerning me as I look over her dark eyes and the white stripe that runs between them. I've overcome with a nagging sensation of having forgotten something, and it's to do with the horse. Something's familiar, I know it. I'm so quickly convinced that I know this horse, somehow, and can almost feel my head ache from trying to figure out how and why. Like ticking items of a checklist, my mind goes through every possibility, and every horse I know. A Thoroughbred, that's what Greg said. And Rose said Greg told her it had raced... I stare at the mare, wondering if I've merely ridden past her on the gallops in the past, when it suddenly clicks.

'Cookiemoon.'

'What?' says Rose, looking over at me as she prepares to approach the mare.

'Cookiemoon,' I say again, pushing past the lump in my throat. 'Is that her name? Cookiemoon?'

Greg squints his eyes as he replies. 'I think they referred to it as Cookie.'

'You know her?' says Rose.

I nod. 'She was at Frank's - the same yard as Loxwood.' *And Nantucket*, I think, but I can't say his name right now. 'I never rode her, she was known as the horse the devil built.' It's true. Lizzie and Graham had both ridden her before, and were rather enthusiastic when the mare left the yard. But back then she had been strong and powerful, never taken out the box without a chifney. But this horse looks nothing like that, and as I compare the two images in my mind I feel like I'm going to be sick. I wasn't particularly keen on Cookiemoon when she was at Frank's, granted, but I never wished her ill. And no horse deserves *this*, no matter how evil they are.

Watching Rose approach the mare with an outstretched hand, I walk forwards to stand beside her. 'Hey,' I say, my voice quiet as I watch Cookiemoon's anxious eyes. 'Cookiemonster,' I say, remembering Lizzie's nickname for her.

'How did she end up here?' says Rose, looking at Greg as she runs a hand down Cookie's skinny neck.

'The people picked it up cheap for their twelve year old daughter. But she couldn't ride it, and then they just left it out here.'

'Of course she couldn't,' I say. 'Almost nobody could.'

'How old is she?' asks Rose.

I don't know which one of us she was addressing, but Greg shrugs at the same time as I say, 'Four. Four this year, anyway, I think. Yeah, she was three last year.'

Rose runs a hand down Cookie's forelimbs before stepping

back to examine her more critically. 'Bad feet,' she says to no one in particular, before sighing. 'What do you want me to do, Greg?'

Greg chuckles. 'You know what I'm suggesting. You don't *have* to do anything, but they're willing to give the thing away. Your call,'

'You know you're not giving me much choice when you show me a horse like this,' Rose says.

'Would you rather I hadn't called?'

'You know the answer to that,' says Rose, running a hand along Cookie's back. Even in her near-death state, the mare pins her ears back.

'Careful she kicks,' I warn. 'She used to, anyway.'

'Not only are you trying to convince to me take in a horse that could collapse tomorrow, Greg, but one that could kill me.'

'I'm not going to make you,' says Greg. 'But it can't keep on living like this.'

While Rose continues looking over Cookie's limbs, I hold a hand out to her nose. Flickering her ears backwards, she stretches her neck out to blow warm breath onto my cold hands, letting out a suspicious snort. 'Haven't changed much, have you?' I mutter, keeping my eyes on her teeth as I run a hand down the front of her head.

'She's very upright behind,' Rose says, and from the expression on her face I can tell that she's trying to look past Cookie's terrible state to get an idea of her conformation, or more to the point, whether or not it's worth even investing time in her.

'She actually did quite well,' I say, remembering her racing results. 'Placed a couple of times when she started out, but then she began refusing to leave the starting stalls. It's her attitude that was the problem.'

As if accentuating the point, Cookie kicks out a hind leg as Rose runs a hand across her croup, before quickly jumping out the way of the oncoming hoof. 'Attitude's everything.'

'I can't believe she ended up here.' I say.

'That's racing for you,' Rose mutters. 'Some of it's great, but then the ones that aren't fast enough - or don't have the right attitude - get chucked out like this…'

I look away, hoping I've done so in time for Rose not to see the tears forming in my eyes. Because although Cookiemoon is the one in this state, standing in front of me, all I keep thinking is that it could have been Nantucket. It could have been Loxwood, too, but I was never going to let that happen. But the pain of the past few months has had me wondering what would have happened if I hadn't spoken up when a certain grey horse was about to be shipped off to a dealer. It's a selfish thing to have thought, and yet the idea persisted. I wouldn't have known the feeling of elation I experienced upon cantering that lap of honour, and the pride in seeing a rosette be pinned to my horse's bridle, but then I wouldn't have had my heart torn in two. I wouldn't have gone to bed every night for the next few weeks in floods of tears, unable to stop the shaking. And I wouldn't resent Loxwood, because he would still make up the entirety of my heart, and I wouldn't have had to give up one of my best friends. None of the pain had seemed worth the reward, but seeing Cookiemoon now reminds me exactly why I got Nantucket. It wasn't about me, it never was. It was about *him*. Just like how my plan was always to save Loxwood, even if it did mean saving myself in the process. I've forgotten that lately, and the hurt I felt losing Nantucket is nothing compared to how I would feel if I hadn't got him, and it were him standing here today without an ounce of muscle or fat on him. Maybe I did do something right after all.

'What do you say?'

I snap back to reality, my thoughts obscured, as I glance at Rose and Greg, both of whom are looking in my direction.

'Sorry?' I say.

Rose grins and nods at Cookiemoon. 'Well? Do you want her or not?'

'I hate that horse!'

'So do I. Or, at least I did.'

'Have you gone mad?'

'I've always been mad.'

'Well, that I can't argue with. But seriously, you've willingly taken on the Cookiemonster!?'

'She's not *that* bad,' I say to Lizzie, pushing my hands deeper into my coat pockets as I lean back against the stone wall. By chance, we both reached the yard gates at the exact same time this morning, and I dragged my friend to one side to fill her in on yesterday's events. 'She loaded well, and she only tried to kick me once in the stable, so I think that's a success.'

Lizzie laughs. 'I can't believe you've bought the Cookiemonster,'

'I didn't *buy* her,' I say. 'I'm not quite that stupid. She was free. Besides, you should see her. She doesn't exactly look like she can do any damage even if she *does* kick,'

'Just wait until Graham hears this,' says Lizzie, shaking her head in disbelief as she pushes herself up from the wall and turns into the yard.

'Unlike you, Graham actually has a soul,' I say, following her. 'And when he hears what state she was in, I assure you he'll be on my side.'

'You say I don't have a soul like it's a bad thing.'

'It's generally considered to be, yeah,' I say, but I'm pretty sure she's stopped listening. Lizzie's walking off towards the stable of her regular ride, and it's so cold that despite not feeling up to riding when I awoke this morning, I suddenly want nothing more than to be hoisted into the saddle and warmed by the effort of galloping up Warren Hill. And with my eyes set on Mackerel's stable door, I stride across the courtyard.

'Hey, boy,' I mutter, pulling my hat on. But as I look over the half door, Mackerel Cloud isn't there.

Other horses are beginning to be led out of their boxes, tacked up and ready to go, and as I look either side of their (mostly bay) bodies, I spot Frank and his clipboard.

'Morning, Boss,' I say, dodging a prancing filly to get to Frank's side. 'Where's Mackerel?'

Frank shakes his head. 'Gone.'

'He's been sold?' I say, my voice coming out pitchy with shock. Mackerel finished the flat season last year as one of the best colts in the yard. I was relieved, in fact, that I wouldn't have to worry about him being chucked out any time soon. But it never occurred to me that the owners would move him.

Frank shakes his head again. 'Dead.'

'What?' I say, my voice barely a whisper as I force the words past the lump in my throat that is beginning to become a permanent feature.

I can tell from the way he sighs before speaking that Frank is upset, but that doesn't change the casualness with which he says it. 'Broke his fetlock on the gallops yesterday. There was nothing we could do. Vet came and put him down.'

'What? How did it happen? He's always been fine...'

All this time, Frank has been standing still, but now he looks down at his clipboard and begins walking. 'These things happen, Georgia,' he says, stepping through the doorway of his office, and the use of my first name makes me feel uneasy as I jog to catch up with him. 'It's all part of the business. Nothing we can do about it, so we move on. Anyway, take the Dazzler filly out today...' My ears switch off at the words, and I come to a stop. Frank hears - or more to the point, doesn't hear footsteps beside him - my switch in attitude, and he turns to look at me. 'What's the problem?'

I've always had great respect for Frank, but right now I almost don't want to look at him. 'He was three years old,' I say, the words coming out with hatred.

'Four this year,' Frank says, frowning in confusion. I don't exactly blame him - I'm not even sure what I'm saying myself.

'He was an amazing horse. He didn't deserve that...'

'It was an accident,' says Frank. 'Like I said, these things happen-'

'But they don't just happen.' I say. 'Mackerel started racing when he was two... That didn't *just happen*. He was trained to!'

'What're you getting at, James?'

'They're horses,' I say, not caring how pathetic the words sound. 'They're not machines. They shouldn't just run until they break a limb, and then get a bullet through the head! Or if they're not fast enough, for that matter.'

I know from the look on Frank's face that I'm pushing my luck, taking to my boss like this, but I don't care anymore. 'Look,' Frank says, his expression softening. 'This whole situation's crap, but there's nothing any of us can do about it now. So go home, James, take a break, and come back in a few days time.'

In the silence that surrounds us, neither of us speaking, and horses moving farther away, I'm aware of my breathing, coming in rapid bursts. Looking back over my shoulder, through the doorway, I see the heads of the horses left behind, waiting to go out in the next string. They may be well looked after, stabled on clean bedding and always fed on time, but they're still business investments. As I stare out at the courtyard, I'm struck by a memory. One of those I haven't forgotten so much as ignored, suddenly playing in high definition. A flashing image of myself walking into the yard and finding a canvas screen propped up around the back of a trailer, and the sound of something heavy being thrust into it, and then the giant pool of dried blood that remained on the concrete long after the vehicle drove away. The grooms scrubbed at it for days, but it was weeks before the stain disappeared. I can still see it now, out there, if I really look. But the point is that one second a horse was in the yard, then it reared up straight and fell over backwards, breaking its neck, and then it was nothing but a load of bones, carted away without a second thought. Nobody mourned for that horse, just the lost money. It was a freak accident, sure, but how can you refer to something as *freak* when it happens so often? The only reason horses are that wired up to begin with is because they're contained in boxes, never being turned out, and fed in a way that elevates their energy levels. And I clearly remember, for one moment as I watched the trailer disappear, that I looked around at everybody else in the yard, for a sign of pain, but the only emotion present was that of annoyance at having to deal with the whole situation. I hadn't been working here for long when that happened, at this job I worshiped, so I pushed the matter from my mind, and my thoughts were quickly occupied by Loxwood's arrival a couple of weeks later. But right now I feel like I have been wearing rose-coloured glasses for the past year, unaware, and now that the lenses have cracked they can never be repaired.

Frank has taken a seat at his desk, either not seeing me or just pretending not to as I glance over at him, watching as he goes over his list of horses and riders. I wonder if rearranging the schedule without Mackerel happened the same way as it does doing so without me. A simple chore, one of many, effected in a matter of seconds without great concern. But any minute Frank will be getting up to follow the horses to the gallops, and I can't bear to be here any longer. He still hasn't looked up when I slip back out the office door, where I stand stranded in the courtyard. There are a couple of grooms around, but there all far too busy with their own jobs to notice me. And yet I can't bring myself to walk away...

'Hey, you,' I say, walking up to the nearest horse. A chestnut - not as nice as Loxwood - with a disproportionate head. It must have a smaller than normal brain, too, because I can barely get a reaction of any sort out of it as I run a hand down its neck over the stable door. Instead I move to the next stable, wishing I hadn't as soon as I look over the door. The filly's name is so unpronounceable that we just shorten it to Fi, but there's a reason I usually stay away from her stall. She's a box-walker, one of the most extreme I have ever seen. If you didn't know any better, you'd think she were possessed. She walks round and round, never reacting to your presence, her body tilted at an angle, both rigid and straight. She almost looks like a broken wind-up toy, stuck turning in circles to no avail. Except the shapes Fi walks look more like triangles. You can call her name and shake food all you want, but she doesn't snap out of it. Being locked up almost every hour but one of the day has driven her to insanity, but she wins races, so nobody cares about this minor inconvenience. In fact, the only person it is an inconvenience to is her. The expression "not an inch to pinch" couldn't be more accurate, because Fi's body is so lean and tight that it's sickening to anyone who knows how horses are supposed to look, though clueless owners and bettors mistake it for fitness.

'Hey, sweetie, it's okay,' I say, leaning against the door and rubbing my fingers together. I know it's useless, but I still try. Soon, a groom will walk in and catch the filly, tack her up, and then she'll get her allocated slot of galloping before being brought in again, and she'll go back to box-walking, and so it goes on. A nervous breakdown she'll probably never recover from - certainly not unless she gets turned out twenty-four-seven in some massive field. But so long as she wins races, that isn't going to happen. The horses are here to earn money, plain and simple

'Come on,' I say, snapping my fingers again. 'You're okay. You don't need to do that.'

I'm still not expecting Fi to cease, but suddenly she looks at me, slowing her pace for a moment, and I feel my heart contract.

'Good girl. Come to me. Come on.'

She almost comes to a halt, contemplating whether or not to come towards me, when Frank walks out of his office, distracting the mare, and the connection is broken as she moves forward again. I give it a few more goes, not caring that I'm just an exercise rider and it's not my place to do anything about it, but my efforts are futile. Fi keeps turning, falling into the middle of her stable, and she's still going when I turn around and leave the yard.

# Chapter 4

Rose has a new horse. After a couple of her working-liveries were sold before Christmas, she was given another youngster to produce. He bears the boringly obvious moniker Midnight Sun, and is as talented as he is feisty. He isn't horrid or anything (if he were, Rose wouldn't have accepted him into her yard), but he thinks he's the most magnificent creature in England, which may well be true but doesn't change the fact that he needs bringing down a peg or two. His stable name is Sunny, which is quite funny considering his serious manner - I think Alex would approve. Sixteen hands tall, the only characteristic of his Thoroughbred dam, but with all the muscle and strength of his Holsteiner sire. Sunny is dark brown, tan shining through a black coat, and amazing under saddle considering he's only been backed for a few months, even though he's five years old. A true warmblood, he excels on the flat, with the kind of natural paces that Thoroughbreds like Loxwood can only hope to achieve with years and years of training, if then. But Sunny does spend the whole time he isn't either in his box or turned out prancing around like an idiot, be it in hand or when ridden. His antics are nothing compared to Cookiemoon's, though.

A month she's been at Rose's, during which she has gained condition, something that has only increased her temper. It takes about ten rears to get her to and from the paddock, something I am now more than accustomed to. I didn't dare turn her out with Loxwood the day she arrived, a decision I have not once regretted. The last thing I need is him being kicked, not to mention lured over to Cookiemoon's dark side. *Cookiemoon.* It's such a ridiculous name. *Cookie* is almost worst. Unsurprisingly, Mackenzie thinks it's the greatest horse name ever. But compared to the classic beauty of *Loxwood*, and the whimsical feel of *Nantucket Winter*, I think it sucks. It's the kind of name a dog gets stuck with when it's named by a two year old, not fit for an event horse. Saying that, I'm sure it's another one that Alex would approve of. Waffles, Fruitloop, *Cookie*. Right up her alley. It'll be a few more weeks at least until she's in good enough condition to begin working, so at least I'm not having to worry about my head being pounded in just yet. There's only one person Cookie doesn't regard with hatred and that's Paige. Suddenly the devil turns into an angel, happily standing to be groomed and caressed. I offered her to Paige outright, an offer I'm pretty sure she would have accepted if she were in a financial position to do so. But she can barely afford to keep Brumby, let alone another horse. And if I'm being honest with myself, Paige is probably too loyal to him to accept another. So here I am, with a nightmare mare in the stable where my lovely grey gelding used to be. The only good things about the situation is that A) I have less time to think about said grey gelding, and B) Nothing Loxwood does looks bad in comparison.

March rolls around before I know it, but with it does not come the spring weather we're all holding our breaths for. If anything, it gets colder. Grey skies become the norm, accompanied by gusts of wind so bitter you can barely breathe, often made worse by sleet or rain, and we're supposed to live in the driest area in England. I entered me and Loxwood for an event at the beginning of April, which basically means that no matter how bad the weather conditions, we're riding. Last year, our competition season didn't have the greatest end, to put it mildly, and I'm not making the same mistake twice. This month is booked with cross country sessions and dressage lessons, neither of which I will be taking lightly. Loxwood lost his confidence last year, something that hasn't exactly boosted my own. A moment to lose, a lifetime to repair. Same old story. But it *can* be repaired. It was there to begin with, so it's just a matter of finding it again.

When I entered the event, it felt like it was an age away. But the weeks building up to it, filled with training outings, tick along quickly, each one seemingly shorter than the next. Thanks to Rose taking Sunny cross country schooling numerous times, I'm able to get a good few sessions in with Loxwood. Things are much improved on last year, though I haven't nailed the problem. There are still times when I think he might stop, and he does, but he'll jump on a second attempt. I'm cautious not to do anything that could cause him to doubt either one of us, wanting Loxwood to trust me, but on the inside I'm terrified. I used to take pride in being fearless, of never being afraid of getting on any horse at the track, regardless of their reputation. And that's irrelevant, really, because that hasn't changed, but there's another kind of fear. Not a fear of falling into a fence or getting crushed beneath a horse, but of failing. I'd take a little pain any day over hurt emotions. A broken limb you can see, shattered belief in yourself is easier to hide, and much harder to repair. I already feel like I've failed, and to do so further, especially when Loxwood is involved, scares me more than any image of myself falling ever could.

'We've got to redeem ourselves,' I tell him Friday evening, running a hand down his neck, his muscled topline accentuated by a newly-plaited mane. The young horse classes don't start until later in the season, so Loxwood is running in a ninety-centimetre, most likely against horses with far more experience than him. I already know Alex has got Tightrope Act in the same section, not to mention her many other horses competing over the course of the weekend. Leni has Lochmere in their first three-star at a different event, so she won't be there tomorrow. But there's another person who will be, which is concerning me far more than my friends' whereabouts. Imogen. And more to the point, Nantucket. The thought of seeing him again, for the first time since he ceased being mine, changes from anticipation to dread every thirty seconds. My heart leaps with joy when I picture his dark eyes, knowing I'll be able to throw my arms around his neck, but then I fear that all the work I've done these past six months, trying to get over him, will be lost. But *six months!* Six months without seeing someone you love, someone you used to spend almost all your time with. Maybe this is what a breakup is like, except I reckon this is far worse.

'I don't know what I'd do if I couldn't see you for that long,' I say to Loxwood, leaning against the stable door as the chestnut Thoroughbred finishes his feed. 'G'night. Sleep tight. I love you.'

I'd forgotten the stress that comes with going to an event. At least it isn't far way, near enough that Rose and I drove to walk the course yesterday, thus saving us having to rush and do it this morning. But it's still an early start, not made any easier by the freezing temperatures. It's so cold that we even keep the horses in their stable rugs for the journey, and I'm wearing not one but two pairs of tracksuit bottoms over my jodhpurs. And even though I'm so worried about today that I can barely believe the fact that my shaking legs haven't given way on me yet, I'm also at ease being back in this competition environment. You have to thrive off it, if you want to ride professionally. The adrenalin and the crowds have to give you a buzz, fuel you on further. I just hope Loxwood remembers that today, too.

Hard as I try not to, my eyes are scanning the other lorries in the park as a volunteer directs Rose to a spot. Part of me wants to fling the passenger door open and run past all the horse boxes, in search of Nantucket. But even if it weren't for the fact that I'm on a tight schedule, and that I have a horse to prepare and a starting fee to go pay, I know I need to forget about him for now. Today's about Loxwood, and I'll think about Nantucket once I've done what I'm here to do. It's easier said than done, though.

We're midway down the order, so that when we ride to the dressage warm-up, the ring is already packed. Hard as I try to concentrate solely on Loxwood, I find myself staring at each grey horse that goes past, feeling my stomach both lift and sink simultaneously. This isn't helped by the fact that the organisers are running behind schedule, leaving me with twenty minutes longer to warm up than I need, providing the perfect opportunity to observe. But then one grey horse walking this way appears familiar, and I brace myself for pain, only to realise that he *is* familiar, but not Nantucket. It's Tightrope Act, and Alex.

'They're running behind,' I call to her as she comes towards me.

'By how much?' says Alex, her voice tense.

'Twenty minutes.'

'Oh, good,' she says, her entire attitude changing. 'He's in crazy mode today, I'm going to need every minute I can get. Anyway, how've you been?'

We exchange stories of riding horses in sub-zero temperatures and having to sit through family Christmas meals for a couple of minutes, all the while Alex is absently watching a horse perform his test in the ring beside us, and her neutral expression turns to a frown.

'What's wrong?' I say, looking over my shoulder at the horse, whose perfect head carriage does little to reassure me about my own chances.

'Do you think she realises her circles are supposed to be twenty metres?' says Alex.

I look at the horse again. 'No, that's right.' I say, turning back to Alex. 'Fifteen metre trot circle.'

'Wait, our test is the ninety-six, right?'

I shake my head. 'Ninety-seven.'

'WHAT!? Are you kidding me?'

'Ninety-seven,' I repeat.

'Oh my god,' Alex says. 'It's not funny,' she continues as I fight back a laugh, but she can barely get the words out without cracking up herself. 'Do you have the test on you?'

'Here,' I say, pulling it out of my jacket pocket. 'How can you not know which test you're supposed to be doing?'

'I *thought* I knew,' says Alex, Waffles jumping beneath her as he spooks at his rider unfolding the piece of paper I've just handed over.

I figure Alex kind of needs to concentrate right now, so I wish her luck as I push Loxwood into a walk. Looking back behind me, I see Alex alternate between looking down at the paper and up at the horse in the ring, her lips moving as she does so, followed by a finger tracing shapes in the air. I laugh again.

Although it's cold, the sun is shining, the warm rays occasionally breaking through the freezing barrier. It's Loxwood's first time out in a big environment since the championships, and thankfully he doesn't seem too overwhelmed by it. If anything, the busier the atmosphere, the more chilled out he is.

I've just collected Loxwood up into a working trot, keeping him supple and responsive to my aids, when Alex rides over to me, dressage test in hand. 'Okay,' she says, handing me the piece of paper as I slow Loxwood to a walk. 'I think I've got it.' She didn't even have the test five minutes, so I highly doubt she "has it", but I don't say that out loud. Instead I go back to working Loxwood, and Waffles is pushed forward into a sitting trot. He looks magnificent, even if he is on fire, and I wonder whether I should start riding Loxwood's tests sitting. At this level, it's the rider's choice whether they sit or rise, and so far I have stuck with the latter. *Next time*, I think. I'm not exactly going to start changing things today.

My attention is focussed on Loxwood throughout the remainder of the warm-up, but I'm unable to stop myself from glancing over at Waffles as he and Alex ride into the ring, and I'm left eating my words as the test is performed to perfection. I spent weeks learning and practicing the test, and here Alex goes, memorising it in two minutes flat, a fact that does not show in the slightest. To her credit, though, she seems equally surprised, riding past me in a fit of laughter, exclaiming that she is "never running through a test again". Granted, on a horse as worked-up as Waffles it works, because he can't anticipate any of the movements. Maybe I'll give it a try next time around.

I don't ride into the arena with an attitude of defeat so much as I'm acknowledging the fact that I can't exactly do any worse than I did last time out, which relaxes me enough to transmit the feeling to Loxwood. I'm not sure about the technical side of the test from a judging perspective, but it's soft and loose, and without major errors. I catch Rose briefly on my way back out of the warm-up area, where she is riding in on Sunny, and she gives me a thumbs up, so I can't have done that badly.

Back at the lorry, I tie Loxwood up beside Paddington while I put on his boots, shorten my stirrups, pull off my gloves, and grab a whip. I offer him a drink from a bucket, but he's uninterested, so I decide to get on with it and ride to the show jumping ring. Rose has planned to come help me warm up once she's down with Sunny, so I work in on the flat while I wait. By the time she appears, in her riding kit, I've cantered Loxwood on each rein, and he feels like he's between my hand and leg. Rose makes sure I have him moving, encouraging me to lengthen his pace down the long sides, before coming to the cross pole. *Increasing stride*, that's what she keeps saying. That doesn't mean taking a flyer, just not hooking in front of the fence. I interpret her instructions the best that I can, and I don't know if I succeed or not, but Loxwood clears the fence reasonably, which as pathetic as it sounds is a relief. I only jump the same obstacle once more, before moving on to the vertical. Whenever I sense Loxwood hesitate, I make sure to keep my legs firm against his sides, encouraging him forward but without pushing him out of his stride. And we make it through the warm-up without any poles (or myself) flying to the ground, which I'm going to consider an accomplishment. Rose looks happy, smiling encouragingly as a steward calls my number to the ring.

'Just keep your leg on,' she says, as I trot to the entrance. 'Shoulders back. Never stop driving to the fence. Do whatever it takes.'

*'Our next starter is Miss Georgia James, riding her own Loxwood.'*

I touch my hand to Loxwood's withers as the starting bell rings, before sliding my outside leg back and pushing him into a canter. The last time the farrier came, I had him put in stud holes, in which I stuffed cotton-wool and oil, and screwed in studs before my dressage test this morning. The grip serves an even greater purpose now, as Loxwood accelerates through the turns, across already churned-up ground, and (for once) I'm glad about my decision. I've got the equipment, now I just need to use it.

Loxwood's ears flicker as we turn to the first fence, and I squeeze my calves in response. *Yes, we're jumping it.* He builds up speed, and I neither push him on nor hold him back. Instead I try to sit steady, keeping an even pressure in the reins, and looking straight ahead at the next fence. I feel Loxwood hesitate on take-off, and I will my attitude to remain the same as we make it over the jump, putting it behind me as we continue onwards to the next jump. This time I ride more positively, determined, and Loxwood picks up on the feeling, jumping far better than he did the last obstacle. We continue on to the next fence, which occurs without incident, and then I turn to the first double. It's a long two stride distance, and I feel Loxwood come up in front of the withers as he eyes up the second element. This time I'm pretty sure I do need to get firm, and I squeeze my legs tighter again, growling under by breath. The chestnut Thoroughbred jumps the first, but he's still unsure of the second element, backing off, and there isn't time to start thinking, so I give him a firm kick in the side, backing it up with a tap on the shoulder with the whip. Loxwood reacts as though I've set a bomb off beneath him, responding by throwing himself into the air, knocking the top rail as he does so. Part of me instantly scolds myself for reacting too strongly, but then the other is pretty sure that he would have stopped if I hadn't. I remember what Rose said, telling me to do whatever it takes, and I'm reassured in my decision.

I almost want to laugh when I turn Loxwood to the last combination and he responds by powering forward, as though saying, "Okay, I get it, I have to jump. I won't mess about this time." And he doesn't, making the distance easily, and I turn him to the last, feeling a lump rise in my throat as I miss my distance, but Loxwood jumps anyway, my back jarred by the awkwardness, but we land clean.

'*Just four faults to add for Georgia James and Loxwood,*' the speakers announce.

Despite a few ugly moments, Rose is clapping when I come out of the ring, and I feel happier than I have after clear rounds in the past. We had some issues, but we fixed them.

'*That* is how you ride yourself out of trouble,' Rose says, and I feel my cheeks redden with pride.

'I did miss that last stride,' I say, running a hand up and down Loxwood's neck.

Rose shakes her head. 'Doesn't matter. So what? We all miss sometimes. But he tested you going through that double and you did the right thing. You should be proud of that round. And *that* is how I want to see you riding cross country. Understand?'

I nod, my mind still buzzing from the sense of accomplishment I feel from that round, and I walk Loxwood off for a few minutes while Rose goes back to the lorry to get Sunny. At almost every event I've done so far, I've had a thirty minute window between show jumping and cross country phases, leading me to ride from one to the next as quickly as possible, but today I have over an hour to wait. After letting Loxwood walk round for ten minutes, I start heading back to the lorry park, passing Rose and Sunny as I do. I untack Loxwood, throwing a cooler over his back and offering him some water, before pulling off my number bib and jacket in favour of a heavy-duty coat. The sun might be out, but it's still freezing, and I relish in the snug fleece lining.

Loxwood is happy munching hay beside Paddington, so I decide to leave him ten minutes to go watch Rose, which still leaves me enough time to take the haynet away early enough before the cross country. I grabbed one of Mackenzie's homemade chocolate crispies from the lorry, which is one of the only things I can even think about eating right now without wanting to be sick, and I nibble on it as I walk.

Sunny is trotting around the warm-up ring when I get there, and I'm so busy watching him that I almost don't see. The figure in my peripheral vision, clouding it like a ghost. I so nearly don't see, because I'm not looking for it, but then I sense it, my body responding to something my mind isn't aware of, and I look to my right, and my heart stops. I want to look away, to turn around and hide before tears fall down my face, but then he sees me too.

'Hey, boy,' I say, because I can't not address him when his eyes are looking right at me.

And Nantucket whickers.

# Chapter 5

Tears spring to my eyes, and I feel goosebumps rise across my arms, which has nothing to do with the cold. At the sound of Nantucket's nicker, Imogen follows his gaze to me, as does the woman she was in the process of talking to, and I only realise then that it's Liz. They're both looking at me now, from where there are on the other side of the rope, and as much as I want to ignore them, I can't.

'Hi,' I say, forcing brightness into my voice as I take a step closer towards them. As I do this, Nantucket whickers again, and I feel my heart falter. To their credit, Imogen and Liz at least have the decency to look affected by Nantucket's outward show of affection, their eyes going from him to me. Imogen recovers first, though.

'Georgia!' she says, smiling. 'I didn't know you were here, how lovely. How's it going? Have you got your chestnut here?' What's even more annoying than standing here and exchanging pleasantries is the fact that Imogen actually sounds sincere.

'Yeah,' I say, feeling uneasy at Liz's silence as she eyes me up. 'He's already been show jumping, and his cross country's in an hour. He's doing great,' I add that last part for Liz's benefit, remembering the way with which she referred to Loxwood during our last meeting.

Nantucket whickers again, and seeing that nobody tells me not to, I crouch beneath the rope to shuffle into the ring, running a hand over his head. 'Hey, buddy,' I say. 'I've missed you.' *Miss* is an understatement, but I'm being watched, so it'll have to do for now. It feels surreal, being here with Nantucket, able to run my hand across his coat, something that has only been a memory during the past six months.

'He's doing great,' says Imogen. 'Everyone loves him. Does everything you ask of him,'

I nod politely, plastering a fake smile across my face, as though I don't already know all of this. Yes, he's perfect, I know, thank you very much. Rub it in, why don't you. Giving him up is the biggest mistake I've ever made, one that worry led me to feel powerless over.

Liz still has yet to say anything, which I'm pretty sure is her way of showing that I'm not welcome here, so after patting Nantucket some more I excuse myself, with excuses of needing to get ready for cross country and I'm sure you need to get warming up and I won't bother you further. What was that? Yes, we'll definitely catch up later. Yes, nice to see you too. Goodbye for now. And I feel like the wound in my heart that has been there ever since Nantucket left is being stretched further and further with every step I take away from him. I don't even stay to watch either him or Sunny jump, because the only thing that can comfort me right now is Loxwood. He's happily pulling at his haynet when I reach the lorry, and I throw my arms around his neck, silent tears running down my face, before pulling myself together and getting him ready for our final phase.

I catch Rose briefly before I ride off to the cross country course, her main concern being whether I'm okay at having seen Nantucket again. I lie, saying yes, and we then move on to the matter at hand as she gives me tips for the impending warm-up. Paddington's dressage is at the same time as my course, so Rose can't be there with me. I've already promised both her and myself that if the warm-up is a complete disaster, I will withdraw. But I really, really don't want it to have to come down to that.

My fingers are webbed through Loxwood's curling mane as we ride to the cross country course, my stomach in knots. Training's been going well, I remind myself. Rose and I have put last season's blunders down to something that started out as a harmless mistake on my part, not helped by stress and fatigue, and I then became worried to the point of self-destruction. I was overly confident, a feeling that soon turned to panic, and the problem became the fixation of my life, but I was too tired and stupid to fix it, until finally acknowledging that things would only get worse if I didn't raise my hand and take the pressure off. But now I'm not worrying about how to afford feed for Loxwood, or worrying about everything being perfect. When I started competing, I promised myself that if years of being on the sidelines had taught me anything it was that you should never take a chance for granted when you finally get one. And yet after one single success, I expected the rest to be handed to me. I sat back, waiting for Loxwood to do the job, and then complained when it didn't happen. I'm not making that same mistake today.

I don't have my own cross country colours, just the plain blue hat silk I normally ride in, paired with competition jodhpurs and whatever top I happen to be wearing, which today is a fleece beneath my body protector. Even riding I'm cold.

Seeing the horses on course gallop past him has sent Loxwood's energy levels up even higher, his neck tensing up as his eyes look about ready to pop out of their sockets, and he prances beneath me. I move one hand forward to touch his withers, but it's a bit like trying to pet a dragon. In other words, he couldn't care less.

Before presenting him at a fence, I make sure that Loxwood is moving away from my leg, stretching out his stride to cover ground. And although I wish Rose were standing in the middle of the ring, ready to help me should I need it, there's also something quite good about warming up alone. You're not just following instructions, or working with the sole goal of earning a few remarks of approval. When there's nobody there telling you what you should be doing, you're fully focussed on the horse beneath you. You have to do what feels right, not what you *think* you should be doing. You work with what you've got, reacting instinctively, and while we all need help sometimes, it's also important to have this time alone, when it's just you and your horse. Let's face it, there's no third person with you when you go out on that course.

I turn Loxwood to the smallest log, his ears flickering as his eyes lock on to the fence. It's nothing he hasn't jumped before, but I can feel his hesitation. And while I'm careful not to hold him back, I also don't want to fire him to the fence, so I try to sit still and let him choose his stride. Loxwood clears it, but the jump's sticky, and certainly not the sensation you want going out onto a course. So when he lands on a right lead I carry on, pushing him into a collected rhythm before turning straight back to the fence. This time Loxwood is more confident, having cleared the jump once already, and I'm satisfied when we land on the other side, pushing a hand forward to scratch his withers.

There's a narrow palisade in the middle of the ring - not particularly big, but the kind of thing a horse is likely to find spooky enough for it to be considered a good one to jump before going on course. This time I ask Loxwood for a left canter lead, keeping my weight over my heels as I push him on down the long side, lowering my seat to the saddle through the turn to the fence. As it did the first time to the log, Loxwood's stride shortens as he comes up in front of the withers, backing off the obstacle. Again I try to ride it the way I did the first fence, careful not to give him any mixed messages. But Loxwood's still backing off the jump, and while my head is screaming at me to do something, to react, I'm merely left clinging on as his front feed slide into the palisade. The sound makes people look in our direction, and as Loxwood jumps away from the fence, I regain my balance in the saddle and turn him out of the way, allowing the horse behind us to jump. I'm still readjusting my reins when the dun flies over effortlessly, making me feel like I've just been slapped in the face. I move a hand to Loxwood's neck, hoping to reassure him as the accelerated rhythm of his breathing beneath me sends my own into a frenzy. I know most people would hit him in this situation, which would probably work, but I just can't bring myself to do it. I don't want to jump a horse that doesn't want to. And I *know* he loves to jump, or else he wouldn't have been so enthusiastic when we started out. I just need to help him believe in himself again-

Rose's words, cutting through my thoughts. She fills my head with plenty of advice, and I can't say that it isn't all useful, but it's very hard to put it all into practice when you're in the moment. But being a competitor herself, she does know how to phrase things, in a way that comes through at moments like these, when you're somewhat fearing for your life. When I was riding away earlier, after mumbling something about not wanting to force Loxwood to jump, she said something so cleverly put that I can't believe I'm only thinking about it now. *When a horse is nervous,* she said, *when he's unsure, it's your job to give him confidence. The more he backs off a fence, the more you attack it. You have to show him there's nothing to be afraid of, and he'll feed off your confidence. You have to have enough courage for the two of you.* It could be a load of fluffy, theatrical mush, granted. But the words, which I've heard before, suddenly click in my head, as though I've been staring at an image for ages, trying to make sense of it, only to realise that it's upside-down. I don't need to *make* Loxwood jump, I just need to show him that there's nothing to be scared of. He's had months to rebuild his confidence, and I've taken it slowly, but maybe now I need to start reacting.

'Two to go until you're up,' the gate steward calls to me, and I set into action.

I click my tongue, pushing Loxwood straight into a canter from a halt. I've already lost my pride, and any belief I had in myself, and I've lost Nantucket. And if nothing changes, I've also lost Loxwood. There's nothing left for me to lose now, so what's the worst that can happen?

As Loxwood hesitates on the approach to the fence, I urge him on. I'm not pushing him out of his stride, or asking him to speed up, but my attitude says *go.* What's the worst that can happen by riding like this, with the certainty that I'm going to get to the other side? I could fall, big whoop. And if I do fall, I'll get up, dust myself off, get back on, and go again. Because that's how it works. Your life doesn't fall into place because you succeed at something once, you keep succeeding because you never give up. But it's amazing how your attitude can change once you realise that you've already lost. Once you hit rock bottom, the only way is up.

It's not a great stride, though to be honest I'm not entirely sure *which* stride we should be taking, because neither of the options in front of me look great, but it doesn't matter, because it's not about being perfect, it's about getting the job done. Every ounce of my body is telling Loxwood to jump, not allowing myself to believe there is any other alternative, and we soar through the air, and by time I get over the shock of landing I'm not even sure which stride we took anymore, but it doesn't matter. I run my hand up and down his neck, saying words of praise, and we turn back to the fence again. This time I see a perfect stride, even though Loxwood is sticky on the approach, but I keep driving, never for one second expecting him to jump the fence on his own, while still holding him together. If the way it felt is anything to go by, the jump isn't pretty, but's that beside the point. This is cross country. If all I cared about was looking nice, then I would be in one of those hunter classes that both bore and confuse me to oblivion.

'Loxwood, you can go to the start box,' the steward calls.

We go to the start box.

# Chapter 6

This time, when Loxwood backs off the first fence, I attack it even harder. *The more he hesitates, the more confident you have to be.* The words whistle through my mind as we move across the course, and I'm not sure if it's that, or the fact I've barely eaten a thing today, or if I'm just going insane, but I feel invincible. *What's the worst that can happen? You fall.*

We get halfway around the course without incident, but then we come to a spooky-looking trakehner, nestled between trees, that no amount of positive thinking can get Loxwood over first time, and he grinds to a halt. I would be lying if I said that I didn't feel my heart sink, disappointment knocking aside the small hope that had formed since clearing the first fence, that I might just redeem myself with a clear. Ten minutes ago, I wasn't sure I would make it to the start box at all. So I don't let it fluster me, and instead take the time to let out a deep breath, putting a hand against Loxwood's neck, before pushing him back into a canter. I take a wide loop, giving myself time to get him back into a good rhythm, while still making sure that when I turn to the obstacle, I'm only a few strides away. Enough to let him see the fence and understand what he's supposed to do, but not so far that either of us have time to second-guess ourselves. Loxwood is still hesitant, his stride shortening as his ears flicker backwards, but my legs are fixed against his sides like iron, and I'm doing everything I can to convey to him that he can do it. And he does,

It's not a pretty round, and even after clearing the trakehner there are a few sticky jumps, where Loxwood gets right to the base of the fence before cat leaping, and I let go of the reins to make sure I don't pull him in the mouth as I'm thrown behind the movement, but we complete. With twenty jumping penalties and who knows how many time, but we *finish*. We got round, we got out of difficult situations instead of letting mistakes control us, and I'm so happy. We won't win, or place, or be anywhere near what is considered a respectable score for that matter, but it doesn't matter. Winning isn't always coming first in the standings, sometimes it's conquering the doubts inside you.

I know nothing is "fixed". Confidence doesn't come back in one round, and it's possible that we'll go out again in a couple weeks time and be eliminated. But for today, it's a small victory, and the fact that I've managed to overcome this blip, and if only for a moment Loxwood trusted me, is all I could hope for. I thought I understood what success was, and even thought I had reached it when we went out and placed at our first event, but I'm realising that I had it all wrong. Success isn't something you reach. It's an ongoing journey, ever-changing, with no fixed destination. It's a way of life.

'Pull yourself together, you're fine.'

The sentence is barely out when Sunny lets out a piercing whinny, so close to my ears that I can feel the warmth of his breath against my face.

'Great,' I say, squinting in pain as the brown horse prances beside me. 'I hope you're happy. I'm probably deaf now.'

This statement obviously doesn't concern Sunny, and all I can do is hang on as he continues to pretend I'm not holding his reins, head in the air and tail lifted. I glance over at the warm-up ring, where Rose is cantering Paddington to an upright, and pray that she'll be called in soon. The times between the two horses are so close that the only option is to have Sunny already tacked up and ready, which is easy in theory, but proving harder in execution. He *is* tacked up, and he *is* ready to be ridden, but he's not exactly making my life very easy. I beat Rose back to the lorry after my cross country round, the two of us way more excited by a twenty penalty round than most are, but there wasn't much time to talk as she quickly swapped Paddington's dressage saddle for a jumping one. Knowing both horses would be away from the lorry at once, I loaded Loxwood in the back once he was cooled off and I had removed his studs, where he happily stood with a haynet, a cooler over his back. As soon as I did that, I turned my attention back to Rose, and barely had time to pull off my hat and body protector before needing to take charge of Sunny. And now that the fear and adrenalin of competing is beginning to wear off, I'm suddenly both very tired and very hungry. My job here's not over yet, though. I'll hand Sunny over to Rose in a minute, but then she'll be giving me Paddington, and I'll need to pull his plaits out and swap his boots before taking him to the cross country course. Maybe I'll just have time to grab myself one of Mackenzie's chocolate crispies from the living compartment while I'm at the lorry. At least looking after

Paddington doesn't come with the same exhaustion that looking after Sunny does.

We're walking along the piece of land reserved for horses to access the warm-up areas, Sunny trying to pull my arms out of their sockets every time one passes, and this time is no exception. A bay gelding comes close by, and Sunny lets out another piercing whinny as he drags me towards him, and I only just manage to swing him away before he lunges himself at the unsuspecting horse.

'Sorry,' I call, leaning into Sunny's shoulder, giving him a shove with my elbow, and by some miracle he comes to a halt. Only then do I look up at the horse and rider he is so obsessed with, and when I see who it is I think I might be sick.

'Bit of a handful, huh?' the guy says, smiling in a casual way.

'Something like that,' I mutter, the words coming out in a stutter. Not only did Sunny almost crash into somebody's horse, he almost crashed into James McDaniels's horse. As in James McDaniels the four-star rider. I've got used to seeing professionals I've spent years admiring riding in the same ring as me, and queuing behind them at concessions stands, but actually talking to them is a different matter. And the last time I did that, I ended up losing one of my horses.

'You've got him listening now, though,' James says, looking relaxed as he lets his reins go slack against his horse's neck - a horse, I now realise, that is called Pemberley, and currently competing at two-star level. *What is happening?* Forget the fact that four-star riders keep talking to me, but why does *anyone?* Seriously, all I ever do is try to look unfriendly and avoid eye contact so that I'm never in these situations.

I look at Sunny, who is standing still, ears forward, but probably only because he's staring at something he will most likely spook at in a minute. 'It won't last,' I say.

'Nice horse, anyway. You riding him?'

I shake my head. Of course this is why he's speaking to me, he's interested in buying a horse. Why else would a rider strike up a conversation? 'I'm done riding for the day, so now I'm playing groom.' As exciting as it is to be talking to someone I practically worship, I really don't want to get stuck making conversation. And if I do, I'm bound to somehow reveal that I know everything there is to know about him. His age (forty-one), or his family (wife Melody, children George and Noah), or point out the fact that he missed out on the Badminton title a few years ago due to knocking down the final show jumping fence (but he still finished third).

'Well,' James says, gathering his reins. 'You clearly know how to handle a horse. What did you say your name was?'

I didn't. 'Georgia,' I say, and realising that's probably not enough I add, 'James.' And then in a panic, wondering if he thinks I was addressing him, I repeat, 'Georgia James.'

He grins slightly before pushing Pemberley into a walk. 'I reckon I can remember that.' And then he's gone, and I'm left wondering what exactly just happened, but it doesn't last long.

As another horse comes up behind him, Sunny spins round, almost knocking me sideways, and I don't even have time to look at who the horse in question is before recognising the rider's voice. 'Oh my god, I love him. Is he yours?'

I jab Sunny in the shoulder again before looking up at Alex. She's on Goji Berry, a beautiful dark KWPN that I'm extremely envious of. 'In case you haven't noticed, he's kind of a pain in the butt.'

'Exactly,' says Alex, grinning. 'I like a bit of attitude.'

'Well, he's Rose's ride, not mine.' I say, the mention of Rose's name reminding me of what I'm supposed to be doing, but glancing at the ring I see that she's still warming up.

'How did you do, anyway?'

'Umm, okay.' I say, knowing what I considered a good round definitely won't sound it to Alex. 'Picked up a twenty, but I was pleased with him. You?'

Alex pulls a face. 'Waffles spooked at the trakehner in the woods. Fine second time round, though.'

'Same thing happened to me!' I say with way too much enthusiasm.

'Stupid trakehner!' Alex says cheerfully. 'It was my fault, though,' she continues. 'Anchor stopped at a trakehner last week, and I let that get to me.'

'Anchor did?' I say, unable to hide my surprise.

'In an Open Novice at that!' cries Alex. 'He's always been a bit of a wuss about airy fences and that. Even ditches he's still afraid of.'

'Really?' God, every time I talk to Alex I end up questioning what she says about her horses. But she's such an amazing rider, and always seems so in control when she's on course, that I can't help wanting to know the truth straight from the source. 'I always think Anchor looks fearless,' I add, hoping to come across as less critical.

I should have remembered that Alex never takes anything to heart, because she laughs. 'Anchor? Not even close. Anchor's brave, not fearless,' she clarifies. 'I don't want to ride a horse that's fearless, because they're stupid enough to jump you both into trouble. You want a horse that has the common sense to be afraid, but then your job is to help him overcome it. Anyway, I've got to go. Catch up later.'

I mumble some sort of agreement, but I'm more focussed on

holding Sunny back from following Goji. And I count my lucky stars when I glance over to the ring to see Rose cantering Paddington through the start flags, and I begin walking towards the exit, ready to swap the beast I'm holding for an easier one.

If I weren't holding Paddington, I would have turned around. But I am, so I have no choice but to watch Nantucket as he trots round the ring, Imogen's riding looking flawless as always. She's obviously still warming in, slowing back to a walk to approach the gate steward as she asks about the delay. Doing this means that we find ourselves feet apart, and once again it's Nantucket who alerts his rider of my presence.

'How did show jumping go?' I say before Imogen can comment, forcing a smile onto my face. Only now do I realise, sensing - as you do in these situations - that somebody's eyes are burning holes into the side of my face, that Liz is standing farther along from me. Still not speaking, I might add.

'He was great,' Imogen beams. 'You've done such a great job with him, he really is a dream to ride!'

Seriously, can't she just be rude and arrogant so that I can hate her? It would be so easier that way. But no, she has to be nice, and an amazing rider, and pretty to top it all off. Twenty-six years old, and already Imogen has achieved more than I could ever hope to in my entire lifetime.

'I'm glad,' I say, not even bothering to make the words sound sincere. Now that I'm looking right at him, I'd walk right up to Nantucket and throw my arms around his neck again if I weren't holding Paddington.

A horse walks past me, and I turn to look at it, as you do, only to see that it's James McDaniels again, and he's recognised me first. I smile weakly, really not wanting to talk right now, before wishing Imogen luck and excusing myself to walk Paddington round. My hands are numb, and I run them up and down his warm neck, hoping to calm myself. When does this get easier? I remember Leni saying that she still hasn't got over selling her European pony, does that mean this pain never goes away? Or is it because Nantucket is the first? Or because he is *Nantucket*, a once in a lifetime horse? I don't know the answers, just that I hate this.

Apparently Sunny is entitled to his attitude problem, because he storms around the course to go clear inside the time. And not only that, but he looks good doing it. I left Rose with Paddington to lead Sunny back to the lorry, though his successful cross country round is doing little to improve my tolerance.

'You're not allowed to have an ego like this yet,' I say, fighting to hold him back. He looks ready to go round a course again. 'You may have done well today, but you're not an advanced eventer yet. *Then* you can be a nightmare. Not now, though.'

I'm still sponging Sunny off when I hear someone say my name, and I look up from where I was crouching to reach his girth passage to see James McDaniels standing beside me. He must have just come from his cross country round, because his hat strap is hanging, and his body protector is unzipped. I feel like I should say something, but I don't know what to say, and he's the one who addressed me, after all.

'I was just chatting to Imogen,' James says, pausing as though this should give me a hint as to what he's going to say next. And as he seems to be waiting for a reaction of sorts, I settle for nodding. 'She said you sold her that grey?' Again I nod, not sure what else I'm supposed to be contributing here. 'You produced him yourself?' At least this is a concrete question.

'Yes,' I say. 'I ex - I *used* to - exercise Thoroughbreds at the track, and he was thrown out because he was too slow.'

'You've done a heck of a job.'

If mention of Nantucket didn't send my heart to the bottom of a pond of sorrow, I might actually register the fact that James McDaniels is praising my riding ability. 'He's a good horse.'

'He was still well produced,' says James, and I feel a wave of gratitude for him. 'Is your horse here?'

'In the lorry,' I say, and seeing James's interest I pull Sunny's lead rope to walk towards the ramp, but the gelding has decided to abandon his nightmarish behaviour in favour of grass, and he pulls me the other way. 'Umm, you can look at him, if you want.' *But he's not for sale.* And then I feel stupid for thinking James would even want to see Loxwood if it weren't with the interest of purchasing him. Nice one, Georgia.

'He's nice,' says James, stepping up onto the ramp to look over the partition. 'He's five?'

'Yep,' I say, bracing myself for the next question.

'What are your ambitions with him?'

Okay, not the question I was expecting. 'What do I want to do with him?' I say, feeling stupid for repeating his question in a different way. Great, now he's really going to think I'm stupid.

But James seems unfazed as he nods, stepping back off the ramp to look me in the eye.

'Well,' I say cautiously. 'I don't really know if I'm going to be good enough…'

'That wasn't the question,' James says shortly. 'What's your end goal? Forget what you think is or isn't possible.'

I feel like answering that question honestly will only make me sound ridiculous, but James is looking right at me, so I go for the truth, covering it up with a nervous laugh. 'Badminton?' As soon as I say it, I wish I hadn't. Especially to someone who's actually *been* round Badminton. About twenty times no less. And I'm cursing myself internally, but James smiles.

'Good. Just what I want to hear. You've got to aim high, right? How else are you going to get there?'

I smile back, feeling myself relax, but I'm still not sure what all of this is about.

'What do you do?' says James. 'You don't work for Rose, do you?'

I hesitate for a second, always forgetting that in the eventing world (and the horse world, for that matter) everyone knows everyone. 'Not really. She just helps me out. I don't live far from her, and I keep my horses there. I wouldn't be able to compete if it weren't for her,' I say, as always, never truly realising just how much I owe Rose until I say it out loud.

'Do you go to school?'

'Unfortunately,' I say, which makes him smile. 'I turned eighteen in February, I just haven't really got round to leaving yet.'

'Well, I don't want to derail an education, but I saw how well you handled that horse, and Imogen gushed about how well that grey has been started off, and now you're telling me that you're used to riding out at the track.' James pauses, and while I don't want to get my hopes up, I'm pretty sure that while he said he didn't want to derail an education, he's going to do just that. 'I'm looking for a second rider.'

'A working pupil?'

James grins. 'Kind of, but without the groom side of it. I need someone to help me keep the horses fit, to ride alongside me and then *for* me when I'm away, and if you're happy to get on anything then even better. You have just the one horse?'

'Two,' I say, remembering Cookie. 'But the other one's not

ready to compete yet.'

'I can offer you living on site, and your horses' board, and I'll have to check, but I think we agreed on something like fifty quid a week on top for your own expenses. You interested?'

*Breathe, Georgia. Breathe.* 'Yeah,' I say, trying to keep my voice calm. 'I mean, I have to think about it.'

'No rush,' James says, taking a few steps back. 'All the details are on my website. Just drop me a message or give me a ring. Melody's in charge of that side of it,'

I nod, still not fully acknowledging what's going on here. 'Shall I give you my number?' I say, managing to regain my senses before he walks off. 'In case you find someone else or change your mind…'

'Are you kidding? I've been trying to fill this position for months!'

'Really?' I say. So much for playing it cool. 'It sounds like the perfect job.'

'You'd think, wouldn't you?' says James with a smile. 'I can find grooms like that,' He snaps his fingers to emphasise his point. 'But nobody wants riding positions. People are too scared of riding anything with a bit of fizz to it, and most of the people that aren't have their own setups. Look, drop me an email, and I'll get Mel to send you all the details. Okay?'

This one I do know the answer to. 'Okay.'

# Chapter 7

The next few weeks pass in a blur. My parents, who I thought would fight me over dropping out of school until I caved just to have some peace and quiet, are thrilled. They know nothing about horses, and probably couldn't distinguish a top eventer from a mule, but as soon as they hear the word "Olympian", there are hugs and stars and words of encouragement. What I find funniest is the fact that me riding has always been referred to reluctantly, and now here's my mum, boasting to anyone who will listen that her daughter is going to train with an Olympic equestrian. I can't blame her, I don't quite believe it myself.

As soon as the joy that came with James's offer wore off, my worry was Rose. I knew she would be happy for me, and encouraging, but the thought of leaving her yard, the place I've come to think of as home, sent my panic levels skyrocketing. But as I knew she would be, she *was* encouraging.

'It's the opportunity of a lifetime,' Rose said. 'You're not going to work as a groom, you're going to *ride* for him. And he's letting you take two horses!'

My stomach flipped at this last part, prompting me to mention in my next email to James that my other horse was somewhat quirky, to say the least, but it was accepted no problem. I then spent ten days in a row lunging Cookie, until I managed to get through an entire session without her rearing, and even started getting her used to a saddle again. To my surprise, she didn't even try to chuck me off the first time I rode her. She did the second time, though.

I think one of the things that frustrated me the most about this whole situation, though, was Imogen's involvement. Or more to the point, the fact that she was involved at all. James went up to her after I left the cross country warm-up, having seen the two of us talking, and it was her words that prompted him to offer me a position. I should be grateful to Imogen, and I feel like a terrible person for not being so, but if she hadn't been watching Nantucket that day, she would never have asked Liz to make an offer. And I know thinking like this is stupid and irrational, because for all I know if it hadn't been Liz and Imogen it would have been someone else, but I can't help it. I could have struggled through the winter, working extra hours *anywhere* whenever I could, and then I would have been riding both Nantucket and Loxwood the day James noticed me, and I would be going to his yard with the two of them. Paid for. The thought makes me sick, and it's the one thing above all else that makes me want to pick up the phone and call the whole thing off. If I'd just waited, just hung on for a little while longer, everything would have worked out. And even though I know there's no way of being sure of this, it doesn't stop me from feeling that, once again, I've failed Nantucket.

If there's one thing I've been warned about these sorts of working pupil situations, it's that professional riders often don't have space for your horse (let alone horses plural) on their lorry, each slot being precious. So I took the plunge, dipping into my savings, and invested in a two-horse trailer. It might not prove necessary, but it makes me feel safe. And at least I'll be able to make the drive to Leicester on my own.

It's on a Friday morning, days before I'm set to leave, that I awake at the crack of dawn, guilt in my stomach, when I realise there's something I need to do before.

'Morning, boss.'

Frank looks up from his clipboard, quite obviously unable to hide his surprise, and I'm thankful for the the sound of trotting horses and speeding cars preventing us from suffering through an awkward silence. His first string is going round the walk and trot track, as I knew they would be at this time, and Frank is standing on the sidelines, watching from the barrier.

For a moment, I'm afraid he'll tell me to get lost, but he doesn't. 'Morning, James.'

'I've been offered a job with a top event rider,' I blurt out, not wanting to enter "pleasantry territory". 'Someone who's been to the Olympics. He wants me to ride his horses, and exchange he'll train me. And Loxwood,' I add.

Frank nods. 'That's good. You deserve it.'

His sincerity is too much. 'About Mackerel–'

'James,' says Frank, interrupting me. 'You were upset, it's fine. Water under the bridge.'

'I am sorry,' I say, glancing over my shoulder at the many Thoroughbreds getting ready to go on the gallops. There are other trainers' strings out, too, but there's no denying that it's

Frank's horses that are in the best condition. For one thing, they're all sound, and I can't get over the fact that nobody seems bothered by some of the hopping lame Thoroughbreds going round. 'It wasn't all about Mackerel, it was just... the past few months had been tough, and Mackerel just pushed me over the edge. And I know I should have come back and talked to you sooner, and I'm sorry about that too.'

'Exercise riders aren't permanent, James. You don't have to worry about hurting my feelings.'

'I know,' I say, only now thinking about how stupid the fact that I'm standing here, doing this, must appear to a trainer. 'But I needed to come say thank you. For the opportunity, and the experience. And Loxwood.'

'You earned it,' Franks says, his face softening further as the early morning wind blows his blond hair back from his forehead.

I nod. 'I'd better get going. But I mean it. Thank you.'

Frank nods back. 'If you ever get fed up with eventing, you know where to find me. I can always use a jockey like you.'

I suppress a grin. 'Sure thing, boss.'

I've already started walking away when I hear Frank call, 'Georgia?'

'Yeah?' I say, pausing to look back down the pavement. I'm just beyond where the horses cross to access the gallops, and another trainer has stepped to the middle of the road to stop the traffic so that his string can go past.

Frank smiles. 'I wanna see you and that horse at the Olympics someday, you hear?'

This time, no amount of biting my lips can stop a grin from spreading across my face. 'Sure thing, boss.'

'Please don't go.'

Okay, I thought I had prepared myself for this, but imagining a sobbing kid and then actually having one standing in front of you are two different things entirely. 'Kenzie..'

'*Please!*' Mackenzie wails, throwing her arms around my waist, and I realise just how much she's grown these past years when I think about the fact that her hugs only used to reach my hips. We went on a final hack together yesterday, and I thought that was upsetting, but this is harder.

'Kenzie,' I say again, wrapping my arms around her shoulders as I fight the tears forming in my own eyes in response to her reaction. 'I have to.'

'No, you don't.' Mackenzie says through sobs. 'You don't have to leave. You can stay here, forever and forever, please.'

'Mackenzie,' says Rose, stepping up beside us. But even her attempt at discipline is clouded by the catch in her throat. 'Don't make this any harder for Georgia.'

'Hey,' I say, unwrapping my arms from around Kenzie to wipe my face with the backs of my hands. I crouch down so that we're at eye level and take hold of her shoulders. 'I get a day off, remember? A whole day of not doing anything. And I'm not that far away. So you know what I'm going to be doing on that day?'

'What?'

'I'm going to be coming here,' I say. 'Do you really think I'm going to be able to go a whole week without any of your fairy cakes?'

This at least makes Mackenzie smile. 'You promise?'

'I promise. And you're going to be helping your mum out at events, aren't you?'

Mackenzie nods.

'Well, I'll be there too. And you *know* that I'm going to need your help.'

'You will?'

'I will,' I say. 'You have to promise me that you'll help me look after Loxwood, because you know how upset he's going to be if he doesn't get to see you.'

'I promise,' Mackenzie says weakly, before her face breaks into sobs again. 'But I still don't want you to go?'

'Neither do I,' I say, hugging her. 'But it's not forever.'

We're standing beside the trailer, in which the horses are already loaded, Tucker's driver's door already open. I already said goodbye to my parents this morning, both of whom were surprisingly teary considering the fact we've barely spoken in eighteen years, but now the fact that I'm leaving actually feels real. And I almost don't want to.

As soon as Mackenzie finally releases me, Rose steps forward to pull me close to her, and that just about does it for my emotions. I break down in the same hiccuping sobs as Kenzie, only reassured by the fact that Rose is doing the same. 'You've always got a home here, you got that?' she says, her arms still around me. 'Whenever you need anything, ever, you come to me.'

'I will.'

'I'm so proud of you,' she says, her grip tightening. 'You've worked so hard, and you're so talented. Don't doubt yourself, Georgia. You're going to make it, I promise you. I know it's been hard, and I know you probably don't believe this, but you are going to go all the way. I believe in you. And Loxwood believes in you. So just believe in yourself now, because you can do this.'

'Okay,' I say, fresh tears falling down my face.

'Stay in touch,' says Rose, squeezing me tighter for a second before releasing me. 'Look at us,' she says, laughing as she wipes her eyes. 'I'll see you in a week's time, and you're not even an hour away.'

'Thank you,' I say. 'Thank you so much. For everything. If it weren't for you, none of this would ever have been possible..'

As to be expected, Rose shakes off the praise. 'You did this. You've worked so hard. You deserve this. I'd say go make me proud, but you already have.'

'Good luck with Sunny,' I say, anything to lighten the mood, sliding into Tucker's front seat as I hear one of the horses (more to the point, Cookie) kick out in the trailer.

'Tell you what,' says Rose, her red cheeks blotchy as she smiles. 'Let's see which one of us can get to Badminton first? Loxwood and Sunny, they're the same age. Fair play. What do you say?'

'Deal.'

I don't know if it's the tearful goodbyes or just the stress of moving, but I'm completely wiped out by the time I pull my old jeep and shabby trailer up beside James's enormous lorry. I'm on a expanse of concrete, having driven through a short driveway off a country lane, and am now facing brick buildings around which a few post and rail paddocks are empty. The building to my right I know from looking at photographs online is an indoor arena, and the excitement that runs through me at the thought of not having to ride in the rain is enough to push aside the doubt I've been feeling since driving away from Rose's. I can see an outdoor ring, too, the tops of the jumps stand peaking out beyond the nearby paddocks. And behind the building that is obviously the stable barn, I can just make out the corner of a mobile home.

As if telling me to get a move on, Loxwood lets out a sharp neigh in the trailer, followed by the sound off Cookie kicking out, and then a whole chorus of whinnies reply from the barn.

'Just give me a minute,' I say, swinging open the top shutter of the trailer. Two sets of ears are visible, and Loxwood, having the edge height wise, lifts his head higher to look out, only to neigh again.

'Pack it in,' I snap, my voice relaxed. 'Let me check there's actually somewhere for you to go first.'

Forget feeling the way you do on your first day of school, this is more like showing up at the Badminton start box on a hamster. Not that I'm in any means referring to Loxwood as a rodent, but the fear and humiliation of being completely out of my depth is the same. This is stupid, I keep telling myself as I stand hesitantly to one side of the barn entrance. They're expecting me. You're being ridiculous. Just walk in. And yet I want to burst into tears, run back to my car, and drive off, all the way back to Rose's. But I can hear footsteps coming towards me, and it's too late to turn around now.

'Georgia?'

'Hi,' I say, what should be one syllable coming out in about three. Standing in front of me is a girl who I would say is only a few years older than me at most. She's short, with a sandy-coloured ponytail pushed back by one of those headbands almost all grooms in this country wear. She's wearing jeans and a sweatshirt, and judging by the fact she's not shivering I would guess that she's in the middle of yard chores, because I've only been stationary for a matter of seconds and I'm already frozen beneath my coat. I thought it was supposed to be spring?

The girl smiles, and her friendliness puts me slightly more at ease. 'I'm Paris, James's head girl. He's riding at the moment, so he asked me to keep an eye out for you and get you settled in.'

'Okay,' I say. 'Thanks.'

Paris smiles again, which I take as a good sign, because it's seriously hard to be that jolly when you work with horses, so James really must be as nice as his reputation suggests. 'Shall we get the horses?'

I want to say no, don't worry, I can manage and I'm sure you're busy, but Paris has already started walking towards my trailer, so I just follow. 'So, do you live on site?' I ask as we each walk to opposite sides of the ramp, pulling back the bolts.

'Yeah. We've got a camper each. There's no one else living on site at the moment, because the other two grooms are local, so we're on our own. And James is only a minute away.'

'Have you worked here long?' I ask, for the sake of being polite, as we lower the front ramp of the trailer to the ground.

'Three years,' says Paris, her words masked by the hight-pitched neigh Loxwood lets out as he sees us.

'Wow,' I say, stepping up the ramp to run a hand down Cookie's neck, to which she decides to respond by making me look bad and pinning her ears. 'You must like it here?'

'It's kind of the perfect job,' Paris says with a shrug, stepping up behind me. 'Which one do you want me to take?'

I'd like to take Loxwood into the barn myself, but having my crazy horse kill James's head girl before I've even been here three minutes isn't exactly going to cut it, so I say, 'You can take the chestnut, if you like. The bay one's a little nuts. Thanks,' I add as an afterthought.

'Was the traffic all right?' Paris asks as she unties Loxwood's lead rope, and I wonder what it must be like to be able to be both polite and friendly so effortlessly.

'Yeah, it was okay,' I say, holding a fretting Cookie back as Loxwood is led down the ramp. It's stupid, but because I'm always the one handling him, I forget just how lucky I am to have a horse like him until I see him with somebody else. He really does look magnificent, but I can't exactly stand back and stare at him for long, because that other horse of mine is trying to hurl us both out of the trailer, and I jump to one side before she can push me down the ramp. Which, as it turns out, is a wise move, because Cookie jumps the whole thing, and I only just manage to hang on to the end of the lead rope.

'You weren't kidding,' Paris says, looking over her shoulder as Loxwood stands perfectly still. But at least she says it with a laugh, reassuring me that Cookie's antics aren't anything this yard hasn't seen before.

I follow Paris and Loxwood into the barn, my gorgeous chestnut seeming to understand the importance of today, walking with the kind of head carriage you'd expect at an international trot-up. A certain mare didn't get the message though, prancing sideways and threatening to go up. At least she gives it a rest when we step into the comfort of the barn, shielded from the cold air, and I'm able to look around.

They aren't the kind of stables you see in the background of glossy magazine pages, but they're smarter than most. The barn is big and open, with flat-pack stables running around the inside permitter, another block in the middle. Simple dark wood, and straight metal grills. The horses that look out are all well cared for, and my heart leaps at the sight of Airforce, James's famous four star ride. Not only am I going to be seeing him on a daily basis, but my own horses are going to be stabled beside him. In a nice, covered barn, sheltered from the cruelty that is English weather.

'These two are yours,' says Paris, as we approach two stables at the end of the row, the doors already slid open. She turns Loxwood into the nearest, so I walk Cookie to the end one. Although the stables are big, bigger than what they're used to, my heart sinks as I look at the bedding. Or more to the point, the lack of. The floors are rubber-lined, and as a consequence there is only a meagre pile of shavings in one corner. I know a lot of people keep their horses like this, but I've become accustomed to Rose's good-old-fashioned deep straw beds, with banks reaching halfway up the walls, that horses love to lie down in. Thinking of Loxwood, and even Cookie, having only this amount of bedding to sleep on makes me feel ill.

I unhook Cookie's lead rope, leaving her head collar and travel boots on for now, and close the door behind me to go to Loxwood. 'I can take all his kit off in a minute,' I say to Paris.

'You sure?'

I nod. 'Yeah, don't worry.'

'Okay,' she says, coming out of Loxwood's box and hanging the lead rope up on a nearby hook.

I peer through the railings, hoping to discover a big bed of shavings, confirming Cookie's stable as a mistake, but I'm met with the same sight. I glance at Paris briefly, not wanting to convey my feelings but hoping that she's a little disturbed by the lack of bedding, which she doesn't appear to be in the slightest. Maybe I'm overreacting, I tell myself. After all, James knows what he's doing, way more than I do, and his way of doing things clearly works, or else he wouldn't have so many horses competing at international level.

With Paris still standing nearby, I slide Loxwood's stable door open to run a hand down his neck, the railings preventing him from putting his head out. Already he is pulling at a haynet, and with a start I realise that what's inside doesn't look like hay.

'Is that haylage?' I ask, fully aware of how panicked I must sound. But switching a horse's feed like that is the surest way of getting colic I know.

But at least Paris shakes her head this time. 'Steamed hay. Why, are they used to haylage?'

'No,' I say quickly, my heart resuming its normal rhythm. 'They're used to hay.'

'Steamed hay's not much different for their systems,' Paris says with a shrug. 'Smells sweeter, and gets rid of the dust.'

I nod, still glancing around Loxwood's stable, and noticing that it's fitted with an automatic water dispenser. He'll only drink out of a bucket, even if lack of means dehydrating himself, but I'll give it a couple more minutes before I complain about something new. And thankfully Paris offers to show me round, thus buying me a little time.

My body feels ready to give way when I collapse onto the small sofa in the mobile home. At least my accommodation is nice - clean, spacious enough, and just mine. I wish I were feeling as enthusiastic about everything else, though.

James was really nice when he came back from riding, just after I'd finished carrying my belongings to the tack room to which Paris had shown me where the key was hidden, immediately making me feel welcome and introducing me to everyone. I met his wife, Melody, when she called by later in the afternoon, who was just as friendly as James, and was shown some of the horses I would be riding. He praised Loxwood's conformation (and even Cookie's), and I wished I could show more enthusiasm. But my worries only increased when I saw the amount of hay that was given at night, which I doubt lasts the horses longer than an hour, and the evening feeds that lacked both bran and sugar beet, so unlike Rose's way of doing things. I made a comment about Loxwood not liking automatic water dispensers, to which I was told that "he would learn" if he had no other choice, and I didn't even get to discussing the bedding. I figured I would at least be able to muck out in a way I find bearable tomorrow, but James crushed that dream, without even realising it, by pointing out that I was here to ride, and under no obligation to muck out or do any yard chores.

'I've got fifteen horses in work,' he said. 'I'm desperate for help.'

And so here I am, sitting on my own in a mobile home, worrying about my horses that are but a short distance away. It had never occurred to me to pack food before getting here, thinking I would have time to shop soon enough, but I am now unbelievably grateful that my mum handed me a bag of groceries this morning, insisting that I wouldn't get round to it yet. And she was right, I realise as I look at the bags of bagels and tins of baked beans. At least I won't starve just yet. And she was also right about needing to bring my own bedding, because if I hadn't then I would be using a bunched up sweatshirt as a pillow tonight.

I'm suddenly aware of how quiet it is. No cars passing by my bedroom window. No sound of Mackenzie and Jemima bickering over who knows what. No sound of the horses, even, tucked away in the barn. I can only see a light on in Paris's camper.

No mucking out, I remind myself, trying to get excited by the prospect. No working like a slave. Just riding. It sounds like a dream come true. So why am I feeling so low?

# Chapter 8

Okay, I could get used to this. The horse I'm sitting on, who goes by the stable name of Trevor, is the easiest I've ever ridden. I've never felt like more of a passenger, because I'm literally just sitting here looking pretty. You don't even have to *make* him go soft and round, he just does it. Is this what it's like to ride a schoolmaster? While I've been struggling, is this what other people have been dealing with - horses you just jump on and let do the job? Are you frigging kidding me?

After Trevor comes a seventeen hand Warmblood who is less enjoyable, and by the end of the session my entire body aches from trying to lift him off the forehand. But then I ride another Warmblood, the kind you watch others go round on with envy, that is so wonderful that I'm pretty sure I spend the whole time grinning. I'm working around James in the indoor arena, and although I was a bit unsure the first time he told me, without great concern, to simply do flatwork, leaving me to my own devices, I've quickly fallen into the rhythm. Especially with a horse like this. Every stride is fuelled by power, the kind of elevation you don't feel on a Thoroughbred, and you spend almost two seconds in the air with every rise in trot. My hands don't move, the horse (whose name I've forgotten) maintaining his balance on his own, flexing his neck and never setting his jaw against the bit.

When I come off that third horse, I can't stop smiling with relief at how well the morning's gone. When I came out at seven A.M. I immediately filled a bucket with water for Loxwood, and he drank the whole thing without raising his head. I felt sick, and angry but mostly with myself for not sticking my ground last night. And then Paris and the other two grooms came into the barn to do the feeds, James arriving by the time we were done, assuring me that Loxwood and Cookie would be looked after, that I didn't need to do any yard chores, and asking Paris to point me towards Trevor and his tack. The fear that had been bubbling through me ever since being offered this position, of riding a professional's horses that I could quite possibly mess up with one wrong movement, was temporarily pushed from my mind as I was handed an expensive-looking saddle, along with a pad and a bridle, and then Paris chucked me four rolled-up bandages before going off to muck out. And that's when I started to panic. I know how to bandage the way any horse person with an average IQ can figure out how to wrap them from one direction to the next, but I'm by no means a pro. Everyone seems to think that they know how to bandage, when really they're doing more damage than good. And I know for a fact that knowing how to bandage *well* is rare, to the point that anyone who understands just how technical it is doesn't let anyone else do so for them. But James clearly doesn't share that philosophy, and I wasn't about to hunt down Paris and ask her to do it for me, so I furiously bit back tears and redid the bandages as many times as I could under the circumstances, hoping they would pass as acceptable. James never mentioned anything about them, so they were either a lot better than I thought, or he really just doesn't care.

All morning, I've been expecting to be asked about turning Loxwood and Cookie out, but by midday there still hasn't been anything said on the matter, and the fact that I haven't seen a single one of James's own horses be led to a paddock has me worrying slightly, but I don't have too much time to dwell. Lunch isn't exactly a word that equestrians are familiar with, and I pause to swallow some mouthfuls of coffee between bandages as I prepare my next horse. James asked me yesterday if I wanted to give my horses a day or two to settle in before riding, to which I replied affirmatively, but I was expecting them to at least spend some time in a paddock when I said that. And right now, if what I've seen so far is anything to go by, that isn't going to happen.

When four o'clock rolls around, the joy of riding so many talented horses does little to ease the cloud of worry hanging over my head. Turnout is definitely not an option now, and I can't even fix the beds to a level I deem satisfactory with everyone around, but I am officially "off the clock", so I decide to put a head collar on Loxwood and take him out to hold him for some grass. He's not used to being cooped up all day, and his energy levels are ready to boil over as I lead him out of the barn, Cookie whinnying behind us, but by some luck he forgets his excitement at the sight of grass, plunging his head down to snatch mouthfuls. I let out what feels like my first breath today, my arms suddenly feeling very shaking as I try to keep a firm grip on the lead rope. I tell myself that I'm being silly, that it's only like this because it's the first day, and even if James believes in little bedding, even less turnout, and small nets of hay, he must be right, because he's a professional and I'm not. And who's an eighteen year old girl to argue with somebody that's been round the Olympics? But I still feel angry at the situation, and myself for not opposing it. I'm worried about Cookie too, but it's Loxwood right now that my heart is thumping for. James has a whole barn full of top-level prospects, but I just have this one. Cookie might be something half decent one day if she stops trying to kill me, but Loxwood's my golden ticket horse. He always has been. Even with everything that's happened with Nantucket. *Nantucket.* My gut twists as the thought enters my head. Imogen and James are obviously friends, certainly enough to trust each other's opinions, so what if Imogen's yard is like this? What if Nantucket has only a corner of shavings so small that he can't lie down in it? What if he's on rations, without unlimited hay, because most of today's event riders seem to think that skinny counts as fit, taking horses that would be deemed anorexic if they were people round advanced tracks? And what if he doesn't get to go out in the field? Each idea crams my head, filling my stomach with dread, and I lean into Loxwood's shoulder to keep myself from collapsing in a heap on the grass.

Even though I'm terrified of making a complete fool of myself, it's a relief to be back on my own horse. Everything fits, the length of neck is what I'm used to, and he's mine to mess up. Today's the first time James will actually be teaching me, as up to now we've only ridden together, mostly taking the horses for their interval training across the hills, and I'm both nervous and excited. I'm pretty sure he's going to say that everything I'm doing is wrong, and that I haven't been helping Loxwood out much, and things like that, but that's okay. He's been to the

Olympics, so as far as I'm concerned he can scream and call me useless all he wants. Not that I really think he's going to be mean, though, from what I've seen so far. If anything he's too laid-back. I asked Paris if he is always this nice (not quite so directly) to which she replied by nodding her head and laughing.

'I swear, all we really do is think for him. His head's in the clouds most of the time,'

I'm not quite sure that's as endearing as Paris seems to find it, but I'd rather a boss who is laid-back than somebody like Amanda Walton. And to be honest I don't really care what he's like so long as he can help me become the best rider I can be.

While I warm up Loxwood, James calls me over to look over my tack. Straight away he cranks the noseband up a hole, tightening both it and the flash, which I kind of knew was coming, but am still a little disappointed by. I always think I should be able to control Loxwood without tying his mouth shut, but clearly most professional event riders find that ridiculous. James then hands me a schooling whip before stepping back to let me continue working in. Again I want to oppose, because Loxwood doesn't exactly lack fizz, and as far as I'm concerned schooling whips are for when you're too lazy to use your legs, but I know this will make me seem even more pathetic, and truthfully I know it is stupid of me, so I keep quiet and carry on. The tighter noseband makes no difference to anything, so I don't see the point in it, and carrying a schooling whip only means that Loxwood shoots forward whenever it moves. But I so badly want to impress James that I stop thinking about this and focus solely on having the horse beneath me moving smoothly, coming up into the hands, and engaging his hindquarters, all while trying to keep my own back straight and my hands together. I keep thinking that James will ask me to get off so that he can sit on

Loxwood himself, in order to assess what I'm doing wrong that makes the gelding chuck his head in canter transitions and rush away from my leg, not to mention the many other things I know need improving, but he doesn't. He tells me some exercises, which I do, and mostly alternates between looking down at his phone and watching me. It's Loxwood first ride here, and I wasn't expecting to launch into full on jumping session or anything, so I'm happy enough with the fact that he remained calm throughout, and I just hope that I didn't make a complete fool of myself. In all, I'm pretty happy and relaxed when I ride over to James to hear what he has to say.

'Remind me what this horse has done,' he says, his tone not giving anything away. 'You said you had some issues with him last year?'

Careful not to drag over the parts that are irrelevant, I tell James about how I picked Loxwood up from the track and the preparation we did in the lead up to our first event. I tell him how confident Loxwood was, and how I ended up finding myself out of my depth with the amount of work I was doing, and honestly describe my mistake the first time he stopped. James is quiet, not interrupting me as I go over the elimination and the fact that I decided to withdraw from the championships. But I explain that Loxwood is finding his trust in me again, and that while we still need help, we managed to fix quite a few things the last time out.

'I'm open to anything,' I say quickly before going on, 'but I think he just needs a few more good outings and he'll have his confidence back. He loves to jump, he just got himself in a bit of a pickle.'

James is silent, and I'm almost not sure he heard me, but then he takes a step back, eyeing up Loxwood. 'I just don't know if it's worth it.'

'Sorry?'

James tilts his head from one side to the next, the way one does so say something is "meh". 'He's a nice enough horse, but there are plenty like that. You'd probably be better off selling him and getting something else. Something that's already going round Novice. There are plenty of nice horses around, no point wasting time on something that's not going to go all the way.'

It's like sirens are blaring in my head, my ears clogged to prevent the sound from escaping. A sickness overcomes me so strongly that it physically hurts. 'It was my fault,' I say cautiously. 'I buried him into the fences, and that's why he started stopping.'

'Maybe,' says James, shrugging. 'But that doesn't mean he should take advantage of you. Plenty of people make mistakes, and horses go anyway. I'm not telling you you *have* to sell him or anything, it's just my suggestion. Like I said, I don't see the point in investing time in a horse that won't go all the way.'

*But he* can *go all the way!* I want to scream it. But shock has paralysed me. 'Even if he doesn't go four-star, I still wouldn't sell him,' I say. 'I want him to go as far as he is capable of.'

'Well, that's your choice,' says James. 'All I'm doing is giving you my opinion, which is that there are plenty of horses out there, so why invest time in something when you shouldn't have to?' He pauses to look at the time on his phone. 'I need to get a move on before my first lesson arrives. I'll tell Paris to get Trevor ready for you while you untack *him*,' he continues, nodding at Loxwood, before walking off.

Even as James disappears, Loxwood remains standing still, ears pricked forwards as the reins rest loosely against his golden neck. The horse of my dreams, the reason I'm even here in the first place, unaware that he's just been referred to as a waste of time.

'Don't listen to him,' I say through the tears that have found their way to my face. 'Don't listen, Loxwood.'

# Chapter 9

The sound of a car door slamming awakes me with a start. I was sound asleep, dreaming but of what I can no longer recall, and yet I'm so certain that the noise I've just heard is a car door that I jump up from the lumpy mattress. In the dark, I fumble for my phone, and when my hand touches the screen the numbers *03:37* flash across it. Why would someone be arriving - or leaving - at half past three in the morning? But I'm so sure that I'm right that I stagger straight through the doorway, and down the narrow space between kitchen units, pulling my coat on at the door and slipping my bare feet into walking boots. My phone is still in my grasp, and I switch on the torch before going outside.

It's cold, so much colder than it should be in spring, but the sensation I feel of something not being right is so strong that I keep walking, even though this is probably crazy. Especially since this is the first night in the two weeks I've been here that I've actually found myself in a heavy slumber.

After that first lesson with James, I've done my best to avoid working Loxwood in front of him. I either go for hacks across the rolling Leicestershire hills, something we're both loving compared to the relatively flat area of Suffolk we're used to, or riding in the outdoor arena in the evening, when James is already back in his house. And there are weekends, of course, when he's away competing, and I'm left with a list of horses to exercise and a lot of free time.

I'm riding youngsters now, which I actually prefer to the foot perfect upper level horses. Not only do I feel like I'm actually doing something when I'm riding, and enjoy working out their quirks, but it's less pressure. Most people would probably think I'm crazy if they heard that I find riding a nutty four year old easier than a three star horse, but it's true. I'm not worrying about doing something wrong, at least not as much, and I feel worthy. Not like a passenger, sitting around while the horse I'm on does all the work, but actually working myself. And feeling like I'm learning something.

While the stable management conditions haven't improved, and it's quite clear that they're not going to, at least I've managed to get Loxwood and Cookie some turnout. James's horses only go in the paddocks every other day at best, and even then for under an hour. But me choosing to put my horses out doesn't seem to be too much of an issue, except for the fact that they keep being brought in after what is no way long enough, and as somebody else usually puts them out while I'm riding, I have little control over anything. What's proving the biggest issue as far as field time is concerned is the fact that they keep being put out with rugs on, which is fine when the weather's as cold as it has been, but there are days when it isn't necessary, and they end up drenched in sweat. I tried to say something, in response to which I was told that the reason was because it takes too long to brush mud off. Even as I pointed out that I would happily be the one to spend the time brushing it off (because my horses keep being groomed for me while I'm riding James's) I was met with a slur about it being a waste of time, and that I had enough to do without spending an hour on something that could be prevented. So I've had to sort of turn a blind eye, biting back frustration whenever I remove a turnout rug to find my horses' shoulders white with sweat.

There's the very minor issue of always thinking I'm being addressed whenever anyone says *James*. Each time, my body swivels round, not catching up to the fact that I'm no longer at Franks's, and nobody here calls me James, and I keep thinking I must come across as really rude because I keep replying for him whenever he's addressed. Of all the riders in the world, I had to pick one with the same name as me.

I've managed to make one thing go my way, though. After my first few days here, I succeeded in convincing Paris to let me take over night check. And this didn't actually require much persuasion, because I'm pretty sure she's quite pleased to not have to leave the comfort of her camper after the day's work finishes at six in the evening. I would have offered to do it even if I didn't have an ulterior motive, but there are benefits that come with having the time alone in the barn. For one, the first thing I do is sneak Loxwood and Cookie some extra hay, rearranging the steamed slices in the machine, ready for the morning, so that it doesn't look like I've taken any. It's all I can do to not give them the whole thing.

Advantage number two is that I've spent almost every evening practising my bandaging techniques on Loxwood, who is too concerned with eating the fresh hay to object. But the third and most important reason for doing all this is that I actually get to spend some time with my horses. They're *my* horses, and the whole point in coming here was to further their training, and yet I can't help but feel that they're not welcome. Whenever I linger, spend a few extra minutes watching Loxwood through the grill of his stable, or take twenty minutes out of my day to pull Cookie's mane, I can feel everybody's eyes on me. And when I tack Loxwood up to ride, or lead Cookie to the school to lunge her (because I haven't even dared ride her here yet), all I see written across everyone's faces - James, Paris, and the other two grooms who look so similar I can barely distinguish them - is *What's the point?* While those words haven't been spoken since my first lesson with James, I can't get them out of my head. I'm convinced it's what everybody is thinking, and the way they regard me and my horses is as though I should feel bad for dedicating time to them. *You're overreacting.* That's probably what anyone I know would say if I told them this, which I haven't because the last thing I want to do is make Rose or Leni or even my mum worry, but I know I'm not imagining it. They don't think my horses deserve attention, I'm so certain of it. Just as certain as I am that right now, something isn't right.

There's that stillness in the air that only comes with night, the kind that is mystical and haunting, and that I usually love, but tonight's different. There's something else in the atmosphere. An uneasiness, the knowledge that something isn't right.

'Hey, guys,' I whisper as I come into the barn, holding up the light on my phone. Already I know I'm right, that there's something around, because every horse has their head pushed up against the sable grills, my torch shining off each panicked eye. My throat clenches with fear, but yet it doesn't paralyse me, it does the opposite. I step up to the first stable, that of Pemberley, and peer in. It takes a moment for my head to make sense of what is amiss, and as soon as it does I shine my torch down the aisle again, and then I see it and I start running. The tack room door is wide open, and I don't even stop to look inside before I'm running out, towards the car park, my mind flashing with what I just saw. It's freezing, cold for any horse, let alone a clipped one, and I overheard Paris and the two other grooms discussing which rugs to choose tonight, and they then addressed me, as the person who does the night check, to see if I could make double sure that everyone was warm enough when I came out. And I did, slipping my hand beneath each cover and then running my fingers to the tops of each horse's ears. But Pemberley doesn't have a rug on now, the idea clicking with the sound of a car door in my head, and then I saw the open tack room.

I'm running, the boots I didn't even bother to put on properly slipping from beneath my feet as my heels fall over the edges. One fall and I could sprain my ankle, temporarily putting me out of action as far as riding is concerned, but I push past all of this as my heart continues to thump louder and louder in my chest. *No. No. NO.* The thought alone makes me want to break down in sobs, yet as I think this I realise just how composed I am under the circumstances. Well, if you ignore the fact that I'm running around a stable yard in the middle of the night wearing pyjamas with cartoon mice printed on them.

At first, I think I'm too late. But through the dark, the beam from my torch lands on a white van, and before the two hooded figures have even finished turning their heads round to see the source of the light, I scream.

'*HEY!*'

If I weren't so concerned with the fact that there is no way I can get to them before they drive off, I would be impressed by how intimidating I sound. It wasn't a high-pitched cry. I sounded strong, confident.

But even as I keep running, I know what's going to happen. I keep screaming, hoping that if it doesn't scare these people it will at least alert Paris, but the figures jump into the front of the van, start the engine, and begin driving off. I can't catch them, there's no way, but I have to try. I keep going, wobbling as I curse myself for not pulling my boots on properly, running and yelling, feeling every emotion I've bottled up during the past seven months rise to the surface. *You're a failure.* That's what I keep thinking. *You're a failure. You're a failure. You're a failure.* And now I'm failing at this, too. I've failed Loxwood, I've failed Nantucket, and I'm even failing Cookie. I don't know how to get out of this situation, and I know that even if my legs suddenly turned into those of an Olympic sprinter I wouldn't be able to catch up with the van. I'm holding my phone out in front of me, hoping to at least read the numberplate, but these people clearly aren't going to make a rookie mistake like that, because it's been covered up. And still I don't stop running.

Alerting Paris with my yelling has clearly worked, because from the corners of my eyes I catch the luminosity that comes from switching on the barn lights. And there Paris will see the rug-less horses, and the open tack room door, and she'll discover just how much damage has been done, something I don't know the answer to. But my legs are moving, my ankles wet from the dew that covers the grass, and for a moment it's not even about the fact that if what's just happened is as bad as I think it is, I have no saddle, no bridles, and my horses have literally been stripped of the clothes on their backs. It's about something more, my chest contracting with every stride, feeling like maybe things never come together. Because that's what you always think, when things get rough. *It will all come together in the end.* But what if it doesn't? What if it never happens, and we're stuck chasing something that is forever out of our grasp. Oh, you'll think you have it at some point. It will be right there, an inch from your fingers, so close you can almost touch it. But then it strikes a leg out and trips you over, and as you fly to the ground you see it - what you think is meant to be - disappearing beyond the horizon, leaving you to start running again. But what if you never catch it? Because things don't always work out, otherwise there wouldn't be horrors in the world.

I reach the end of the driveway, coming to a stop as I look left and right, wondering which way they could have gone. But everything is silent, not a car on the road, and I know I'm beat. My breath is coming in heavy gasps, only made worse by the cold air, and I remember that Loxwood and Cookie are probably without rugs. And even if I hurry back to them now, I won't have any to put on them. And while none of this has actually been confirmed, I just *know*. The way I knew something wasn't right when the sound of a car door woke me up. The same way I know that this whole situation, being here, isn't working out.

Raising my hands to my head, I turn around. But my luck has worn out, and in one swift motion the back of my right heel slips off the side of my boot, and I go flying. At least I miss the tarmac, landing in the grass on the verge, and if I had just fallen off a horse I would already be up, because lying there is never an option. But now I'm already wet, dew soaking through my pyjamas, and feeling suffocated by my coat, so I stay still for a moment, closing my eyes, knowing that in a minute I'll have to go and face reality.

I knew it, it was inevitable, and yet the truth is still a blow.

They took everything. The saddles, the bridles, and the rugs from the horses' backs. Paris is hysterical, and when James and Melody arrive, James in jeans and the rest of us in pyjamas, they're in tears. James's saddles were insured, but the odds of getting the company to pay up, he says, are next to none. They always find something to fault, and admittedly keeping the key to the tack room a few feet away doesn't fit the bill. But he has tack sponsors, who will send him new, luxury saddles. And the rugs, that will have cost a few hundred quid each, will be replaced. I'm the one who is left with nothing. My saddle isn't insured, and certainly not the bridles, and bar the fact that they had been cheap to begin with, my rugs had been ripped and repaired so many times that they weren't even worth taking. But these people clearly weren't picky. At least they didn't get my travel boots, safe in the back of my car, or my riding jacket and boots that are in my camper along with my body protector. They did get my hat, though, so I can't even ride Loxwood round in a head collar until I dish out the money needed to replace it.

As soon as James and Melody begin making phone calls, I go to my mobile home and gather the duvet and blankets from my bed, watching that they don't trail in the wet grass as I carry them to the stables. The duvet I put over Cookie, securing it round her girth passage with one of the travel straps that the vandals were kind enough not to take (among a few other boxes of bits and pieces), and do the same on Loxwood with the blankets. I didn't notice Melody leave, but she must have had the same idea as me because she comes into the barn a few minutes later with an armful of folded blankets she obviously just went home to collect.

Police arrive, and I'm the one who has to speak to them and describe what I saw, which isn't much. Two people, a white van.

What kind of van? A white one. It we were talking about a horse, I would have only needed one glance to say that it was a Thoroughbred with a hint of something heavier, Irish Draught maybe? Fifteen-three, tad long in the back, quite an upright shoulder. But car makes elude me, which is what I tell the policeman as he keeps asking me the same question again and again, as though if he does so enough times I'll remember. But it's futile.

We're all standing around the hay steamer at seven A.M., warming our cold and tired hands against the machine that is preparing another load, because we've already fed the horses what was supposed to be for this morning, when the other grooms arrive. I watch the shock on their faces, as James fills them in on the night we've had, like an outsider. Pretending, just for a moment, that all this doesn't affect me. That it's just another tack-theft story, the kind you read about in *Horse and Hound* every so often, never believing it will actually happen to you. And even though I'm exhausted, all I want to do is tack up Loxwood and take him for a ride across the hills, the only way I know how to clear my head. But, guess what? I can't. Save going off with a head collar and lead rope without a hat, and even I'm not stupid enough to do that. If I had a hat, maybe, but not without one.

James and Melody leave not long after, telling us all to take it easy. They're going to spend the day sourcing tack and rugs, they say, but as nice as they are I'm pretty sure that doesn't include a saddle for me. And then I remember that today is my day off, and I had plans to go see my parents and Rose. But right now all I want to do is be with my horses. Except that hanging around the barn, the bareness of it like another person, is too much to bear.

Another thing that wasn't stolen were my brushing boots, which doesn't say much about the thieves so much as it does about what a state they're in. They're fastened to the stable railings, muddy and missing straps, not even considered good enough to steal.

Although it's cold now, it's supposed to warm up later this afternoon, so I put the boots on my horses and turn them out. At least not owning any rugs means that nobody can complain about Loxwood and Cookie not having any on in the field, and I watch as they each find a patch of mud in their respective paddocks to roll in, not even caring that I'm going to have my work cut out for me later.

My plan was to get to Rose's for ten, only for a quick catchup over tea between her rides, which still leaves me an hour until I need to leave, after the worst of rush hour. And since everybody is too shocked and depressed to tell me otherwise, I spend the time mucking out my horses' stables, spreading shavings out across the whole box. I still don't consider it enough, and it can hardly be described as a bed, but at least the thought of them lying down in boxes like this is a little less sickening.

So now I'll drive to Newmarket, spending an hour or so with Rose and my mother in turn. It's not enough to keep me busy all day, but it's something.

I'm climbing into Tucker, having swapped my pyjamas for jeans and a jumper, not even addressing the tangled, tied-up mess that is my hair. I've only just put the key in the ignition when my phone buzzes, alerting me of a text, and I look at the screen to see the name *Leni Cullen* flash up. **Oh my god, is it true? Just saw the news online. Are you OK? Are the horses OK? It's my day off, do you want me to come and give you guys a hand or something?**

Of course the news is online. One of the first things James (or Melody) will have done after speaking to the police is alert the horse world press. Yet I'm still surprised, almost hoping that if nobody else knew I would be able to pretend, for a little while, that it hadn't happened. **Yeah, everything's fine. They took the rugs right from the horses' backs, but they're all ok. My day off too, am going to Newmarket. Just need to get out.**

Leni's response comes seconds later. **What else did they take?**

I stare at the screen a moment, wondering how best to reply to this, but it's simple. **Everything**

This time, it's a while until Leni's next message comes through, and for a moment I think she isn't going to reply, because there isn't anything to reply to that, and I turn the key in the ignition, but then my phone makes a sound again. **Do you wanna come round? To the yard. Clear your head, and I have some spare stuff you could use. Plus I've made a really good batch of choc chip cookies :)**

I laugh reading that last line, and answer right away. **Yeah. That sounds great!**

# Chapter 10

The fact that I'm about to drive into Amanda Walton's yard doesn't really dawn on me until I'm faced with the automatic gates that open when I get near them. As Leni said I would, I almost missed the turning. You'd expect a fifty acre equestrian setup to be in the middle of nowhere, but I'm in a village, having just passed a convenience store with an old-fashioned front, and too many storybook cottages to count. But these are undoubtably the gates I've been looking for, leading right off the narrow country road, and suddenly, as they open, I'm in paradise.

I'm still in the typically English village, yet here I am, staring at rows and rows of post and rail paddocks, facing the short, white driveway that runs between them. The gates start closing once I've driven through, and already I can see the stable yard. Stone buildings, running in a U, with horses' heads peaking over the half doors, looking happy and relaxed. There's a big house, with the kind of facade you only see in period dramas on TV or at event venues, set at the farthest visible boundary, and between it and the stable block is a wooden chalet. I can't see an arena, which is enough to suggest that the land stretches on for quite a way behind the buildings. It's so… not how I pictured Amanda Walton's yard to be.

Not quite sure where I'm supposed to go, I park my car beside another jeep that is near the stables, hoping this is what I'm supposed to do. I can't see any lorries, so there must be another parking area somewhere, but I don't see that I'm causing any trouble here. And luckily before the thought of running into Amanda makes me panic further, Leni appears.

'Hey!' she calls, bright and happy as always. Seriously, how are some people that happy? 'Did you find it easily?'

'Good thing you warned me about those gates coming out of nowhere,'

'I know, right?' With the exception of the couple of times I've seen her in Newmarket, I almost only see Leni at competitions, when she's kitted out in luxury riding clothes. But today she's in full on "day off" apparel. Tracksuit bottoms, shoes that look like slippers, an overstretched jumper that practically hangs off her, and thick curls pulled back in a high ponytail.

'So,' I say, before Leni can ask something along the lines of how I'm doing, because I've cried enough today. 'This place is not what I was expecting.'

'Yeah?' says Leni, easily picking up on my conversation starter.

'Yeah,' I repeat. 'I was expecting something more… you know…'

'Glass and chrome and prison uniforms?'

'Exactly,' I say, laughing. Amanda Walton, unlike James, isn't known for niceness. Laid-back is the last way you would describe her, yet that is exactly how the yard feels, and I've only been here sixty seconds.

'The thing about Amanda,' Leni says, speaking quietly as she steps closer. 'Is that she isn't good with people. Horses, on the other hand, she's great. I mean, come on, how many times has she been round Badminton? She knows what she's doing. And I'm not so desperate that I'd put up with her if my horses weren't happy here.'

I try not to let my reaction to that last sentence show on my face. Without even realising it, Leni has struck the idea that has been on my mind ever since arriving at James's yard. I thought maybe I was just being ridiculous, but that's exactly what I feel. My horses don't seem happy there. Though I could be getting ahead of myself, I remember, because James's yard looks fine from a distance too, and for all I know Amanda's is the same, and up close will be a different story.

'Do you wanna look around before we go get a drink or something?' Leni says.

'Yeah,' I say, before adding, 'Amanda won't mind?'

Leni shakes her head, already walking towards the stables in front of us. 'You know, she's not actually *that* bad. Not if you don't work for her, or don't do anything to put yourself in her bad books.'

I grin. 'Like throw a bucket of water over her?' I say, remembering the story of Ryan, a fellow competitor, mistaking Amanda for Alex during a water fight.

'Yep! Exactly. Just stay clear of water buckets, and you should be fine.'

Most of the horses are in their stables, though a few are still moping around the paddocks, and Leni explains that they each get three hours of turnout.

'Every day?' I say.

Leni nods, continuing to walk past the first row of stables. 'Yep. I mean, if it's pouring down or snowing then maybe we'll give the odd day a miss, and if it's really hot then they'll come in earlier - but let's face it, that doesn't exactly happen often.'

We go see Lochmere first, who is munching on some hay that has been shaken out at the front of his stable. The boxes are rubber lined, like James's, but unlike James, Amanda obviously believes in horses having enough bedding to lie down in, because five inches worth of shavings cover the mats, not to mention the big banks built up around. The walls have been painted in black gloss paint up to shoulder height, the top halves white. And I even notice that Lochmere has a bucket of water by his stable door.

'Does Amanda not have automatics?' I say, nodding at the bucket.

'Oh, she does,' says Leni, pointing at one on the other side of the doorway that I hadn't noticed. 'But Olly's not that keen on them. We've got a few like that, actually, and Amanda doesn't even like automatics that much, but at least you know they've got the option if ever they tip over a bucket.'

Lochmere raises his head from the hay, stretching his neck out to nudge Leni and me in turn over the half door, happy and relaxed, before lowering his nose for another mouthful.

'He only cares about food,' Leni says.

'He looks well,' I say, staring at the black horse's glossy, well muscled coat.

Leni shrugs. 'Amanda wouldn't have it any other way.'

After touring the stables, getting introduced to each horse, and walking to see the arena, we go to the wooden chalet I saw when I drove in. It turns out this is where Leni lives, along with two other grooms, and while I'm no expert I'm pretty sure it has to be one of the best working pupil accommodations in existence. It's one of those buildings that comes as a flatpack, Leni informs me as I gape at the perfect living conditions. It's not fancy, far from it, but that's what I like. An open plan sitting room and kitchen, with wooden floors, and walls you can barely make out beneath cross country photographs.

'Pretty much everyone who's ever been here,' Leni says as I admire the many horses that surround me. A lot I don't recognise, but I also see a lot of pictures of Amanda, jumping some of Badminton's most iconic fences, and people she's trained to go on and do the same. There are pictures of Leni, mostly on Lochmere, some from the last European Championships that have been framed complete with congratulatory messages, suggesting they were hung as a surprise for her when she got back.

Dog hair covered throws are on the sofas, and what is supposed to be a dining table is hidden beneath printed dressage tests, rosettes, about fifty different copies of *Horse and Hound*, and cardboard boxes with the names of famous equestrian brands printed on the sides.

'I'm not even going to lie and tell you it isn't normally like this,' Leni says as she pushes items to one side of the table.

'No, I like it,' I say, as my eyes fall on the packages Leni is now holding. 'Are those what I think they are?'

Leni looks down at the expensive jodhpurs, still folded and wrapped in plastic through which a label is visible. 'Crazy, isn't it? The box arrived today. Apparently, my sponsor thinks I need not one, but *six* pairs.'

'Nice sponsor,' I say, looking at the jodhpurs that should come with a lifetime guarantee for what I know they cost.

'Take some,' Leni says, all casual as she pushes a couple pairs towards me.

'Oh,' Suddenly I feel really stupid for saying everything I just have. Now I sound like I was begging so she would offer me some out of pity, which was the last thing on my mind. 'I didn't mean it like that. I wasn't trying to make you give me any.'

'You didn't,' Leni says, walking over to the kitchen area to fill a kettle with water. 'I offered.'

'No, I couldn't.'

'Seriously. You see how many pairs there are. And I've already got however many upstairs. I'd need a second set of legs to get through them all. And I'm sure were the same size. Ten?'

I nod.

'There you go, then. I'm not taking no for an answer, so will you hurry up and accept?'

It's only the fact that Leni's grinning, waiting for my response before switching the kettle on, that I nod. 'Fine. But I owe you. When I get some fancy sponsor, you have to accept a pair of jodhpurs from me. Deal?'

'Deal,' says Leni, carrying a biscuit tin over to me.

'You realise jodhpurs are pretty much the only thing that didn't get stolen?' I say, a remark that sounded funny in my head but not so much now that I'm saying it out loud.

'Don't let me forget to give you some stuff,' Leni says. 'I've got some spare bridles and rugs..'

I shake my head. 'Don't worry about it. I went to see Rose this morning, and my car's practically overflowing. I think I have more tack now than I started out with.' It's true. While I told her it wasn't necessary, Rose spent almost the whole time I was there removing things from her tack room and piling them into my arms. Granted, I was glad to be able to borrow some rugs for tonight, but I was completely taken aback when she went on to carry both a saddle and two bridles to the back of my car.

'I can't accept that,' I said.

'At the very least borrow them if it makes you feel better,' Rose said. 'The saddle should fit Loxwood, anyway. It's what I usually use on Thoroughbreds.'

And by some miracle, Rose and I have the same sized head, and she gave me one of her crash caps, so at least I'll be able to start riding Loxwood again tomorrow.

For the next hour, Leni and I drink tea and eat biscuits, mostly discussing James. I try not to make it sound like I'm completely miserable, but the small things I do mention seem to earn the same reaction from Leni as they did from me. So at least I'm not the only one that feels that way.

It's only when I'm driving away that I remember that I forgot to ask Leni about the other thing on my mind. Nantucket. Or more to the point, ask her what she knows about the way Imogen runs her yard. I know Leni knows her, because she said before that she was lovely, so maybe she would have at least been able to reassure me that Nantucket gets fed well. I could text and ask, obviously, but I can just see the words, **Hey, do you know if Imogen is looking after my horse right?** popping up on her phone and making me look completely crazy. Of course Imogen knows how to look after horses, she's been round four-star tracks, but I still wish I had thought to ask.

The moonlight casts shadows against the walls, and I stare at the patterns until I can bear it no more. All my (or Rose's, I should say) tack is piled on the sofa, even though I know the thieves aren't exactly going to be back, seeing as they've already taken everything worth stealing, but you never know. But

Loxwood is still out there, and I can't sleep, and all I want is to be with him. After all, isn't the whole point of sleeping a few feet away from your horse being able to go see him in the middle of the night?

Even though I'm not expecting another high speed chase, I make sure my boots are on properly should I need to run. But when I step outside this time, the night holds only the dark magic it's supposed to. There's no anxiety, and I smile as I inhale the cool air.

'Hey, buddies, it's just me,' I say as I walk into the barn. I'm pretty sure wandering around the stable aisle at night isn't exactly something James or anyone else that works here would approve of, but if anybody finds out I'll just say that I heard a noise. After last night, they can't exactly argue with that.

'Lox?' I say, pushing my face up to the railings. Stupid railings, I think. He can't even look out of his stable.

I'm greeted with a low whicker, the same huh-huh-huh I got from Nantucket when I saw him. The surest way to my heart there is.

'Hey,' I say, sliding the door open. Moonlight has cast a canopy of shadows across the barn, and they dance across Loxwood as he moves forwards to greet me, nudging my coat pockets. 'I don't have anything for you,' I say. 'Sorry. I didn't exactly plan this. I just wanted to see you.'

Loxwood stands beside me, neck arched as though he were in a dressage test, directly in line with the brightest beam from above, lighting up his head.

'This isn't very good, is it?' I say, kicking at the thin layer of shavings. 'None of this is going to plan. And I don't quite know what I'm going to do yet, but I'm going to do something. Okay? Even if I have to go running back to Rose and beg for her help.

So please just hang on a little bit longer. All right? We're not going to stay here. And James is wrong, you hear me? Even if he wasn't, I would never sell you. Even if it meant never going any higher than Novice. But that doesn't matter, because I know you can do it. We might not be the best, but we're going to work the hardest. Because there's no reason we can't be. You're the horse of my dreams, Loxwood. Don't you forget that. My golden ticket dream horse. And you can refuse every fence I point you at for all I care, because it won't stop me from loving you. And I know you really do think I'm crazy now, and I'll try to stop these random babbling heart-to-hearts, but I just wanted to tell you that. I love you so much. I even love Cookie, although all she does is try to kill me.' I laugh at this, wiping away the tears that have found their way to my cheeks. 'I'm gonna get us out of here, Lox. I'm going to get you out of here. Just give me some time.'

# Chapter 11

My supposed escape plan gets put on hold when James asks me if I'm taking Loxwood to an event he's got six horses entered at, three weeks away. Doing so ties my hands for that time period at least, but I also need to get him out again, so I enter. And for the next twenty-one days I make the most of each session as though it were my last. I go to sleep thinking about dressage movements, and I awake from cross country dreams. James gives me jumping lessons, which admittedly are hugely helpful, and I wonder if I've been too hasty, wanting to leave already, but then I look at Loxwood in his stable, without that same sparkle in his eye, and I'm reassured. So I might as well do what I came here for and make the most of what James can actually teach me.

Even though there's a spot on the lorry the day Loxwood is competing, I decide to take him in my own trailer. At least that way I don't have to worry about my tack and belongings getting in the way, and I'm freer to do as I wish. And the evening before,

I'm neither confident nor defeatist. Because whatever happens, I know that I've done everything I can. It will be down to Loxwood.

Of course, I was still hoping that I wouldn't pull up at the venue to find it pouring down. Rain splatters against Tucker's windscreen, the wipers working overtime to keep me seeing. The tractors are going to be busy today, because I have a feeling we're all going to be getting stuck.

* * *

'Three, two, one.. *GO!* Good luck!'

We fly out of the start box, not waisting a second. It took everything I had to stop Loxwood from taking off early, and I barely even came to a halt between the barriers. And I don't try to hold him back. It's wet, and the ground is muddy, but this is cross country, after all. You're supposed to go fast.

Loxwood's ears prick as soon as he locks on to the first fence, and I lower my seat to the saddle, without sitting, as we move on a forward stride. *The first fence is supposed to give them confidence.* My attitude is saying "Go!", and Loxwood's response is, "One step ahead of you,".

I try to stick to the edge of the track, avoiding the churned up ground that many other horses have already been down. My weight shifts in my stirrups, and Loxwood moves with me. Feeling our way across the ground, his stride powering forward. We're working together. I'm not overthinking, or hesitating, or expecting everything to be perfect. I'm just doing my best. We both are.

When we come to the trakehner, I feel Loxwood's hesitation

as he begins to back off, remembering last time. But I know he can do it, we both can. And what's the worst that can happen? I click my tongue, encouraging him, remembering those words of Rose's that have helped me out so much recently. *The more he backs off a fence, the more you attack it. You have to show him there's nothing to be afraid of, and he'll feed off your confidence.* I repeat it to myself over and over again. *Give him confidence. Give him confidence.*

'Go on!' I yell, pushing my hands up Loxwood's wet neck. 'Go on!' I yell again.

Loxwood's ears flicker back, but I keep pushing towards the fence, right up to the last stride. *We're getting over,* I think. *We're getting over. We're getting over. We're getting over.* And we do.

'Good boy!' I scream, running a hand up and down his neck as we gallop to the next fence. 'You can do this!'

Soon we're galloping through the finish line, and I'm practically sobbing as I call words of praise. If Loxwood didn't hate having his neck patted, my hands would be numb from doing so. Instead, I slide from his back, running up the stirrups and loosening the girth at top speed, and throw my arms around his neck

'I knew you could do it,' I say, jogging beside him as he walks. 'I've always known. Now we've just go to show everyone else.'

I'm sure everyone passing by is wondering what the heck somebody who was halfway up the dressage order, and knocked a fence show jumping, is so happy about a clear round ninety centimetres for, because they're probably still not going to be placed, but it doesn't matter. This is everything. This is me and Loxwood succeeding. This is our victory. And it should also be enough to qualify for the Five Year Old Championships.

For a moment, I wonder if this is a mistake, but I've put it off for too long. Loxwood is safe and dry in one of the stables James has hired for the day, eating hay and drying off. My focus has been on him all day, and I just need to do this for myself right now.

It doesn't matter how many times I've seen this before, or how many times I prepare myself, rehearsing this moment in my mind, because seeing the grey horse canter round still takes my breath away. Nantucket, my Nantucket. Beautiful and trusting and brave. And *kind*. That's the main thing, the reason I was drawn to him in the first place. One of the kindest souls I'll ever know.

For perhaps the first time since I've known her, Leni isn't riding today. Lochmere and Cooper are both entered in big classes next week, and Arturo is off for a few days with an abscess, so she's here as a supporter. She's standing in a raincoat, hood pulled up over her head, beside Amanda, who is helping someone warm up. But I'll talk to Leni in a minute. Right now, I just want to watch Nantucket alone.

I stand to one side, watching my horse jump the warm-up fences, and I'm still here when he gets called to the start box, watching as he trots over calmly, and then sets off at a gallop, clearing the first fence without hesitation. It's an open course, one you can see a lot of without wandering very far, and I watch him jump every fence he's pointed at, completely unflustered. And when the grey horse comes through the finish flags, ears pricked, I find myself crying. Not loud sobs, just silent tears running down my face. And realising that I'm suddenly staring into space, crying, no less, I turn back to the warm-up, wiping tears on my sleeves. Only then do I see Liz, who has so obviously been watching me, but now turns away. She really has got to be the rudest person I've ever met. But I don't want to get into that now.

More horses come and go, and soon Imogen is riding back into the ring on another, a beautiful bay with a white diamond on his head. He looks more like a dressage horse than an eventer to me, but then even with his unorthodox action he clears the fences in the ring easily, so what do I know?

Liz has walked away now, probably to go drink champagne or whatever it is that rich people spend their time doing, and Imogen is trotting by the start box when Leni makes her way over to me.

'You look busy,' I say.

It was supposed to be a joke, but Leni is smiling widely. 'This is really fun! Seriously, getting to enjoy an event without competing yourself. I mean, I wouldn't want to do it too often, but every once in a while is great. Anyway, that's boring. A way better topic is your awesome cross country round.'

I grin. 'He was great. If only there were no dressage and show jumping!'

'Oh, I'm with you on that one. I saw Nantucket, too. He looks good.'

'Yeah,' I say. 'Nantucket and his unbelievably rude owner. I've seen her twice now, and she doesn't even say hello to me. Are all rich that rude?'

Leni shrugs. 'I dunno. Because then you've got someone like Erin,' she says, referring to a fellow competitor I tend to just think of as "the one that's always cold", 'and she's probably richer than everyone here today put together, and yet she's one of the nicest people you'll ever meet. So who knows?' She smiles as she says this last word, but it fades as her eyes lock on to something behind me, and I turn to see what it is. But even as I do, I'm left none the wiser as I see only an empty start box, realising that Imogen has set off again.

'What's wrong?' I say.

'Nothing,' Leni says, rain falling from her hood as she shakes her head. But she's started walking, and I follow her. 'I just never know if I want to watch this or not,' She clearly does today, though, because her eyes are glued to the moving horse.

'Imogen?' I say, confused. 'That reminds me, actually, I keep meaning to ask you if you know anything about her yard. Because you said something about her being nice before..'

'Oh, she really is lovely,' says Leni, still waking and looking ahead as she does so, her eyes on the moving body of Imogen's horse. 'And her horses are really well looked after. I just don't like watching *this* horse.'

I look back at the bay in the distance. 'Why?'

'It's Motown.'

She says this like it should mean something to me. 'Who?'

'Motown. You know, Made in Motown.' Leni frowns at my confusion, going on. 'You know, the horse that used to belong to Alex.' And seeing that I'm none the wiser, she goes on. 'Have I really never told you this? You know, the horse Alex used to have with the dangly front legs. The one she had a crashing fall with, and her parents sold.'

'That's him!?' I say. 'They sold him to Imogen?'

Leni nods. 'She really liked him. But if you ask me, Alex is right. It's just an accident waiting to happen.'

My head is fuzzy with new information, trying to process all this and whether or not it's actually relevant. Somehow, Leni and I have made are way farther onto the course, watching as the bay moves along. I can see it now - the big, scopey jump, but no snap. He doesn't know how to get his legs out of the way.

Motown is in our range of vision as he slips on the landing side of a log, the first part of a combination. Not his fault, only the bad weather's. But then, because they've lost momentum, Imogen pushes him on. I feel my body go still, and Leni gasps. It's a mistake, anyone can see it. But she keeps going, pushing him to the next element. She shouldn't do it, I think. She should have held back and added a stride. Maybe it would be all right on a horse that is quick with his feet, but this one clearly isn't.

It all happens slowly, with the sense that it's inevitable. Motown taking off, trying to make height, but it's not enough to make up for his dangling forelegs, Imogen going with him. For a second, it looks like it's going to be all right. But then Motown hits the fence, and the impacts swings him over. And they're falling, falling, falling. Imogen's body on the ground is the last thing I see of her before Motown's body lands on top.

And even in the panic, and the shock, and the want to run over and do something, my head is still able to think. And a sentence, six words, flashes through my mind.

*What's the worst that can happen?*

# LAP OF HONOUR

BOOK 5

*'Don't be pushed by your problems. Be led by your dreams.'*
Ralph Waldo Emerson

# Chapter 1

The fence judges get there first. Two people, who have up to this point been sitting in the comfort of a car, running over to crouch beside Imogen's limp body, as Motown struggles to his feet.

One of the women, the one who reached Imogen one step ahead of the other, is hunched over her for a second before turning round, walkie-talkie in hand, and yelling, 'We need an ambulance!' And if witnessing the fall wasn't enough to inform us that this isn't good, the panic in the fence judge's voice certainly does it.

'Should we do something?' I ask Leni, watching as more people begin making their way over to the fence, Imogen hidden behind their bodies.

'We could get Motown,' Leni says, but as soon as the words are out, a groom appears to take the horse. 'At least he's okay,' she continues, as we watch the bay horse be led off the course. He's moving stiffly, and even from here you can see the rise and fall of his breathing, but he's all right.

Leni and I stay where we are, standing on the sidelines of the cross country course, the patter of rain hitting our coats accompanying the sound of tires rolling over wet ground and voices. The speakers announce a hold on course, reassuring spectators that Motown in "on his feet" and that "paramedics are assessing Imogen, and we'll have news on her condition shortly".

'Have you seen her move yet?' I say to Leni, just as paramedics clear to reveal a stretcher being lifted into the back of an ambulance. 'She must be conscious,' I continue, not waiting for a response. 'Because her leg's up. See?' Imogen is lying flat except for her right leg, which is bent at the knee.

'Paramedics position bodies like that,' Leni says the words, her voice flat and disconnected as though belonging to an automatic recording. 'It's not good,' she goes on, shaking her head. 'You *know* when it's not good. And we both saw the fall - he landed on top of her.'

'You don't think she's...' *Dead*. Not a word I've ever been afraid of before. If anything, I'm used to it. A word thrown around so loosely in racing yards. One that is said too many times to count on the radio, whether it be one person down the road from you or seventy-one in a country not that far away. And then the category that is almost more terrifying. *Riders*. Cross country is dangerous, always has been and always will be as far as I'm concerned, and every time a news update pops up on my phone, informing me of another young person with the same goals and aspirations as me, falling at a seemingly uncomplicated fence, there's a feeling of sickness. Once again reminded of the risks of this sport, but when you read of these fatalities, whether people admit it or not, you always think *at least it's not me*. Or maybe more to the point, you never believe it will be you. I'll be different, you think. Of all the riders in the world, what are the chances of me being the one? But then whoever got crushed beneath their horse will have thought the same thing. And you expect these sorts of things to happen at four-star level, it's almost part of the game, but at two-star? One? Or, like today, Novice? And when fatalities do happen, it's always to people you don't know. And I realise that's a silly thing to say, because of course a lot of people will know whomever the person in question is, but up to now I haven't, and nor have the fatalities happened this close to home. Yet here I am, witnessing the consequences, and not saying the word is ridiculous considering I'm pretty sure that's what I've just seen.

'I…' Leni shakes her head. 'I can't. Not until… I just can't think about it unless we know for sure.'

'I know.'

'My god,' she says, raising a hand to her face. 'I know I just said I don't want to think about it, and this is the least important thing right now, but if anything *has* happened, Alex will be crushed.'

'I can't believe I didn't realise Imogen's the one who bought him,' I say, just to say something.

'I thought I'd told you,' Leni says. 'I meant to, anyway. When you said Nantucket was going to Imogen, I thought I told you.. I obviously didn't. Anyway, yeah. Imogen had always liked him, and like I said he's great on the flat, and he does have a lot of scope. Alex just always said that he could never get his feet out of the way when it mattered..'

'Alex can't blame herself though, can she? Not that we know anything. I mean, Imogen's probably fine. But it's not Alex's fault.. Didn't she say that she had a crashing fall with him once?'

Leni nods, and I can't help but think she looks rather cold

and pale beneath her coat hood. 'It was coming out of water. Up a step and one stride to the next fence, and he left a leg at the second element.' *Like today*, I think. 'And of course, sometimes those things just happen and it's nobody's fault, but he was *always* dangling his legs. And as far as Alex was concerned, it was just a matter of waiting for him to keep falling. But he would quite easily fall once and then go double clear nine times. But Alex was adamant after that fall - it was a rotational - and you know Alex, she's not exactly fainthearted. She'd have to really be worried to refuse to ride something.'

'And she thought he could show jump,' I say, remembering the conversation. 'Right?'

'Yeah. Because he actually had, *has*, a lot of scope. And he can jump plenty high enough to clear any fence you point him at, but when he gets himself into a tricky situation, like earlier, he just doesn't have that natural ability to snap his knees up around his chin.'

'But surely Alex's parents knew that, too.' I say. 'I mean, they're Joan and Ridley Evans for goodness' sake! They know nobody would want to ride a cross country horse like that.'

Leni sucks in a breath as she shakes her head slowly. 'They started out back when eventing was long format. Their motto was ride however you had to to get any and every horse round. They didn't care if it looked dangerous. Cross country was supposed to be risky. And now that dressage and show jumping are so influential, they thought it was ridiculous that Alex pass on a horse that's so reliable in those two phases.'

'Well, why didn't one of *them* ride him, then?' I say angrily, as not too far away another horse sets off from the start box, cross country action resumed.

'Ridley would have, I think. At first they were just angry at

Alex for refusing to ride him, and she so nearly fell out with them over it. And then Ridley thought he would take on the ride to prove a point, but then they got offered a ridiculous amount of money for him. And the fact that he'd been doing so well up to now they considered a " we told you so" to Alex. But she really did fight for him. I mean, fight to say that he shouldn't be going cross country. And I know she's kind of loud and outspoken, and she does overreact sometimes, but she's fair, and she'll do whatever she thinks is right, whatever that means for her.'

'But then, if anything *has* happened, it's not like she didn't say something.'

'It's probably nothing,' Leni says with a swing of her arms. 'I'm sure she's just winded. Or broken an ankle or something.'

'Right,' I say. But it's quite clear that neither of us believe the words.

As quickly as Imogen fell, competition resumes. Nothing is said, good or bad, as everyone moves on. Yet there's an unspoken edge, the stereotypical elephant in the room, that something is terribly wrong.

'You're all right, aren't you, buddy?' I say to Loxwood, going into his stable and wrapping my arms around his neck. I had planned on leaving after watching Nantucket, assuming James and Paris didn't need my help with anything, but now I've convinced myself that I'll go once I hear something, anything, about Imogen.

'Do you know how Imogen's doing?' I ask James when I walk out the stable to see him riding over on Trevor, coming back from the show jumping ring.

He looks at me blankly,

'Imogen Hollis-Rye,' I add, wondering if it's necessary. 'She had a rotational on course.'

'I didn't hear anything,' says James, still looking confused but I'm not sure why seeing as it's quite a simple question. 'I'm sure it's just a fall.'

'No,' I say. 'This was bad. Seriously. She... never moved. They carried her off on a stretcher, but there hasn't been a word said since.'

I can see that this does at least alarm James a little more, but before he can say anything else Paris is there, leading a tacked-up horse towards him, and he's off again.

'It'll be nothing,' Paris says briskly, undoing Trevor's throat lash while he tries to rub his head up and down against her arm.

'But the commentators didn't say anything,' I say. But now Paris has shot Trevor a look of annoyance which I am pretty sure is actually directed at me, so I drop the matter.

As Trevor is led away, I'm left standing in front of the collapsable stables, jodhpurs soaked through and water dripping from my ponytail, watching as everyone goes about with their day - filling water bucket, pulling out plaits, unscrewing studs. And I'm just standing here, wondering if anyone else is aware of the casualty that may or may not have just taken place. Until I can bear it no longer, and I go off in search of somebody I know. If anything has happened, Alex will be my best bet. Not only because Motown was once hers, but because I'm pretty sure there is no news on the eventing circuit that doesn't reach the Evans horse box first.

My boots squelch in the mud, splattering dirt onto my beige jodhpurs. The washing machine in the horse barn, which both Paris and I have access to for our own washing, is mediocre at best, so trying to get those stains out will be fun. Maybe I'll take a load of washing back home, my mum seems to enjoy that sort of thing...

Tractors are towing cars and lorries from the field, wheels spinning madly until the strength finally pulls them free. Is that why Imogen fell? Was it really just too slippery? I make a quick step left to avoid a puddle, wondering what *any* of us are doing running in this weather. But then again, that's what cross country is about. Rain or shine, snow or thunderstorm, you ride. End of. Those sorts of conditions are what distinguish the pros from the pack. It's part of the whole "riding by the seat of your pants" thing. If it rains, you get wet. If you break a limb, you strap it up and jump on your next horse. You have to be crazy to ride cross country. It's the sport of the brave. Pushing you and your horse to the limit of your capabilities, doing things most people wouldn't even consider possible. The sport of warriors... everybody knows this, and they laugh and say things like, "you're mad" or "you've got nerves of steel", because everyone knows it's a sport for the adrenalin obsessed. And you gape at footage of crazy falls, as riders stand up without a scratch and completely unfazed. But what about when that doesn't happen?

As I round the corner, sidestepping another puddle, I feel my insides twist. The ramp to Alex's lorry is down, the horses standing inside out of the rain, and neither her parents nor any of the grooms are in sight. But Alex is there, sitting in the doorway of the living compartment, feet on the step below, arms resting on her legs. The first give-away is that her shoulders are hunched - Alex, who has probably spent more hours of her life riding than she has sleeping, does not hunch her shoulders. I didn't even think she *could*, the muscle mass she has amounted from years in the saddle leaving her unable to do so, but I was wrong.

And then there are the figures in front of her. Standing around the steps, in a huddle, soaked white jodhpurs covered by raincoats, bar one person in jeans. Three people, who turn at the sound of someone approaching - Leni, Thomas, and Zach. Both Thomas and Zach look relatively composed, but even though it's pouring down I can distinguish tears from rain on Leni's face.

The twisting in my stomach increases, wringing my insides like a wet tea towel, but still I feel calm. I don't have the sensation of falling apart, collapsing in a heap on the wet ground and breaking down in tears. Rather I feel like none of this is real. I know what I'm about to be told, I've known since I saw it happen, and yet I can't get myself to process it. It's like I'm hearing about the incident as an impartial observer, not somebody who knows the sound of Imogen's voice or the way she looks when she's on horseback. And even though my mind knows what has happened, and I can believe it, I still don't see how it's possible to process the fact that the person I saw just an hour ago is gone forever. How is that possible? How can such a life changing thing, the *most* life changing thing there is, happen so quickly? No buildup, no warning, no do over. How can something that happens so instantly not be reversible?

I don't ask, and nobody needs to say it. We all know. The way we're all standing still, as though aware that the slightest movement, one wrong movement, can end our own lives just as quickly. And now that the uncertainty is over, the agony of not knowing, I feel all the emotions leave my body as I allow the news to sink in, ink dripping through the cloth of naivety. *Imogen is dead.*

# Chapter 2

Leni's standing on this side of the circle, closest to me, and Zach, who is beside her, takes a step closer to Thomas to make room for me to join them.

'You're sure?' I say, my voice so much quieter and shakier than I expect it to be.

Leni nods, fresh tears filling her eyes, and I take a step closer. 'Yeah.'

'Has it been announced?' I ask, looking over at Thomas and Zach because I'm not sure Leni can manage sentences containing more than one word.

'Not yet,' says Zach. 'Competition's being cancelled, though. Everyone behind the scenes knows, and they're announcing that the event is called off "due to weather". And then they'll have to say something soon, but I'm sure people have figured it out.'

'And how do you guys know?' I say, still stretching my question around the circle, but again Zach seems to be the only one composed enough to reply.

'Ridley found out right away.'

At the mention of her father, I glance up at Alex, having almost forgotten she was there. And that realisation suddenly makes me feel sick, and this whole situation that much more real, because Alex isn't exactly a person whose presence often goes unnoticed. But she's sitting at the top of the steps, eyes down, and for what is possibly the first time since I've known her, she is silent.

'Where are Joan and Ridley now?' I say, because I can't bear the thought of succumbing to nothing but the sound of rainfall.

'Making the social rounds.' It's Alex, who I would have pegged as the last person to reply. And at least she doesn't sound in the least bit teary, because that really would be too strange to deal with. Instead, she sounds how I feel - detached, as though this discussion, this incident, were taking place in a movie, affecting fictional characters.

'O-kay,' I say slowly, because the way that she says it makes it seem like she's expecting a reaction.

Alex laughs, but not at what I said. 'Because it's not like I *warned* them this would happen!'

'Alex,' Leni says, her voice catching.

'I *told* them!' Alex yells. 'I knew this would happen! I *told them so!* All they had to do was sell him for dressage or show jumping, but *no*, they got offered some huge cheque and they were too greedy to refuse it!'

'Imogen knew the risks,' says Thomas. 'She knew he dangled his forelegs, and she knew you had a fall with him. Nobody should pay this price, but she was aware of the risk she was taking.'

'That's not the point!' cries Alex, looking up now. 'THEY

SHOULD HAVE LISTENED TO ME! I knew it! I knew it wasn't safe, but no one paid me any attention! No, they all just thought I was being pathetic about one fall. But one of Imogen's rich owners just had to open a chequebook!'

My head shoots up, heart pounding. Is she talking about Liz? Probably not, I'm sure Imogen has - *had*, I realise a beat too late - a whole army of rich owners. But for the first time since seeing Imogen's body disappear beneath her horse's, another thought enters my head. Nantucket.

'What's going to happen to her horses?'

'They'll just get distributed between other pros,' says Leni, her voice containing a bitter edge to it, and I understand what she means right away. She means that's what *always* happens. That's the protocol, when a rider dies, which happens often enough for there to even be such a thing as a protocol.

'Huh, do you think people might actually listen to me this time?' says Alex. 'Or will they send Motown to another eventer and put today down as fluke?'

'It could be fluke,' says Thomas.

'But it's dangerous enough as it is,' says Alex. 'You don't need to take unnecessary risks. Maybe another horse would have fallen too, maybe not. But you *don't need to take the risk.*'

'Cross country *is* dangerous,' says Leni, seeming to gather her wits a bit more. 'There are always risks. And if we thought about them, we'd never be able to set off out that start box.'

'But it doesn't need to be made even more dangerous.'

'Alex,' says Thomas. 'It's not quite that simple-'

'Don't!' she says, with enough anger that Thomas doesn't go on. 'Don't you get it? I have to believe that's how it works. I *have* to think that you make yourself safe by picking your horses carefully, because if I didn't I wouldn't be able to keep doing this.

What if I hadn't refused to ride Motown?' Alex continues, and I think I speak for everyone when I say she sends us each further into our shells. 'Would that have been me today? Would I be the one being carted off in a body bag right now?'

Those two words send a lump to my throat. I saw the fall happen, I *saw* Imogen's body disappear beneath a horse, and with it her life. And yet these two, simple words, and the image that comes with them, make reality even clearer.

'You might think I'm wrong for saying this,' says Alex. 'But this could have been *avoided.*'

None of us reply to this, and I'm not sure there even is anything to say. But in the silence - or at least, *our* silence, as tractor engines continue to roar and rain continues to fall, I remember the thing that keeps popping to mind. I see Nantucket, standing tied to the lorry, wondering why his person hasn't come back yet. Because while he may whicker a greeting whenever he sees me, I know he loves Imogen. He has always looked happy when she's riding him, and he's spent more time with her than he ever did with me, and that horse is so trusting that I know he'll have become attached to her. And now, he'll be left wondering forever where she is, because she's never coming back.

'I've got to go do something,' I say suddenly, saying the words quickly because I'm not sure if anyone's really listening anyway. 'I'll be back later.' And with that I turn around, off in search of Imogen's lorry.


'Hey, Tuck.'

The grey horse whinnies in recognition, nostrils fluttering as raindrops run down his fine head. And because nothing even matters anymore, I run right up to him and fling my arms around his neck. Nobody's going to care right now, and after today I realise life's too short to not do the things that you want to, especially when your heart is concerned.

'What're you doing, out here in the rain?' I say, rubbing my knuckles against his forehead. There are three horses tied to the side of the lorry, including Nantucket and Motown, all with almost empty haynets and wet coolers.

'You all right, buddy? I continue, running my hands down his neck. The only times I've seen Nantucket since he stopped being mine, I've had to control myself. *He's not yours anymore,* I could hear people around me thinking - at least I imagined I did. So I would resign myself to a quick pat on the neck, all casual, as though my heart wasn't breaking from trying to refrain myself from throwing my arms around him. But that doesn't matter now.

'I'm so sorry, Tuck. All I've done is think badly of Imogen these past months, but I never wanted this. I know you were happy with her, and I'm sorry she's gone. Neither one of you deserve this. You're gonna be all right, though, you hear me? You're going to go to another four star rider, who'll look after you just as well, and you're still going to end up going round Badminton. Okay? Unless Liz decides to sell you, in which case I promise I'll do everything I can to buy you back. But I doubt that's going to happen. Apart from the fact that she seems to hate me, you'll probably be more expensive now. I don't know. But you're going to be all right. You're going to be well taken care of, I'll make sure of it.'

'I'm sure he will be.'

I jump so violently that even Nantucket is startled, and I run a hand down his neck before addressing the person in question. Liz. Standing there, her fancy clothes soaked through, and for the first time since I've known her not looking as though money can buy the world.

'I'm sorry,' I say quickly. For Imogen, for standing here with her horse when I have no right to. It's all the same.

Liz holds up her hands as she shakes her head, trying to stop a fresh onslaught of tears. 'I can't…' she says. 'We're waiting for her parents to get here… But she went out doing something she loved.'

I nod. 'It's still not fair.'

'No,' says Liz, looking at me with something that almost resembles respect, or at least not disapproval. 'It's not.'

'Okay,' I say, looking around to buy a little time, but I don't have anything else to say, really. Except one thing. 'Can you.. Keep me updated, about Nantucket? Please make sure he goes somewhere good.' As I say the last word, I find myself fighting to remain calm with his whole situation, so I start to turn away.

'Georgia.'

I stop, turning back round to face Liz. I almost wish the snotty, arrogant woman were still in front of me. At least I knew where I stood then. But this blubbering person is more confusing. 'Yeah?'

Liz is looking me right in the eye, looking almost human behind the mascara-stained skin. 'I should be asking *you* to keep me updated.'

'What?'

'I'd like him to go to you,' says Liz, smiling past the tears. 'If that's okay,' she adds.

I can hear what she's saying, and understand the meaning of the words, but I can't believe it. I can't believe it because to do so would mean to hope, and I've faced too much disappointment to ever allow myself that. 'Why?' I say finally. 'Why would you want to put him with me? Plenty of pros would be happy to take him on, or if you wanted to I'm sure you could sell him for a profit.'

As I say all this, there's a voice in my head going, *Well done, Georgia. You're being offered the one thing you want, and you're talking the woman out of it!* But I'm not letting myself be ambushed, or blindly accepting any proposition that comes my way without getting the facts first. Not this time.

Liz looks like she's about to reply, only to pause and pull a handkerchief - yes, a handkerchief, because a tissue is clearly not good enough - from her coat pocket, blowing her nose before speaking. 'I forced that cheque on you. I know I did, and it certainly wasn't the first time I've done that, either. And I didn't think about it... but then, when I saw you at that first event a few months ago, and the look in your eyes when he neighed, I felt sick. I thought, maybe, I'd done the wrong thing.'

I laugh. 'Seriously?' *Shut up*, the voice inside my head is telling me. *Shut up. Shut up. Shut up.* And yet I go on. 'You know, no offence, but while leading Nantucket up onto your lorry is the hardest thing I've ever done, I'm not the first person it's ever happened to.'

'You're right,' says Liz, actually looking sincere. 'You're not the only person who's ever sold a horse when they didn't want to. In fact, a young girl who must be about your age tried to talk me out of buying a horse a while ago, but I gave the cheque to her parents and she was promptly dismissed.'

'Is this relevant?' I snap. The anger at being in this position in the first place - the combination of selling Nantucket and Imogen's life having just been taken from her - has overridden any self-control I possessed.

'That same horse has just broken Imogen's neck, so what do you think?'

That nauseating feeling again, the one the word "death" cannot provoke, but other, seemingly less intimidating, words can.

*Body bag. Broken neck.* 'Are you talking about Alex?'

'Joan and Ridley's daughter,' says Liz. 'Do you know her?'

'Yeah. She's a friend, I guess.'

'Well, she must be rubbing off on you, because I recall being spoken to in a similar fashion. Anyway, she begged me not to buy him. Motown, that is. Imogen had seen him on the flat, and he's just such a beautiful horse. Always led the dressage by miles. Joan and Ridley said their daughter had lost her bottle… But then she burst into our conversation yelling. She… she came right up to me and pleaded with me not to buy him. She just kept saying, over and over, that he wasn't a cross country horse. He needs to do pure dressage or show jump, she said. She told me he was too kind, because he would try to jump any cross country fence you pointed him at even if he wasn't capable of doing so. And then she got yelled at by Joan and Ridley, but of course I already knew he'd had one bad fall, but Imogen wasn't bothered by it. She said you couldn't have a horse that was only good at cross country anymore. She wanted the one that would lead the dressage.'

'Alex isn't afraid of much,' I say. Of all that Liz has just said, that's what I pick up on. 'She doesn't lose her bottle. She didn't think it was safe. In fact,' I continue, becoming hysterical, 'she's a mess right now! She knew this would happen, and she warned you all, but nobody would listen!'

'And now we all have to live with that,' says Liz. 'We're going to have to live with that guilt. So, please, ease that guilt a little and let me right one wrong.' As I realise what topic the conversation is shifting back to, I freeze. But Liz goes on. 'You never wanted to sell him. And it seems quite clear to me that you still haven't got over it. I should have listened. The same way I should have listened to Alex. Maybe you youngsters speak more sense than we give you credit for.'

'You don't like me,' I say, wanting to get this off my chest. My eyes dart to Nantucket, watching me, and I worry that I'm jeopardising his future, his future with *me*, but I've spent the past seven months of my life feeling worthless. 'And you made it quite clear that I would only end up wrecking him, the way I did my other horse.'

'First of all,' says Liz, an edge to a voice. *Well, Georgia, you've done it now. If you had any chance you've just blown it.* 'I've never disliked you. Though that might still change.. But I saw you ride that chestnut today. That was some seriously impressive riding.'

'Uh, thank you,' I say. *Thank you?* My god, why can't I think before I speak.

'When I saw him last year, I thought, "well, that horse clearly isn't going". I didn't, and still don't, know any of the details, but I certainly didn't think that horse would ever jump again, and seeing that, it was possible to assume that Tuck might end up the same way.

'So when I saw that chestnut go out the start box today, and the commentator announce your name, I did a double take. Not long ago, I thought that horse would never even be good enough for a riding school. And yet, somehow, you've made him into a cross country horse. If you can manage *that*, then yes, I think Nantucket will be in good hands.'

The lump in my throat turns to pride, and I swallow it down just as quickly. 'I don't want pity-'

'It's not pity. It's an owner giving a talented young rider the ride on a horse.' Liz pauses, a small and sad smile coming to her face. 'That horse loves you. And it's what Imogen would have wanted.'

*Imogen.* Somebody who's been nothing but nice to me, to Tuck, and yet I've spent every minute of this year so far hating her. Guilt wraps its slimy fingers around my gut, wringing it out until it's so twisted that it's rigid. Something I've never even dared to imagine is happening, and it's only happening because Imogen has paid her life. Why couldn't I have just been nicer to her? I mean, I know I *was* nice to her, but only to her face. Inside I was hating her with all my being. And for what? Because she got to see fences come to life between a pair of silver ears. As did I, at one point, but I chose to give it up.

'What about Motown?' I say suddenly. And then, worried that Liz might think I'm asking about him for myself, I add, 'I mean, what's going to happen to him?'

'I think it's about time I listen to Alex, don't you? Maybe Motown would like to try his hand at pure dressage.'

'Really?'

'I'm not a monster, Georgia. What, did you think I was going to shoot him?'

I shrug. 'Other things have shocked me more.'

'I do have a heart, you know,' Liz says, but she doesn't sound particularly offended.

'I didn't mean it like that-'

'I know you didn't. Anyway, back to right now. Do you want to take him back with you today? Or sort things out with James first and come pick him up in a few days time? Things are obviously going to be a bit up in air for some weeks, so it doesn't matter what you decide.'

'You'd let me take him now?' I say, the reality sinking in. *I've got Nantucket back.*

'Has James got any empty stables?'

*James.* That whole situation. It needs sorting out. And now I've got an extra reason to. 'I'll check with him first,' I say. I'm shaking now, as it settles that this is actually taking place. Not falling through, not even a dream.

'I need to go see some more people,' says Liz. 'I'll be around. Let me know.'

'Okay. Wait! Umm, do you think you could speak to Alex? I know nobody can do anything about it, but.' I shrug. 'I dunno. Just thought maybe it could help.'

'I'll do that right away,' says Liz, turning to walk away.

'Wait!' I call again. 'I just...' How do I say this under the circumstances? Tragedy hangs in the air like a virus, but there's this shining light fighting it away. 'It's just... thank you. That's all. Thank you.'

Liz nods. 'You two just make me and Imogen proud. Okay?'

'Okay.'

As Liz walks away, I turn my attention back to the grey horse beside me, with drops of water running down his neck. Today's events have made me feel sick to my stomach, a feeling I know will return tonight when I go to bed, and many more nights to come. So now, just for one moment, I allow myself to push the feeling aside as I soak up the other one. I'm actually getting Nantucket back. If you'd told me this morning that I would be ending the competition getting back the silver horse I've cried over more than just about anything, I would have asked what exactly had been put in your coffee.

'Tuck,' I say, and he whickers as I hold my hands out to him. And I lean my head against his, tears threatening to fill my eyes. 'You're coming back with me. You're going to see your brother again. And your new sister, who probably won't like you, but it doesn't matter.'

I step back, taking in the wet horse in front of me, and this time tears do blind my vision. *I'm getting him back. I'm getting him back. I'm getting him back.* Except I need to talk to James first, to see if I really can bring him back tonight.

'I'll be back,' I say to Nantucket. 'From now on, I'll always be back.'

As I make my way though the lorries, knowing James will probably be getting filled in on the news somewhere while Paris looks after his horses, I find myself making a detour. Speaking to James is kind of important right now, granted, but there's someone else I need to speak to more.

'Loxwood,' I say, opening the stable door. He looks at me, my ears filled only with the sound of him grinding a mouthful of hay, and I feel my limbs go weak. Have I eaten anything today? Who knows? I'll do that in a minute, but for now I steady myself against Loxwood's neck, slinging my arms around him. 'Hey, buddy,' I say. 'Your brother's coming home.'

Now just to figure out where home is.

# Chapter 3

Tucker bounces around as we drive down the potholed track, swinging me from side to side in the driver's seat. I can see far enough down the drive to know that there are no cars coming the other way, and I make the most of it to take my eyes off the road and look out the windows at the scenery. To my left, the land is immaculately maintained, with topiary shrubs running in geometrical shapes, an orchard of apple trees planted in perfect rows, and gravel paths winding through formal gardens. The view to my right is different, and it is the one that I prefer. Pasture land stretches out in a wave of rolling hills, the grass dotted by sheep. There are old trees, their shadows casting shade on this unseasonably hot day. The one thing both sides of the property have in common is the old stone wall that runs around the estate's perimeter. It really is like entering a different world, the wall letting you into your own.

The sun is warm against my skin, the breeze coming in

through the open windows barely enough to keep me cool. It's not often in England that you can honestly say that there is truly not a cloud in sight.

After almost a mile, during which I pass the main estate house, with its gated entrance and many turrets, some smaller buildings come into view, and the car parked outside them tells me I'm in the right place. I pull up next to the Mercedes, keeping Tucker a safe distance away so as not to risk denting the expensive car beside me, and climb out of my seat. There's a woman waiting for me, middle aged, wearing a pink cardigan and carrying a couple of brochures.

'Miss James,' she says tentatively. She's still eying me with as much suspicion as she did on our first meeting in the office. I'm not in the mood to comment on her rudeness, though to be fair you can't blame her for being dubious. 'Where do you want to start?'

'Anywhere,' I say, folding my arms across my chest. In contrast to the woman's bright colours, floral patterns, and shiny shoes, I'm in a simple V-neck sweater, dark jeans, and walkings boots.

There's a slight breeze in the air, and I tuck my hair behind my ears as it blows strands across my face. I pulled it free from its usual elastic band so that it wouldn't look like I've just come from riding horses, which I have, but I'm kind of regretting the decision now. The woman in pink is rattling on about technicalities and I remind myself to pay attention, even though the childlike butterflies in my stomach are overpowering.

'It's a little tired, obviously,' she says as I follow her through the door. 'But it's got charm.'

We find ourselves in the kitchen, with a utility and cloakroom leading off to the left. The kitchen itself is a nice size, with original red tiles stretching out unevenly across the floor, and small windows running all around. There are no built-in units, but rather various mismatched pieces of furniture. A big butler sink, and old enamel stove with a red and white checkered tea towel hanging from its side, a cream wardrobe, a narrow table serving as a counter, with another, also old and wooden, in the middle of the room, with four chairs around it. I walk slowly towards the table, letting my fingers rest on its top as I look around.

'It comes with it,' the woman says. 'There are a couple pieces of furniture that fit in too well to be moved.'

I go to the sink and peer out the window above it, the fluttering in my stomach returning when I see the view.

At the end of the kitchen, a doorway leads into a sitting room, nestled nicely at the back of the house. Here there is no furniture, without counting the three sets of curtains that hang either side of each window, or the pans hanging on hooks beside the open fireplace. There's a simple staircase in one corner, with the kind of banister I would have wanted to slide down as a kid. Dust shimmers over the wooden floorboards with the light that shines in, and while the figure beside me apologises for the lack of cleanliness, I only think it adds to the charm.

The steps creak as we go up them, each one louder than the next. The landing is small, only two steps each way, but with a window from which I can see rolling hills. There are two opposite doorways, both leading to bedrooms.

'This is the larger one,' I am told, following the woman into the room on the right.

Natural light floods the space, sending patterns across the floorboards. There's a bed frame against the middle wall, with a wooden headboard covered in faded blue paint, which looks about as old as the rest of the house. A large wardrobe also stands in one corner, the kind in which I could imagine climbing inside to discover Narnia. There are a couple windows, but I'm drawn to one in particular, from which I see the same view as I did standing at the kitchen sink.

A doorway leads off into a small en-suite, again with floorboards. There's a standing sink of white porcelain, and both windows are complete with white cotton curtains embroidered with blue botanical prints. The bath is enamel, balanced on feet that remind me of door knockers.

The other bedroom is of a similar style, just a little smaller. There is also an empty bed frame, this one wooden too, but white, with hand painted flowers running along the edges.

'They're both en-suites,' the woman says. 'Old plumbing, of course, but that's to be expected in a house of this age. Are you ready to see outside?'

We go back out the door we came in, and as we turn a corner I am faced with the view I saw from inside. The one that made my stomach flip.

A row of five stables runs in a straight line, the building consisting of old red bricks, and the doors of dark wood. I approach them slowly, as though the building were a fragment of a dream, and getting too close would mean that they cease to exist. Each box is a good size, four strides wide, and solidly built even if they are showing their age.

'There's a tack room round here, and a hay barn.'

I walk round the stable block, a building covered in climbing red roses, to where there are more matching brick structures. There's a voice rattling on beside me, but I only hear half of what comes out. Nothing she says matters anymore.

Paddocks surround the house and stable, with slanting posts, and missing railings here and there. Nothing a hammer and a box of nails can't fix.

'The manège is round here,' she says pretentiously. I don't point out that a manège is technically an indoor arena, because frankly it would be a waste of my time. 'As you know, it does flood in winter, but it's better than nothing.'

The sand school, (much more fitting), is small, twenty by forty if that, and framed by a hedge. I can see that the surface isn't ideal, the sand unevenly deep in places, and weeds coming up, but it doesn't matter.

We wander back towards the house, and I stand silently to take in the view. The grey farmhouse, with the painted front door and the many windows with rattling panes of glass. An image like something out of a movie, the stereotypical English cottage. The red stone stable block, with shabby wooden doors, and roses climbing along it. And the paddocks, in need of some TLC but more peaceful than most you'll find in this area of the country. Everything is silent, in this beautiful corner of the estate.

'If you think you're interested,' the agent says. 'I'll take you up to the main house so that Vera can talk over the ponies with you.'

My mind is yelling, *I'll take it.* But I remember to compose myself. 'Okay.'

In the end, everything was simple. Almost like it was meant to be.

When I traipsed into my camper that evening, drained from the day's tragedy, the first thing I did was call Rose. The news of what happened to Imogen had already reached her, had already reached every horse-interested person in the world with an

Internet connection, but it was worse for Rose than me. I felt guilt over what happened because of my own personal feelings towards Imogen, maybe, but it didn't come with fear. Whether I admitted it or not, like all young people I had that false idea of invincibility. People died riding horses, but it wasn't us young and fit dreamers. You don't expect it to be pros, either. And safety has always been a big issue for Rose, and part of the reason she hasn't pursued three-star level more seriously since having Mackenzie. Not only was Imogen more experienced than Rose results wise, but she was only going round a Novice track.

I told Rose that I had seen the fall, and we discussed the details, until it was all too painful, and I said, 'Do you want to hear some happier news?' And then we were both crying for completely different reasons.

Having a third horse meant that not only was I no longer getting paid, but I actually owed James money at the end of the month. Even if my mind hadn't been set on it already, I needed to find somewhere else to go.

The thought of crawling back to my parents, admitting defeat and carrying my belongings back up to my tiny room, was almost as hard as trying to stick it out here. I would have done it, though, for my horses' sakes. But that wasn't even an option anymore, because Rose only had two spare stables.

I needed my own place, that conclusion was easy to come to. How hard could it be? It's not like I lived in England, where there's next to no land to speak of, and any equestrian properties to rent are snapped up in seconds… oh, wait a minute. I did. Still, I went to the agents, and asked around. Single eighteen year old girl looking to rent an entire property. At least they seemed to remember me each time I called, because apparently I was a one of a kind. Who knew?

But then, only six days after I first started looking, during which time I had lost track of how many phone calls I'd made, my phone rang.

'Miss James?'

'Yes.'

(They said their name, that they were from so-and-so agency, all useless information to me. I just needed to know *why* they were calling)

'So Vera Addington got in touch with us this morning,' the woman said, in a way suggesting that I should have known who Vera Addington was.

'Right,'

'Mr and Mrs Addington own the Ballowmoore Estate,' she continued, and this name I did know. *The* Ballowmoore estate, referred to simply as Ballowmoore, some twelve miles from Newmarket. But only eight from Rose…

'Yes,' I said, holding on to my phone with a death grip.

'Some of their longtime tenants have decided to downgrade, moving to a town. So they are now renting out a two bedroom cottage, with five stables, a couple paddocks, and I think there's even a small ring.'

'Okay,' My mind was buzzing. *Don't get excited. Don't get excited.* A place like that had to be a fortune per month.

'I thought of you, because there's a catch.'

Of course there was. There's always a catch. Something I had come to discover during my short time as a hopeful tenant was that random demands seemed to be a characteristic of any property on an estate. So I waited to be told what exactly the catch was this time. My horses aren't allowed to leave the property on weekends? I have to work full-time in the estate house as a cleaner? Speak a foreign language so that I can tutor the people's kids four times a week? Crazy things I had already heard, so what was it going to be this time?

'The youngest daughter, Delilah, is at boarding school during the week, and they would be keen to have someone that can keep her two ponies fit while she's away. And I remembered you saying you were an eventer, and you're not too big to ride a pony.'

'That's it?' I said, too surprised to hide it.

'They're lovely ponies, I'm told,' the woman continued, obviously misunderstanding my reaction for annoyance. 'The been there done that kind of sort. As you know, properties like this don't come up very often. But Vera is really keen to rent it out to somebody who can ride the ponies. The monthly rent would be very fair as a consequence.' The woman named the price, and my limbs trembled. 'Would you be interested?'

After hanging up that call, slipping the phone back into my pocket, I stood where I was for a moment, looking at the horse I had been in the middle of tacking up. My eyes drifted across all the unhappy-looking horses in the barn, and then down to the nonexistent bedding, and I wept with relief. Finally, it felt like everything was going to work out.

# Chapter 4

'What do you think, boys?'

I pull off Loxwood's head collar with one hand, sliding the bolt across the door with the other, and step back. He immediately pushes his chest up against the half door, holding his neck as high as he can, eyes wide and nostrils flared. His ears swivel to the right, where Nantucket is looking out of his new stable, and Loxwood lets out a high-pitched whinny.

'Does that mean you like it?' I say, watching as he proceeds to walk around the stable, trailing his nose across the straw bedding until it reaches the pile of hay by the door, and he snatches a mouthful.

'You two going to be calm?'

Loxwood's head shoots up, hay still dangling from his lips, as he stares into the distance. I laugh at how pathetic he is, walking over to the grey horse farther along. Unsurprisingly, Nantucket doesn't seem the least bit bothered by the move. He's standing in the red brick stable as though he's always been there, looking content as he ducks his head for hay.

'You know I need to go again,' I say. 'I'll stay a bit longer to check you aren't about to do something stupid, but I need to go pick up your sister.'

It made the most sense to bring Loxwood and Nantucket together first, allowing them to settle in, with each other, the plan being that they're perfectly relaxed when I bring Cookie into the mix later today. Two trips is unavoidable, because of only having a two horse trailer, but I'm hoping I've planned this the right way round.

All of yesterday was spent here, getting things ready. Finding a hay and straw supplier was easy, and I organised to have a truckload delivered in the morning, during which time I swept out the stables and hosed cobwebs off the walls, laying down three beds once they were dry. It was then that I realised I hadn't thought of my own bed, and drove to dish out money on a mattress that would fit the frame upstairs. After putting so much effort into my horses' beds, for myself I got the cheapest one that could fit in my car. It was compressed in a bag, designed for easy transport, and I dragged it up the cottage stairs before driving back to the yard.

I haven't bought myself any food yet today, but if worst comes to worst then I'll massacre the raspberry bush I saw in the garden. Details I'll think of once I have Cookie here, all my horses safe in one place, and I'll be able to breathe again.

'Look at you, getting all fancy!'

I grin as I turn around from Cookie's stable door, having slid the evening feed through, already knowing who's standing behind me because I glimpsed the car coming down the drive. 'I know, right? I'm a lady on an estate.'

'You might lure me away from racing yet if this is the kind of life you event riders live,' says Graham, eyeing the location with a look of awe, while Lizzie pulls a face beside him at the remark.

'Don't give her another reason to boast,' she snaps. 'Anyway,' She turns back to me. 'Happy house warming! Or, whatever you're supposed to say when someone moves house. We brought bubbly!'

'By "bubbly"', Graham cuts in. 'She means lemonade.'

'The idea's the same,' says Lizzie. 'It's just the only kind of bubbly either of us can afford. You almost done out here?'

I smile, snapping my head back to look at the three horses, happily eating up their evening feeds. 'A glass of lemonade sounds perfect.'

It's only once we're inside, huddled around the wooden table of my little farmhouse kitchen that I remember I don't actually have anything to serve drinks in. But I'm saved by Lizzie setting down not only the bottle of lemonade, but a packet of plastic wine glasses.

'I figured you wouldn't have any,' she says.

'You figured right. Since when are you so organised?'

'Since never,' interrupts Graham, glaring at Lizzie. 'I told her you wouldn't have any glasses yet, to which she responded that I was a moron, and she went to wait in the car while I ran back to buy some.'

'Would it seriously kill you to let me have some credit sometimes?' says Lizzie, accompanying the statement with dramatic hand gestures.

Graham laughs. 'Are you kidding me?'

'Need all the glory for yourself, don't you?'

'Do you two ever not sound like an old married couple?' I

say, removing the cups from the plastic packaging. At least that makes them shut up, and they both sit in silence looking awkward until our drinks are poured, and Lizzie perks up to propose a toast.

'I thought it was bad luck to make a toast with anything other than alcohol?' I say, watching as she stands up from her chair.

'It's only bad luck with water, I think,' says Graham.

'I still don't think we should risk it.'

'Georgia James!' snaps Lizzie. 'You've had, like, the most ridiculous year ever. I'm pretty sure you've already got bad luck.'

'But look at this,' I say, holding out my arms. 'My luck's going good, now. And I don't need it being messed up.'

After some more bickering, debating what exactly consists of bad luck, and where exactly this superstition came from in the first place, it's Graham who comes up with a solution.

'Hey,' he says, reaching across the table for the handful of raspberries I put down earlier. 'Fermented fruit is alcohol, so what if we put a raspberry in each glass and then *technically* it's just alcohol that hasn't become alcohol yet. Would that work?'

'Are you joking?' Lizzie says, as she watches me happily hold my glass of lemonade out for Graham to drop a raspberry into it.

'It's a good idea,' I say. 'Are you making a toast or not?'

'You think one raspberry in a glass is going to stop you from having bad luck? Are you actually kidding me? You think a piece of fruit is going to change the order of the universe?'

'Just get on with it,' I snap, at the same time as Graham says, 'Hurry up.'

Because she can't actually refrain from reciting whatever speech she has concocted in her head, Lizzie goes on, and soon we're actually able to drink the lemonade.

'So,' Lizzie says after we've all had a few sips. 'Now that you have a house, you need a dog.'

'I don't need a dog.'

'Do you want to get all your tack stolen again?'

'I don't need a dog,' I say again, unsure why exactly Lizzie is bringing this up, but knowing her well enough to suspect an ulterior motive behind the topic. 'I don't even like dogs.'

'Of course you like dogs. Everyone likes dogs.'

'I'm not getting a dog, Lizzie,' I say.

'But she's really sweet!' cries Lizzie, and beside her Graham laughs into his hands.

'Who's really sweet?' I say.

'Your dog.'

'I don't *have* a dog.'

'You *didn't*,' says Lizzie. 'But this is the point I've been trying to make. You do now!'

'Lizzie...'

'She's really sweet, I swear! And you need a guard dog. Do you seriously think you're safe here on your own?'

'Lizzie,' I snap. 'Can you actually tell me what the heck you're going on about?'

Lizzie sighs, as though I'm really useless for not understanding what's going on. 'I got you a dog.'

'Well, take it back. What do you mean you got me a dog?'

'My cousin was driving down to visit today, remember? Anyway, she found a greyhound abandoned on the side of the road.'

'It'll belong to someone-'

'It doesn't! She took it to the vets, and it's had its ears sliced off!'

'Why would the vet slice its ears off?'

'Not the vet, stupid. Its ears had already been sliced off.

Apparently people do that so nobody can trace the identity tattoo. It's definitely been abandoned.'

'Why would someone do that?' I say, sensing myself fall deeper into the trap Lizzie has set for me.

'Because it was a racing greyhound! They get abandoned or killed once they're done racing, you know that.'

*And she's got me.* 'You sure?'

Lizzie smiles, and Graham laughs at the tone of my voice. 'Yes,' she says. 'See, it couldn't be more appropriate! An ex-racing-dog to go with your ex-racehorses. Perfect!'

'I still don't need a dog,' I say, trying to regain some control of this situation. 'I told you, I don't even like dogs.'

'Yes, you do. Just come outside and see her-'

'You brought her with you!? Where is she?'

'In the car,' says Lizzie, standing up. 'You coming to meet your new dog then?'

I don't know if it's the warm evening weather, or the relief of today being over, and finally feeling at ease, or that I actually do feel sorry for this dog, but I cave. As soon as I see her, two nervous eyes looking up from the curled-up ball on the backseat of Lizzie's car. Lying like that, and not having any ears, she almost looks like a snake.

'I don't need a dog,' I say, with as much conviction as I can. I reach a hand out to stroke the dog, and she responds by shying away, ducking her head.

'She thinks you're going to hit her,' says Lizzie, smiling in spite of the awfulness of the words, because she knows she's going to win this one. 'You won't even notice she's here.'

'She won't exactly be much use as a guard dog, then,' I say.

'Sure she will. She'll still bark if some crazy axe murderer breaks into your house. Besides, look at her! Not only is she a racing reject, but she's the same colour as Loxwood! Loxwood in dog form.'

Why did she have to go and say that? Great. Not only was I thinking that this dog is in exactly the same position as all my horses have been, but Lizzie has to point out that she *is* the same colour as Loxwood. Her coat is red, dull across her skeletal body. And that isn't a speck of white on her forehead, is it?

'Just take her on a trial run,' says Lizzie. 'A week or two, see how you get on, and if you really don't want her by the end of it then I'll take her back and find another home. Come on, that's fair!'

I look down at the dog, curled up on the car seat. There's no point even fighting it anymore. 'Fine. One week. But you'd better have food! I'm not going off to buy dog food now.'

Lizzie grins triumphantly. 'Full bag in the back!'

The dog is curled up on a folded blanket on the kitchen floor, Lizzie and Graham having driven off a few minutes ago, when I hear another car roll up outside. For a moment, I worry they've come back for the dog, only to get annoyed at myself for being upset about that. I don't want this dog, after all. And when I glance out the window, I see that it isn't Lizzie and Graham, anyway.

'GEORGIA!'

Mackenzie runs up to me, and I'm so happy to see her that I return her embrace. 'You've grown,' I say, holding my hand out to measure where her head comes up against me, and she laughs.

'No I haven't.'

'Yeah, you have.'

'Maybe,' Mackenzie concedes, her attention caught by the horses looking out of their stables, and she runs to see them.

'No running!' Rose calls as she climbs out her jeep, holding a plastic bag with one hand, and closing the car door with the other. 'I wanted to get here earlier,' she says to me, now. 'But Sunny pulled a shoe, and the farrier was two hours later than he said he would be.'

'It's fine,' I say, glancing over my shoulder to see Mackenzie stroking Loxwood. 'You didn't have to come at all. I'm glad you did,' I add quickly.

'You kidding? As if we'd miss this! And,' She holds up the plastic bag. 'I doubted that you'd have any food in.'

'Am I that predictable?' I say.

'Oh my god,' Mackenzie says, running back towards us. 'This place is *amazing!* Is it really yours? Is that your house? Can we go inside?'

'Yes,' I say. 'Let's go inside.'

Of course, the first thing I hear upon opening the kitchen door for my guests is Mackenzie yelling, 'Oh, you got a dog!'

'I'm just… looking after her, for a week.' I say.

'She's so *sweet*,' says Kenzie, crouching down beside the dog, who seems to curl up into an even tighter ball. 'Why doesn't she have any ears?'

'Some mean person cut them off.'

'That's horrible! Oh, you poor thing.'

'Careful,' I say. 'I don't know her yet, I don't know what she's like.'

'Leave her alone, Kenz,' says Rose, looking round at the kitchen. 'Isn't this lovely?'

Mackenzie leaves the dog's side long enough to follow me as I give Rose a tour, both of them seeming as besotted with the house as I am, Mackenzie even going as far as suggesting that she move into the spare room to help me out with the horses.

Back downstairs, Rose empties the contents of the shopping

bag to reveal tortilla crisps, pots of hummus, and a Tupperware box of home-made flapjacks. 'I've got some bags of apples in the car, too, for the horses.'

'What's her name?' Mackenzie says, interrupting the conversation. She's returned to the dog, sitting cross-legged beside it on the floor.

'Umm, I don't know.'

'How can you not know her name?' says Mackenzie, looking horrified.

'I don't think she has one,' I say.

'You need to give her one, then.'

'Tell you what, you can name her.'

For some reason, this is the most exciting thing I could have said, because Mackenzie makes more squealing noises, and brainstorms aloud while Rose and I continue to talk. We're discussing the event we're both entered for in a few weeks time, as Mackenzie interjects with things like, 'Sprinkles? Missy? Lulu?' and I'm beginning to regret giving her freewill to name the dog, when she finally comes out with something that I actually like the sound of.

'Lily,' I repeat.

'Goes with Loxwood,' says Kenzie. 'Lily and Loxwood.'

It's classic, and simple, and almost an ode to Rose, though I don't say this out loud. Having an earless dog named after you might not seem like a compliment. 'Okay, then. Lily it is.'

Later that day, when evening has faded into night, after going out to check on the horses, I'm ready to go to bed. I'm exhausted, and surprisingly, even to me, not at all nervous about being on my own. Being realistic with myself, while the idea of sleeping alone in the middle of nowhere didn't scare me, I was expecting it to be different once I was actually faced with having to do so. But I'm not. Everything I love is just a few paces away, so why would I be?

But as I walk through the sitting room, something is stopping me from going upstairs. I wander back to the kitchen, switching on the light, and look at her. It's not that she's begging, with wide eyes that one associates with the image, because she wouldn't know how to. She expects the worst from people, and I doubt it would occur to her to ever asking for something so long as she isn't being beaten. But her quietness, the way she is huddled in the corner of the kitchen, not daring to hope for anything more, is the stumbling block preventing me from going to bed.

'Hey,' I say. 'Lily.'

She doesn't lift her head, eyes barely flickering.

'It's okay. Do you want to come upstairs with me? I won't hurt you.' I tap a hand against my leg and click my tongue. 'Come on, let's go.'

She walks slowly at first, seeming to expect a blow to the head at any moment, but I encourage her to follow. We walk up the stairs, and Lily retreats in fear every time I make a sudden movement, until we get to my room.

'Go on,' I say, patting the bed. 'Up you get.'

Her eyes flicker to me again, then back to the bed, and she pauses, as though weighing up the options. But even an abused dog can't resist a new mattress, and understanding what I'm saying, Lily jumps onto the bed, circles once, and curls up into a ball.

I shake my head, smiling to myself, as I walk to the bathroom. *Lizzie, I hate you.*

# Chapter 5

As I was expecting, the horses behave like complete idiots the next morning. Because, of course, calmly walking around a new paddock is overrated. So they spend an hour galloping like lunatics, while I muck out the stables as quickly as I can, by which point I decide to bring them in while all their shoes are intact. How many days of this will I have to go through? Three? Four? A week? I don't know, but I did know it was to be expected. They'll get a little longer out each day, until they finally decide to give up revisiting their former lives as racehorses. As much as part of me would like to leave them out until they calm down, the last thing I need is an injury right now, not to mention a vet bill.

'You guys settle down,' I say to the three horses eating hay. 'I've got some ponies to go ride.'

When I first visited the property, I was introduced to Vera Addington, who showed me the two ponies I would be expected to ride. As the estate agent had said on the phone, they really did seem like nice, bombproof ponies. Both about fourteen hands - one a pie named Zebra Swallowtail, the other a dun called Dun For The Day. They went by Zebra and Dun, which at least meant I wouldn't be forgetting their names any time soon.

Delilah Addington is twelve years old, and the photos I've seen of her riding put me to shame. Her ponies are going round bigger tracks than Loxwood and Nantucket, even though she only started going affiliated this year. She's also part of the local pony club, and hunts throughout the winter, and all this without even exercising her own ponies. During the week, Delilah's away at a boarding school that costs the same per term as a Novice event horse (I looked the school up). An all-girls school where plaid skirts are compulsory, and there's a riding school on-site, and, according to the website, a school which allows you to bring your own pets (horses, rabbits, and guinea pigs) with you. I didn't think those sorts of places even existed outside of children's books, but I was proven wrong after hours of browsing the website, trying to imagine just what it would be like to attend a school like that. But if that's your start in life, I'm pretty sure you're going to be toast once you enter the real world.

Some local girl from the village had been exercising the ponies before, but she had apparently become too flaky to count on, and when my home's former tenants moved out, Vera Addington saw an opportunity to hit two birds with one stone. And hacking two idiot-proof ponies four times a week will probably forever be the easiest job I'll ever have. Plus, Vera doesn't have a problem with there being an odd day I might have to miss due to events. Another bonus of riding the Addingtons' ponies? I get free roam across the entire estate - which, I'm soon discovering, could also be referred to as hacking heaven.

I'm back inside, having just come back from riding the

ponies, drinking a cup of tea at the kitchen table before going back out to groom the horses, when my parents show up. I obviously must be more exhausted than I think, because I'm both thrilled and relieved to see them, the way I remember being when I was little and I was reunited with my mum in the supermarket after wandering around lost for ten minutes.

After feeding the horses this morning, when I realised with horror that not only did I have no coffee, but no mugs to drink any from, I drove to buy some essentials. Cheap cutlery, teabags, cans of baked beans... So now, I'm at least able to offer my parents a cup of tea each, and even a biscuit.

The best present I could have got would be another bag of food shopping, thus preventing me from needing to leave for a while, but alas, that is not the house warming gift I receive. Instead, my mum hands me a bag printed with the name of her favourite shop, and from it I remove a matching set of porcelain horses. Having been dragged to said shop many times, I can say that I've escaped lightly. Now I just need to buy some furniture that these items can actually be displayed on.

'You know what? I'm beginning to see why Lizzie doesn't like you.'

Oblivious to my words, Cookie spins round again, turning her left shoulder towards me in protest. I click my tongue, pulling my hand that is holding the lunge line out further to the right, stepping behind her with the whip. As she has already done six times today, Cookie responds by rearing. It isn't intimidating, nor is she aiming for me, it's just her way of saying "no".

'Come on,' I say, alternating between a pull on the lunge line and a tap with the whip, until, as she has done each of those other six times, Cookie gives up and takes a step forward.

'Honestly,' I say. 'You're only causing yourself more work with this whole act. We both know you only end up by giving in. Think how much time you'd save yourself if you just did what I asked first time round.'

I spent most of yesterday weeding the small sand school, pulling up roots until neither my hands nor my back could take any more. At least it actually looks like an arena now, even if it's small and the surface isn't great. I doubt I'll ever use it for anything other than lungeing (and maybe Cookie's first rides here so that if I fall it will at least be onto a soft surface), but that's fine. Why would I want to ride Loxwood and Nantucket in a school when I have three hundred acres to roam across? Event horses need uphill gallops and hours going across rough terrain, not endless circles on a sand surface. But this ring is perfect for young horses.

After succeeding in getting Cookie to go a full ten minutes without trying to rear, I decide to call it a day and quit while I'm ahead. I rode both Loxwood and Nantucket earlier today - Nantucket was as good as gold, while Loxwood decided to pretend Secretariat's ghost was following him, and that his job was to always stay ahead, and I deemed the fact that I didn't fall off at any point during the ride as much as I could have hoped for.

I'm spongeing Cookie off when Lily suddenly starts barking, running past the stables, towards the driveway, and I look up to see a woman walking down it. She looks about sixty, with the typical haircut of someone her age, and she's carrying a canvas bag. If a passerby saw the way she smiles and waves at me, they would think we've known each other for years, when really I haven't a clue who she is. But how do you respond to someone smiling and waving at you without doing the same back? Though

I'm not quite sure what I'm going to say to her. Thankfully, she takes care of that.

'Hello, dear! I'm Lydia, I live in the coach house.' I nod, recalling the house at the entrance to the estate. 'My husband's the main gamekeeper,' she continues. Gamekeeper? Those people really exist? What the heck is this place.. 'I couldn't believe it when Vera said a young girl had moved here *alone!* And I told her, I said, "Goodness, I'd better let her know that I'm just up the road if she needs anything," so here I am! And I mean it, if you need anything, anything at all, just shout. And if you need a hand with anything outside, just give Bill, my husband, a call. He'll be right down here right away to fix whatever it is! Vera said you ride? You event, like Delilah? This is all so exciting! How are you liking living here so far?'

So as it turns out, speaking to Lydia is relatively easy, seeing as she spends the whole time she's here asking direct questions. And it also turns out that the bag she was carrying is filled with jars of her homemade blackberry jelly, which she insists I take because she has a pantry overflowing with the stuff. It goes without saying that I accept the jam happily, because I'm not exactly in the position to turn down any free food at the moment. I mumble something along the lines of being in need of groceries as a thank you, to which Lydia responds by going into a frantic speech about how she should have thought to brought more food, and going on to quiz me over what I do or do not eat.

'Do you eat pasta? Most young people these days don't eat pasta. I was going to make a pasta salad tonight, I can bring you a helping. What about crumble? Do you like apples? I cold bring an apple crumble round...'

I soon realise that any attempt at insisting that I am just fine is futile, and by the time Lydia leaves I have the promise of home cooked meals for the foreseeable future. Okay, so I'm just going to put this out there, but I've kind of won the neighbour lottery.

After my first week at Ballowmoore, I set about finding and buying jump stands and poles. It turns out this is not a cheap task, and instead of spending four figures on a handful of plastic fences, I opt for empty molasses cans and plain wooden poles that I paint myself. It's not much, but it's enough to keep the horses ticking. Loxwood and Nantucket are competing in a couple of weeks, the idea of which was starting to seem like more hassle than it's worth considering the fact that I've been trying to get back on track after the minor detail of moving, but I'm glad now. A deadline is good, because it forces you to keep moving. And it's only three months until the Five Year Old Championships. *Three months.* It's crazy. This time last year, I was still going to school, still riding at Rose's. I had only just got Nantucket, unsure exactly what was going to happen there, and I was convinced that I had already done enough for Loxwood to be foolproof, and that everything would be easy. The idea is laughable now. But then, after the Four Year Old Championships, I wouldn't have believed it if I had known that I would be riding Nantucket again the next year. To think how much heartache I could have saved myself if I had known. Things don't always work out the way you expect them to, but sometimes that's not such a bad thing.

The horses are seriously benefiting from this new lifestyle, as much, if not more, than I am. It's true that Nantucket has been straightforward since the first time I rode him at James's. Better than he was when I had him, I realised straight away with a pang. He was better because Imogen had been working him for the better part of a year, improving his flatwork and jumping technique. He used to be unbalanced through the turns, something that has now been completely ironed out. I've done my best not to think about the situation, averting my eyes each time a new article on safety measures pops up, usually featuring a recap of the body protector brand Imogen was wearing that day, and an analysis of the obstacle at which she fell. I ignore the pictures that get printed of her other horses competing with new riders, and especially pay no attention to the lines that say something about young prospect Nantucket Winter being ridden by the amateur rider who started him off. Because it's all too hard. Riding Nantucket, and acknowledging the progress he's made as a result of hours and hours of time being invested in him by somebody who thought she would be benefitting from it, is hard enough. Imogen took care of my horse, now it's time for me to do the same for her.

So Nantucket only really needs keeping fit. He's happy with anything. And Loxwood, in this new atmosphere, is thriving.

We'll go off for hours, riding across the paths that run through the estate. Trotting down alleyways, galloping up rolling hills. Anything remotely resembling something you would find on a cross country course - log, ditch, puddle - we go towards. I point him at fallen trees and hanging branches, encourage him to go up and down any steep incline, let him stand in shallow rainwater that has flooded the tracks. And while I'm still cautious, I'm also careful not to take any of it too seriously. I'll let Loxwood choose his own stride when we jump a small log, and not worry about my own position when he cat leaps a ditch. And when we're doing fitness work, trotting down a path, I'll allow myself to take a hand from the reins and let him find his own balance, both of us enjoying the ride.

I still ride Loxwood in the field, whether it be running through dressage movements or popping a few fences, but I think hacking is where we're making the most progress. He's certainly more willing as a consequence, paying attention when I school him, so I'll just have to see how things go when we start competing again.

Five days before the event, I panic. I'm online, looking though the entries and start times, when I realise something that makes me sick. How is it possible? *No no no...*

My section is over two days. Dressage on the Friday, at eight o'clock in the morning no less, show jumping and cross country on the Saturday. How did I not pay attention to that when I was making the entries? The venue is far away enough as it is, and driving there and back, four journeys in two days, would be enough to put the horses off. I would have to leave at three in the morning to get there early enough to not be rushed on Friday, and I can't expect to go round a cross country course having spent almost eight hours travelling in the last twenty-four hours...

The first thing I do is ring the event secretary, asking to book two stables. But, of course, everything's booked. Rose has already said in the past that should I need to stay overnight at an event, I could drop Cookie off at hers while I'm away. Leah is competent, and she's seen her quirks enough times to know how to handle them. So at least Cookie will be all right with me having to stay away, but I still don't have anywhere for Loxwood and Nantucket to stay...

After another hour of ringing every nearby yard I can find online, I'm despairing. I'll have to withdraw, because there's no way I can drive there and back… Then I think of one person I haven't tried to contact. If there is anywhere I might be able to stable the horses, I'm sure she'll know.

**Hey! I know this is really last minute, but do you**

**know anywhere with 2 stables free Thurs and Fri night? Didn't realise it was over 2 days - haven't booked anywhere!! Don't worry if not x**

Leni replies straight away. **Yes! Give me 2 secs to check...**

By two seconds, she means three minutes, which are the longest three minutes in history. **70£ per horse incl bedding + hay available to buy on site. I've got mine there too. Sound OK?**

Right now, I'm so desperate that I would say yes to seven *hundred*. **Yes yes yes! You're a lifesaver! Where?**

**Evans based right down the road from the event. We're staying at Alex's.**

# Chapter 6

I've imagined the yard many times in my head. The fact that Joan and Ridley are two of the best event riders in the world alone is reason to think their setup is going to be ridiculous, not to mention the things I've heard from Leni and Alex. While Joan doesn't have quite the same reputation as Amanda Walton, she isn't far off. It's said that there's a reason she and Ridley got to the top, and that's because they're ruthless. They're tough with their staff, and won't think twice about accepting a large sum for a horse, or selling one that isn't deemed good enough for that matter. So naturally, I expected my directions to lead me to a large pair of wrought iron gates, beyond which lies a sweeping driveway lined with poplar trees, post and rail paddocks either side, picturesque Gloucestershire countryside. The barns new, stables of green railings complete with brass knobs either side of each door.

If it weren't for the large horse box I see as soon as I ease my way into the turning, the one with the name *EVANS* printed along the side, I would think I'm in the wrong place. Surprise number one.

For the past five minutes, I've been driving past rows and rows of ugly, semi-detached bungalow, each one with a small garden crowded with broken swing sets and piles of rubbish. None of the rolling hills I had pictured, or any big country houses. But then I saw the name of the farm, the red sign I was supposed to look out for, and there's no doubting the fact that I'm in the right place.

The paddocks border the road I've just turned off, and the thought of my own horses being so near cars makes me shudder. There are more, farther away, but if the churned up ground is anything to go by, these ones still get used. There's a house right by the road too, two storeys and bigger than most, but certainly not fancy, with paint peeling from the window frames. Beyond it is an outdoor school, in the middle of which jump stands and colourful fillers are stacked, poles lying on the ground. The surface is sand, unlike James's which left me pulling small pieces of rubber and fibre free from the space between the edge of Loxwood's shoe and his frog. It's the kind of arena everyone dreams of, and it looks out of place in this shabby area.

The image I had in my mind of a brand new American barn, with a wide aisle and sliding doors, is shattered by the sight of various outbuildings. These barns are no more than forty paces from the road, that space between being where cars are supposed to park. I don't know if there's somewhere else those renting stables today are supposed to station trailers and horse boxes, so I pull up here for now, turning the key in the ignition. Leni said she would be arriving today, and also that there were about ten other stables occupied, so I wasn't exactly expecting to find myself deserted, but there's nobody in sight.

Without the hum of the engine keeping them quiet, the horses kick out and neigh in the back, prompting me to climb out the car.

'I'll be back in a minute,' I call, leaving Lily on the passenger seat as I walk towards the buildings.

Now that I'm out in the open, I have a better idea of the layout of the place. While the side I came in is still very much public, with neighbouring houses visible through the trees, the property seems to stretch out towards the back, revealing more land than I would have thought possible in such an area. The post and rail fencing is reserved only for the paddocks that border the road, though, because everything else is white tape and plastic posts. But I was right about thinking there was more than one building, because the yard seems to be a whole jumble of structures. No main barn or courtyard, just lots of walls and roofs. Some made of grey building blocks, others old red bricks. When I step round the corner of the nearest building, it reveals itself to be simply a row of three stables, heads looking out. There's nobody around, so I step up to the horse closest to me and peer into the stable, keeping a hand on its head as I do so. The place might be scruffy, but surely Joan and Ridley Evans' stable management is second to none? If this box is anything to go by, it would appear not. The bedding doesn't even look like shavings, more like sawdust from a mill. And there's no hay that I can see. Surprise number two.

I step past a couple more stable blocks, both resembling the first, and glance more horse-filled buildings to my right, but I don't recognise any of the heads that look over the doors, and still no sign of people. But this place really is deceptive, because more buildings still stretch out farther to the back. Despite the fact that I saw Alex's lorry out front, I'm beginning to wonder if there's some way I've made a mistake. Is this really the right place? I consider turning back, to get my phone from the car and call Leni, but then I hear something. Voices? Yes, voices. And music.

There are more bored-looking horses, and I walk past them as I follow the sound. The music gets louder the closer I get, and the buildings back here aren't quite so sorry looking. Old and made of stone, but without the genericness of the building blocks. There are twelve of them, four separate rows running in a square, and the first horse I see looking out of one is definitely Anchor Lane. There are loud voices calling over the radio, which is currently playing *Counting Stars,* and then I see Alex. She's carrying a saddle from a tack room, looking over her shoulder as she does so, seeming to speak to someone inside the building. I've already walked closer to the stables, holding a hand out to whom I recognise as Tightrope Act, and straight away I notice the fact that he isn't on sawdust like the other horses I passed, but a deep straw bed, with banks reaching a quarter of the way up the walls. There's a broken-handled plastic bucket at his feet, filled with shaken-out hay, and he looks content. I still haven't been noticed by anybody, so I take a step towards the next horse, Goji Berry, and look over the door to see the same sight again. Immaculate bed, unlimited hay, healthy horse. I walk away from the stables, glancing around the yard, and notice just how tidy everything is. Swept concrete, head collars and boots hanging neatly. Every horse that looks out I recognise as one of Alex's, confirming that she and her parents run their own yards separately, something I hadn't expected considering how much they try to keep control of her. I can't quite get my head around what I'm seeing - not only do Joan and Ridley not run a spotless yard, but Alex *does*! If

I had known that they kept their horses separate from each other, I would have said with certainty that while Alex's would be well looked after, her yard would be disorganised. Because she is disorganised, isn't she? Learning the wrong dressage test for her class at an event, seeming to have her head in the clouds the whole time and yet able to pull off faultless rounds. But there's no denying the fact that she seems to be running this place to a T. Maybe she isn't as careless as she lets on…

'Hey!' Alex calls as she spots me, swinging the saddle in her arms onto her hip.

'Hi!' I say back, over the sound of the music. 'I wasn't sure where to go, and I couldn't find anyone…'

'Yeah, no worries,' she says, pulling a saddle rack out beside the stable of a bright bay horse, balancing the load on it. 'You'll give me an excuse to take a break. I've still got four left to ride.'

'Four?' I repeat. It's already that time of the afternoon.

'I know,' Alex sighs. 'I was going to pan one off on Leni, but she's running late. Hey, you busy? Wanna take one out with me? And if Leni decides to get here this century she can take one too, then I'll only have two to do!'

'Really? I mean, yeah, sure, if you want me to.' Alex thinks I'm good enough to ride one of her horses? *You rode James's horses,* I remind myself. And he didn't even see me ride before putting me on one of them.

'I've got these three project ponies. We can hack them together.' Alex nods at the row of stables on the other side of the concrete. 'Anyway, I'll show you where to go first.'

'Your stables are immaculate, by the way,' I say as we walk.

'Unlike my parents',' Alex finishes for me.

'Well, I wasn't going to say that.'

'No, I did. I wouldn't sleep if my horses were on the same

bedding and rations. I literally have nightmares about badly built straw banks.'

I follow Alex through a space that cuts between two buildings, entering again what she refers to as "parent territory", and as we take another left I find myself faced with a yellow row of temporary stables.

'This was Dad's business idea,' she says. 'There's always a shortage of stabling at events round here, so he charges people a fortune to use these.'

'Clever,' I say.

There's an open patch of grass opposite, clearly destined as a small lorry park, and I see now that there's a track running back to where my own trailer is.

'I always tell them to put signs up,' Alex grumbles. 'But do they listen?'

'It's fine,' I say.

'Well, just give me a shout if you need anything. Leni should show up soon, too. And then we'll go for a ride?'

'Sounds good.'

Leni arrives just after I've finished settling the horses in, her huge lorry being driven by her mum. Both Leni and Poppy wave, a gesture I return, as they pull up onto the grass.

'I thought we'd never get here,' Poppy says as she climbs out of the cab, shooting her daughter a mocking glance.

'I forgot Cooper's dressage saddle,' Leni explains.

'Something she only remembered after we'd already been driving an hour-'

'It wasn't an hour!' says Leni. 'Forty minutes, tops.'

'So we had to wait on the side of the motorway,' Poppy continues. 'For Kelly to bring it to us.'

'She *offered*. And it got her out of poo picking the fields, so she'll probably thank us.'

Poppy frowns, clearly still not seeing the funny side of the story. 'Just go put the beds down so we can unload these guys.'

'I can give you a hand,' I say.

'Maybe we should all *stop* giving Leni a hand,' says Poppy. 'And she'll actually remember to do things for herself!'

'You're so mean!' Leni calls from the opposite side of the lorry, where she is now opening a tack locker to pull out a pitchfork.

'I don't mind, I've already done mine.' I say to Poppy. 'And I think Alex is hoping Leni and I will go hack some ponies with her.'

'Yes! The ponies!' Leni cries, as though she's just won a prize. 'I love the ponies,' she continues, walking towards the stables with a pitchfork in her right hand.

'Why does Alex have ponies?' I ask, hoping that question doesn't sound stupid.

'She's always got about three ponies in the yard,' Leni says over the sound of slices of straw separating, and I step closer to hear. 'Buys them straight over from Ireland most of the time, puts a few months work into them, then sells them for a profit. I swear, I don't know why *everyone* doesn't do that. So much easier than horses, not to mention less chance of them going wrong.'

I'm still not quite sure I understand the point of this whole pony thing, but when we walk round to Alex's yard half an hour later, I sense that I'm going to be converted. I didn't get a good look when she pointed to the stables earlier, but now that I'm nearer I see just how nice these ponies are. At a glance, I'm pretty sure they're all Connemaras. There are two greys, one of which is obviously younger than the other if the darkness of his coat is anything to go by, and a dun. All three of them look to be just shy of fourteen hands two, and while they are small ponies, there is something reminiscent of event horses about them. Neatly pulled manes, well-muscled necks, coats shining.

'What happened to Stanley?' says Leni as she frowns at the three ponies opposite us.

Alex is walking this way, a saddle under each arm. 'I sold him months ago!'

'You didn't tell me!' cries Leni. 'I loved that one!'

'Well, what did you expect?' Alex says indignantly.

'You should've seen him,' Leni says to me. 'He was so gorgeous.'

'And *because* he was gorgeous, I got twenty grand for him. Anyway, which one do you want?'

It takes me a second to realise Alex is looking at me. 'Uh, I don't mind.'

'Leni?'

'I'm not speaking to you anymore.'

'Get over it,' Alex sighs, before walking over to me. 'Pick a saddle.'

'Umm,' So that she doesn't think I'm trying to eye up which is nicer, I take the one nearest to me as Alex holds it out.

'Okay, that's Howie's. The lighter grey on the end. I'll be nice, Leni, and take the dun because he's a pig. So you take Ziggy.'

We follow Alex back to the tack room, which is better organised than any I've ever been in, and she hands each of us a bridle and saddle pad. 'Boots and brushes in their box by the stable door,' she says. There's a big whiteboard up on one of the walls, divided into columns and boxes in which many things have been scribbled in different coloured markers. During the time we're standing for Alex to hand out tack, I make out the stable names of all her horses, followed by their last shoeing dates, as well as a list of their upcoming events. There's also a small wooden table below the board, on which a large diary lies open.

Howie is as sweet in the stable as he seemed from outside, standing perfectly still while I flick dust off him with one of the brushes found in the box outside his stable (horses clearly don't share brushes in Alex's yard, because there's an identical box by each door). I put on the the boots provided, as well as pick out his feet, before tacking up. Alex is a tad taller than me, but she must have done some fast work or something last time she rode Howie because the stirrups are short, and I decide they'll be fine for me.

'Come on,' Alex says to the dun, standing outside the stable door as she waits for him to step out. 'Seriously, can you move any slower?' There's a pause, followed by the sound of front hooves stretching out onto the concrete. 'Oh, finally,' she says with a flare of the arms. 'Thank you for gracing us with your presence! Am I disturbing you?'

Leni looks like she is holding back a laugh, so I decide to not listen to anything Alex says too carefully. Though I can't quite imagine talking to my own horses like that. Well, maybe Cookie…

I pull down Howie's stirrups and tighten the girth, wondering if we're supposed to get on here, getting my answer as I watch Leni swing straight up onto the dark grey's back. As soon as her seat touches the saddle, a grin spreads across her face.

'Oh, I love ponies!' she says, her voice sounding very much the way it did when she found out we would be riding them. 'Why do we even bother with horses?'

I swing a leg over my own pony, settling into the saddle as my feet find the stirrups. 'I do not know,' I say, almost laughing as I feel the perfectly proportioned Connemara beneath me.

'That's why I ride Anchor,' says Alex. 'You'll have to have a sit on him sometime,' to me, now. 'He really is just like riding a big pony. He's awesome. Ponies aren't always that cute, though' she concludes, raising her left foot to the stirrup. As if to reinforce what she just said, the dun shoots forward, Alex's hold on the reins enough to stop him taking off before she falls over. 'Oh, so *now* you want to move, do you?' she says loudly.

'He's really nice,' says Leni, cocking her head at the dun pony. I was thinking the exact same thing - beautiful colour, good natural head carriage, and flashy to look at. 'Why is he a pig?'

'Because he could give Veni a run for his money as far as strength goes,' she says, referring to Veni Vidi Amavi, a seventeen hand Warmblood. 'Totally bears down on you when he wants to. So far, I've had to do every dressage warm-up in a Pessoa, and swap it for a snaffle two minutes before going in the ring.'

'Does he jump?' I say.

'Oh, yeah, he'll jump anything you point him at, but you might not feel your arms by the end of it.'

'How are you going to sell him, then?'

'I'll either sell him to hunt, but I'll get less money, or find a boy that's strong enough to ride him. Or I'll keep hold of him for another season and sell him as an FEI prospect, but I could be worse off by doing that. I dunno. I'll just see how he goes, I guess.' Alex clicks her tongue to send the dun forward, and the two greys follow. 'Those two, on the other hand,' she says, looking at Howie and Ziggy as we walk out of the stable courtyard, towards a dirt track leading past the back paddocks. 'Are goldmines. They've never even refused a fence. They're both going double clear round BE100. Shame they'll end up being sold to people who can't ride.'

'How do you know the people who'll buy them won't be able

to ride?' I say.

'Because if you have to spend over five figures on a pony, then you clearly don't know how to ride one.' Alex says.

'Do people seriously pay that much for ponies?'

'More,' Leni says, and Alex nods in agreement.

'My European pony, Otto - Lakota - sold for a hundred and fifty,' says Alex. Not bragging, just stating a fact. 'And the girl who's got him can't ride worth a damn.'

'Leo sold for a hundred,' says Leni, 'and Olivia can ride him, at least.'

'I also had Accel and Lorcan,' Alex continues. 'Accel didn't sell for as much because he never made a team, and he went to someone nice. But Lorcan was my reserve, so he went for a crazy price too. And again, to somebody who thought they could just buy their way onto the team. I mean, hello, you still have to ride the pony! He isn't going to do it all by himself!'

'And Sophia,' says Leni, 'the girl who bought Otto,' she adds to me. 'Bought Ryan's European pony, too.'

'Is that Fendigo?' I say.

'Yeah, Fendi.'

'And she can't ride her, either,' Alex scoffs. 'And Fendi is seriously idiot-proof. I mean, if you can't ride Fendi then you can't ride a donkey. Her parents spent three hundred grand on two ponies, and she's wrecked them both. I can't believe it. It makes me so angry… I mean, I seriously can't get over this - if you have to buy your kid, who you think is going to go pro, a pony that's already been in a European team, then you're wasting your money, because your kid is never going to go pro!'

'So,' I say. 'It's like, "Give someone a top horse and they'll win once, teach them to produce one and they'll be unbeatable?"'

'Oh my god, we should put that on a t-shirt!' says Leni. 'We'd make a fortune!'

'Can we have bumper stickers that say, "If you have to buy your kid a hundred grand pony then they're obviously crap"?' says Alex.

'I think we might get in trouble for that one,' I say.

'Thomas's parents bought him two ponies that had been long listed for Euros, and he succeeded,' Leni points out.

'Yeah, but that's just not even fair,' says Alex. 'Anyway, shall we trot up here?'

Riding Howie isn't much different than riding Zebra and Dun, but the hack is made more fun by the fact that I'm not alone. Alex never stops talking, even when her pony decides to take off in a bucking fit, she finishes her sentence while trying to pull his head up, completely unperturbed.

It turns out that the property backs onto farmland riddled with bridle paths, offering the kind of hacking you wouldn't think possible based on the approach to the yard.

A chorus of neighs greet us when we ride back to the stables, Alex's top event horses looking at the trio of ponies as if to say, "Why are you bothering with them when you've got us?" Especially Anchor Lane, the horse that always looks so laid-back at competitions, who is now kicking his stable door and pushing his weight against it. I watch him lower his lips to the top bolt, shake the handle so that it clanks, only to give up and kick the door again.

'Dream on,' Alex calls, though she looks as him as though he's the best thing since sliced bread. 'He's an escape artist,' she adds to me, and I look back at the top bolt of the door to notice a clip securing it so that it can't be lifted. 'He doesn't actually go anywhere, just likes wandering about the stables. Walks *just* far enough from the other horses that they can't reach him. I can't decide whether he's evil or a genius.'

I'm about to turn my eyes away from Anchor when a cat jumps up onto the half door, from inside the stable, and carelessly walks along the narrow ledge.

'He likes cats?' I say.

Alex nods. 'Yeah - or more to the point, Evie likes *him*. She sleeps in the stable with him. And comes to events with him, too. It's ridiculous-'

'ALEX!' a voice shouts, interrupting the discussion.

'WHAT!?' Alex screams back, sounding as fed up as she looks.

There's silence for a moment, until Joan Evans steps round a stable block, face to face with the three ponies. She doesn't even acknowledge me and Leni. 'I thought you were doing flatwork with them today,' she says.

Alex shrugs. 'Changed my mind.'

As Joan starts telling Alex off for "lack of commitment", I follow Leni's lead as she excuses herself by leading Ziggy back to his stable. We untack at the same speed, and by the time we're carrying our kit back to the tack room, Joan has left, and Alex comes in as I'm sliding the saddle onto the wooden rack on which a label reads *Howie*.

'Oh my god, she drives me crazy!' she says, taking off her riding hat and pulling a hair free from its elastic band. 'In case she hasn't noticed, I run my own yard just fine!' Alex continues, tying her hair up in a high bun, and then picking a pen up from the table beneath the whiteboard.

'Just ignore her,' Leni says offhandedly, and I'm guessing the words are only to try to calm Alex down.

'She'd better never retire,' Alex says as she sits on a chair and starts scribbling something down in the open diary. 'Can you imagine? She'd have nothing better to do than annoy me.' Her hand pauses on the page, and she raises the opposite one to her head, squeezing her eyes closed as though she's going through something painful. 'What's the pony you rode called?' she asks, opening one eye to look at me.

'Howie?'

'Howie,' Alex repeats triumphantly, removing the hand from her face as the pen starts moving across the page again. '...*Ziggy, and Howie, hack. Moderate,*' she murmurs as she writes.

'Alex!?' another voice calls, and somebody I recognise as a groom who is often at competitions appears in the doorway. She shoots both me and Leni a polite smile before going on. 'Shall I start plaiting Waffles?'

'No,' Alex says, standing up. 'I'll do it in a sec. I just need to finish untacking...' and with that she walks off out the tack room.

'Crap, I haven't plaited either,' says Leni.

I shake my head. 'Neither have I.'

It's almost six o'clock, and as soon as the ponies are cooled off we hurry to get started on the first of many jobs left to do.

## Chapter 7

It turns out that not only did Poppy plait all of Leni's horses for her while we were riding, but she even moved on to mine. When we reach the stables, I find Nantucket with a row of plaits way better than any I could have done myself, and Poppy halfway through Loxwood's mane.

'I hope you don't mind,' she says. 'I thought I'd give you girls a hand.'

'It's great!' I say, looking at the perfect plaits. 'Thank you so much. Mine are nowhere near that good.'

'Thirty years of practice,' says Poppy through the elastic bands between her teeth.

When we finish feeding our horses, and I've taken Lily for a walk, Leni and I go back to Alex's yard to see if we can help her out with anything, leaving Poppy to unpack the many dishes of food she seems to have brought. The music's still playing when we step round the corner of the first stable block, the Black Eyed

Peas this time, except that now the soundtrack is accompanied by a very off-key voice singing along to the lyrics.

'You gave me a heart attack, I thought somebody was being tortured!' Leni yells with a grin.

Alex is standing beside a tied-up Waffles, wrapping an elastic band around what appears to be the last plait. In response to Leni's comment, she goes to great lengths to sing the next lyric of the song even louder.

'You're scaring Waffles,' says Leni as the grey horse pins his ears back.

'It's called bombproofing,' Alex says, clicking her tongue to pull Waffles forwards a step.

Leni steps forward to rub her knuckles against the horse's forehead. 'It's called tone-deaf,' she whispers to him, just loud enough that Alex can still hear.

'Did you come here to insult my musical ability?'

'No, actually, we came to offer our help because we're nice like that,' says Leni. 'Also, my mum has enough food to feed an army, and she said to invite you all for something to eat.'

'I've only got Cash left to do after this, and he's practically got no mane so it won't take long,' says Alex, stepping back to admire Waffles's mane.

'Ooh, I haven't seen him yet. Is that the one from France?'

Alex nods, pointing at a stable block across the yard. 'Second on the left.'

A bright bay head, dished like an Arab, with a white stripe running down it looks out over the half door.

'Hey,' I say, remembering something. 'Did you get that horse you were looking at last year? Chevalier?'

'Ugh, failed the vet,' says Alex. 'Three hundred quid spent for nothing. Oh.' She snaps her fingers, the words seeming to remind her of something as she looks around the yard. 'Polly!' she calls. 'Did you get more bute?'

A groom appears from what looks to be a feed room, nodding as she pulls a piece of paper out of her pocket. 'I've got the receipt.'

'Put one in the morning feed too, yeah?' Alex says as she holds a hand out for the invoice. 'Fruitloop gave himself a whack this morning,' she mutters to me as her eyes look down at the page. 'That stuff must have platinum in it,' she comments before folding the receipt up once more. 'I need to advertise Howie again.'

I'm pretty sure I know the answer to this, but I ask anyway. 'Do you have to pay for everything yourself?'

'Yep. I make sure I've always got a few specifically to train and sell on, and that pretty much funds the rest. It's not like my parents wouldn't help me if I asked, but I don't like them having any control. For instance, Anchor is still fifty per cent theirs on paper, so they'll try to have a say, but I've obviously managed to keep hold of him this long. The last horse I rode that belonged to them was Motown, and you know how that went down. So for the past two years I've been building a team up on my own. I got a percentage of the money when we sold the ponies - peanuts compared to what my parents got, though - and I used it to invest in horses, making a profit on each one until it got to the stage that it was enough to run the others, and now I run it all myself.'

I thought I was doing pretty well for my age, succeeding in moving to my own yard with three horses. But Alex is barely a year older than me, and she's running a business that finances her entire team of event horses. 'That's pretty impressive.'

Alex shrugs. 'Not really.'

'I'm not sure I'd ever be able to sell them, though.'

'The thing is, I treat the ones I'm going to sell differently to my own,' says Alex. 'I mean, obviously they're all cared for to the same standard, but I don't ride them the same way.'

'In what way?' I say.

'Well, umm, take Anchor, for example. I didn't start with him from scratch, and the person who rode him before had really crap hands, so he has a tendency to sit on the left rein. I obviously tried to work it out of him, and still do, but I've kind of come to accept it. I mean, he's fourteen now, so he's never going to change. And I basically ride every test with the right rein.'

'Seriously?' I say. Anchor Lane is competing at three-star level, and he certainly isn't at the bottom of the leader board after dressage.

'Exactly! You can't tell. But if he had been a project horse to sell on, I wouldn't be able to accept that. I can't train horses that will go just for me. They have to know this leg means move and that one means bend. Know what I mean? I can't let them do things their own way, or have them not respond to an aid, or anything like that. Because at the end of the day, I don't know who they're going to end up with in the saddle, so they have to respond to commands, end of. I can't rely on a partnership, or for that matter even build one, when I'm not producing them for myself.'

'Is that not tough?'

'Yeah,' sighs Alex. 'But what can you do?'

The event venue is only five minutes away, and I'm one of the first trailers to pull into the lorry park. Alex was loading horses onto the lorry when I left, though, so she won't be far behind. I've left myself forty-five minutes to pay entry fees and collect numbers, and the same time again to warm up. At least

I'll be finished early, allowing me to drive the horses back, and then return to walk the cross country course later in the day. I can't decide whether having the stress of competing spread out across two days is better or worse than one. Rain is predicted for this weekend, but so far the weather has held off, and I just hope that it does at least for tonight. Needing somewhere to sleep, I borrowed a tent and sleeping bag from Clara, whose family has a thing for occasional camping trips, and set it up beside my car. Both Leni and Alex offered me a bed in their respective lorries upon seeing my sleeping arrangements, which I declined despite how tempting it was to experience the luxurious living accommodations for a few hours. If it does rain tonight, though, I might just take one of them up on the offer.

I forgot how much work getting greys clean is, but I'm so happy to be competing Nantucket again that I'm smiling almost the whole time I spend scrubbing at manure stains. Every time a person walks by, I'm hoping that Nantucket didn't go to enough competitions with Imogen to be recognised by association. I'm doing an all right job at pushing the incident to the back of my mind, but I'm not sure I could handle anyone wanting to exchange condolences. I've got myself under enough pressure to make her proud as it is.

Everything feels right when I ride Nantucket to the warm-up area. He isn't Loxwood, but he means more to me than I ever thought another horse would. Rose isn't here because her horses are only competing tomorrow, so I'm on my own. Except with Nantucket beneath me, I don't feel so alone.

Imogen has done a beautiful job. The Thoroughbred moves with elegance, balancing himself through the turns while keeping his hindquarters engaged. The contact in the reins is the same pressure you feel when slicing into soft butter, never heavy but enough to know it's there. Nantucket's canter strike-offs are immediate, his shoulder lifting up into the gait the second I slide my outside leg back. His halts are square, due in no part to me. I always thought he was a special horse, and he's confirming it.

'Hey!'

I've just brought Nantucket back to a walk, and I look over my shoulder to see Alex riding this way on Waffles. 'Yeah?'

'How the heck am I supposed to compete with that?' she says with a grin. 'I thought Waffles's selling point was that he's grey, but yours is grey *and* good. No fair.'

Tightrope Act looks amazing, a far cry from what he was when he started competing, and I tell Alex so, but she shrugs it off.

'Just try and pick up some time penalties or something to give us a chance,' she jokes before riding off to focus on warming up.

I laugh, and lean forward to run my hand down Nantucket's neck. 'Not likely.'

The buzz from Nantucket's brilliant test hasn't worn off when I start warming up Loxwood. I don't know if it's the schooling we did with James, or the past weeks of hacking, or just the many hours of work starting to show, but he feels the best he's ever felt.

'Or maybe,' I say to him. 'You heard Nantucket brag about how well he did, and you're feeling left out?'

I know which hypothesis I think is correct, but it doesn't matter. He's working well, and that's all that is important.

When we're called by the steward, and I trot Loxwood over towards the white boards of the dressage arena, I feel him tense up with excitement. His stride shortens, his stomach making that *glug glug* sound, but I stay calm. This is what we've practiced for. This is why halfway through a hack I have turned into an open field and begun running through a dressage test, so that I know I can get my leg on him any time, any place.

I never expected Loxwood's test to be better than Nantucket's, but he still does a good job. His neck remains supple, forward movement always coming through from behind. The canter transitions aren't great, because he still sees them coming from a mile away, jiggling with anticipation and then throwing his head when I ask for a strike-off, but that's okay. We're a work in progress.

As soon as Loxwood has cooled down, I run him and Nantucket back to Alex's in the trailer. They're quite happy to return to their respective stables, where they each bury their heads in piles of hay and don't look up. Once it's clear that they're settled, I unhook the trailer and drive back.

With Lily on a lead, I walk the cross country course. It's a rolling course, with long galloping stretches, and enough hills to distinguish the fit competition horses from those ridden only at weekends. In other words, the perfect track for ex-racehorses.

'It looks like the storm's going to pass,' Leni says, scrolling down the weather forecast on her phone. 'It says on here that it's going to be in the twenties now tomorrow.'

'Ugh. I'll take the rain, please,' says Alex, lifting a forkful of couscous to her mouth.

Leni frowns. 'All English do is complain about the rain, but then when it's hot we don't know what to do with ourselves.'

'And we drink tea,' says Alex. 'Don't forget the tea.'

I'm sitting on a camping chair outside Leni's lorry, back at Alex's, watching the horses finish off their dinners as I eat my own. True to Leni's weather report, it's warm. The heaviness that has been in the air all day is starting to disperse, promising even hotter weather to come. I ended up going back to the event a third time, after Alex asked if Leni and I wanted to join her for the three-star course walk, insisting it would be "so fun". Because apparently that's what looking at enormous fences you'll be expected to jump in a matter of hours is. Leni has still got this last year in Juniors, and as a consequence is having to run in the classes selectors choose, but Alex is aiming some of her other horses at Young Riders, thus leaving Anchor free to pursue the higher levels. Her plan is Badminton in spring, which makes racking up more experience at three-star a priority.

There are more lorries and horses here now. Riders competing over the course of several days, clearly having come here straight from a dressage test, are in their own horse boxes around us, voices drifting through the air.

'Don't stay up too late, girls,' says Poppy, stepping out of the living compartment behind Leni. 'You've all got a lot of riding to do tomorrow.'

'Oh, I can't go to bed early,' says Alex. 'I only ride well when I'm tired.'

Poppy nods as though Alex has just reminded her of something obvious. 'Right. Sorry, Lexie, I forgot.'

'Am I missing something?' I say.

Leni shoots Alex a mocking look, just as the latter launches into what I can already tell is going to be a rant. 'I've always ridden better when I'm tired-'

'You're imagining it,' interrupts Leni.

'...And about five years ago - was it five years ago, Leni?'

'Yeah.'

'Okay, so five years ago we were competing at the Haras du Pin pony one star, over in France, and the team trainer at the time was there too - that *stupid* woman.'

'I can't stand her,' says Leni.

'Nobody can stand her,' says Alex, and behind her Poppy nods in agreement. 'Anyway, she was there, and so obviously all of us who went over stuck together, and the day before cross country, when we were sitting around the lorry park having dinner, and she starts going on about how we should all be asleep already, and she had our parents send us to bed at nine o'clock! Nine! Can you believe it?'

'I'd give just about anything to be in bed by nine most days,' I say.

'Well, so do I,' Alex concedes. 'But not in the middle of summer, and certainly not the day before a competition. And not when it's light out and we're all buzzing with adrenalin like that.'

'Keep going,' says Leni, stabbing her fork into a piece of courgette.

'Okay,' says Alex. 'So my parents make me go to bed, and I end up lying awake until one in the morning, because I am normal and I don't go to sleep that early the day before a competition.'

'Uh huh,' I say, still not seeing how this is relevant.

'Well, long story short, I fell off the next day.'

'Because… you went to bed early?' I venture, thinking I might be catching on.

'Yes! Exactly. So now I stay up until I can't keep my eyes open.' Alex swallows down another mouthful of couscous before speaking. 'Hey, do you guys wanna watch a movie in the lorry?'

Almost two hours later, having watched *Pitch Perfect* in the living compartment of Alex's horse box, I wriggle into my sleeping bag, Lily by my side, and fall asleep as soon as my head hits the pillow.

*'And that is a clear round inside the time for Georgia James and Nantucket Winter.'*

'Good boy!' I yell, leaning across Nantucket's neck as we pass the finish line, standing in the stirrups to bring him back to a trot. 'Good boy, good boy, good boy!' I pat his neck with both hands, my bare fingers sliding against the sweat. Alex was right - rain is better than this heat.

Liz is standing nearby, looking this way, and as my eyes meet hers she holds up her thumbs, smiling, and I respond by doing the same. My first time out with Nantucket since getting him back, and we've gone double clear. I can't ask for anything else. I just hope Loxwood can do the same.

The show jumping went well, and while his round wasn't as polished as Nantucket's, it was clean. All the poles stayed in their cups, so I can't complain. And looking pretty doesn't matter across the country.

The warm-up is uneventful. Loxwood jumps every fence first time, without neither hesitation nor overconfidence. I make sure I'm always asking him to move forwards while still keeping him collected and coming through, careful not to send any mixed messages. I've been round the course once already, so I know where the ground is hard, and which fences have shadows cast over them at this time of day.

'Five, four, three, two, one, GO! Good luck!'

Loxwood is off, moving away from my leg as soon as I tell him to go. The first fence is a nice one, inviting, the perfect confidence booster. We clear it on an easy, forward stride, and then we're on to the next. And the next. With each jump, Loxwood seems to take the next one on with more self-assurance, and I feel my own confidence grow with it.

But then we come to the white palisade. It's neither big nor technical, but in the middle of an open field, with the sunlight glinting right off it, it's spooky. Nantucket didn't give it a second look, but I feel Loxwood back off as soon as he realises I'm turning him towards it.

'Go on!' I shout, clicking my tongue.

I'm squeezing with my legs, and I give his shoulder a tap with the whip as we move towards the fence, sensing his hesitation. I know he isn't sold, but I keep going, attacking the obstacle with everything I've got. The stride's right, and I lean forward on take-off, except there is no take-off, only me flying over Loxwood's shoulder and landing on the fence. My body protector takes the worst of it, and I'm on my feet in no time, walking forwards to catch Loxwood. Every ounce of confidence I've gained up to now seems to roll to the edge of a cliff, not falling over the edge and plummeting but instead waiting there. Waiting for me to do something.

I run a hand down Loxwood's neck, trying to steady my breathing. So much for two double clears. I glance over my shoulder, checking the next horse isn't anywhere close, but I don't have all day. It would be so easy to raise a hand and withdraw. It would be so easy to wallow in a puddle of self-pity, but nothing is ever achieved by taking the easy route. *I will not give up*, I think, chanting the words to myself like an intimidating coach in a movie. *I. Will. Not. Fail.* So I push past every thought of doubt I have, running a hand down Loxwood's neck again before swinging back into the saddle, shortening my reins and pushing him back into a canter before I can change my mind.

The fence still needs to be ridden strongly, and moving forward, but I try not to override it this time. I keep my shoulders back, all while making sure Loxwood knows he has to jump it. And this time he does.

We complete the course with the sixty penalties I got for falling, but that's okay. I'm annoyed at myself for making such a rookie mistake, but I am also relieved that I managed to come back from it. We fell down, but we got right back up. Once you manage to overcome failure, there's nothing it can do to scare you.

'Next time,' I say to Loxwood as I give him an apple back at the trailer. *Next time.*

# Chapter 8

I let Loxwood and Nantucket take it easy the next week, giving me time to focus on Cookie. I start introducing her to poles, which she is surprisingly okay with. The thing with Cookie is that she's not actually fazed or scared of anything, it's just a question of having her on your side to do what you ask. It only takes two sessions to have her perfectly jumping a small upright, and at the weekend I even attempt hacking her for the first time, and while she naps and rears when I first ask her to leave the invisible boundary she is used to staying within, the rest of the ride isn't completely terrible. Sure, she prances the whole time and I can barely keep a hold of her, but it's still a hack, and I'm in one piece at the end of it.

There's a four year old class at a nearby event in a few weeks time, and that evening I decide to enter her. She might not be ready when the time comes, but if that's the case then we'll only do the dressage. But at least I've got something to work Cookie towards.

It's the next Wednesday that I find myself sitting in the kitchen at three o'clock in the afternoon, having worked all five horses, overcome with the need to get out. Boredom isn't something I exactly have time for, but that seems to be what strikes me today.

'Hey, Lily,' I say, watching as the dog lifts her head from her bed at the sound of her name. I walk over to the back door, where trainers lie discarded beside a pair of boots. 'Wanna go for a walk?'

We drive with the windows half open, me resting my elbow against the sill while Lily stares out the glass at the countryside we pass. 'Do you know where we're going?' I say, pushing aside the thought that I really do need to get out more if I've reached the desperate stage of having one-sided conversations with my dog. 'We're going to a racetrack, but not the kind you're used to.'

There are no other cars on Warren Hill, Tucker the only one as we pull up onto the parking area. Just to be safe, I clip a lead to Lily's collar before opening the door, and then we run. Across the sand track, over the grass, me struggling for breath while she finds it easy. We run all the way to the top of the hill, by which point I collapse onto the grass.

'That's way easier on a horse,' I wheeze, while Lily seems unaffected by the effort.

Pulling my knees up to my chest, I sit up, looking down at the view that stretches out below. Seeing that I'm not about to get up any time soon, Lily lies beside me, stretching her front legs out in front of her and holding her head up like a lion.

'I used to come here every day,' I say, running a hand down her back. 'With your brothers.'

How long has it been now? A year and a half? Back when

Loxwood wasn't mine, and I lived for that one morning ride on him. I can still see it - his eyes watching me when I arrived at Frank's in the morning, warming up round the small track while cars sped by, crossing the road to the gallops. And galloping, galloping up this ground I'm sitting on right now, just one of thousands that did the same thing every morning, unbeknown to us both how drastically our lives would change.

As I look down at the rolling hill, I can see the past two years laid out before me, dotted like racehorses along the grass track. From first seeing Loxwood, to riding him, and taking him back to Rose's... the triumph of our first event, the disappointment that followed, the heartache of last year... it's all there, moving towards me. But then I'm at the top, living a life I could only imagine before. Each obstacle, every setback, has been just that. We fell, we hurt, we learned, we got up, and we kept going. It's all part of the journey, and I wish I had realised, when I felt like a failure, that challenges are part of success. Every blow has toughened my skin, and shown me that there is no such thing as failing if you don't give up. A legend is never born from having everything come easily.

Lily pushes into my thoughts, moving closer to nudge me with her nose. I laugh. 'I'd better actually give you a walk, hey? Come on, then. I'll race you. Ready?' I get to my feet, watching as Lily braces her body. 'On your marks, get set... GO!"

The day of Cookie's event, I turn Loxwood and Nantucket out early, which does not go down well with her.

'Hey, you're the one getting all the attention today,' I say, pausing to pop my head round the door of the stable I'm mucking out. '*They* don't get to go gallop around a cross country course. Joke's on them!'

This doesn't stop Cookie from shrieking the entire time I'm mucking out, which means I'm fed up with her before we've even got to the event. At least she loads well, even if she does almost knock me over on her way up the ramp. Loxwood and Nantucket trot to the fence at the sight of the horse trailer, nostrils flared and tails held high.

'Oh, don't start being idiots,' I grumble. 'Please, for me, be the calm, sensible horses I know you are capable of being.'

Loxwood responds to this by spinning on his hocks and taking off in a full on bronco fit. *Great.*

'If either of you are injured when I get back,' I say before climbing into the jeep. 'I'm disowning you.'

While the event is affiliated, it seems to be pretty low-key. Few enormous lorries, and more small horse boxes and trailers. I don't really know anyone here today, which is great because it means nobody will see the catastrophe that is Cookiemoon.

'You look pretty nice, though,' I say, stepping back to admire the tacked-up mare. Her good conformation is accentuated by a muscled top line, and her bay coat is shining. I see her as a walking disaster because I know too much about her, but if you saw her for the first time you probably wouldn't think she looks half bad.

I'm prepared for the absolute worst today. She could stop at every fence cross country, or crash through the show jumping, or even jump out of the dressage ring, and I wouldn't be surprised. So when a few hours later, I find myself loading up the trailer with a double clear under my belt, I can't quite believe it.

I've always known Cookie isn't afraid of anything, but I didn't expect her to actually use that to my advantage today. Nothing fazed her, and she performed the dressage test with confidence, even if it was a bit scrappy, and kept that attitude right through the remaining phases. And the two clear rounds were enough to bring Cookie up in the placings, meaning we even won our entry fee back.

That evening, I enter her for the Four Year Old Championships.

In the month leading up to the Young Event Horse Championships, I think of nothing else. My main focus every day is riding. Though I'm also careful not to turn them sour. Instead, ignoring the voices in my head telling me that everyone else will probably be going all out on flatwork, I hack. And I do do flatwork, but on a hilltop halfway through a ride. And every time I trot down a track, I focus on having my horse balanced and responsive, their attention on me and not the distractions around them. Dressage is important, but I don't think endless circles is a way to achieve anything. I do one serious session, though, two weeks before the championships. I trailer Loxwood to Rose's for a lesson, having her point out and correct any bad habits I've acquired, giving me plenty to work on for the next couple weeks of hacking. But overall, she thinks Loxwood is looking great.

I'm definitely not confident that everything is going to go to plan at the event, but I'm confident in what I'm doing. I've seen the way other people train their horses, and I know what I believe. If it backfires, then it backfires. But I believe in my way of doing things, and for once I'm not going to doubt myself. I've just got to keep going.

*But*, I think as I wait by the gate for Loxwood and Nantucket to come to me, a week exactly before the Championships, *I definitely do not need* this.

I hope I saw wrong, or that it was just a stumble, but there's no doubting it as he gets closer. Nantucket is lame.

'Hey, buddy, what have you done?'

He's got all four shoes on, which I almost wish he didn't because that would at least explain what's wrong. But he's definitely reluctant to put weight on his hind left.

*Oh, what have you done?*

The only thing I'm sure about is that it's coming from the foot, and I call the farrier straight away. By some miracle, he's in the area, and promises to be round within an hour. When does that ever happen?

I'm pretty sure I know what it is, but the farrier confirms it. He finds an abscess, blood dripping onto the concrete in front of the stable block as he cuts it out. Nothing major, pretty common, certainly lucky that it's been found. But it will need poulticing, protected so that no dirt can get in. And as I listen to the farrier rattle on about how many days rest and how long the wound needs to be bandaged for, all I can hear is the truth of what this means: no Young Event Horse Championships for Nantucket.

I've learnt by now that nothing can ever just be simple. Nothing can go according to plan, no matter how much you work. So if this is the curveball of the week, then at least it's out the way. Get the bad luck over with, so that I'm not waiting for something to go wrong. I'm disappointed, of course I am, because once again I feel like all the work I've done has been for nothing, but it's not the end of the world. I'm training to go round Badminton someday, not just for tomorrow's win. So through the tears, I remind myself that this is just another setback to look back on in a year's time. Another event in the timeline to victory.

Rose was going to drive one of the horses to the event for me, along with Sunny, but instead I now drop Nantucket at hers early in the morning before I leave, confident in the knowledge that he will be spoilt rotten by Leah, Mackenzie, and Paige. Everybody loves Nantucket.

Most of the competition takes place on the Friday, except that Loxwood's dressage is scheduled for Thursday. He's isn't up until late in the afternoon, and I've only got just over an hour to drive, which means that I have a relatively laid-back morning as far as competition mornings go. It's warm today, but I know that a rapid drop in temperature is scheduled for this evening.

'You two ready?' I say, as Loxwood and Cookie look at me over their half doors. I'll plait Cookie's mane tonight, but Loxwood's is already done, perfect bunches running along the top of his neck.

I walk up to Loxwood's stable, running a hand down his neck over the half door. 'Hey, my little superstar,' I say. 'We've made it this far. And I couldn't be prouder of you. I don't expect anything of you, okay? We're just going to go and do our best. But I really would like to stick it to James, though. How dare he call you average? It's ridiculous. We're *all* average. Everyone's ordinary, it's only hard work that puts the *extra* in front of it. So, are you two ready to go show those expensive Warmbloods how it's done?'

# Chapter 9

It's already packed when I arrive. Rows of horse boxes, speakers crackling as horses and riders are announced, ambition so thick in the air you can almost smell it. This is where I belong.

Tacking up a horse has never taken so long. My limbs keep shaking, refusing to cooperate with my brain, and after it takes me three tries to get the reins over his head the right way round, Loxwood tilts his head towards me as if to say, "what's wrong with you?"

What would Rose say now? *Breathe.* I close my eyes for a moment, inhaling the smell of shavings and hoof oil. *Breathe, Georgia.* I want to do well so badly, for Loxwood, for Rose, for *myself.* I just want to achieve something I can be proud of. And I'm beginning to regret my decision to not run through the dressage test beforehand... I've ridden parts of it, of course, but never the whole thing in succession. Part of the reason the phase hasn't always worked out in the past is that Loxwood gets too worked-up as the test progresses, particularly anticipating canter strike-offs and no longer executing them correctly as a consequence. So instead of giving him the opportunity to learn the test, I've decided to do the complete opposite. He's practiced the movements - working on leg-yielding in the paddock, riding into an open field on a hack to execute twelve, fifteen, and twenty metre circles, and walking with his nose to the ground down alleyways in the woods. And I've read the test through so many times myself that I go to sleep imagining the movements, Loxwood's ears pricked in front of me as we trot down the centre line.

Cookie neighs when I lead Loxwood out the stable beside her, spinning once in the box to press her head against the grid of the door. But Loxwood ignores her, keeping his attention directed straight ahead, soaking up the competition atmosphere. I feel claustrophobic beneath my jacket and gloves, wondering, for the millionth time, why on earth I choose to do this when I could just ride for pleasure, hacking on weekends without the pressure of competing. But that would mean not working with horses, and having to succumb to the conformity of a nine-to-five job. No, I chose a five-to-nine job instead. One filled with danger and disappointment. And I used to think that if I worked hard enough, and wanted it badly enough, that I would be victorious. But it doesn't always work out that way. You can chase something your whole life without ever catching it, or you can also achieve everything you ever hoped and more, and then have your life taken away from you with a single error in judgment. Or you can *almost* make it. You can *almost* get the right horse, and *almost* ride round Badminton, and while you don't fail, you just never quite get there. And then sometimes, *sometimes,* everything comes together. Whether it be laid out by the universe in such a way that we can never understand, or pure luck, or the fact that you never give up. It *can* all come together. All the blood, sweat, and tears will be distant memories, as hard work pays off. I don't know yet which one of those outcomes awaits me, the thought of which is terrifying if I allow myself to think about it, but I do know one thing. Nothing is as terrifying as the thought of finding myself looking back at the dreams I had, in a few years time, and wondering what could have been. What if I *had* dared to set up a yard on my own? What if I *had* left school to accept an opportunity to train with a top rider? Or even, what if I *had* said yes when Frank asked me if I wanted Loxwood? It's been hard, and I would be lying if I said there have never been times when I've wondered why I put myself through it all. But if ever it doesn't work out, if in twenty, or ten, or even two years time I find myself a complete failure, I'll know I've tried. I'll know that I gave it my all, that I fought back at every obstacle, that I got up every time I was knocked down. I'll know that instead of resigning myself to imagining an alternate universe in which I was riding round Badminton, I had the courage to actually go after that dream and try to make it a reality.

And right now, standing before me, is the chestnut horse that started it all. The horse I am riding in all those daydreams, imagining his victory even more than my own. Because at the end of the day, I wasn't picturing myself going round Badminton. It was *him*. I didn't think about how nice it must be to be such an amazing rider that I could hop on a horse one day and take it round a four-star track the next. I loved Loxwood, and I wanted to train him to the top level, the two of us a team. And then, sure, I've thought about riding other horses too, and wishing I were like Alex and Leni, able to get any horse going beautifully, but that's not how it started, and it's certainly not as important. I want *Loxwood* to succeed. Hearing James tell me that I would be better off selling him didn't make me upset so much as it did angry. Yes, the reality is that Loxwood may never make it to the top, but why should that mean that he doesn't get to try? What is with this idea people have of horses being born "winners"? Athletes are created, not born. It comes more easily to some than others, sure. That doesn't mean those others should just give up. Thinking like this probably means I'll never be a top rider, but I don't care. I'm not going to be the kind of person who gives up on a horse because they feel that getting the best out of them is a waste of their time. I believe every horse can be something special if only given the chance. I think about Paddington, Rose's horse, who we're always saying will never go all the way. But nobody thought he'd make it to two-star, and he did. And even though Rose doesn't think he'll make it to four-star, she has still kept going. She hasn't given up on him.

'And you, Loxwood,' I say quietly, pulling down the stirrups of the saddle that isn't even mine, 'are never going to be given up on.'

All the endless evenings spent riding the test in my mind, and the random dressage sessions across the estate, come down to this. Loxwood has warmed in well enough, and I know I've done everything I can. I've done my best, and if it's not good enough then it's not good enough. So I take a deep breath, and we turn down the centre line.

'It's too hot, I can't take it anymore,' says Alex, leaning back in her chair and holding her arm over her eyes to shield her face from the sun. 'I'm moving to Alaska. Is there an eventing circuit in Alaska?'

'Sure, but instead of riding in a sand school you ride on ice.'

'Why can't you ever take anything seriously, Leni? I thought you were supposed to be the smart one, why can't you just answer a question normally?'

'Why can't you just ask *normal* questions?'

'Whoa, wait a minute,' comes Thomas's voice as he appears round the side of the lorry, striding up to us with a bottle of Lucozade in one hand, and a Tupperware box in the other. 'Did you just imply that Alex is normal?'

'*Imply,*' scoffs Alex, lifting her arm just long enough to glance Thomas, before covering her eyes again. 'Who even talks like that? I mean, apart from Leni.'

'Joke all you want,' says Leni. 'But I've aced all my A-levels, so I don't even care.'

A shadow casts over where we're sitting as clouds shift to cover the sun, and Alex sits up again, frowning at Thomas. 'You selling cookies or something?'

'No,' he says, pulling the lid off the box. 'But since you asked so nicely, you may have one.'

Alex goes to take a baked-good from the container, only to pause with her hand in midair, crinkling up her nose in disgust. 'That's not a cookie. What the heck is that supposed to be?'

'Let's see,' says Leni, stretching her neck to peer into the box.

'These, Lennon,' says Thomas. 'Are gluten-free, chia seed, goji berry, and courgette vegan muffins.'

Alex's look of horror does not subside. 'And why would you eat that instead of chocolate cookies?'

'Because these are healthier. And let's face it, I'm not going to look like this forever.'

Leni snorts into her cup of water, loud enough to earn a glare from Thomas. 'That reminds me,' she says to me. 'I can't remember if I ever told you that Alex and Thomas spent the whole time we were in Italy last year arguing over who had the best abs.'

'I don't think you can call it an argument,' says Alex, 'since there's no debating the fact that the answer's me.'

'How can you even say that?' cries Thomas. 'That's not even possible.'

'Um, yes it is. It's called riding horses that don't just do everything on their own. *Cough, cough.* Hence why I do not need to eat that disgusting looking thing when I have a cupboard full of chocolate in the lorry.'

'Just try some,' says Thomas, holding out the Tupperware box again. 'And also,' he adds, 'Alex didn't spend as much time arguing with me at Euros as she did complaining about that French horse having a bad back.'

'It *did* have a bad back!' shouts Alex. 'Anyone with half a brain could see that! Not to mention the fact it was swishing its tail non stop! It was a joke. How could anyone in their right mind think that horse was fit to be ridden? Horses don't buck and swish their tails for no reason.'

'Waffles,' says Leni.

'Fine, there are some exceptions. But he doesn't swish his tail. And I had his back x-rayed, because *I know* that horses don't usually buck and kick out under saddle for no reason. But in his case, the reason is that he is crazy. You know as well as I do that that horse's back in Italy was completely shot.'

'Oh, I know,' says Leni.

'Everyone in Italy knows, too, the way you were talking about it,' mutters Thomas. 'Anyway,' he continues, changing the subject as he holds out the Tupperware box once more. 'Do you want a muffin or not?'

'What do I get if I eat one?' says Alex, glancing over Thomas's right shoulder at the approaching figures of Ryan and Erin as she speaks.

'What do you mean what do you *get*? You get the muffin! I'm being nice by offering it to you.'

Still not looking convinced, Alex takes one from the container, pulling tentatively at the paper case, as though touching it would infect her with some sort of disease.

'Gluten-free muffin?' says Thomas, holding the box out to Ryan and Erin.

'What is gluten, anyway?' says Ryan.

I see Leni open her mouth to answer, but before she can there's the sound of Alex spitting something out. 'It's what makes food taste good,' she says, grimacing as she holds the muffin out as far away from her as she can.

'That's just unfair. They're good, I've had some. You're just being pathetic,' says Thomas. He holds the container out to me and Leni. 'Come on, try one.'

With reluctance, Leni helps herself to a portion, and upon seeing that Thomas isn't going to give up until I do so, I take one as well. I'm prepared for the worst, but the first bite is a pleasant surprise.

'That's actually not bad,' I say.

'Oh, don't humour him,' says Alex. 'You don't have to be polite. Tell him it tastes like gravel.'

'It's really all right,' I say, nodding my approval at Thomas, who grins smugly.

'If you really like it, at least lie and say you don't so that his ego doesn't get any bigger!'

Even Leni admits that it isn't half bad when she takes a bite, and our reaction is enough to convince Ryan and Erin to try some.

'Hey,' says Ryan as he pulls the paper case free, laughing at his own thoughts. 'I just remembered something.'

'What?' says Thomas.

'Don't,' warns Leni, the expression on her face enough to see that she knows just what Ryan is referring to.

'What is it?' says Alex.

'Don't do it,' Leni says, and this seems to be enough for Thomas to cotton on.

'Oh, I forgot about that,' he says.

'Can I tell her?' says Ryan.

Thomas shrugs, as if to say "whatever".

'Guys, think about this,' says Leni. 'Once you say it, there's no going back. Are you really sure you want to go there?'

'Okay,' says Alex, seeming to understand that whatever this secret topic is it concerns her. 'Now you have to tell me.'

'Remember the brownies I made a few years ago?' says Thomas.

Alex snorts. 'No.'

'Okay, well a few years ago I made some brownies, and you ate about ten. Still don't remember?'

'I've eaten a lot of brownies in my lifetime,' says Alex, 'so I'm not quite sure how to answer that.'

'It was the weekend Otto won the last pony trial,' says Leni.

'Oh, those brownies I ate after cross country? See, Thomas, why didn't you lead with that?'

'Because I don't have Leni's freakish eidetic memory,' he says, eyeing Leni with apprehension.

'Wait,' says Erin. 'Leni doesn't have a good memory, she's always forgetting things.'

'She doesn't remember day-to-day things,' says Thomas. 'She

remembers details that seem pointless, and that happened ages ago.'

'*She* is sitting right here,' says Leni.

'And *she* is going to shut up so that Thomas can get on with his story,' says Alex.

Thomas sighs. 'Anyway, you remember, then?'

'I just said that I did,' Alex snaps.

'Okay, well, you remember Connie?'

'Your pushbutton European pony? I think I do, yes. Get on with it, Donnelly.'

'Well,' says Thomas, hesitating slightly. 'I was talking to Leni and Ryan-'

'Oh, why do you have to bring us into it?' cries Leni. And then to Alex she says, 'For the record, I told him not to do it.'

'I don't care who did what, but will someone just hurry up and tell me what the point of all this is!?'

'I was trying to before Helena interrupted me!' says Thomas. 'Anyway, I was talking to them about Connie-'

'Actually,' Ryan interrupts. 'You were making feeds, that's how it came up.'

'Since when does Thomas make his own horses' feeds?' says Erin.

'Can I finish before Alex starts throwing things at me?' says Thomas. 'Whatever, talking, making feeds - does it matter? *Somehow*, the fact that Connie was on one of those stroppy mare products came up. You know what I mean? Those herbal remedy things?'

I'm pretty sure we all know what he means by now, and I cover my face with my hands to not let laughter show, as I watch Alex's expression tighten. 'I know what stroppy mare products are,' she says through clenched teeth. 'But you'd better come up with an explanation different to the one I am imagining.'

'Don't say I didn't warn you,' Leni says to Thomas.

'I asked Ryan and Leni-'

'SERIOUSLY! *STOP* bringing me into this!'

'...if they thought it would work on humans, because it says it cures bad moods, and Ryan joked that I should try giving you some to see if it made you jollier...'

My own laughter is masked by everyone else's - well, everyone except Alex.

'Are you seriously telling me that you fed me stroppy mare?'

'Man,' Ryan says through gasps of laughter. 'I forgot how funny that was.'

'Why are you guys laughing?' cries Alex. 'You ate it too if it was in the brownies!'

'Actually,' says Leni. 'We didn't. Thomas gave them all to you, we didn't touch them.'

'Are you kidding me?'

'You didn't have to eat all ten,' Thomas points out.

'If it makes you feel any better,' says Ryan, momentarily recovering from his hysteria, 'it didn't work.' And that sets us all off again, everyone except Alex, laughing until tears are running down our faces and we're clenching our sides.

The mere thought of earlier's laughter is enough to stop me from keeping a straight face as I walk around the venue. I keep trying to think of something, anything else to stop me from looking insane. *Think about the fact that you're competing tomorrow.* Yep, that does it. Goofy smile gone, replaced with a look of terror. Dressage was as good as it could be, though with so many combinations still left to go tomorrow I don't know how we will fare in the standings. But one phase at a time, I remind myself.

One phase at a time.

## Chapter 10

It's not the sound of rain falling that wakes me, but the wet fabric my arm collides with when I roll over. I turn back the other way just as quickly, and *now* I hear it. The pitter-patter of raindrops, the outlines of which I can make out through the material of the tent.

With one arm keeping Lily close to my chest, holding on to her warmth, I slide the other down the side of the blowup mattress, fingers searching for my phone. I know it can't be late, because I set an alarm for six *A.M.* just in case I didn't wake up, and sure enough it's only five.

Climbing out the tent proves impossible without soaking myself in the process, and I make a mental note to get Clara to define what the word "waterproof" means in her world as I make my way to the trailer to stir sugar beet pulp into the already prepared feed buckets. I pulled on the boots that were at the foot of my sleeping bag, and I grab a coat from the car, pulling it on over my pyjamas, before carrying feeds and hay round to the horses. They both nicker when they see me coming, and I check their water buckets and skip out before going off in search of coffee.

*Except*, I soon discover, no coffee stands are open at half past five in the morning, even though every groom will already be up. We're talking about horses here, the five-to-nine job, and the only reason we as riders are able to function at five in the morning is because we have coffee. And right now, I don't.

I walk back to the stables via the lorry park, which is the best decision I could have made because I come face to face with Leni and Alex, sitting on folding chairs beneath the overhang of the latter's horse box, mugs in their hands. Leni might as well be heading out for a jog, dressed in a sports top, leggings, and running shoes, and I wonder if I should have thought to get dressed before wandering about, but then I see Alex, and I'm reminded that I'm not the only one. She's also in her pyjamas, a fleece pulled on over the top, a blanket across her lap, and her dark hair stands up at all angles. And despite all the signs and speaker announcements that say something along the lines of "please keep your dogs on leads, and somebody with half a brain tied to the other end", Alex's dog is running loose around them.

'Early risers unite,' Alex says, sounding much more awake than she looks as she lifts her mug up in the air. 'Want a drink?'

'You're a lifesaver if you have coffee,' I say.

'Mmm,' Alex holds her other hand up as she swallows down the mouthful she just took. 'That's Leni's department.'

Even before she's said the words, Leni has already sat up from her chair, putting the cup down on the camping table. 'Alex hates coffee,' she explains as she goes up the steps into the living compartment, which I take as a sign that Joan and Ridley aren't inside.'

'Because coffee tastes like mud! Actually, I've swallowed enough mouthfuls of dirt to know that it's actually nicer than coffee.'

'Are you having tea, then?' I say, looking at her mug.

'Are you kidding? Tea's for the afternoon. *This,*' Alex says, holding the cup up again. 'Is the drink of champions.'

'*Breakfast of champions,*' Leni recites, stepping back into view and leaning against the doorway.

'No, I'm just talking about the drink,'

Leni shakes her head as she steps back further into the living compartment. 'Never mind.'

Alex frowns at me. 'Do you know what she's going on about?'

'Umm, I think it's a book…' I let my voice drift, wondering if that question was supposed to be rhetorical. 'So what's the drink of champions?'

'Hot chocolate! Obviously.'

'Quick, Alex,' Leni calls teasingly from the lorry. 'Name two things you can't live without.'

'Chocolate and horses,' Alex replies, which I'm pretty sure is what Leni thought she would say. 'You already fed?' she says to me, and straight away I realise the conversation has gone back to horses.

'Yeah, did it as soon as I got up. You?'

Alex nods. 'My first one's up at quarter past eight.' She pauses to look up at the fabric overhang, rain falling against it. 'Hey, Leni,' she calls. 'Why are we sitting out here again?'

'You're going to have to ride in this later,' a voice yells back. 'You might as well get used to it.'

'I like riding in the rain, I just don't like sitting in it.' Alex pauses, pulling a face as she looks up at the wet canopy again.

546

'Remind me why I'm not an accountant? Come on, let's go inside.'

Accepting the invitation, I follow Alex up the steps, letting her go a few paces ahead so as not to risk stepping on the blanket she's allowing to trail, only to have the dog dart in front of me.

'Winnie,' Alex scolds.

You can tell the lorry's being slept in, and not just used for the day, because clothes and duvets seem to cover every surface, with the odd magnetic stud tray balanced here and there.

'Here,' says Leni, turning round from the kitchen counter to hand me a cup of milky coffee.

'Just push anything aside to make room,' says Alex, lifting a pillow from the sofa and throwing it carelessly up onto the bed above the cab. 'You guys hungry?'

'I'm not sure I could eat anything,' I say, reminded of the sickness in my stomach, and Leni nods in agreement.

'Rubbish,' Alex says. She opens a few cupboards, pulling something different out of each one, before dumping everything she's collected onto the table, where one packet of biscuits promptly rolls off the pile of clothes it was thrown on, thumping to the floor. 'Oh, peanut butter.' She turns back to a draw, pulling out both a jar of peanut butter and three spoons. 'This is good when you don't feel like eating.'

My stomach begs to differ, judging by the lump that rises in my throat at the thought (even though I love peanut butter). Alex seems pretty adamant we eat something, though, staring at both me and Leni until we give in and reach for something. I opt for a digestive biscuit, enough to keep Alex happy, and something I can dunk in my coffee.

'How many have you got today?' I ask Alex. I already know Leni has got Cooper and Arturo in the two-star.

'Only three.'

'You've got Cash in the five year olds, right?'

Alex laughs. 'Yeah, that'll be interesting.'

'Have you walked the course? What do you think?' I ask.

'It's not too bad. Just be wary of number eight, maybe, because you're turning back on yourself, and it's near the warm-up so they might get a bit nappy.'

*Number eight.* I hadn't even thought twice about that fence when I walked the course. A small roll top, flowers along the bottom of it, in quite an open space. Great, if I missed that then what else have I neglected to pick up on. 'You think?'

'Well.' Alex shrugs. '*I* paid attention to it because I know what Cash is like, and he's likely to look at the other horses. But what I think isn't necessarily what's right.'

'So, what are you going to do? How are you going to ride it?'

'I'll just attack it a bit,' Alex says offhandedly, breaking off a piece of the flapjack she's eating and feeding it to Winnie. 'Give him a tap on the shoulder through the turn, before he even thinks of backing off, and just make sure I keep my leg on him. Make sure he's paying attention and listening to you. But I do that in front of every fence, so…' She shrugs again. 'I'll ride strongly, but without throwing myself in front of him, either.'

We discuss the other fences on course, none of which Alex seems particularly concerned by, and then move on to the two-star track.

'I'm gonna die,' Leni says, leaning her forehead into her hand. 'I mean,' she continues quickly, and I only realise a beat later that she's regretting the unfortunate choice of words. 'That combination in the woods. It's three short strides, and Arturo's got a really long stride, but even for him two would be a flyer.'

I wonder if Alex is nervous at all about the fact she'll be

going round a two-star cross country course in a matter of hours, but when I look over at her she's piling studs up in their tray to build a tower.

'He can do three if you stick to the outside,' she says, without looking up from the stud tower.

'Do you really think I can think about that while I'm trying to get him over those brushes!?' Leni says.

'I should expect you to,'

'That was rhetorical,' Leni answers back, and as Alex pulls out another witty reply, I let my eyes wander over the pile of stuff beside me, and they settle on an open copy of *Horse and Hound*. It's showing a dressage report, also known as the feature I usually skip over (though it still beats showing), but there's something about the picture that is familiar. I pick the magazine up, staring at the beautiful bay horse depicted, and inexplicably feel tears prickle my eyes as I read the caption beneath. *Former eventer Made in Motown wins...* I don't read the rest, because I don't care about percentages and I don't understand the names of dressage classes. But it's Motown, looking magnificent, getting a new start. And for a reason I cannot comprehend, I suddenly feel a lot more at ease about today.

'You know, I'm not sure I like you that much anymore.'

My diminishing affection clearly doesn't worry Cookie much, as she spins her quarters towards me, craning her neck to let out a piercing whinny.

'If you stood still, I'd be done by now and we'd already be on our way,' I snap, trying to secure a brushing boot as she paws the ground.

The sweet, sensible mare I had at our last event seems to have missed the memo, and I now have the beast that earned

Cookiemoon the nickname Cookiemonster. It started before we even got to the dressage warm-up, when she decided to nap upon the realisation that I was riding her away from the stable blocks. When she realised that rearing wasn't going to phase me, Cookie started backing up, no amount of kicking enough to send her forward. I didn't have a whip on me, which would have done it, so when we had gone backwards so much that she was only a few feet way from smashing into a very expensive-looking Range Rover, I jumped off her back and leapt to her quarters, coaxing her forward. And because everything with Cookie is a game, a power struggle, she obeyed. She doesn't fight because she wants to cause harm, and she isn't actually that stubborn, she just likes to see what she can get away with.

Warming up was terrible, though by this point I wasn't exactly expecting anything else, which did at least mean that I rode into the test feeling relaxed, because I wasn't hoping for anything. But then, surprise surprise, Cookie transformed. She knew what she was doing, and that she was being watched, and she only went and did a foot perfect test. At least I will have got extra marks for smiling, because I was practically laughing by the end of it. Back behind the scenes now, though, she's reverted to being a nightmare.

'If we hadn't saved you, you'd be dead now,' I say coldly, shortening the stirrups a couple holes. 'Remember? You could at least try to show some appreciation.'

*Okay, I didn't mean quite so much,* I think as Cookie canters round the show jumping warm-up. Apparently she took my words to heart, because since seeing the fences she has put her game fence on, approaching each obstacle with the same determination needed to tackle a Hickstead bank.

'Whoa,' I call, sitting up from the jar the impact of landing caused, as Cookie accelerates, tucking her nose to her chest. I click my tongue, keeping one hand firmly against her neck as I use the other to lift her up. 'Good girl,' I say, moving my hand forward to touch in front of her withers.

The steward calls my number, and we canter one last circle before making our way to the gate. Despite the rainfall we've had, the ground doesn't look too bad. It's still drizzling, and later in the day might be a different story, but for now it doesn't look too churned up. I've put studs in anyway, just in case Cookie decides to take off through a turn and forget to balance herself, which is highly likely.

The sound of the starting bell ignites Cookie's determination further. She might possess many characteristics that I could do without, but she also has grit, and it's her quirks that make her who she is, good and bad. All the best horses have an attitude. The ones that don't, like Nantucket, are few and far between.

Even if I weren't on her back, I'm pretty sure Cookie would have gone round clear regardless. Her temper, which was her demise in racing, is also her strongest quality when directed the right way. It doesn't matter how high or how small a fence is, she jumps them all the same - with everything she's got.

I take Cookie back to the stables, where I offer her a drink and swap her boots, and get straight back on to head to the cross country. Not too long a warm-up, just enough to get her moving, before we're off again. And it's with the same determination she had show jumping that we fly around the cross country course to finish clear.

'Good girl,' I yell as I gallop across the finish line, letting my reins out to pat her wet neck, only to shorten them again with the realisation that Cookie isn't done yet. She's still trying to go, even though there's nowhere to go *to*, and it takes me a minute of circling for her to fall back from a canter into a trot, eventually coming to what is supposed to be a walk but is more of a jog.

'Chill out,' I say. I swing from the saddle, jogging a step to stop Cookie from walking farther away from me, and somehow manage to put the stirrups up and loosen the girth without losing her. 'You goof,' I mutter,

'Handful much?'

I look over my shoulder to see Alex grinning at me. I noticed her at the edge of the warm-up ring earlier, watching Joan on a young horse, but I didn't stop to talk to her.

'Something like that,' I say, smiling. 'She went double clear, so she can get away with it.'

'She's nice,' Alex says, stepping back as she looks at Cookie's build.

'She has to look nice, she's a pain in the neck.'

'She's just feisty,' Alex says defensively, stepping forward to scratch Cookie's shoulder. 'But seriously, she was on fire out there.' At her touch, Cookie stopped fidgeting and turned her head to rest her nose against Alex's arm.

'I thought you didn't like mares?'

'Well, truthfully *they* don't like *me.*' Alex pauses as Cookie rubs her head against her arm. 'At least, they don't usually, anyway. What's her name?'

'Cookie. Cookiemoon.'

'Ha, that's awesome!'

'I thought you'd like it,' I say, laughing at the sight before me. Cookie, the horse made by the devil, cosying up to none other than Alex. 'You want her?'

It was an offhand remark, not expected to be taken seriously, but Alex's eyes widen. 'Really, you'd sell her?'

'You're actually interested?' I say, not quite able to process what is happening.

'If you actually want to sell her, then yeah. She's my type. Like I said, I normally stay away from mares, but, I dunno.' She shrugs, running a hand over Cookie's forehead. 'I feel like we've clicked.'

I never particularly thought of Cookie as saleable. And while I love her, and would happily look after her until her dying day, I've never felt that connection. That *click*, as Alex says. The way I did with Loxwood, and Nantucket. Like my heart's been tugged. And part of that is the fact that I know Cookie has never felt that way with me, either.

Selling Nantucket broke my heart, and the thought of selling Loxwood is even worse. And I've been wondering how exactly I'm going to make it in the horse world, financially, without ever selling a horse. Unless you're rich, or have an army of sponsors, it's almost an impossibility to make a living competing without doing so. But after Nantucket, I wasn't sure I would ever be able to face that again.

Yet now, I'm standing here, both my horse and an offer to buy her in front of me, and I feel excited. If Rose and I hadn't come across her, Cookie would most likely be dead by now. By getting her back to health, I've given her a second chance. We never clicked, and probably never will, but she could have that with someone else. Every horse deserves to have that special connection with somebody. And because I invested time in her, because I put her back on the road, she's going to get that chance.

'You realise she's a nightmare, right?' I say, grinning. 'She's not mean, but she naps, and rears - not very high, though.'

Alex nods. 'I saw her earlier. But I like a bit of crazy. How much do you want for her?'

This time I do laugh. 'You actually want to *pay* me for her?'

'Well, obviously.'

A second ago, I was prepared to give her away for nothing, but now I remind myself that I have a living to earn, other horses to feed. And there's what I've invested already in feed, and entry fees. 'I don't know,' I reply honestly. 'She's only done two events, but she went double clear today...' my voice drifts. 'I honestly don't know.'

'Well,' Alex says, pausing to look at Cookie's conformation once more. 'I'd give you four grand for her. I know you might get more for her after today, but that's the most I can offer at the moment...'

'Done.'

Alex smiles. 'I've got to run. Talk it over later?'

My mind is whirling with ideas as I lead Cookie back to the stables. Maybe I could produce and sell horses, ones I don't get so attached to. Ex-racehorses, who would end up in the same state as Cookie, or worse, if not given another chance. Because selling a horse isn't nearly so bad when you know that their alternative would have been death. I'll have to call by to see Frank when I get back, maybe we could work something out-

*Not now,* I remind myself, seeing Loxwood's eyes watching me through the railings of the stable a we walk up the block. I need to cool Cookie off and focus on the task at hand. Right now, I've got something to do.

# Chapter 11

I already know halfway round the course that it's going to be all right. All the rails are in their cups, and not only is Loxwood jumping his socks off, but he's working *with* me.

The warm-up was good, but not so much so that I was waiting for something to go wrong. A perfect warm-up can be terrifying, no matter how much you claim not to be superstitious. But today, it was just right. No hiccups, correct strides, not so great that I was burdened by the knowledge that I would never be able to top it in the ring. And now that we are, it's all coming together.

I soften my seat as Loxwood rushes to the last fence, taking a quick check on one rein before releasing it again, pushing my hands forwards as he takes off.

'A clear round for Georgia James and Loxwood, and they shall move forward to the cross country phase on their dressage score of twenty-nine.'

Loxwood lowers his head to the ground as we trot out the

ring, and I run my hands up and down his neck. I haven't been thinking about the placings, only about our performance, but there's still a voice in my head reminding me that we're doing pretty well so far.

'Where's Georgia gone?' calls Rose, walking Sunny near the warm-up entrance. She arrived early this morning, and while I didn't get to see her ride, I know that she's done a very good test.

I grin. 'Told her to take a hike!'

Rose points at the show jumping ring. 'Never let her come back if that's the result.'

'I'll do my best.'

Back at the stables, I swap Loxwood's show jumping boots for cross country ones before changing out of my own jacket. I offer him a drink, while he waits with a loosened girth, and I also check Lily's water bowl, having left her in Tucker with the windows open, not that they need to be when the weather's like this. As predicted, temperatures plummeted last night. At least it hasn't rained again, even though the sky is still grey.

'You ready, Lox?' I say, leading him back out the stable again, Cookie spinning in her box as I do so. 'You can do it. I trust you. I know you can. I know I've said that it doesn't matter what happens, and it doesn't, but just know that I believe in you. Okay? Don't go out there thinking that I'm expecting you to stop, because I'm not. I think you're braver than you realise, and you're going to go out there and show everyone else that. We didn't run here last year. I pulled out. So let's go out there and prove that was the right decision.'

My fear and worry levels seem to have peaked so high that I no longer feel anything. Because I've been a complete wreck all week, yet now, trotting around the start box, I no longer feel any of it. I think there comes a point when you worry so much that you stop feeling sick. Besides, almost everything I've ever feared has already happened. I now know that I can come back from failure, that I can get up every time I'm knocked down, and there's no reason that should change.

'Thirty seconds.'

*Breathe.*

Loxwood warmed up well, both bold and respectful, and I'm at least confident in the thought that there's nothing else I could have done.

'Fifteen seconds.'

'Georgia!'

I've brought Loxwood back to a walk, and I look behind me, towards the warm-up, and see Sunny's dark face looking this way, Rose on top. 'You can do this,' she calls.

I nod, my tongue feeling like it's about to choke me. *You can do this.*

The steward motions me to the start box, and I trot Loxwood up to it, turning him sideways a step before setting off. I don't have a stopwatch, so I'm not worrying about that. I just want to get round.

His ears are pricked as we approach the first fence, the sound of his breathing, the Thoroughbred rumbling exhale, filling my ears. *You can do this. We can do this.* I squeeze my legs firmly against his sides, and Loxwood powers over the first fence. As soon as we land, I click my tongue and urge him forwards, meaning business.

We make it over the second fence, and the third, and the fourth - the first combination on course. And I decide that no matter what happens, even if we fall at the next, it will all have been worth it for those few moments in the air. That feeling of invincibility, of escaping a mundane existence. Because trusting a horse, and having him trust you, to soar over a solid fence provides the sort of exhilaration and freedom that some spend a lifetime searching for.

It's a rolling course, and after the seventh fence we're turning back on ourselves, heading for a roll top isolated in a clearing. As Loxwood's balance shifts at the change in direction, I remember Alex's earlier words. I would never have thought about this fence being a problem, proof that I haven't walked or ridden anywhere near the same number of courses that she has. I'm still learning, and things like this, noticing every detail a horse is going to pick up on, can only be mastered with time. If I hadn't spoken to Alex, if I hadn't been warned, there are two different scenarios that could play out right now. One is that I freeze, too frazzled by the surprise to react. The other is that I go into overdrive, kicking and flapping with everything I've got. But Alex's words come back to me, and while she may not be right about everything, she knows a lot more than I do. *Tap on the shoulder, make sure you've got his concentration. Ride strongly, but don't override.*

'Come on,' I growl, keeping my shoulders back and my legs steady as I drive him towards the fence, throwing in a tap on the shoulder with the whip for good measure. And while I've been telling myself this whole time that I won't allow myself to ever believe that we're scot-free, to never get ahead of myself, I can't help the feeling that when Loxwood lands clear on the other side of the roll top, we're going to be all right. We've found our way.

When Loxwood jumps the final fence, still full of running as he heads towards the finish line, I can't hold it in any longer. Tears run down my face, and I throw one arm into the air, wrapping the other round his neck. I yell "good boy" too many times to count, the words becoming more and more jumbled as relief washes over me. *We did it.* Every fall, every moment of heartbreak, of feeling like the biggest failure to ever walk the planet, and all those moments when I wasn't sure I'd ever succeed. And there are bound to be more of those moments, because I've realised that one single triumph does not mean that you can't fail again. But just for now, everything's okay. A spot on the podium is not permanent, and success is not the end game. Success is getting up every time you fall. It's not giving up on your dreams. It's working hard to achieve your goals.

'Good boy,' I say again, sliding out the saddle to wrap my arms around his neck. Loxwood turns his head to look at me, and I plant a kiss on his forehead, tears still running down my face. 'You did it,' I say. 'You did it, Lox.'

And then I feel an arm wrap around me, and I turn to see Rose with cheeks as wet as my own, her spare hand holding Sunny's reins. She releases me to praise Loxwood, saying the words "you star" over and over again, which does little to stop me from crying.

'I'll come see you in the stables when I'm done,' she says, getting back on Sunny.

'Good luck,' I say. 'I'll try to come back in time to watch.'

As Rose rides away, I run up my stirrups to lead Loxwood back to the stables, unzipping my body protector as I walk. I don't even need to hold the reins - Loxwood walks with his head low, pushing into me every other step. His body is wet with sweat, but the course was nothing compared to the treks across Ballowmoore he's used to, and he looks fit enough to go again.

'I love you,' I say, leaning into his neck. 'I don't regret a thing. You hear me? Every time I've cried, and failed, and fallen... I would do it all again. Even if the same thing had happened again today. I would do it all again, Loxwood. I would go through it all again.'

I don't think I've made it more than three minutes at a time without crying, and right now is no exception. Sitting in the saddle, watching the third place ribbon be pinned to Loxwood's bridle. I meant it when I said I didn't care about the standings. I don't. I just wanted to do well, to do myself proud, to do right by Loxwood. But coming third, having Loxwood named as the third best five year old event horse in the country, is a pretty nice extra. And what makes me even happier, is coming third to a winner as worthy as Rose. Sunny blew it out of the park, finishing two marks ahead of second place, nobody having been able to catch him up after the dressage. Years ago, Rose gave up her shot at making it big time so that she could build a life for herself and her family. She sold her own top horse, but unlike Nantucket he didn't come back to her. Orion was her Loxwood, and the pain I experienced in the seven months after selling Nantucket she has lived with for years. But she has her own yard, and raised a family, and put her own dreams on hold to help everyone else. Without her, I wouldn't be where I am today. And now she's in a position that she can pursue the higher levels more seriously again and although he is a pain the in the neck, Sunny has the potential. I've often felt during the past years that I deserve to succeed, that it wasn't fair that I didn't when I worked harder than most. But Rose deserves it even more.

Between the two of us is a rider with a Badminton title to their name, and I can't quite believe that I am here, behind these two incredible riders. More to the point, Loxwood is here. James said he would never make four-star, that I'm wasting my time, but nothing can be predicted so easily. And even if it's true, we're still going to try.

I can't hold the tears back as we canter the lap of honour, Loxwood spicing up with the knowledge that he is being watched, carrying his neck high and round. Last year, when I was in this same spot with Nantucket, I thought I was as happy as I could be. But this is different. Everything came easily with Nantucket, even if finishing so high up the standings was a surprise. But *this* victory, this triumph, has taken so much time and work to achieve. I'm by no means the best rider here, and in many ways I'm not a great rider full stop. Talent didn't get me here, hard work did.

Outside the ring, as I ride out, I slide from the saddle, wrapping my arms around Loxwood's neck again. 'You're the dream horse,' I say. 'You always have been.'

'Excuse me?'

There's a woman standing in front of me, a girl beside her who can't be more than a couple of years younger than me, and definitely her daughter. I'm pretty sure I know where this is going, but I force myself to be polite regardless. 'Yes?'

'I don't suppose you'd be interested in selling your horse?'

I smile, shaking my head. 'Sorry. He's not for sale.'

'Are you sure?' the woman says, her daughter standing silently beside her. 'Every horse has a price.'

I don't answer right away, letting my gaze linger on Loxwood, and the ribbon hanging from his bridle. 'Actually,' I say, clicking my tongue for Loxwood to start walking away with me, 'they don't.'

* * *

I noticed him straight away. As I was given a leg up into the saddle, and proceeded to walk in circles on the concrete until everyone was ready to go, all I could see was him. A chestnut horse, one I hadn't seen before, being ridden around me. He wasn't spindly like most of the other horses in this string, but big and muscular. A gleaming coat, a round neck-carriage, and a dash of white between wide eyes that seemed to take in everything around him. Most of the horses looked brain dead most of the time, like clones, but not this one. There was an intelligence to him, I could tell, and I just wanted to stare at him. I saw hundreds of horses a day, occasionally thinking that one was nicer than another, but I had never felt like this.

Throughout the whole ride, my eyes were far ahead, watching this chestnut horse move. I was too nervous to ask Frank about him, and I tried to get some information out of another exercise rider, but his English was limited and he ended up ignoring me, so I gave up. I just watched this beautiful horse, barely thinking about the one beneath me.

Back at the yard, my eyes sought him out as I untacked my ride. I watched which stable he was taken to, feeling sick with nerves at the thought of going to see him. Not to mention that I was running late as it was, with only twenty minutes to get home and change for school. But as soon as my horse was cooled off, and the other riders were getting the next string of horses out of their stables, I went up to him.

'Hey, buddy,' I whispered, looking over the stable door. He looked up at me from his hay, and for a moment I was worried that the illusion would be shattered. Maybe he looked nice from a distance, and I would now discover that the dream horse my mind had concocted during the past hour didn't exist. He would pin his ears back and lunge at me, or the tingling in my limbs would disappear once I saw him up close. But that didn't happen. Instead he stretched his nose out towards me, sniffing my arms until lifting his nose to my chin. I smiled.

'Hey,' I said again, feeling a fluttering in my chest. 'Do you have a name?' I looked down at the half door, where each horse had a square of paper printed with their information. Quite often, new ones would arrive without names. The piece of paper would indicate their sire's name, and grandsire's, and owner's, but not the horse's. Names were a technicality. They got named once it was known they were going to run. But this one did have a name.

'Loxwood,' I read, looking back up at the chestnut Thoroughbred.

The sound of shod hooves walking on concrete echoed behind me, and I glanced over my shoulder to see the next group of horses walking around the courtyard.

'I've got to go,' I whispered, running a hand down his neck as he took a step closer to me. 'But I'll be back tomorrow. Loxwood.'

I could have stayed there all day, overcome with the feeling of there being some sort of magnet pull between us, two figures in a crowd that inexplicably find themselves drawn to each other. But the horses getting ready to head out reminded me of just how late I was, and I hurried across the courtyard, trying to remember whether I had done the history assignment that was due today.

Sidestepping the group of horses, I made it to the gates, each step farther away from the chestnut horse feeling like it was taking a part of my soul with it. This was ridiculous. He was a horse, one of many. And while I knew there was no reason to, I turned back. If he was looking at anything, I knew Loxwood would be looking at the group of jockeys and horses on the right, the figures crowding the courtyard. But as I turned back, looking the opposite way of the riders, I saw Loxwood's pricked ears, but he wasn't watching the horses.

He was looking at me.

# ABOUT THE AUTHOR

Grace lives near Newmarket, where she works with horses full time, and writes early in the morning or late at night. Follow her on Facebook and Twitter for news on all the latest book releases (as well as the odd horse picture).

https://www.facebook.com/GraceWilkinsonWrites

https://twitter.com/gracewwrites

Or send an email to gracewilkinsonwrites@gmail.com

*Also by the author*

Confetti Horses

Eventing Bay

Printed in Great Britain
by Amazon